PARADISE PENDING

KRIS PURDY

About the Author

Kris Purdy is a former singer-songwriter and public broadcaster. She spent a big chunk of her growing-up years in Tucson, Arizona. She calls Canada home and at present, resides in Toronto with her partner and their dog, Maggie. This is Kris's first novel.

PARADISE PENDING

KRIS PURDY

BELLA
B O O K S
2023

Bella Books, Inc.
P.O. Box 10543
Tallahassee, FL 32302

First Edition - 2023

Editor: Ann Roberts
Cover Designer: Kayla Mancuso
Photo Credit: Moe Laverty

ISBN: 978-1-64247-438-1

PUBLISHER'S NOTE

Acknowledgments

The author would like to thank the following for their help and contributions to this novel: Firstly, my spouse and partner, Susan, without whom this book would have been impossible, as well as Ann Roberts, Dinah Forbes, Joy Fielding, Joan Barfoot, Steen Starr, Francisco Berney Comandone, Mary Lou Creechan, Margo Charlton and Nick DeCarlo.

Any factual shortcuts or mistakes in history, politics, geography and the Spanish language are entirely the fault of the author.

Dedication

For Kathryn, tiny badass angel.

PROLOGUE

The ambulance pushed deeper into Old Town, emergency beacon splashing red across white stucco walls, siren seesawing Euro-style. Root to fifth her musician ear noted despite her fear. Dani's hand dropped to the seat for balance as the ambulance manoeuvred its way through the medieval maze of Cádiz, Spain. Late night revellers backed out of the way. No mean feat on cobblestone streets built for carts.

She wanted to scream. *Move! Move faster!* But these men, the paramedics, gave her pause.

The younger one was driving. He was slim with a pale complexion marred by acne scars. He avoided eye contact when she caught him glancing back at her in the rearview mirror.

The older one sitting in the front passenger seat was not so reticent. Brutish in profile, his head and neck formed a solid block of flesh, as if a sculptor had forgotten to finish that part of him, making a turn of the head impossible. Except that he could, and when he did, he looked directly at her, eyes dead cold.

Dani held his stare, gut clenching under his scrutiny.

"¿Hay algún problema, señora?"

"No, señor. Pero, ¿más rápido?"

"¿Más rápido?" He looked back at the narrow road and shook his head. "Guiri loca," he muttered under his breath. Guiri. Not a nice word for tourists.

He's an ass. So chill. This is normal emergency procedure. Another language, another culture, another place, is all.

She reached back to touch the stretcher as much for her own comfort as for Jo's. Her Jo. Brilliant. Some said visionary. She managed an NGO back home in Toronto. It was called HomeStart and it served newcomers, immigrants and refugees from all kinds of backgrounds, helping them find homes in their new city. Jo had achieved what few had at the time: changed an overwhelmingly white Anglo agency into one that not only reflected the people it served, but had become one with them. She was now called upon by organizations everywhere to share her path to success. This was her first invitation to Europe.

Dani shook her head slowly. *And to think I pushed her to do this. Take a vacation. Finally.* The first week Jo spent at her conference, as planned. The second week was going to be pure relaxation amid the beauty of southern Spain. *Instead, she's flat on her back on a stretcher being rushed to a hospital.* Dani sighed, looking at her lying there, face pale, skin clammy. *But a heart attack can happen anywhere, right? Even sitting on the couch at home. I should have made her take time off long before this.* She grimaced. *Yeah right. Like I can "make" Jo do anything.*

She braced herself as the ambulance took another corner, siren bouncing off stone walls so close she could almost touch them. Jo moaned and Dani took her hand. *Hang in there, kiddo.* Corner after corner they turned, winding deeper and deeper like some slo-mo slalom into oblivion.

CHAPTER ONE

The maître d' moved his finger slowly down the page, his mouth making little sucking noises at each entry. El Alabado, The Acclaimed, required a reservation, as most good restaurants in Cádiz, Spain, did on busy nights. Dani Papineau had made one, just not here. She would never have picked this place. It was convenient enough, located right inside their hotel, Casa Colón, but it was upscale, pretentious even, and undoubtedly way over their budget. Dani's pick had been a sweet little boîte that featured flamenco jazz and great wine. This place, El Alabado, was the choice of one of Jo's new conference contacts. He'd succeeded in dragging her into a working dinner despite the fact that her conference was now officially over. Dani gritted her teeth. This was their first free night and the beginning of their vacation. *Am I pissed? You betcha*. Dani took a deep breath. *But no complaining, girlie. You married the workaholic, eyes wide open.*

Jo grabbed her arm. "Dani, I'm so sorry. He came up to me just as the conference was winding down and was, well, almost pushy. I said yes before I realized it."

Dani shrugged and thought of how she'd envisioned tonight, just the two of them, sipping wine and listening to a great guitarist.

The maître d' cleared his throat and shook his head with exaggerated sadness. "Qué lástima, señoras. What a pity. There is nothing under Gasperi. But perhaps under your name?" he said, looking hopefully to Dani. "What is your name, señora?"

"Me? Uh, it's Papineau. But it's definitely not under my name." She turned to Jo, no longer able to contain herself. "Face it. Conference guy screwed up. It's Friday night in Old Town. Hell, Friday night anywhere. No one gets a table last minute, except maybe some squeeze-'em-in spot behind a swinging kitchen door. And I'd found such a great place for us. It wasn't fancy but it was charming and on Plaza San Antonio, right next to your conference site. We had reservations and everything and now we have nada, nothing."

The maître d' raised an eyebrow and Jo frowned. She held up her hand. "Dani. Stop talking, please." She turned back to the man who was clearly tiring of this exchange. "You're sure there's nothing under the name Gasperi?" The man shook his head and sighed. "Okay, sorry. Uh, let me think back. Maybe I misunderstood. Maybe he said his…" She closed her eyes. The maître d's finger began tapping the page of the reservation book he held. "Is there anything under Ed…wahr…doh Moon… yoz." Jo struggled, Spanish not being one of her many skills.

The man's face lit up. Without hesitation, he picked up three menus and motioned them to follow him.

Dani whispered in Jo's ear, "kitchen door."

The maître d' wove his way through the packed main room, squeezing behind chairs and waiters holding heavy trays of food and drink aloft, past the dreaded and thankfully occupied kitchen-door spot and out onto an equally crowded patio. He kept going right by the guitarist playing muted riffs appropriate for diners and ushered them behind a hedge at the far end. A lone table stood there set for a dinner party of three, hidden from the rest on three sides. Dani stood motionless, jaw agape at what she saw on the fourth side. She placed her things on the chair held out by the waiter, while Jo flopped into the one offered her by the maître d'. The waiter opened and served a bottle of wine while the maître d' explained that it was an apology from their host for running late. Their tasks completed, they nodded and left the two women to enjoy their own private-*ish* outdoor dining room.

Dani picked up a glass of wine and walked over to the end of the deck. She felt the breeze blow over her, washing away her disappointment. She heard Jo back at the table say something about exhaustion, but she was rapt standing there as if at the edge of the world. The wind was blowing off the Atlantic that evening, one of those humid westerlies that thwarts sailors and thrills the makers of manzanilla sherry. The Spaniards call it el Poniente after the setting sun, hot during the day and chilling as the sky darkens, leaving diners on the patios of Cádiz shifting in their seats and pulling their light wraps closer against the sudden nip in the air.

Dani felt it. She tugged her blazer collar higher and batted down the wind-crafted spikes in her hair. She saw Jo scrunch up her shoulders too. "Hey, babe. Here." She went back to the table and handed her a navy-blue shirt jacket she'd brought from their hotel room. She sat down, thinking the table Jo's guy had reserved looked like the best in the house, all set for three. *Three. Wow. Me. Jo. And the guy. Great.*

"Okay, so tell me. Who is this guy? Ed-wahr-doh Moon-yoz?"

"Babe. Don't mock me. I don't have the energy for it." But she smiled nonetheless. "Oh my god, what a day. And it's not over. Please don't forget, this is a working dinner."

"How could I possibly forget? Instead of celebrating your first night off work, we have to play nice with some guy who's what? Come on. Who is he anyway?"

"He goes by Eddie, gratefully. He fronts some organization that builds immigrant housing or renovates it or something. I don't know exactly. All I know is the group has money and I would fall on my knees, almost, to bring some hard cash back for HomeStart."

"So you're hustling him. That's kind of weird because this setup is amazing, more like he's hustling you. I mean this table, the vino"—she tipped the bottle to better see the label—"Pago Negralada Tempranillo Abadia Retuerta 2006. And that view. It's all impressive."

Jo looked up and spoke, as if seeing the sea view for the first time. "Damn. That is stunning."

"Right? And try the wine. It's very good. It'll warm you up too. And seriously? You look like you could use it."

Jo grimaced. "If I start drinking, I'll probably fall asleep. Between my speech and getting lost walking back here through Old Town, I'm pretty much spent."

Dani froze midway to her third sip and stared at Jo, the meaning of her words sinking in. "Oh my god, Jo. Your speech. I was so, uh, *frustrated* by your 'cancel all plans' message, I totally forgot about your speech. How did it go? I want to hear everything."

"It was fine. No technical problems, thank god, and no one heckled."

"My, how we've lowered the bar." They both laughed. "And that's it? That's all you've got to say after weeks of angst over your first international keynote address?"

"Too tired. I'll tell you about it later."

"Well, congratulations, I think. And that makes me even more surprised you agreed to a meeting tonight of all nights. The official start of our vacation. You remember the concept, right? One week's work, yours, for one week's play, ours?"

"I'll say it again. I am so sorry. So very sorry to ruin your plans. They sounded great." She reached over and gently stroked Dani's cheek. "And thanks, babe, for the congrats. I am so glad that speech is behind me." She pushed her black hair behind her ears, picked up her glass of wine and took a cautious sip. "Mmm. This *is* good." She sighed, her face softened, and Dani's heart warmed. She picked up the menu to keep from getting emotional. She'd loved this woman from the moment they'd met.

"You know what, babe? Your Eddie guy is not here. So you aren't working *yet*. And I don't really mind giving up Nuñez."

Jo's head jerked up, black eyes flashing.

"Who?"

"Down girl." Dani smiled. "Gerardo Nuñez. He's the guitarist at the jazz joint I booked for tonight. His pulgar. Oh my god. It's to die for."

"What are you saying? Pull-something?"

"It's an amazing bit of guitar technique I would love to add to my repertoire. But no worries, my love. There's always YouTube. And he's just one of the wonders of this place. As you can see"—Dani thrust her chin toward the view—"there are many."

They gazed out their private window on the world. The Atlantic Ocean was the scene stealer but the city's ancient buildings crammed along the cliff's edge drew their eyes too.

"See that big one?" Dani pointed to the massive cathedral, the alpha building overshadowing all the others. "See how it's facing out to sea?" Jo nodded. "It's positioned that way because the invaders always came from the sea. And there were many."

"And you know this…?"

"I know this because I spent way too much time in museums waiting for your conference to wrap up. I even prepped a little synopsis to get you in vacation mode, but I'll save that for later." She reached over and took Jo's hand. "I love you, babe."

"And I love you. And you may kind of enjoy tonight. As you say, the setting is pretty spectacular and the food should be good here. The work talk is kind of unavoidable but I can't imagine it'll go on all evening. Eddie's kind of an interesting guy. Very nice. A tad pushy. But he did include you in the invitation. And by the way, do *not* under any circumstances give him our cell number. He's just the type to completely take over our vacation time. It shouldn't be too bad, though, just for this dinner. And he is a Spaniard after all. A good chance for you to spend some time with someone actually from here." She took another sip of wine. "And guess what. He's…" She stopped and looked up.

"He's what?" said Dani, following her gaze.

A little parade marched through the hedge opening. First, the waiter who placed another wine glass on the table. Next, the maître d' who pulled out a chair for a third man, the man for whom they'd been waiting. Eddie.

He was taller than Dani, just under six feet, heavily tanned, neatly coiffed and manicured. His clothes looked expensive but with that casual flair that only the wealthy seem to manage. His white cotton slacks and shirt were remarkably unwrinkled, as was the black linen jacket thrown casually over his shoulders. It's all in the material, Dani remembered someone saying.

"Thank you, León, for squeezing us in," Eddie said, touching the maître d's arm. He turned to their table and perched his sunglasses on top of his head, revealing piercing blue eyes. "Dani Papineau. It is so wonderful to meet you." He took her extended hand between both of his. "You're a musician. And an expert in Spanish, I understand."

Dani shook her head. "Musician yes. Spanish expert? Jo exaggerates."

"Nonetheless, how delightful you could join us."

I could join you? Dani bit her tongue.

"And you, Josefina Gasperi." He air-kissed her on both cheeks. "Congratulations, my dear. Such a gift you were to that conference, not only a bright light in the rather serious world of immigration policy but a sister, if you don't mind my referring to you as such."

"What?" Dani asked, as they all sat down.

"That's what I was about to tell you just before Eddie arrived."

"Oh yes, my dear." His face was serious, his eyes laughing. "We danced around it for a while, Jo referring to her partner without gender-specific pronouns. Isn't that true, Josefina?"

Jo laughed. "I had no idea how open people would be here, so I was cautious."

"No need, especially in the cities. Spain legalized same-sex marriage in 2005, the same year as you Canadians. And now here we are." Eddie brushed back a lock of copper-gold hair with flourish. "A handsome gay man and two charming lesbians."

Dani cringed. "Gee, Eddie. Only charming? You don't think we're handsome too?"

Jo grimaced. Eddie threw back his head and laughed. Dani took a sip of wine. *Not that funny.*

"Your Jo certainly charmed them today. Did she tell you they gave her a standing ovation?"

Dani's eyebrows rose as she looked at Jo. "She did not."

"Oh, yes. Her final summation moved them to their feet. How did it go, Jo? To empower newcomers, we must reflect them. To reflect...Josefina. Give us your closing lines."

Jo groaned but complied, launching into it with a muted stage-style delivery. "To empower newcomers, we must include them. To reflect them, we must look like them. Correction, we must *be* them and they us, in staffing, in management, at every decision-making level. We must see the world through a variety of lenses. Perspective is everything. Lived experience counts. This involves big change throughout our organizations, change in hiring and promotion and cultural shifts to actually *be* more inclusive and equitable. Change can cause fear. To succeed, we must manage that fear."

"Manage the fear! Brilliant. They loved it," Eddie said to Dani. "They even stood up to applaud her. They went wild for it."

"Wow. Talk about burying the lede. Congratulations, Jo. That's fantastic. I'm having a bit of trouble, though, imagining a room full of social work types going wild."

Eddie's laugh was too hearty yet again.

"Ah, Dani, you'd be surprised at the passion tucked inside that earnest crowd. Your presentation," he said, turning back toward Jo, "took them out of their procedures and protocols. You reminded them of that passion."

"You're exaggerating, Eddie," Jo countered, waving him off with a wine-softened dismissal. "But thank you. It did feel good when they stood."

"Time to celebrate your success. I suggest a crisp cool manzanilla to accompany the first course."

"So that means food? Please?" Jo raised her glass. "This is delicious but potent stuff. I need to eat."

"Oh, yeah," said Dani. "Must eat. Getting too, uh, relaxed."

"That was my plan," their host said with a wink. "El Alabado is famous for its traditional Spanish cuisine. When I called for my table, I took the liberty of ordering some especialidades andalucianas, Andalusian specialties."

Jo's eyes widened. Dani laughed recognizing the look of fear from she-of-the-childlike-tastebuds. Eddie rose from his chair and snapped his fingers vigorously above the hedge line. A waiter appeared and nodded.

Within minutes, their table was laden with food—an appetizer platter of tortillas de camarones: shrimp fritters, followed by an earthenware bowl filled with biftec estofado: beef stewed with charred garlic, tomatoes and chorizo. In another dish were papas bravas: brave potatoes roasted with olive oil and garlic, al estilo andaluciano, Eddie explained. On separate plates were small tomatoes stuffed with a date and walnut mixture, a cold marinated carrot dish and a basket of breads. It was a feast. They drank the second bottle of wine and most of a third and finished with coffees and Spanish brandies. He was wining and dining them extravagantly, but by the end of the meal, he still hadn't mentioned work. They talked about food, the challenges of speaking a second language, the challenges of not speaking one, politics and the current governments in Spain and Canada, back to food, music, and eventually, the personal.

"Bueno. Dani, I understand you are a famous performer in Canada?"

Dani squelched a guffaw. "Uh, well, famous is a bit strong. I've never broken through to the *big time*. So, the answer is no. Not famous."

"Don't let her kid you, Eddie. She's a well-known performer in Toronto. Gets great reviews. Has a voice to die for."

Dani rolled her eyes and lifted her snifter.

"Please, honour us with a song."

Dani almost choked on her brandy. "A song? Now?"

"Sí, sí. Sing. I want to hear this voice."

"No, no, no, no. I don't do impromptu."

"It's true," said Jo, "she only sings on stage. Won't even entertain dinner guests at home."

"What can I say? I feel comfortable on a stage. Off stage? Not so much. It'd take mucho más vino for that."

"That can be arranged."

"Sweet idea, Eddie. But nope. I'm happy just sitting here enjoying our conversation."

"And so that is a definite no?" Dani nodded and Eddie dropped his head to his chest in mock defeat. "I am very disappointed."

"You'll survive."

Eddie's head snapped back up. A sharp look slid across his face. *Well, well, Mr. Marvelous. Not refused much?* His eyes carried a dark intensity, as if being denied were a personal insult. *Gee. And I was just getting to kind of like you. What's up with you, Eddie. All warm and friendly. And then…cold as ice.* A chill swept through her. It was an unpleasant sensation, one she'd learned not to ignore. Advice from her mum. "Always trust your gut." *Shit.*

He turned his chair and shifted his attention to Jo, clearly dismissing Dani. "Now, la estrella del congreso. The star of the conference. Tell me, Jo, how a talented woman with such a potentially lucrative skill set as a manager, innovator *and* public speaker, tell me how you chose the admittedly noble career of social work."

"Oh man," said Jo, rubbing the heel of her hand against her forehead. "I'm almost as bad as Dan. I hate self-revelation."

Dani leaned back and folded her arms, waiting to see how Jo would sidestep Eddie's probing, but tonight, the wine, the praise, the work done and done well, all that seemed to help her open up. Jo sighed and started talking.

"Business jobs never appealed to me. I come from simple folks of mixed heritage. And the bigots in my hometown never let me forget that or the fact that I was a lesbian. School was not that much fun for me. Being seen as the other is mostly horrible and I decided I wanted to do something to change that."

Eddie became pensive, rolled the stem of his glass between his fingers and raised his eyes and his drink toward Jo. "To you, Josefina, for forging your own path to success. I respect that."

Dani looked at him anew. "Yeah, Eddie. I'll drink to that." She held up her glass to Jo. "To you, mi amor."

"Okay, enough about me," said Jo. "Over to you, Dan. You can't avoid the spotlight completely. Do the piece on Cádiz you mentioned. That's an order."

"Geez, if it's an *order*. But only the first bit. It's too long."

Eddie turned to Dani. "¡Soy todo oídos!"

Dani laughed. "All ears. Okay, okay. Here goes." She stood, cleared her throat, and began:

"Hercules founded Cádiz, the legends say, over 3,000 years ago and it's considered Europe's oldest continuously inhabited community. It was named Gadir—the Stronghold—by the Phoenicians, Gades by the Romans, Quadis by the Moors. This tiny finger of land was the gateway to the western Mediterranean and the launching point to the Americas. Hugely strategic. Everybody wanted it and everybody attacked it, at one time or another." She ended with a fancy bow.

"That was great but is that all?"

"That's all I'm prepared to do right now."

Eddie smiled and clapped. "Bravo. Bravo. And no stage. Bien hecho. Well done." He turned serious. "I am from Seville. But I know these people here. Los gaditanos. It is true what you describe. And they still struggle, you know. Not against foreign invaders. These days the threat is more of a homegrown nature."

"What do you mean?" asked Dani.

"The city and this entire province remain an active gateway, but now twice over. People still come but not to conquer. They come legally and illegally in search of better lives for themselves, their children. Como todos, no?"

"Absolutely. Like everyone, everywhere," said Jo. "However, you said 'twice over.' What did you mean?"

"Cádiz is also a gateway for drugs. Hashish. Cocaine. The result is the rise of una cultura de los narcos and all the illegal activities that come with it."

"Narco culture? Here?" asked Dani.

"Yes. It is here and it is homegrown and it is growing in strength, increasing the divide between rich and poor, scandalously exploiting the desperate. It is a fairly recent development. There is much discussion about solutions. The kind of work you do, Jo, is one way. And my company is another."

"Okay, Eddie. A perfect opening. Time to turn the spotlight on you. What exactly do you do?"

"I am the brand ambassador for a company called Caballero Andante. CA for short. It means a gentleman who dedicates his life to defending the less fortunate."

"Like Don Quixote?"

"Exacto, Dani."

"What does CA do?" asked Jo.

"We are involved in many things but mostly in housing. My organization believes safe, affordable housing is one of the best methods of fighting back against the criminal element. Less vulnerable people can resist the lure of the criminal life. And now that it has come up, would you mind very much, Dani?" Without waiting for an answer, he turned his chair sideways and began speaking only to Jo. "As I mentioned at the conference, we deal with organizations providing housing."

"I understand. So, you want to give us loads of money? Is that it?" She snorted and put her hand on Eddie's arm. "Sorry. I'm too direct right now. Well, too drunk actually."

He laughed. "Yo también. Me too. To your question, Josefina. No. We do not give money. We *invest* in housing. We do not actually build buildings. We take over solid structures that already exist and are underutilized or abandoned. We renovate them for the specific needs of organizations like your HomeStart. In other words, we make properties useable for you. But we only do this with a guaranteed buyback, or in some cases, a leasing arrangement. The arrangement must offer us some remuneration for our work. Nothing exorbitant. We are not greedy but we are neither an NGO nor a charity. We need assurance of a return on investment. Altruistic entrepreneurs, if you will."

There's a spin. Dani listened to them talk about Eddie's proposal and nibbled on some pineapple and papaya still on the table. Gradually her thoughts drifted to their planned outing on the beach tomorrow. The weather was fantastic, a classic Andalusian spring. A bit windy, that Poniente, but she liked it. Stirred up her soul. She tuned back in when Eddie pushed his chair around to include her.

"When you two finish your holiday," he said, "you will go through Seville on your way home, yes?"

"Yes, we will."

"I could show you one of the residences my company has handled there."

Jo hesitated and looked at Dani who shrugged.

"I would love to see one of your places, Eddie. But only a quick visit at the end of the trip. I promised Dani one solid week and I don't want to cut into that."

Eddie nodded and reached into a pocket. "Excellent. You have my card and my email, Jo, so we can stay in touch. And here, Dani. My card for you as well. Do you have a cell phone number for use here in Spain?"

A kick from Jo under the table. Dani barely held a straight face. "Not yet," she said. "But when I get the damn thing set up, we'll send it to you."

"Excelente. Where will you be staying?"

"The conference people booked us a room right here at the Casa Colón," said Jo. "We're streetside so we don't have this view but that doesn't matter. It's convenient and the conference rate is great. They're even extending it for us, for the next week."

"I am glad they are making it work for you. Well, my new friends, this has been a thoroughly enjoyable evening. I thank you for allowing me the pleasure of hosting it. But it's time for me to go. The dawn and my flight home to Seville will come too soon. Josefina, we will talk again, yes? We have much to plan. Now, please stay and enjoy this wonderful place for as long as you wish. The bill is paid, of course."

He waved off their objections, air-kissed them, left and right, walked through the hedge opening and was gone.

They sat for another hour talking and staring out at the dark ocean. When the briny night air proved too chilly to ignore, they made their way back into the building. Just before getting on the elevator, Jo decided she needed a smoke. They walked together out the main glass doors and into the hotel's lush tropical garden. She lit up immediately. Dani took her free hand and they stood, silent. Jo threw her head back, closed her eyes and exhaled smoke from her cigarette. It floated up and was swept away by the fronds of the tall date palms waving in the breeze. Dani hated Jo's addiction but loved seeing her relax. Her skin glowed and the curve of her neck arched just so as she tilted her face skyward. It was a peaceful moment broken when Dani suddenly pulled Jo back hard.

"What?"

An ambulance tucked in the shadows had abruptly started moving and narrowly missed them as it sped off the hotel grounds. Its flashing lights and wailing siren popped on as it pulled into the street. They covered their ears.

"Geez. Let's go back to the room."

Jo mashed her cigarette out in an outdoor ashtray. "Sounds good. I'm wiped."

No sooner had the doors swooshed closed behind them than the clerk at the front desk called out, "Señoras. Señoras. ¿Podrían acercaros aquí por favor?"

They walked over, as requested.

"Con permiso, señoras. ¿Ustedes son, you are, Jo Gasperi y Dani Papineau?"

"Sí, sí."

"Ah, bueno. Un momento, por favor." He tapped away on his computer. "Ah sí, señoras, su sala ya está lista." Your room is ready.

"Uh, right. We've been in it for five days already." Dani pulled out her key card and put it on the desk.

He asked for permission as he took the card. "Si me permite, ya tenemos una habitación nueva para Uds. Es la mejor del hotel, muy lujosa. Cortesía del señor Eduardo Muñoz."

Jo touched Dani's arm. "Did I hear Eddie's name?"

"Yeah. I think he said we have a new room. He said 'courtesy of' so I believe Eddie booked it for us. *And* he described it as the best in the house."

"What? That's ridiculous. It must be some mistake. God, I hate not being able to understand."

Dani spoke again with the clerk.

"No mistake."

"No. No. Absolutely not, Dan. If HomeStart ever does business with his company, I can't have accepted expensive gifts. Too easily misconstrued. Even his paying for dinner was ethically iffy."

"Right. Damn. He did say the best in the house, though." She saw the concern on Jo's face. "Okay, okay. I'll tell him we don't want it."

Dani explained to the front desk guy as well as she could in Spanish. He gave her a lengthy reply. She turned back to Jo. "The problem is, they've already reassigned our old room. And they've moved our bags into the new one."

"We weren't even packed. I don't like that."

Dani turned back to the desk and the discussion continued. "He says they're booked solid because some cruise ship got hung up in port and our old room is already gone. I don't think we have much choice here, Jo."

"Oh for fuck sake, how much is it?" Jo started fumbling through her briefcase. Dani dropped the expletive in her translation for the desk clerk. He quoted the price. Dani blanched and told Jo, who promptly slapped down her credit card, signed the paperwork and took the key card.

"Done," said Jo. "Now let's go see what we'll be remortgaging the house for."

It was on the eighth floor and plain as toast: a small room, terracotta tile floor, double bed under a cotton coverlet, side lamps and an accent table on the far side. Jo immediately checked the contents of their bags while Dani went out the door to the balcony.

"Oh my god. Jo. You gotta see this."

Jo rushed to Dani's side. "What? What's wrong?"

It was more terrace than balcony, spanning the width of the building and furnished with wrought iron lounge chairs and a coffee table. They stepped outside. The moon was high in the sky now, bright and full, silver-plating waves that hurled themselves onto the rough black rocks directly below, rolled onto the white sand beach to the left and crashed into the malecón to the right. The sound rendered them silent, words yielding to surf. They stood enthralled and moved back inside with reluctance. Jo immediately crumpled onto the bed.

"I wish you'd let him pay for this," Dani said as she lay down beside her.

"Eddie? I don't want to be beholden to him in any way mainly because of what he was suggesting. He says his company buys, renovates and rents to governments and NGO's solely for newcomers or whomever is in need. It sounds fantastic and after a whole lot of due diligence, we might actually do a deal. But you know what, Dan? I'm going to take your advice and stop thinking about all that. I'm on holidays now."

"Excellent. You are now the proud owner of five days without computers or cell phones, other than our secret burner. You are completely disconnected. Freedom, my love. This week will change your life."

CHAPTER TWO

Dani bolted upright out of a deep sleep and looked over at Jo. Her eyes were pressed closed, her breath short, hair plastered against pallid skin.

"I...I...can't...breathe. Pain...in my...chest."

Dani put her hand on Jo's forehead and felt cold sweat.

"Stabbing...pain," Jo said, lightly touching her chest.

"Try to sit up."

"No. No. Can't. Pain...worse...when I move."

"Maybe it's indigestion. We overdid it at the Eddie extravaganza. Or maybe there was something wrong with the food."

"But...are...you...?"

"Sick? No. Good point. I feel fine. Let me get you a drink of water."

"No. Hurts to swallow." Long pause. "I think...it's...my heart."

Dani didn't move. Couldn't. She was immobilized by the memory of her father's heart attacks, the last one in particular. She hesitated only long enough to rehearse the Spanish words she would need, took a deep breath, picked up the phone and called the front desk. After she hung up, she got a damp cloth and sat next to Jo, gently wiping her forehead.

A sharp rap on the door surprised her. *Fast.* Dani opened the door expecting paramedics. Instead, the front desk clerk stood there, craning his neck to see around her and into the room.

"¿Dónde están los paramédicos?" Dani asked.

"Pues, señora, tengo que verificar su condición."

"Verify her condition? Are you a doctor?"

"Perdón, señora, pero quizá este problema no necesita de un doctor. Quizá bebió demasiado vino en la cena anoche?" *Perhaps this problem does not require a doctor. Perhaps too much wine at dinner?*

Dani was incredulous, rage surging. "Óigame." *Listen to me. You idiot.* "She's sick. She can't…" *Damn, what's the word for breathe?* "…respirar. Llame a los paramédicos inmediatamente, por favor. Call the paramedics right away, please."

He nodded, pulled out his cell phone and left.

Fifteen minutes later—the longest fifteen minutes of Dani's life—there was another pounding on the door. They stormed in like an occupying force, equipment clanking, orange vests blaring. One stood at Jo's bedside, gruffly giving orders to the other: connect her to the monitor, take her pulse, check her eyes. Preliminaries complete, the lead guy started asking Dani questions. All in Spanish.

"¿Cómo os llamáis?" *What are your names?*

"¿Nosotras dos?"

"Yes, both of you," he replied brusquely.

"Josefina Gasperi and I'm Danielle Papineau."

"How old is the sick one?"

"Forty-four."

"Has she ever had an episode like this before? What did she do this evening past? Today? Yesterday?"

It went on and on, his questions coming rapid-fire, all in Spanish. This was no casual exchange, no "cerveza, por favor." There was no margin for error. This was Jo's life. Dani answered as best she could, but she was shaky. She started missing words.

"¿Qué comió? ¿Bebió? ¿Ha tomado drogas? ¿Farmacéuticas? ¿Ilícitas? ¿Cómo sé siente ahora mismo? ¿Cuándo comenzaron los síntomas? ¿Tiene seguro médico?"

Their questions became a jumble of sounds. Her mind seized up, refusing to translate. She stared at them. They stared at her, waiting, until finally, the meaning of the last words, *seguro médico*, filtered through to her brain.

"Yes, she has insurance."

And the treatment continued. Lead guy picked up a needle and drove it into the skin between Jo's thumb and forefinger. Jo cried out. Dani cringed.

"Señor," Dani began, wanting to tell him to be gentle, desperately searching for the word, and only managing a pathetic, "no lo haga, por favor." Please don't do that. She cursed her own powerlessness, all the while wondering what that needle was for. They stuck small white discs on Jo's upper chest and attached the wires to a portable machine they'd set up next to the bed.

"Un electrocardiograma," the subordinate offered.

The ECG machine spit out results which the paramedics took to the small table next to the terrace door. After a brief study, lead guy pulled out his cell phone and punched in a number. He stood as he began to talk, turned to stare out the window. There was a short exchange with someone on the other end, inaudible except for the paramedic's replies, staccato bursts of "Seguro, el privado, ah sí, emergencia, entiendo, claro." Sure. The private one. Ah, yes. Emergency. Understood. Of course.

He turned back to Jo and Dani. "Pues, señoras," he said, slapping his flip phone shut. "Es un infarto."

A heart attack. Confirmed. It meant, he explained, she had to go to the hospital. Dani felt her own heart grow heavy. She translated for Jo, who closed her eyes without a word.

Lead guy produced a small patch, which he applied just above Jo's breast.

"Nitroglicerina," number two guy explained, smiling and rubbing his hands together like some creepy sycophant.

Dani prayed she'd translated everything correctly, understood it all. One word seemed out of place. "You said *privado*. What does el privado, the private, mean?"

"That is the private hospital. There are private and public hospitals," the subordinate explained.

"Why a private one?"

"Lo más cerca," grumbled the larger man. The closest.

Dani hesitated. She'd read that medical care in Spain's public system was excellent. *And private hospitals are even better, right? Only the best for the privileged?*

He asked for Jo's passport and insurance policy. Dani looked at him, wondering if she should actually hand them over, something travellers are advised not to do. But one look at Jo and she pushed her misgivings aside. She reluctantly placed the documents in the big guy's hand. He copied down information from both documents, returned the insurance card and explained he would keep the passport because hospital admitting would need it. *Shit.* They lifted a miserable Jo into a sling and slowly carried her out of the room and onto the stretcher they'd left in the hallway.

Once on the main floor, the paramedics hit full stride. The night clerk glanced up and away with apparent discomfort. The glass doors of Casa Colón swooshed open, as if eager to hurry this unpleasant business off the premises. The two men loaded Jo's stretcher and Dani climbed into the rear passenger seat with the paramedics seated up front. The ambulance lumbered off the hotel grounds, carefree garden palms cheerily waving them bye-bye.

They drove a short distance along the ocean-side boulevard, siren on full. They changed direction and headed into the city centre. After a couple of normal streets, their route deteriorated into the labyrinth of Old Town, endless passageways requiring slowing and turning and slowing and turning.

Dani berated herself the whole way. *Maybe the trip was too much for Jo.* She winced as she remembered poking her chest in the heat of the discussion.

"Don't you get it? This is a gift from the gods, a holiday mostly paid for and with no strings attached, well, aside from the fact you have to give a speech at the conference. But you're good at that, right? So come on." Dani held her arms out, palms up and curved, like some carnival preacher rousing the faithful. "What more could you possibly ask for?" Jo had finally agreed despite her misgivings: not speaking Spanish, boarding out the dog and leaving her never-ending work in Toronto. *Way to go.* She sighed.

The ambulance came to a full stop, siren silenced.

Out her window was a well-lit entrance with the sign Entrada de la Clínica Emergencia Ortega. Entrance. Ortega Emergency Clinic.

She got out quickly to watch the two men she now thought of as Scrawny Guy and Thug. They swung the rear doors open and pulled Jo out. They went in the main entrance and through a wide, empty lobby. They kept going, rolling Jo through a room labeled Emergencia and into a smaller examination room, no staff or other patients anywhere to be seen.

"Don't leave me," Jo said, voice taut and low.

"I won't. I'm here," Dani replied, resting her hand on Jo's arm. She looked so pale.

The paramedics asked for Dani's signature on some papers and turned to leave.

"Perdón. Where is everyone? She needs to be seen by someone."

"The nurse will come soon," Scrawny Guy answered. "This is a very good hospital."

"Are you sure? It doesn't even look open."

"Sí, sí. Ya viene," he repeated as the two men left the room.

Dani leaned against the stretcher and took Jo's hand. Ten minutes went by and still they were alone and waiting. Ten minutes more and Dani's apprehension became unbearable.

"This is ridiculous. I'm going to find someone."

"No. Don't leave me."

"Maybe I could find a cab and take you somewhere else."

Jo groaned. "Where? You know where there's another hospital?"

"No, I don't. But nothing's happening. He said this was a private hospital. I figured you'd be swarmed by nurses and doctors and getting the best of care."

"I'm scared, Dani. Don't leave me."

"Okay. I won't." She squeezed Jo's hand. Her breathing was getting more laboured again. Dani shuddered. "Are you okay? Your breathing is…" Jo moved her head slowly indicating "no." *Thank god. She's not getting worse. It must be her fear. That's causing the breathing. Shit. I'm scared too. Gotta distract ourselves.* "Babe. Why don't I finish my piece on Cádiz?" She launched right into it without waiting for an answer.

"We've got this city in an incredible location, gateway to this and that and all? Remember? And everyone wanted a piece of it. Guys like Napoleon, no less. His crew parked their ships in the harbour and stayed there for two years, lobbing bombs all over town. Two years. Can you imagine? And we think construction in Toronto is bad. Of course, what this did to the collective psyche of the locals, called gaditanos by the way, is anyone's guess. However, and here's the pitch, contemporary Cádiz has emerged as a vibrant and unique city, known for its jambalaya of cultural histories, in part thanks to those nasty invaders but also to today's immigrants and emigrants. And there's its ancient Old Town which we just had a horrific ride through, may I say. A bunch of grand plazas like San Antonio where your conference was held. They've got the naval yards, whopping unemployment, generally left-leaning politicos with the occasional rightist blip, Paco de Lucía on the cultural front along with my Gerardo of course and Manual de Falla, flamenco, etcetera etcetera and bonus!, trees Columbus allegedly brought back from the 'new world' as the Europeans so charmingly called it. And let's not forget the sun, the sand and the malecón, a.k.a. seawall. The wine and the wind."

"I know what you're doing." Jo's voice came out just above a groan. "Sweet, but not working. Actually it's making me feel ill. Rather have silence."

"Wow. The pitch is that bad eh? Just kidding. I'll shut up."

Another ten minutes ticked by. Dani stood up. "I can't stand it. I'm going to go check the lobby. I won't leave the area, Jo, I promise."

She started toward the door as it burst open. Two nurses entered the room: a long-legged young woman in a skimpy pink uniform pushing a cart and a rather severe-looking older woman in a more modest, yet still short and ill-fitting pink getup. Her name tag said Enfermería Jefa Montoya, Head Nurse Montoya. She nodded at Dani while the younger one leaned over to take Jo's wrist, the hem of her uniform riding high. She tracked Jo's pulse against the clock and checked her heart with a stethoscope.

Jefa Montoya turned to Dani. "Por favor, may I have your friend's passport and insurance information please?"

Dani's eyebrows scrunched together. "The paramedics have the passport. Didn't they give it to you? And the insurance card is, uh, I put it back into the leather pouch." Dani looked at the handful of things she'd grabbed as they'd left the hotel. The backpack and the slouch bag. Wallets were there. But no leather pouch. "Damn, I didn't bring it. It must still be at the hotel."

"No se preocupes, señora. Don't worry. I will get the passport and insurance information from the paramedics. Bueno," she said turning back to Jo. "Dime. ¿Qué pasó?" What happened?

"Don't you have the paramedics report?" Dani said, incredulous at having to go through it all again.

"Sí, claro," she said, unfazed. "But I need to hear it directly."

"Okay. A friend took us for dinner at El Gato…"

"El Gato?" The younger nurse turned toward Dani. "Gerardo is playing there right now." She sighed. "Ay dios, ¡qué pulgar!"

"What is she saying?" Jo whispered, annoyed. "Did she say that word, pull something?"

"Shit. Yeah. She did. Sorry." Dani raised both her hands to the nurse. "Sorry. Not El Gato. My mind is mush. We had a reservation there and we cancelled it. Oh geez. Doesn't matter. Ignore all that. We didn't go there. We went to, uh, uh…shit. I'm losing it."

"Take your time, señora," said the head nurse.

Dani nodded. "Right. Right. Okay. Thank you." She took a deep breath, exhaled and started again. "We ate at uh, the hotel restaurant on the cliff. El, uh, El Alabado. That's the name. And after that, we were exhausted and went to bed."

The older nurse asked what they had eaten.

"Biftec estofado with vegetables. Some sides. Lots of wine. Probably too much. We finished with coffee and brandies."

Dani told Jo what she'd said.

"Just tell her I feel like shit."

"Pues, señora," Montoya said directly to Jo, "you must be admitted to the hospital. We will do a blood test and wait for the doctor to decide what needs to be done from there."

Dani translated again for Jo. She groaned. "I guess that's good, though. I need to know what's going on. That pain, oh my god."

"Is it less now?" asked Dani.

Jo nodded. "A little, but still there."

"It is the nitro. It will lessen the pain," said the head nurse as she checked Jo's patch. The other nurse took a blood sample. She helped Jo sit up, gave her a glass of water and a couple of tiny white pills.

"What are they?" asked Jo, fingering the first pill.

"Aspirina. Until you see the doctor and we get test results, we won't be giving you anything more than the nitroglycerine and aspirin."

"When will the doctor come?"

"Soon, señora. Paciencia."

Montoya turned sharply and left, her colleague hot on her heels.

The door no sooner closed than Scrawny Guy burst in. He didn't give them a word or a glance while he prepped the stretcher for moving. He was listening intently to a small device emitting a tiny, disembodied torrent of Spanish. Dani eventually caught a few words: final, Atlético Madrid. Guadalajara. A soccer game. "Fútbol," she said out loud, before she could stop herself.

"Sí, sí señora," he said. "Están jugando en Estados Unidos." A game in the U.S.

"Ah, sí." She paused. "Pues, señor, por favor, ¿puede Ud. decirme cuándo Uds. van a devolvernos el pasaporte de Jo?"

"Más tarde. Más tarde." Later. They weren't returning Jo's passport until later. Dani was about to ask when *later* would be when he pushed past her with Jo's stretcher and moved quickly into the main hall. Montoya joined them and he quickly muted his game. There was silence. *Okay, now's my chance. Maybe she'll help me get an answer.* But the head nurse had her own issues. She let loose a streak of nonstop Spanish directed at Scrawny Guy about something or other. It was too fast for Dani to understand or interrupt. By the time Montoya stopped talking, they were at the elevator. It was smaller than the hotel's and after they pushed Jo's stretcher on, there was no room left for Dani.

"I'll take the stairs. What floor?"

"El tres. The third. Pero no, señora. Don't take the stairs. Hay construcción." As the doors slid shut, Montoya said, "I will send the elevator back down to you."

Dani waited and stared as the floor indicator numbers rose, her apprehension with them. It seemed to take forever to get to three. After a brief pause, it began an excruciatingly slow descent. By the time the doors finally opened on the ground floor, Dani was frantic, rushing on, stabbing the button repeatedly. The doors closed slowly. A cheery tune with a samba beat filled the space. She knew it but couldn't remember the name. She saw herself reflected in its glossy walls. Wrinkled blazer. Hair shoved back. Pained expression. Distraught dyke chastising herself for allowing them to take Jo ahead without her.

When she reached the third floor, she bolted off and looked both ways. It was a curved hall and completely empty. Small sounds came from the right. She ran in that direction and caught sight of the tail end of the stretcher just as it disappeared around the bend. She reached the little caravan and took Jo's hand. They made eye contact. *Whatever happens, we're together.*

They continued along the highly polished tile floors, the only sound the plumpf, plumpf of the orderly's soft-soled shoes, the slap of the nurse's harder rubber ones, the slight squeak of the stretcher wheels. Beyond that, all was silent. All was still. No other nurses, no other patients, no medical carts in the hall, no machines beeping, no televisions, no radios. Nobody. Nothing. Nada. *Fuck.*

They stopped at Room 312.

CHAPTER THREE

As the head nurse pushed open the door and flicked a wall switch, Dani felt an overwhelming impulse to grab the stretcher and Jo and race back to the elevator. The whole place creeped her out and Room 312 did nothing to change that. A blinding bare bulb lit up an old-fashioned room: high ceiling, glossy green plaster walls, a bed with a rounded white-iron frame, a closet and a second door. A reclining chair slouched in the corner and a straight-back chair pushed against the bed. A small chest of drawers was tucked in on the other side. High up on the wall was a small reading light. Below, within the patient's reach, hung an old-fashioned black wall phone. It made Dani think of a scene from an old-time TB sanitorium. Grim. The only pleasant feature was a large double window with a view of the street by day. Now it was a wall of darkness.

Scrawny Guy helped Jo move to the bed. Montoya brought her a hospital gown, suggesting Dani take Jo's clothes to the hotel and bring back any items she would need: underwear, toothbrush, hairbrush. The nurse turned toward the door to leave.

"Uh, señora?" Dani said. "How long do you think she'll have to stay in the hospital?"

"It's up to the doctor. She will come later today."

"Wait. What? Excuse me? The doctor isn't coming now? No one is going to see her right away?" Dani asked, stunned. "She was rushed here because the paramedics said she had a heart attack. She needs to see a doctor now."

"She is stable, señora."

"And what happens if she has another episode?"

Clearly unconcerned, the nurse repeated herself.

"Tell her I have to pee, really bad," Jo said.

"Sí sí," Montoya replied to Dani's translation. "There is a bathroom there," she said pointing to the second door.

"Could you bring her a…a…*bedpan*…urinal…so she doesn't have to move?"

"No, señora. It is good for her to get out of bed for such things. To keep her blood moving."

"Ohh-kay," Dani said slowly, her voice rising with doubt. She sifted through her memories of heart attacks. *Never heard that bit of cardiac advice before.*

The nurse noticed Dani's hesitation. "I will return right away to help her." She left with the paramedic and his stretcher.

"What did she say about the doctor?" Jo asked as Dani out held the hospital gown for her.

"She said she'll come back to help you to the bathroom."

"No, no. About the doctor. What was she saying about the doctor?"

"She said you're stable now and that the doctor will see you later in the day."

"Later in the day? Oh man, that sounds like so long. I thought being admitted would only mean some testing, a prescription and off we go. I know I know. I guess I'm dreaming, dreaming of that glorious hotel room and my week off in…in…" She sighed.

"In paradise," Dani finished her thought, heart aching at Jo's tone. Fragile. Frantic. Sick and not able to communicate. Not able to manage her own affairs. *Jo's nightmare. Anyone's nightmare, really.*

"How are you feeling now, babe? That's the important thing. How's your chest, your breathing?"

"Not great. My stomach's queasy and my chest is still heavy. But I feel better than when I woke up. At least I can breathe." Jo turned her head away. Was she crying? Dani put her hand on Jo's shoulder. Jo grabbed it, pulled her closer and whispered, "You have to call the insurance people."

Nope. Not crying.

"You know, babe, insurance shouldn't be your biggest concern."

"It's not. But it will be if we get a bill for a few hundred thousand dollars."

"C'mon. Cost is not something to worry about right now, okay? We can remortgage the house if it comes to that."

"We already did that for the room with a view, remember?"

"Aha. Your sense of humour is intact. That's good."

"I'm not joking. The insurance card is in the leather pouch."

"I left the pouch at the hotel so we don't have the insurance card. I told the head nurse all this downstairs. Remember?"

"No. I don't remember. And my passport?"

"The paramedic kept it. He said the hospital people would need it."

"I hate this, Dani. I really hate it."

"I know. I hate it too." She couldn't think of anything more reassuring to say.

"You've got to go back for the insurance card. You need to call the insurance people."

"Seriously? You want me to leave you alone? I'm not even sure I can find the hotel from here. Why don't I do it by daylight? Tomorrow first thing?"

"No, they need to be contacted right away. It's one of their rules. They're in Los Angeles. This is a good time to call because of the time difference. And maybe I could call my mum or my sister in case, you know, something unexpected happens, so they won't hear about it after I'm dead."

"Geez, Jo. Don't think like that."

"How do I work the phone?"

Dani rounded the bed to reach the phone and grabbed the receiver. She listened for a second, flicked the metal cradle a few times and put the receiver back.

"No dial tone."

"We probably have to set up an account or something."

"I can't imagine the phone activation person is working in the middle of the night if the doctor isn't. I can check downstairs. Or we could use our new cell."

"I forgot we had that. Yeah. Use it."

Dani pulled it from her pocket, turned it on.

"I got an error message. No service. Fuck. I know I did the setup right."

"Maybe it's the building. Old buildings do that sometimes. Just grab a cab and go back to the hotel, get the insurance card and make the call. And a quick one to my sister too. And then just stay there, Dani, and get a good night's sleep."

"No way I'm leaving you here alone all night. I'd never be able to sleep anyway. I'd worry the whole time."

"And I'll worry about you walking around Old Town in the middle of the night. Take a cab and stay in that gorgeous room with a view. I'll be fine. I have my own little room now. And that head nurse seems okay. Crusty but benign. And I feel a tiny bit better than before. I just need to pee. Where is she?"

"Here, I'll help you."

Just as Dani leaned over to help Jo sit up, the door flew open. Montoya returned.

"Señoras, what is happening? Where are you going?"

"To the bathroom? Like you suggested?"

Montoya didn't move, simply stared at them.

"So, like, do you think you could help us here?"

"Sí, sí."

"Gracias. And one more thing, señora. Is there a working phone in the hospital? The one here doesn't work."

Montoya shrugged but didn't respond.

"So, is there? A working phone?" *What is wrong with this woman?*

"I do not know which ones are working and which ones are not."

"How about the phone in the emergency department?"

"Perhaps, señora."

Helpful, aren't you? "So if something happens up here on this empty floor, how do we get a hold of you?"

"You will be here, will you not, señora?"

"Eventually. But as you suggested, I have to make a quick run back to the hotel."

"Sí, sí, claro. I will check on her while you are gone."

"Okay, babe. I'm off. I'm going to see if I can find a phone first. After that, I'll go to the hotel to get your things and that insurance number." Dani moved her head close to Jo until their foreheads touched. A ripple of fear ran through her at the thought of leaving. "But I will be back, ASAP," she whispered.

She stopped and watched the nurse deftly maneuver Jo to the bathroom.

"Don't talk to strangers," Jo called out weakly.

Dani forced a laugh. It was a joke. Jo knew her fears all too well. "Not that funny, babe. See you soon."

Dani left Room 312 and started down the hall. She walked by a room with a stretcher left next to the door. *That wasn't there before.* She heard voices. One was soft and low. Another voice was loud, almost crying. *A woman in pain, and afraid.* She hurried on. She didn't even want to know what was going on there but she was marginally glad someone else was on the floor. She hated leaving Jo here, alone. *Just go, Dan. Find the number, make the calls and get back here. Fast.*

She checked the third-floor nursing station. No phone. She went to the elevator and pressed the down button. She could hear the mechanical beast moving sluggishly behind the wall. Just when she figured it had arrived and the door was about to slide open, it continued on to a higher floor. She groaned and decided to take the stairs. *How bad can it be?*

She charged through the stairwell door next to the elevator and almost fell over a ladder leaning against the wall. A fine white dust swirled around her. Montoya wasn't kidding. It was a construction zone. She heard the door behind her move, the column of light from the hall narrowing as it drifted shut. She turned to stop it, but a moment too late. The door closed with a convincing click.

Darkness enveloped her. She searched for the doorknob. *Where is the damn thing?* She patted down the entire surface to make sure it wasn't in some weird designer location. No. There was no doorknob. *Aargh! I hate you people.*

Her lungs grew heavy. Her breaths shortened. She couldn't see in front of herself, not one step. Panic swelled inside her. What if she were trapped? She flashed on her skeletal remains discovered centuries later by paleontologists who would puzzle over her dying in a stairwell. *Oh, shut up, Dani. You're being ridiculous.*

As her eyes grew accustomed to the darkness and her surroundings became a bit more visible, her breathing normalized and she decided she could see enough to keep going. She started down the stairs. Very carefully. She wended her way past various construction materials lying helter-skelter: big plastic buckets, little pans and trowels, an old cloth. Her foot landed in a mud pan and practically sent her flying face first to her grave. She pondered the fire code violations of all this junk blocking an exit route and almost laughed. *Right. People who remove doorknobs probably don't care.*

At the second-floor landing, the door was propped open onto a huge dark space. Dani hurried past it and continued down to the next landing. The door there had a glass window on which was painted primera planta, first floor. She was elated to find a doorknob, right where it should be, at hand level. And bonus, it turned. She opened the door and walked into the lobby. She sucked in a lung's worth of air, revelling in her freedom before heading for the emergency room.

Still empty. There was a phone on the counter but it didn't have a recognizable dial tone, only a solid drone. She tried each number on the keypad, thinking one should connect to an outside line but none worked. In frustration she slammed the handset down and stormed out the main doors.

The street was dark and empty. A smell triggered something close to solace. Cigarettes. Less comforting was the sound of male voices speaking low. An exchange between familiars. The ambulance was parked to one side of the building. The two paramedics leaned against it. Scrawny Guy and Thug. *Ugh!* She forced herself to approach them, taking cold comfort in the fact they weren't complete strangers.

"Hola. Perdón. ¿Hay un teléfono público en el hospital?"

Thug ignored her, looking away, smoke sifting through the fingers of the hand that cupped his cigarette in so manly a fashion. Scrawny Guy shrugged, his lips stretching into a thin smile.

"Allá. There is a public phone," he said, pointing down the street.

Dani peered in that direction and saw a bright blue kiosk under a streetlamp at the intersection. "Ah sí, Okay. Gracias. And where can I grab a cab to the hotel?"

"There are no late-night cabs in this area except the ones that drop people at El Popular. That is the bar"—he pointed— "across the street from the phone booth. But, señora, Casa Colón is not far. It is allá, allá, down the street past the bar. Se puede caminar."

"Really? I can walk to it? And yet it took so long to get here."

Scrawny Guy raised his shoulders and spread his hands. "Ay sí, señora. It is the streets. They are crazy in Old Town." Thug exhaled a smoky cloud that enveloped her.

She stifled a cough and went over to the phone kiosk. Across the street was the bar the paramedic had mentioned. El Popular. Its hanging sign creaked along to a muted thump-thump-thump of music bleeding through the walls. She watched a couple go into the bar, the rowdy sound of a party zone pouring onto the street as the door opened. *Popular indeed.*

She looked back at the paramedics next to the ambulance. *No. Not the public phone with you two and who-knows-who-else within earshot. Use the hotel phone. You have to go to there anyway.*

She turned her attention back to the street. It was long, narrow, and completely deserted.

Fuck. My nightmare.

Literally.

It was always the same, her dream: she was alone in the middle of the night, in danger, wandering through a seedy warehouse district with darkened tractor-trailers and no people.

Dani didn't know why she had this dream, suspecting the origin was some forgotten childhood trauma or scary story at a tender age. Or maybe it was because of her mother's dire "warnings" as Dani called them. Every time she was about to go out, her mum would launch into something cringeworthy, like "keep your knees together" or "don't talk to strangers."

Ghastly tales from the news were another source of inspiration, stories about braids caught in machinery and dead bodies dumped in the woods. They changed, of course, as Dani grew older, becoming vaguer allusions to pending doom like, "stay in well-lit places" and "make sure you have a ride home." Dani's favourite, though, and the only one that made her laugh, was the "never-pose-in-the-nude-because-you-never-know-where-that-image-will-end-up" exhortation. She'd scoffed at that one at the time but never had, posed in the nude that is, despite dalliances with several artists. The worst horror story, however, was the one her mother never mentioned, couldn't even have imagined. That was the one that took her life and scarred Dani forever.

She stared down the dark, dodgy route, shook her head, gritted her teeth and goaded herself into moving forward, her blood pressure rising, her breathing accelerating. *Dani, you aren't that timid little kid anymore. And you're strong now. Definitely not a weakling.*

She *was* strong. Her arms had hardened from years of hauling amps and guitars and various sound equipment. And her legs? After deeming them a fashion liability like *for-e-ver*, she had lately come to consider those stocky appendages a genetic gift from her ancestral Celts, excellent for climbing crags and running down deer. Granted, those skills weren't in high demand these days, although running *from* something could always come in handy.

Come on, Dan. Running from what? Drunken sailors? Rapists and murderers? Ultra-right-wing homophobic racist misogynist goons? Wild animals? There are no animals salvajes here, waiting to pounce.

She wasn't so sure about the rest and moved quickly past each darkened space, scanning as much for places to hide as for signs of danger. Her heart raced. She was scared, scaring herself. She remembered the breathing trick a therapist had taught her and pulled the air deep into her belly, then slowly exhaled it.

It was warm and sweet, that night air, seductively so, laced with vestiges of the day's heat, of humidity and green things growing. And brine. The ocean was close. She could taste it, feel its pulse.

This was Cádiz asleep in the embrace of its elements. Dani realized it was beautiful and that *she* was the whirling dervish of fear, terrified for Jo and what lay ahead of them. She breathed in and out again, adding prayers to whatever gods/goddesses/he/she/theys were on duty: *protect me, protect us.* Protéjanme. Protéjannos.

She caught a glimpse of a yellow glow further down. It was the sign for their hotel blazing in bright neon letters calling to her like a beacon of safe harbour. When she reached the end of the street, all was quiet. A traffic light blinked in nighttime mode. Cars were tucked in next to the curb. Across the wide boulevard the hotel palms, those fickle fronds, waved at her manically in the brisk westerly. "Come on over," they said, "and enjoy La Casa Colón."

She spoke briefly to the night clerk, explaining that Jo was in the hospital but that they would keep their room. She found Jo's leather pouch right there on the table by the bed. Inside was the insurance card. The bedclothes were rumpled. The impression of Jo's body was still visible. She sat down and cried. Her heart was breaking. *She's on this trip because I wanted it. A gift from the gods, I said. The Promised Land all warm and Latin. Cádiz, Spain. Paradise. That's what I called it. Shit.* That idea of a paradise pending, just around the seasonal corner, had fuelled

Dani through a bitter winter, hauling her guitar and equipment through minus-twenty temperatures and thirty-plus winds around ever-growing piles of snow just to get herself to her crazy assortment of gigs all over Toronto. Lying on the beach had never been Jo's dream.

What if they have to keep her there indefinitely? What if there's surgery? What if Jo dies? Anguish surged through her like it did the night her mum died. An accident, the police had said. Her dad had disagreed. Said it was no accident. She saw herself sitting alone, like he did after that night, soul in despair. *No. No. Stop. You can't think about all that. You've got to find a way to stay strong instead.*

She went into the bathroom, splashed water on her face and drank some from her hand. She tried to think about how she'd dealt with her fears in the past. She remembered her talisman. She'd actually tucked it in a side pocket of her suitcase for the trip, out of habit. She always had it with her at home. Just in case. She would touch it for comfort when she was nervous or afraid. Things like doctor's appointments, exams, some performances, she had it close at hand to give herself comfort. It was a bit alternative, she knew, and definitely gave Jo a chuckle, but she didn't care. It helped her deal with her *stuff.* But she never thought she'd need it here. She pulled it out of the pocket and looked it. It was a tiny angel figure no bigger than a thumbnail. *Hmmm. This situation may require something bigger than you, little darlin'.* She clutched the little angel statue tightly in her hand and went out onto the terrace. She sat down on a big wrought iron chaise lounge and listened to the ocean, automatically starting her deep-breathing practice. With apologies to her tiny friend, she imagined the powerhouse woman she wanted to be, needed to be for Jo. Her first big angel image wore a long white gossamer gown and sported huge white wings. *Nah. Try again.* The image of a tall muscular woman popped in her head, skin glinting in the moonlight, hair pulled back tight and out of the way, eyes narrowed, jaw tensing, arms ripped, stance aggressive, kind of Michelle Rodriguez meets Serena Williams. Dani's mouth screwed up in a twisted smile. *You're crazy, you know that?* She put her head in her hands and sighed. *But anything for you, my beloved Jo. I will not let you down. I will protect you.* She went inside, made the calls and headed back to the hospital, badass angel top of mind.

CHAPTER FOUR

She hurried along the long dark street. Her fear intensified with each step, that same old terror now added to a gut-level feeling that she'd left Jo alone far too long. She felt the little angel in her pocket and made herself walk like the big one, fists clenching and unclenching.

The street in front of the hospital was dark and still, the light on the sign over the door off. *Geez. Closed for the night?* The ambulance was parked in the same spot, no paramedics in sight. She went into the hospital lobby. Empty, as was emergency. But the elevator was there, its door open as if it was waiting just for her. She pushed the button for the third floor. The door closed and the music started. In her present mood it sounded like the score of a horror movie. *Hard for a samba.*

She got off on the third and the elevator closed immediately behind her. She started down the hall, her own footsteps echoing back at her. She was alone. It seemed darker than before. She shook her head. *No, you're imagining it.* She came around the curve near Jo's room and stopped cold. It was the stretcher, now positioned sideways and spanning the width of the hall, preventing her from passing.

It carried a form, an unmistakeably human form, covered by a large white sheet. A hand had dislodged and fallen into view. She couldn't pull her eyes away from it. She edged nearer, leaned forward and peered at it. White skin with brown age spots. Squarish fingers. Chewed nails. Not Jo. She reached out and grabbed the corner of the stretcher pushing it back against the wall so she could get by. She heard the elevator door roll open back down the hall. She turned and walked quickly to room 312.

It was still. Unlit. The glow from the streetlamp just outside barely nudged the shadows aside. The room appeared empty.

"Jo?" Dani whispered. She got no response. Her heart flip-flopped. "Jo?" she called out louder this time.

"Dani?" came a small voice.

"Where are you?"

"In the bathroom."

"Geez, Jo, you totally freaked me out. I thought you were gone." She pulled open the bathroom door. "Why is the light off? I can't see a thing."

A soft, snuffling sound. Dani flipped on the light to see Jo huddled on the toilet.

"You're crying?" she asked.

"Please get me out of here. I've been here since you left."

"Oh my god. What the hell happened to Montoya?"

"Her pager went off right after you left. She got me on the toilet and took off. She hit the light switch. Without thinking, I imagine."

"Without thinking? That's only marginally better than on purpose. I can't believe you've been in here all this time. Did you try standing up?"

"Of course. But I got dizzy. I was afraid I'd fall or pass out so I just stayed still."

"Dizzy? That's new. I think we should get you out of here, Jo. You've been abandoned on the toilet for god's sake, and they've done nothing at all for you. Besides, it's disturbing out there"—she jerked her head toward the door—"and uh, I'm not sure you'll get, uh, the *quality* treatment you want, if you get any at all."

"Okay, I want to know more about what you're saying, but can I first get the hell out of the bathroom? Please?"

"Right." Dani positioned herself in front of Jo and put her arms under Jo's armpits. "This is ridiculous." She bent her knees and pulled Jo into a standing position. Jo grunted. "Are you okay?" Dani asked.

"Yeah."

They shuffled into the main room like some bizarre two-faced arachnid and eventually reached the bed. Jo lay back gingerly and let out a big sigh. Dani sat down next to her and took her hand.

"I really think we should find another hospital. There's something very off here."

"Yeah. But I'm now even more afraid of leaving. My chest pain is only slightly better and I've got a headache too." She pressed her hand to her head.

"Headache *and* dizzy?" She gave Jo a long look.

"Dani? What did you mean that it's disturbing out there?"

She didn't answer at first. She didn't want to freak Jo out. Thug notwithstanding, there might be a logical explanation for what she'd seen and heard down the hall. "Uh, well, it's just so empty of people here and it's all taking too long. You need to be checked out immediately, not whenever some doctor decides to stroll in. I know you're scared, Jo, but I *really* think we should leave."

"Please, Dan. Just a little longer." Jo took a deep breath. "Did you make the calls?"

Dani told her about the conversation with Carmen, the woman at the insurance company.

"They're only waiting on the doctor's name and your passport number."

"But you got the file started. That's great. And my sister?"

"She was worried. She started to cry."

"My sister? Wow. That's out of character."

"She loves you, babe."

Jo squeezed her hand.

"I am so angry with that nurse for leaving you. I'll take a strip off her when I see her, trust me, although I may not have the Spanish to do a proper harangue. I'd have to look up the words first."

They laughed softly, Jo still fragile, Dani still pissed.

"Maybe let's not blow off the head nurse yet. At least until I see the doc, okay?"

"Okay, babe. How about some sleep? You must be exhausted. And you know that recliner is looking rather inviting."

"Oh my god, it looks awful."

"Nah. It's perfecto."

She grabbed a blanket from the foot of Jo's bed, sat down, pulled off her runners, lifted her legs to the footrest and pushed the chair to recline. Jo rolled on her side and looked over at her.

"You know what's odd, Dan?"

"Aside from a heart attack, an ambulance ride to an almost vacant hospital and…wait for it…no doctor?"

"Yes, aside from all that. It's how quiet this place is. Hospitals are never quiet. They have machines and heart monitors and all sort of things beeping. And people coming into the room at all hours to do stuff. Nothing's going on here. What if I had another attack? How would they ever know?"

Dani tensed. She saw the image of the body on the stretcher, the hand dangling. *Shit, how would they know? Maybe they don't know.* "All the stuff I read said Spain has a great health care…" she slowed, seeing Jo's eyes closing, her breathing smooth out "…system. But more later."

Dani couldn't sleep. She started to think about possible scenarios but forced herself to stop. She tapped her talisman. *There is only one outcome. Jo will see the doctor, get a diagnosis and some meds. She'll be fine. And then we'll get the hell out of here. I will make sure of that.*

She drifted off and woke up a short while later needing to pee. She decided to brave the hallway and head to the public bathroom near the elevator. Less likely to wake Jo. And she wanted to see if *it* was still there. *Please god no.* She put on her sneakers and moved as quietly as she could out of the room. The smell of coffee hit her. *Hallelujah. Humans and stimulants. Life on the planet.* She patted the wallet in her hip pocket. She'd find that coffee, post.

She moved slowly along, one hand against the reassuring curved wall, half-expecting the stretcher-corpse combo to suddenly roll out in front of her. But it was gone. The hall was empty and the body apparently disposed of. She shuddered. *Better to be alone than—what is that?* She stopped and listened. A breathy gasping came from behind the empty nurses' station. The hair stood up on the back of her neck. She walked past the WC door, edged slowly toward the counter and peered behind the desk.

A man with stringy gray shoulder-length hair squatted there, his slim frame in a red jogging suit, his hands clutching his arms, partly covering a colourful ship patch stitched on the sleeves. He rocked back and forth without sound, except for sharp snatches of breath, just enough to continue silently weeping.

"¿Está usted bien?" Dani asked softly. Are you all right?

The man started at her voice, lifting his face, wet with tears. "No. No. No estoy *bien*," he said almost spitting the last word. An Anglo.

"You speak English." A statement, not a question. He didn't respond. "Can I help you?"

He opened his mouth and began making a small sound that grew to a keening so alarming, Dani moved back from the desk to put more distance between them. He lifted his hands to his hair and pulled and twisted the mucky strands in all directions. *Is he crazy?* She wasn't going to hang around to find out and made a hasty retreat back to the room. Dani closed the door quietly and sat down on the recliner, her fists clenching unclenching, on guard.

"What's going on?" Jo stared at her through bleary eyes.

"Uh, well, this guy is down the hall. He may be insane."

"More details, please."

"I went to use the washroom and this guy was on the floor behind the nurses' station having a meltdown."

"That head nurse woman was probably taking care of him."

"Montoya?" Dani laughed. "He did look totally abandoned. Uh, there was something going on in one of the rooms when I came back from the hotel. That might have something to do with it. But it's pretty dark out there. Maybe I won't investigate just yet."

"Good. Use the can here," Jo said drowsily. "You can figure out crazy guy in the morning."

CHAPTER FIVE

"Buenos Deeee-aahhhssss, señoras."

The singsong voice was high and sharp, shattering sleep like a hammer to glass. Dani's eyes snapped open. A young woman entered the room, wielding a broad smile and wearing a very short and low-cut nurse's uniform along with oddly practical clogs. She pushed a small stainless-steel cart with one hand while the other steadied the nurse's cap precariously attached to a high pile of frothy blond hair.

"Buenos días," she repeated in a more normal tone. "Yo me llamo, Leona."

Dani roused herself. *Not the name I would have guessed.* "Buenos días, Leona."

"It is late, señoras, and we have much to do."

"Is the doctor coming?" replied Dani.

"Sí, sí. Soon. Perhaps this morning. Perhaps this afternoon."

"Perhaps?" Dani's eyebrows shot up. "What do you mean? Last night the nurse, uh, Montoya, said the doctor would be here today."

"Yes, yes, of course. The doctor will come. Do not worry. What is more important right now," she said, handing sleepy-eyed Jo a small plastic container, "is that we require a urine sample. And I must take some blood."

"More blood?" Jo's words came crusted with sleep.

"Sí, sí, señora. And we must change your patch."

"Nurse, Jo now has headaches and she had a dizzy spell last night after that idiot jefa abandoned her on the toilet."

The nurse's eyebrows shot up.

She stared quizzically at Dani. "¿Qué dices, señora?"

Over Leona's shoulder, Dani could see Jo vigorously wagging her finger.

"The headache is new. And the dizziness? Maybe if she ate something she'd feel better?"

"No food and no water for now." She turned to Jo. "Except for your pill, of course."

"No water?" Annoyance slipped into Jo's voice.

"It is because you will go later this morning for more tests. It is important. No food and no water. You, señora," she said, turning back to Dani, "you can go to the cafeteria. They have coffee and snacks and right now they serve breakfast. It is just down the hall past the elevator."

"I smelled the coffee a couple of hours ago. The cafeteria is on this floor?"

"It is. Because of the construction."

"I have another question for you, Leona. Is it normal in this hospital to leave a heart patient alone and stranded on the toilet with a crazy man crying in the hall at all hours?"

"Not now, Dani." Jo spoke through gritted teeth.

Leona didn't respond immediately. She looked up at Dani while she took Jo's pulse. "We had una emergencia here at the hospital last night. Perhaps this is what you are referring to. But you can ask the doctor."

"I will if he or she or they ever shows up."

Leona widened her mascara-laden eyes. "She. La doctora Nieves-Félix," she said.

"Okay. If *she* ever shows up."

"Es seguro, señoras. Como dije. As I said. She *will* show up. When she can. She has many responsibilities with the hospitals and clinics. La Dra. Nieves is in charge of both Ortega facilities, here and near Jerez." She began the bloodletting ritual, taking eight vials.

"Wow. That's a lot you're taking. The nurse last night took blood too. No wonder Jo is dizzy."

"There are many tests to do. And don't forget the urine sample when you are ready."

Leona casually lifted Jo's gown. "Con permiso, señora." Before Jo could resist, the nurse pinched the flesh of her belly and pierced her skin with a needle that appeared out of nowhere. Jo yelped.

"Fuck. Nothing like a needle to the gut to get me going in the morning."

"I must give you an injection to prevent blood clots."

Jo shivered. "I thought that shot was only for surgery."

Leona didn't respond. "I will bring una aspirina for your headache."

She finished taking Jo's vitals, jotting her readings in a notebook. She changed the patch on her chest, packed up her equipment and left the room.

"Are you *sure* you don't want to leave this place?"

Jo didn't speak. She only pressed her lips together, shook her head, alarm flashing in those eyes before she turned toward the wall.

The cafeteria surprised Dani. It looked normal, even pleasant. It was a long, narrow room with glass walls providing glimpses of blue sky and white stucco buildings on one side and the hospital hallway on the other. Its wooden tables and chairs were in disarray. She could almost see a cast of hospital characters crammed in for their much-needed morning cafecito. *But where did they all go?*

The hiss of an espresso maker drew her attention to the counter. She ordered a coffee for herself and tea and a plain bun for Jo.

The barista nodded. "Tres euros, por favor, señora." He passed her a tray with a sturdy glass of espresso and hot milk, another glass with tea and a plate with Jo's bun.

Dani carried the load carefully back down the corridor and found Jo sitting up in bed holding a glass of water.

"I brought you tea and a bun. To hell with Leona." She noticed the pitcher of water and a tiny, fluted paper cup on the tray. "She brought you the aspirin?"

"Yeah, but I'm afraid I'll throw them up along with that stuff you've got there too."

Dani took a closer look at Jo. She was pale and covered with a sweaty sheen.

"You look like you have a serious fever. And you are nauseous? That's new, isn't it?" Jo gave her a small nod and blinked. "Is the chest pain back?"

"It never completely left. But it's a little better than last night. This headache is killing me, though. I think that's why I'm nauseated."

"Have a bit of the bun first and then take the aspirin. That might make it easier on your stomach. And I can always get more if you throw up."

"Great. Love the reboot plan." Jo dutifully ate a small bit of bread, sipped some tea, tossed the two pills from the paper cup into her mouth and downed them with water.

"Maybe the headache is withdrawal? No caffeine or nicotine since last night?"

"Don't remind me."

"I got myself a coffee. I hope that's okay. I really need some caffeine but I can drink it in the hall if you think the smell will bother you."

"No, no. Drink it."

Dani took a sip. "It's incredible, actually. It's like a latte with no foam, but strong. Really delicious."

"I said drink it. Don't flaunt it."

"Shit. Right. Sorry."

Their heads turned in unison as the door banged open. A bucket entered the room followed by a mop handle, and finally, the person pushing the whole affair.

"Con permiso…pardon me, señoras. My name is Zapa. I will wash your floor if you do not mind the interruption."

She was tall, athletic, with a mass of natural red hair secured by a wide metal clasp against the nape of her neck. Her blue uniform was similar to Leona's, but to different effect. While the morning nurse looked naughty, this woman was all business. The hem was still mid-thigh, making bending over awkward, but the relaxed fit allowed for greater ease of movement. She manoeuvred the heavy bucket and mop with panache, arm and leg muscles flexing under copper-brown skin. She broke the rhythm only to dunk her mop into the pail, squeeze out the rinse water and slap it back onto the floor. Dani sat down and raised her feet to give her room to mop.

"Gracias, señora," Zapa said with a brilliant smile.

"De nada," Dani replied. *You're welcome.* "Señora, may I ask you a question?"

Zapa stopped mid-swab. *"¿Una pregunta? Sí, cómo no."*

"Do you know if the doctor is in the building?"

"No sé. I do not know. I am sorry. She comes and goes at all hours."

"How about an older Anglo man acting kind of crazy, crying? He was on this floor early this morning, around three? And some, uh, activity at a room just down the hall?"

Zapa considered the questions, looked over at Jo and spoke. "Señora, es que, uh, I am sorry, but I have not seen such a man. And I do not know about the room down the hall." She looked away and returned to her work. Dani's eyes narrowed. *You do know something about that man I saw. Why are you saying you don't?*

Dani was unnerved by her and watched her closely as she cleaned the room. She was impressive with that damn mop, swishing the wet ropey tendrils about, allowing them to curl into the corners and around the legs of the bed, pulling them back before they clung too tightly. She quickly worked her way back to the door and stopped before leaving.

"Señoras, if you need anything, you will find me working on the first and third floors. I clean the lobby, the emergency room, the administration office, all the public washrooms, patient rooms, the cafeteria and the hallways. I sometimes must go to the basement laundry but I am not there long. I take my cafecitos in the cafeteria, claro. But that is not as often as I like," she said with a laugh. "If you cannot find me, please leave a message with Miguel. I am here to be of assistance. Me entienden? You understand?"

Dani nodded slowly but remained silent. Zapa nodded back and pulled the bucket out of the room and closed the door softly. Only a faint vapour trail of disinfectant remained.

"This is the oddest place," said Jo. "Getting anything from the medical staff is like pulling teeth while the maintenance crew seems eager to help."

"Yeah, well, not that eager. She knew *exactly* what I was referring to. And *odd* just doesn't cover it. This place is fucking bizarre. I mean, come on, the woman I heard, and that stretcher thing alone…"

"What stretcher thing? You didn't tell me about any stretcher thing."

"Uh, shit, actually, babe, I didn't mean to mention that. I didn't want to, you know, upset you, because it's kind of…well…upsetting."

"Spill."

Dani took a deep breath. "Okay." She told her the whole story in detail, seeing the stretcher, hearing the woman in pain, and then, later, the scene in the same hallway when she returned from the hotel. "The stretcher was still there, and okay, so this next part is what I didn't want to tell you."

Jo's brows were furrowed together. "Geez, Dani. Stop stalling. Just tell me."

Dani's cheeks puffed and she blew out air again, this time hard as if to steel herself. "Well, the stretcher was still there but now it had a body on it."

Jo didn't say anything.

"Jo?"

"The woman you heard died?" she said finally, eyes narrowed.

"Yeah. She was right there under a sheet. And a hand was hanging down. I was so scared it was you. But then I knew it wasn't. The hand, uh, her hand had brown spots and her nails were—"

"Okay, enough with the descriptives. Go on."

"Well, that's pretty much it. I heard the elevator door open and I just hightailed it back here. I didn't want to run into anyone, especially that horrible paramedic—"

"What horrible paramedic?"

"Oh my god, Jo. I guess you were too out if it to notice. He came to the hotel. He's a big guy with a thick neck. Cold eyes. Nasty. Everything seems kind of creepy here. Like the stairwell. No doorknobs. I mean, come on. Who does that? Who removes doorknobs? That's why I've been pushing to leave."

"Okay, one? I can't believe you haven't told me any of this. And two? This *is* a hospital. So odds are someone will die. And three? The way you're talking has me seriously worried about *you*. You're sounding a tad, you know, stressed?"

"I know, I know. I am stressed. Of course I'm stressed. What else could I be but stressed."

"Okay, take it easy."

"And I'm also feeling kind of crazy. This *place* is making me feel crazy. You've been sitting here in your room and I've been roaming around. And I assure you, it's weird out there. And honestly, Jo, it makes me wonder if we'll ever set eyes on a fucking doctor, but also, when we do, do you even *want* to see a doctor who's part of this place."

"Now you've got me weirded out. Dammit. I just want to get this"—she gestured to her heart—"a little more figured out before I go traipsing about town. That's all. Dammit all to hell." Jo flopped back on her pillow and shaded her eyes against the light. Neither spoke for at least a minute until Jo said, "So, who's Miguel?"

"No idea."

More silence.

"That nurse with the boobs hanging out? Lee-ona?"

"Lay," said Dani.

"What?"

"It's pronounced lay-o-nuh."

"Really? You're correcting my pronunciation? I have a brutal headache. I'm dying for a cigarette. I'm ravenous and nauseous all at once. And you just finished telling me the building is filled with lunatics and dead bodies and knobless doors, although I still don't quite understand that *last* one, and you're giving me a pronunciation lesson? News flash, babe. I don't care *how* you say LAY-oh-nuh. Geez, Dan. The *only* thing I care about is seeing the doctor. Any doctor. Here. In this building. And right now I feel horrible."

"Uh, yeah. Got it. So I take it that means you are still determined to stay here?"

"This headache makes it almost impossible for me to open my eyes, let alone roam around the streets looking for another hospital. So yes. I *need* to stay."

"Okay, okay," said Dani, unconvinced. "So why did you mention Leona in the first place?"

"When you were getting coffee, she came in and started talking to me and I couldn't understand what she was saying. I presume it was about the tests they're going to do. I don't even know what they are or what they're for. Why don't I know? Because there's no one to ask except nurse foo-foo, a.k.a. LAY-oh-nuh, and oh yeah, the woman who washes the floor. And even if there *was* a doctor I could ask, it doesn't really matter, because I *can't speak the language*. Fuck."

"You know what you need?"

"Aside from a strong coffee and a cigarette?"

"You need a note to explain the fact you don't speak Spanish."

"Really. Never would've thought *that* was what I'm lacking."

Dani rummaged in Jo's bag for a pen and something to write on. "Oh, look. Here's Eddie's card. Hey. Why don't I phone Eddie and ask him if he knows this place, you know, its reputation?"

"No no. I do not want him dragged into all this. It's too messed up as it is, let alone involving a business associate. Correction. A *possible* business associate."

"Got it. I'm going to keep this card, just in case. I can't remember where I shoved the one he gave me. A lot has happened since that dinner." She stuffed it in her pocket and went back to searching the bag. She found one of Jo's business cards, flipped it over, wrote on the blank side and propped it up against a tray sitting on the bedside chest. "There. That should give them pause. For when I'm not here. Just point to it. You could say, 'espera mi amiga, por favor,' which means wait for my friend. Okay?" Jo nodded. "Repeat after me. Ess-pair-uh mee ahh-mee-guh." Dani paused, waiting for a response. Jo gave her a dirty look. "Okay. I think I'll leave now. See if I can find out about the doctor."

"Yes. Find the doctor. And please be back before they take me for the tests."

"I will. I promise."

Dani left the room, headed down to the lobby via the samba machine and strode directly out the front doors. She went straight for the blue pay phone kiosk. She decided she didn't care what Jo said. She wanted to get her out of la Clínica Ortega and into a better hospital. She could think of only one person who might be able to help.

"Diga." A male voice.

"Eddie? Eddie Muñoz?"

"Sí. Para servirle."

"Eddie, es Dani, Dani Papineau, la amiga de Jo."

"Dani. I am delighted to hear from you. You are enjoying your vacation, I trust?"

"Not exactly."

"What has happened?"

"It's Jo. She had a heart attack."

"Ay, dios mío. Is she all right?"

The concern in his voice wrapped around her like a warm blanket.

"Her heart seems to have stabilized but now she's got this blinding headache. It started when she was admitted to hospital, which was last night. It's now morning and she hasn't seen a doctor yet."

"What? That does not sound good."

"Yes. They keep saying the doctor will be there soon."

"What hospital is she in?"

"It's called the uh…" She looked over to the sign on the front of the building. "Hospital Traumáticos Clínica Ortega."

"Ah, sí. The Clínica in Cádiz. Lo conozco."

There was a long silence. "Eddie?"

"Why did they take her there?"

"The closest, they said."

Eddie said nothing. Dani heard music in the background, the silken voice of Andy Bey. *Oh, to sit quietly across from Jo, sip a latte while listening to some great music…*

"When did she get sick?"

"A few hours after dinner. I can't believe that was just last night. It seems like a lifetime ago. And by the way, Eddie, the hotel room is magnificent. That was very generous of you. Jo insisted on paying for it, though."

"Of course she did." He chuckled but immediately cut it off. "I am so sorry, Dani, that all this has happened. I know how much you both wanted this vacation."

"We've moved past the vacation. Right now, I just want Jo, well, looked after."

"How can I be of assistance?"

"I need to take her to another hospital as soon as possible, like maybe a public hospital?"

"Yes. I understand. There is Puerta del Mar? It has an excellent reputation. It is on Avenida de Ana de Viya. It runs off Avenida de Andalucía along the peninsula away from the city centre. It will be about five kilómetros, more or less. Much too far to find yourselves. But you could call a cab."

"That will be hard for me, Eddie. I could try to flag one down at the pub next door. I can't call directly, well, except from the public phone. My cell isn't working and the hospital doesn't seem to have any phones for public use."

"No phones? Ay dios. Pues, sí, the public phone. But that sounds very inconvenient. Perhaps someone could help you with this."

"Any help would be truly appreciated."

The phone line went quiet. She waited for his response, listening to the street sounds, people walking by, car tires rumbling over cobblestone and the dull roar from across the street. It was El Popular of course, the daytime version.

"Bueno, Dani. I have an idea but I must check to see if this gentleman is available. Can you call me back later? Give me a couple of hours with this."

"Yes, yes. I will for sure. Thanks so much, Eddie." Dani hung up, holding the glimmer of hope close. Her only dilemma—should she tell Jo that she'd called Eddie and he was now involved?

Scrawny Guy arrived just before ten a.m., pushing a wheelchair into Jo's room. He said nothing, merely raised a finger and pointed to Jo and to the wheelchair, like the wordless command of an orange grim reaper. Finally, he spoke.

"Electrocardiograma. La doctora lo quiere. We must go to the fifth floor. Necesita ayuda?" Do you need help?

"No, thank you," said Dani. "I will help her." Jo braced against Dani for support and swung herself from the bed to the chair.

The paramedic rolled her out of the room, down the hall and onto the elevator while Dani followed close behind. He swiped his access card, hit the fourth-floor button, cursed, and hit the fifth-floor button. Predictably, the elevator stopped at the fourth floor and the door opened. The man came apart right in front of her, letting loose a string of mierda—shit—and puta—whore—and one coño—that "c" word that Dani detested—as he repeatedly punched the button to close the door. It finally slid shut, but not before Dani got a good look at el cuatro, the fourth.

The elevator resumed its climb.

"Is there music playing?" Jo asked, eyes lowered, hand over her eyes.

"Oh yeah. One of the hospital amenities, I believe."

The door opened on the fifth. Scrawny Guy charged off the elevator with Jo in her wheelchair and careened down the hallway like a Paralympic racer. Dani hustled just to keep up. They slowed at a long and narrow room, painted orange, with moulded plastic chairs lining the walls. A waiting area with no one waiting. The paramedic pushed the wheelchair through a pair of swinging doors and into a room with an examining table. He left without a word.

Almost immediately, he returned with a small cart. He asked if Jo could get up on the table herself.

"I'll help her," said Dani, and she did so, gingerly. He opened the front of her gown to access the nitro patch and continued with the now familiar routine, squeezing puddles of goo on her upper torso, pressing little plastic discs into place. To the discs, he attached cables running from a computer and screen next to the table. He flicked the switch. Nothing happened. He pressed a few buttons and flicked the switch a few more times. He leaned over and, shaking his head, pulled the machine's electrical cord up. The plug dangled uselessly at its end. About three metres across the room was the wall outlet. He cursed, Dani presumed, recognizing the tone if not the actual word, and then stood up and walked out of the room. Dani and Jo look at each other.

"Oh. My. God," Dani said under her breath.

He returned with a long extension cord which he plugged in and declared with great joy, "Electricidad. Electricity."

Once the readings were taken, he removed the cables and discs and wiped the gunk from Jo's body.

"Ahora, el ultrasonido," he said as he smeared different gel onto her entire torso and readied to take the ultrasound.

"That's a big area you're covering there. What are you looking for?" Jo asked.

"It is part of the test the doctor requested for your heart," he said, "to make sure it is clear, the blood that approaches."

"Really? With an ultrasound?"

"Sí, sí, es muy efectivo."

Dani stood behind him and rolled her eyes at Jo.

When he finished, he gave Jo a cloth to clean up the gel before she closed her gown. Dani took it and helped Jo. He took her blood pressure and more blood samples and left. He returned to help Jo back into the wheelchair and started off along the same route back to the elevator. This time he paused at the panel, finger held in a moment's consideration before pressing the number three button with great precision. He nodded, satisfied. The doors closed and the music started up.

"'Blue Moon,'" said Dani. "That's what it is. I didn't recognize it all samba'd up. It's been bugging me." She turned to Scrawny Guy. "So, señor, tell me. Is the doctor in the hospital yet?"

"No sé."

"But you said she ordered the tests, like the ultrasound."

"Pues, pues…" he stuttered and fell silent.

"When do you think the doctor will come to see Jo?"

"Ay señora, no sé," he muttered, staring at the floor,

When the doors opened on the third floor, Scrawny Guy pushed the wheelchair out and down the corridor at breakneck speed.

"That fourth floor looks pretty impressive," Dani said, raising her voice as she booted it to keep up. "What goes on there?"

He shook his head. "Nada. Nada. I know nothing." He kept his eyes forward.

"Who the hell does?"

Back at room 312, he helped Jo back into bed and made a quick exit.

"Wow, Jo, did you see that floor? The fourth floor?"

"Yes, but I can't talk about it right now. I feel like I'm going to throw up."

"Oh god. You do look pale. Have some water."

"Am I allowed water? Am I done with the tests?"

"Yeah. I think so. And besides, you already had tea and a bun. Remember? You're going to get dehydrated if you don't drink anything. But just in case, I'll go see if I can find someone to confirm that."

Not surprisingly, no one was in the hall near Jo's room. Dani hurried toward the cafeteria, thinking maybe she could find someone there. Rounding the bend, she saw two nurses in beige uniforms heading for the stairwell, coffees in hand. Before she could reach them to ask about the water, they'd gone through the door. She opened the stairwell door and peered up and down, but too late. They'd disappeared. She backed out the door and looked into the cafeteria. Zapa sat at a table in the far corner.

"Buenos días, señora," Zapa said, voice elevated, coffee in hand.

"Hola, Zapa. Listen, uh, you said maybe you could help us. I have a question. Do you know where I can find a nurse? I won't even ask for a doctor. Jo is really hungry and I want to make sure she's done with her tests. Leona told her she wasn't supposed to eat or even drink water until then."

"Someone may be in the emergency department now. And if Jo *is* allowed to eat, well, you must leave the building to find food. The cafeteria only serves food earlier in the day. I suggest El Popular across the street. Perhaps you have seen it?" Dani nodded. "But it will be busy now. Right, compa?"

The barista responded, "Es verdad. It is true. A lot of people go there during the day from the hospital and the university next door."

"Sí. It is muy popular," she said, smiling. "Like its name. I recommend the chicken sandwich. It is very good."

"Thanks, Zapa. And you too, señor." She turned to the barista. "I have noticed the place."

As she turned to leave, Zapa waved her back. "Señora. ¿Un momento? I have something to tell you if you have the time. You asked about a man, a very upset man in the hall last night."

"Yes."

"I didn't want to speak of this in front of your sick friend. I myself was not here last night but Miguel told me about it."

"Who *is* Miguel?"

"The barista." She pointed to the man behind the counter, who waved.

"Oh." Dani waved back. "And *he* knows about the guy in the hall?"

"Yes. People were talking about it when they had their morning coffees."

"What people? I haven't seen anyone but you and Leona and the two nurses who took those stairs out there." Dani nodded toward the hallway.

"Sí, sí. They come down here from the clinic upstairs, on the fourth floor. It is more, uh, equipado allí."

"Equipado?"

"Es privado. Hay más dinero. Más empleados. Más de todo. ¿Me entiendes?"

"It's a private clinic with more money. More staff. More everything. I thought the whole place was private."

"Yes. It is. But the fourth floor is *more* private. Pues, señora, that man on your floor last night? I believe you saw the husband of the patient, Benning. They say he went a little crazy when the hospital started blaming him."

"Blaming him? For what?"

"For the death of his wife."

Dani chilled. "Oh god. She was the body on the stretcher. I saw her."

"Yes. She was in a room on the third floor, just down from yours. She must have died after you arrived."

"Why would they blame the husband?"

"I do not know the illness she struggled with. But I understand they told the husband that it was his responsibility to stay with his esposa, his wife, and watch her. He went back to his hotel to rest. And because of this, there was no one to alert the nurse when she had a problem."

"Is that how hospitals operate here in Spain? The relatives have to monitor the patients? Because that's what it's like for Jo. No one monitors her except me."

"No. Absolutamente no, señora. It is not like that in most hospitals. But here at la Clínica Ortega, things can run quite differently from other places. Just last month at another hospital west of here, part of the same chain you understand, another patient died under similar circumstances. This is what I am told."

Dani stared at Zapa. "That sounds like what's going on with Jo. She was rushed here last night but no doctor ever showed up. Everybody just kind of abandoned her. Nobody said anything about me keeping an eye on her. As a matter of fact, the head nurse told me to leave, go back to the hotel to get her stuff, which I did. But then that nurse just deserted her. I found her still in the bathroom over an hour later. Had to crab-walk her back to her bed. And now this story of the woman who died? I'm getting really scared for her. I better get back there." Dani started to get up and stopped. "Zapa, do you have any idea when this uh, Dr. Nieves, *usually* shows up?"

A short snort came from Zapa. "No one knows her schedule. La suprema is not an easy one to pin down. Ask anyone."

Dani was surprised by her tone. "You don't like her?"

"I am sorry, señora, if I sound harsh. She is everywhere and she is nowhere. Confía en mí." Trust me.

Dani hurried back to room 312. She wanted to make sure Jo was okay before she headed down to the ER, but one look at Jo's pale face said it all.

"It's the headache. It's brutal," Jo said.

"If you could eat, that would probably make you feel better. But I'm having trouble finding a nurse, let alone a doctor. I'm going to check the emergency room down—"

"I've never had a headache like this." Jo's skin was flushed and her eyes were dull. "It makes me, well, I think I'm losing it. I'm sick of the endless bloodletting and ECG's. I hate not being able to understand anything being said…about *me*. I hate waiting for the doctor. I would kill, almost, for a cigarette. I feel like shit and I could tear someone a new asshole right now."

Dani cringed. This was not the woman Dani knew. Not because of the swearing. She was from Cape Breton Island after all. Swearing was an art form there. But she, like her island compatriots, was not a complainer, not a negative thinker. *She's afraid and she's hiding it behind her anger.* "Hang in there, babe. We'll get you better. You could be less whiny, though."

Jo looked up, irritation flaring in those squinting eyes.

"Just kidding. Wanted to see if the fighter was still in there. Et voilà, there she is. Good. I'm going to find a nurse or"—Dani rolled her eyes—"maybe even a doctor."

"Yes. Get the doctor. Any doctor. Please, Dan." Jo eyes were virtually closed when she looked up. "I now have a profound understanding of the term *blinding headache*. And I'm scared. I wish we could just leave but the idea of us being out there, trying to find our way on those winding streets...and what if something happened? I can't do it. I can't even think about it. So, you've got to find help and bring it here to me."

CHAPTER SIX

Dani marched into the emergency department. She was angry and she was determined. She touched her tiny angel and clenched her fists. She was now armed and dangerous. She would find a doctor for Jo or damn the consequences. She found Leona instead, leaning on the counter reading a book.

"Leona." Dani threw the name down like a gauntlet.

The nurse looked up, startled. "¿Señora? How may I help you?"

"There are a few ways you could help me, Leona. But let's start with the obvious and most urgent. Jo needs to see the doctor. Now."

"She will come soon, señora."

"No. Not good enough. I repeat. Her patient, Jo Gasperi, who has been in the hospital for, what, oh yeah, almost twelve hours, needs to see the woman, needs to see her *now*. She is in pain. She is nauseous. She needs medical attention and by that I mean someone beyond nurse qualifications, no disrespect intended, and something more than nitro and aspirin. Please contact the doctor, *any* doctor, immediately and get her or him to come *NOW*."

"La Dra. Nieves is the only one treating patients and I have no idea when she will make her rounds and that—"

"Rounds?" Dani's voice rose. "Rounds? What are you talking about? Rounds. To see whom? Jo is the only patient she's got."

"That could change at any moment, señora. This *is* the emergency clinic."

"Jo is the only emergency you have right now."

"Señora, if your friend doesn't see the doctor today, she will definitely see her tomorrow. La doctora is a very busy woman."

Dani's jaw dropped. She made a sound she'd never made before. Something between a growl and a yell. "Tomorrow?"

"Cálmese, por favor."

"No. I will not *cálme-me*. Why the fuck isn't the doctor here to treat Jo? The insurance people won't be happy to hear about this. They won't pay if there isn't some actual medical care happening." Her fury spiraled. "Maybe the only thing you understand is outside pressure. Maybe I should get in touch with a lawyer. Or maybe the Canadian embassy. No, better than that. I'll call the Cádiz newspapers, tell them what a scam you've got going on here. Wouldn't that be a nice follow-up to the story of last night's clinic disaster."

"Señora, please. I don't know what you are talking about."

"Uh, the dead patient? On the third floor?"

The nurse blanched. "That was a complex situation, señora. Do not make threats about things you do not understand."

"I certainly *understand* lack of care, perhaps even malpractice. Jo's had an ultrasound and two ECGs. Where are the results? And the blood samples. Tubes and tubes of it. And a urine sample. When will we get *those* results?"

"I do not know. The blood work is done at a lab at the Hospital Puerta del Mar across town."

"You don't have a lab for testing here?"

"No, we do not."

"So, what the hell *do* you have here? Certainly no monitoring equipment, no lab, no staff to speak of and as for doctors, no doctor here as far as I can see. No patients. Maybe this whole place is a tourist trap."

Dani stopped. She was so outraged she could barely breathe. She had to find a way to calm herself before she had her own heart attack or leapt over the counter and strangled the woman behind it. She took a few deep breaths and forced herself to change her tone. "Look, Leona. I'm asking for your help here. If this were your sister or mother, what would you do?"

The woman visibly softened. "Well, I suppose I would call around to see if I could find her, la doctora."

Dani struggled to contain her reaction to this casual solution to a medical emergency. "And how would I do that? The phones don't work."

Leona pursed her lips and said, "All the phones work."

"Not the one in Room 312. There is no dial tone."

"I see. I will have to leave a message for Luci about the phone. Of course she—"

"Who's Luci?"

"Luci Nieves is the administrator. She doesn't work on the weekend."

"Nieves? As in Nieves the doctor?"

"Luci is her niece."

"A family affair, eh?"

"¿Como, señora?"

"Never mind. I'll use the pay phone on the street. Again. Where should I call?"

"She could be at el Hospital Gran Puerto."

"That's a different hospital than the one where you get blood tested?"

"Sí, sí, Puerta del Mar is a public hospital. El Gran Puerto, which is close to Jerez, is parto of el Grupo Hospitalario Ortega, the Ortega Hospital Group, just like la Clínica Ortega. And we have others to the east and north in Andalusía. We are six hospitals in total," she said, puffing ever so slightly. "Dr. Nieves-Félix works at two of them but of course she must leave the city for el Gran Puerto. Another place you could call is her office, which is near the port, of course."

"Of course. So, she's either across town or out of town all together. How convenient for us," said Dani in English.

"And, and sometimes she is in the private clinic."

"Where's that? Seville?"

"No, señora. It…it…it is on the fourth floor."

"The fourth floor?"

"Yes."

"The fourth floor clinic as in right-here-in-this-building fourth floor?"

"Yes."

"You're saying she could be upstairs right now?"

"Yes. In fact I believe she is now in the Clínica."

Dani's jaw dropped. Her eyes narrowed. "So you're telling me the doctor we've been asking for all day is right here on the fourth floor of this building? Why didn't you say so? All this time you've been what, stalling? Lying?"

"Claro que no, señora. I do not lie. You asked when she will visit your friend and where to make calls. You did not ask me where she was right now."

"What possible reason could you have for not getting the doctor to come down one floor to check on a patient in distress?"

"La doctora does not like to be disturbed when she is in the Clínica privada."

"Are you people on drugs? This is ridiculous. No, it's criminal. You know what? I'm going to go up there and get her myself."

"No. No," Leona said, waving her hands at Dani. "You cannot, señora. The fourth floor is restricted access."

"Do you have access?"

"No."

"And you refuse to call."

Nurse Leona did not respond.

Dani's hands formed claws and she let out a strangled groan. She leaned forward across the counter as if she were about to catapult herself over it.

"Ay dios mío," the nurse said, leaning away from Dani. "Please leave or I will call Chaco."

"Good. Call Chaco, whoever that is."

"No, no, no. You do not want me to call Chaco. He is not a very nice man." She held up her hand over her mouth and whispered, "Es un monstruo. A monster. La jefa Montoya says he has anger issues." She trembled, eyes wide. "He scares me."

Dani shook her head in frustration. "Okay. Can you please tell me this? Just this? Is the testing done? Can she eat something and have some water?"

"Oh no, señora. She must wait to see the doctor."

Dani's own eyes widened in disbelief. She felt like she was trapped in a Groundhog Day loop. Fists clenched, she stomped out of emergency, across the lobby and out the main doors. She needed to let her rage die down so she could think clearly. After a few deep breaths, she knew what she had to do, restricted access be damned. *Get your sorry ass to the fourth floor and find that fucking doctor and if necessary, drag her by force down to the third.*

She went back into the building and looked around. *Okay, let's start with the obvious.* She got on the elevator and pressed the button for the fourth floor. The door closed. "Blue Moon" kicked exuberantly but the elevator did not move.

"Aargh. Fine then."

She pressed the button for the third floor. The elevator lurched into its painfully slow ascent, at half-time to the relentless samba. When it reached the third floor, she didn't wait for the door to fully open but still seething mad, squeezed herself out and hard-turned into the stairwell, the words *hay construcción* coming to mind. She tried to ignore the ominous click of the door closing behind her but her body took over, her heart rate and breathing instantly quickening. She slammed her mouth shut to keep from inhaling construction dust, and clenched up her fists. *I will do this.* And she started up the stairs despite being virtually blind, repeating one mantra over and over. *Find the doctor. For Jo. Find the doctor. For Jo.*

She reached the fourth-floor door only to discover it was unopenable like the one on the third. Quelle surprise. It did however have a glass window. She peered through it and saw nothing. Blacked out, perhaps. She moved her hand along the outer edges of the door, just in case. *Nope. No knob.* She forced herself to go farther up the stairs to the fifth floor. Again, same story. Just like the third-floor door. Her head dropped, her shoulders sagged and she fell against the wall in defeat. No exit.

No exit. The very words and her panic bubbled up inside. She forced herself to focus yet again on Jo and reminded herself of something she knew for certain. *The first-floor door has a fucking knob. Head downstairs.*

She retraced her steps past the fourth- and third-floor doors and continued on to the second-floor landing. Its door was still propped open. The wide empty space was bright now thanks to daytime sunshine pouring through the huge windows on the opposite wall. It was almost cheery except that it was gutted, wires hanging, lathe and plaster exposed, the bones of the building laid bare. She checked for any back-door access to other floors, but there was only the elevator. It was completely closed off by plywood except for the doors, which were blocked by crisscrossed two-by-fours. She pressed her ear to the wall and could hear the big machine plugging along inside the shaft accompanied by the faintest sound of congas.

She went back into the stairwell, rushed down to first floor and into the elevator to go back to the third floor. She was beginning to consider "Blue Moon" a la samba the soundtrack of her madness. Or her rage. *Yes. Rage. That's where I am.*

Once on the third, she marched defiantly around the circular hallway, hands clenched at her sides. She charged into the stairwell next to the cafeteria, the one the nurses in beige had used. She took its clean and well-lit stairs two at a time, spirits rising. At the fourth-floor landing, she found a key card box and no doorknob. *What is it with this place and doorknobs?* Leona's voice rang annoyingly in her ears: *restricted access restricted access restricted access.* She returned to the third floor and was relieved to find a knob on the stairwell side of the door, no doubt there to facilitate cafeteria access for the fourth-floor crew. She looked through the dining area windows and saw Zapa waving her over to a table she shared with the barista. Maybe they could help her get to the fourth floor. She started toward them when a high and piercing voice stopped her cold.

"¡Señora! ¡Señora Canadiense!"

Leona was running toward her, clogs clacking, hands waving. "You must come back to room 312."

Terrified at the tone in the nurse's voice, Dani hurried back to Jo's room. She walked in and emitted a mighty lip-flapping breath of relief at seeing Jo alive in the bed. Dani sat on the chair next to her and took her hand.

"Is the doctor coming, Leona? Is that why you came for me?"

Leona spoke guardedly. "Pues, la doctora has decided on a course of action for you, Jo."

"She has?" asked Jo. "She hasn't even seen me yet."

"That's right. When is she coming here to see Jo?"

"Ah, pues, no sé. I don't know. Pero, ah, but she has seen the test results. And she is prescribing continued nitroglycerine. You are also complaining about a headache. For this, la doctora will give you aspirin. And—"

"Okay. This is ridiculous. How can she prescribe things in absentia? We need to know how serious her heart attack was! And why is she getting headaches? Headaches can be serious. It could be blood pressure or well, sorry, Jo, like maybe a brain tumor or…or maybe whatever's in those patches?"

"Nitro," said Jo.

"Yeah. What about the nitro? She's been on it since last night at the hotel. Maybe the last thing she should be doing is taking more nitro."

Leona looked more agitated. "No sé. I don't know." She shook her head rapidly as if clearing her brain and asked Jo where the headache hurt most.

"All across the base of my skull and up over the top. Pretty much my entire head. And my eyes ache. I can't keep them open for long because the light hurts. Sometimes it lets up for a while, but it comes back with a vengeance."

"Headaches can occur with the patch, especially in the beginning. I will tell la doctora. Perhaps she can adjust your nitroglycerine dosage."

Dani growled. "Can't the doctor just come down one floor and you know, actually *see* her patient? And then, hey, she could ask her *own* questions and get answers directly, rather than through a medium. This sounds like a lawsuit in the making and you, Leona, are right in the middle of it." Leona looked scared. "Tell the doctor *that*!" Leona nodded vigorously. "Yes. Tell her that we are considering legal action and she better get her fat ass down here." Jo looked quizzical. Dani took a deep breath and continued in an almost normal tone, "Okay, back to the nitro issue. Maybe she should be taken off it completely."

"No, no, that is not possible. But a higher dose of aspirina. Perhaps that will help the headaches. Also, la doctora has ordered extra tests to determine what is happening with your heart."

"What sort of *extra* tests?"

A long rattle of words poured forth, of which Dani could only catch: prueba, sangre, orina. Tests. Blood and urine tests. On and on Leona went, but it was at her last word that Jo erupted.

"What did you say?"

"Angiograma. Angiogram."

"Yeah, I figured. An angiogram? Absolutely not."

"Yes, señora. This is what the doctor has ordered."

Jo's face went rigid and her voice hard. "No. I will not have an angiogram. Small veins and arteries. It runs in my family. The risks are too high."

"Uh, nh," stammered Leona. "But we are already booking el especialista."

"I repeat. I am *not* having an angiogram."

"Pero la doctora me dijo…the doctor told me to tell you that you must have the angiogram. At that point, they will decide if you are healthy enough to be released from the hospital. Without the angiogram, you will not be released and we will hold your papers."

"Papers?" asked Dani.

"My passport. I'm sure that's what she means. Right, Leona?"

"I am sorry, señoras, I must leave now. I will return with your new patch and aspirina." Leona turned and hustled out of the room.

They stared at the slowly closing door, stunned.

"That was unbelievable," Dani said, moving to shut it completely.

"And was that a threat? I mean it sounded like she said I *have to have* the angio."

"No angio, no release, no passport? What kind of place *is* this?"

They stared at each other.

"You know what's really freaking me out here? She hasn't even *seen* me and she's making pronouncements on my care. It is impossible for her to know what's happening with me when she hasn't talked to me. And speaking of the invisible doctor, what did you mean about getting her fat ass—can't believe you said that—down a floor?"

"Hey. It's the new me and I've had it. I am going to keep showing how pissed I am because you know what?"

"No? But I'm afraid to ask."

"Do you remember the fourth floor? On the way to your ECG, when the paramedic stopped the elevator there by mistake?"

"Yeah. Kind of."

"Well, la doctora is there as we speak, tending to patients in a private private clinic, just for the extraordinarily wealthy, evidently. At least that's what I've gleaned from what Zapa and later Leona said."

"You're kidding."

"I wonder if that's why that woman died. The extraordinary lack of care? Her husband is claiming negligence, by the way."

"What are you talking about? What woman?"

"Remember? The body down the hall? I now have the whole story thanks to Zapa. She didn't want to get into it in front of you. Sweet, eh?"

"Uh, sure. Now, just tell me."

Dani sat next to the bed. Jo lowered her head onto the pillow, covered her eyes with her arm and listened to Dani's story.

When she finished, Jo said, "That's horrible. She was alone and dying when I was rolled into this room."

"Yup. That guy in the hall last night? Zapa told me he was the woman's husband. No wonder he was in agony. And I'll bet that's the emergency Montoya went off to deal with when she left you stuck on the toilet."

"Oh my god."

"Zapa said a similar incident happened at the other Ortega hospital too, a patient dying because they weren't properly monitored. The hospital claims that monitoring is the responsibility of family members."

Jo moaned, covering her eyes.

"I'm so sorry, Jo. Maybe I shouldn't have told you all that."

"It's okay. You *have* to tell me this stuff. It's just my head is pounding again. Now who is this Zapa person?"

"She's the woman who mopped the floor in here. Remember?"

"Right. Right. I do. When did she tell you all this?"

"When I went to get you the tea."

"And you didn't tell me."

"You were suffering so much with the headache. I just charged off to find the doctor. That's when Leona happened."

"Right. I have something to tell you too." Jo leaned over and opened the top drawer of the bedside chest. "Something that happened while you were gone. A weird guy in gloves came in the room and handed me this." Jo waved a business card weakly in front of Dani.

"What? In your room? Who was he? What did he say?"

"Beats me. It was all in Spanish, but it sounded like he was saying…protection?"

Dani's eyebrows rose. "Protection? Was he talking about insurance? Probably the hospital covering all angles. Offering their own insurance against their own lousy medical care? What did you say?"

"Uh, nothing. Did you miss the part about all in Spanish? I pointed to the little sign and yelled at him to get out. He looked at it and laughed this kind of low, unsettling laugh. And then he left."

Dani stuffed the business card in her pocket.

"What are you doing?"

"Just in case. I'm surprised he could just walk in like that."

"Well, there is no security to speak of and if there's no real medical care going on, maybe there's good reason someone is selling protection or insurance, or whatever it is. And this Zapa? Do you trust her?"

"Yes, I think I do. I mean, she's the only one giving me *any* information. And she seems so normal compared to everyone else."

"That isn't a high bar in this place. And normal doesn't necessarily mean trustworthy."

"Right, but we're desperate."

"Yes, we are."

"Okay, let's talk about our options, given the angio ultimatum." Dani took Jo's hand, looked directly into her eyes and braced herself. "Option one, my love? We simply leave."

"And option two?"

Dani looked at the floor and back at Jo.

"Given the doc's ghosting you and the place seems to have a bad reputation, I don't really think there *is* an option two, except maybe something Protection Guy might be offering. I could call him and find out."

Jo sighed. "Oh man, I don't know about that. He really was really, well, unsettling. But you know what? Option one? Just leaving? *That* makes me more nervous I think."

"More nervous than staying?"

"The problem is I don't know how serious my heart attack was. Like, was there any damage? Do I need surgery? Will drugs handle it going forward? I'd like to get those answers."

"That's why they're doing the angio. Are you *sure* it's a bad call?"

"Yes. Mum almost died because of that procedure. It caused a stroke. And I've been told I have the same condition. Anyway, the angiogram isn't the only course of action and certainly not the first step. There are options when an angio is considered dangerous. Why don't they give me a monitored stress test or an MRI or a CT scan or—"

"Honestly, Jo. Do you think they've got the skills for that? Or even the equipment? Remember when buddy had to go searching for an outlet to plug in the ECG machine? Not confidence inspiring."

"Yeah. You're right. But if they're bringing in someone to do the angio, why can't they do the same…"

Dani shrugged. "I don't know, babe. What can I say?"

"And what about my passport? I can't leave without that."

"Fuck the passport. I mean really, your well-being and safety are paramount, Jo. We can throw ourselves on the mercy of the Canadian embassy, god help us, or hire a lawyer. Actually, maybe we should call the embassy, wherever it is. And maybe that other place, the public hospital, can help us. The thing is, and I'm sorry to say this, but I'm afraid. Afraid for your life. If you stay here, that is."

"Now you're freaking me out."

"Good. You didn't see that widower guy. I'd say he was pretty much destroyed by his wife's death. And we don't know why she died. Or how she died. I don't want to end up like him. But more importantly, I don't want *you* to end up like his wife."

"Okay. Okay. You've won your case, Ms. Papineau. We'll leave."

She sighed and gave Jo a big hug. "We can do this, babe. The only question is how do we leave? Are you strong enough to walk out of the building?"

"I think so. I haven't moved on my own since, well, since the hotel. But I have to do it. That's all there is to it."

"Here." She helped her sit up, her legs dangling over the side. "Why don't you start flexing those muscles while I pack your bag. We'll go very, very slowly. I'll call a cab from the pay phone. Or maybe one will be outside El Popular. We'll hightail it to Puerta del Mar."

Bag packed, Dani helped Jo to a standing position.

"I feel pretty shaky."

"Try walking over to the door."

Jo took a couple of steps, holding on to Dani's arm. When they reached the door, they stood and stared down the long hall.

"I don't know, Dan. That's a long, long walk. I can't believe I'm so weak already. How is that even possible?"

"Maybe we're walking too fast."

"We go any slower, it'll take us until tomorrow to get the out of here. So, we better get going."

They moved into the hall and started inching along, Jo's toes dragged as she pulled each foot forward. About ten steps along, she crumpled to the floor. "Shit. Shit. Shit. I can't do it. My feet feel so heavy. How can that be?"

"We'll just have to figure something else out."

Dani hauled Jo up from the floor and half-carried half-dragged Jo back to the bed.

"We need a wheelchair."

"That'll make for a subtle exit."

Dani snorted. "Wouldn't want to do this the easy way."

She roamed around the third floor but found nothing. She went down to the first floor and spotted a wheelchair near the emergency room entrance. She waved at Montoya and as casually as possible, left with the wheelchair in tow. Back in the room, she helped Jo into the chair, put her bag on her lap and rolled down the hall where not a person was in sight.

When the elevator opened on the main floor to the fading strains of "Blue Moon," Thug stood in front of the main doors, facing them. He called over his shoulder to the emergency room. Head nurse Montoya joined him and together they blocked the way out of the building.

"Señora, you have to return to your room," she said.

"She's fine, jefa. Just wants to get some air and sunshine."

"What's the bag for?" Thug asked sharply.

"Silencio," Montoya said to him just as sharply. She turned back to them. "The doctor has said Josefina should stay in her room for her own safety. Do you understand? She is being monitored right now and cannot be allowed to leave. It is for her own good."

"Monitored?" Dani snapped back. "By whom? With what? She is the most *un*-monitored patient in the history of medicine."

Montoya didn't answer. She turned to the paramedic. "Chaco."

Dani paled. Thug was the infamous Chaco. Leona had blanched at his name.

He put his hands on the armrests of Jo's chair, like a bulldozer at the ready. Dani was silent. In shock. He was going to keep Jo here by force. Fury flooded her system. She hated bullies. Her first impulse right now was to ram the wheelchair into his fucking junk and disable him so they could make a run for it through the doors. *With our luck, he'd probably fall on top of Jo.* She must have had a similar vision. "Let's go back," she said quietly.

The episode left Jo a frightening shade of gray.

"Jo. You look awful."

"I feel awful." Tears filled her eyes. "Oh, babe, I'm so sorry. I should've listened to you and tried to leave before this."

"No worries, mi amor. We had to learn stuff about this place first. And now we know too much. I mean really, this is forceable confinement. Hell, it's kidnapping. Maybe we should call the embassy."

"And tell them what? That the hospital won't let me leave? They'd probably just tell them I'm too sick to be allowed to leave."

The door burst open and Leona rushed in.

"Here are your pills, señora," she said, holding out a little paper cup. "The aspirina and a sedative, as requested by la jefa Montoya. She thought you might need something to help you rest. You must get some rest. And la doctora asked me to remind you. No food or water before surgery."

"Surgery?"

"The angiogram, señora."

"When is the angio booked for?" Dani asked.

"I do not know. Perhaps tomorrow. It will depend on the schedule of the specialista from Puerta. I will return in a few minutes with your new nitro patch."

As soon as the door closed behind the nurse, Jo grabbed Dani's hand.

"Okay, you have to get me the fuck out of here. Now. And toss this in the toilet." She picked the sedative out of the paper cup.

"Will do." Dani kept talking as she went into the bathroom. "I guess this is a good time to tell you, babe. I called Eddie from the pay phone before you went for the ECG."

"You did?"

"Yeah. You were determined to stay put but I wanted to see what options we might have in case you changed your mind. I figured if anyone would know what is possible, Mr. I-Have-Contacts-Everywhere would."

"I hate involving him but I'm way past that now. So, what did he suggest?"

"That we take a cab to Puerta. Of course, that's no longer possible given they won't let you out the front door. He also mentioned he might know someone who could facilitate your transfer but he said he needed to check with the guy first. I'm supposed to call him back right about now."

"Do it. And use that damn cell phone, would you?"

"I'll try, but I didn't have much luck last night." She pulled out the phone and dialed Eddie's number.

"Et voilà! It says no service. I'm doing exactly what they told me to do at the store. I don't know why it isn't working."

"It'll take the rest of the day to figure out the cell phone issue. Just go to the public phone, Dani, and then, while you're there, give the Canadian embassy a call too, if you can find a number. They must at least be able to give us some advice if not actual help."

"Good idea. There's an emergency number on the back page of the passport that might work."

"I hope those yahoos at the front door won't give *you* a hard time leaving."

"I'll just tell them I'm going to El Popular for sandwiches. Correction. Sandwich. You can't have one. But I could sneak one in for you. I hear the chicken is great."

"I'm not supposed to eat. And I'm not the slightest bit interested in food right now anyway. I can't believe you are."

"I'm not. It's the details that are important when lying."

CHAPTER SEVEN

"Diga."

"Hi, Eddie. It's—"

Beeeeeeeep.

"Damn."

Dani pulled away from the loud sound, annoyed and disappointed. She left a short message saying the hospital wouldn't allow Jo to leave and had even blocked her attempt to leave. She hung up and started across the street toward El Popular. She stopped and looked back at the kiosk. She went back to the phone, pulled "protección" guy's card out of her pocket and dialed the number. It went straight to voice mail. Frustrated yet again, she left another short message, essentially a "who are you and what service do you offer" query and then, remembering she had no number to leave for him, she hung up in disgust.

Next, she tried the number on the back page of her passport. It was an Ottawa area code, in the nation's capitol, and that meant it was about five hours earlier there. The voice mail message had numerous options which Dani listened to carefully. She pressed one, the number offering assistance to Canadians in a foreign country experiencing an emergency. The number was transferred. It went directly to another voice message telling the caller there was an unusually high volume of calls and to try later. After the forewarning, the call was immediately disconnected. Dani stared at the phone for a few seconds, brows furrowed. *Unbelievable.* And then, head shaking, she headed for the bar. *Unfortunately, not for a drink, girlie.*

El Popular took up the whole corner of the ground-floor retail space of its building. It was a classic neighbourhood tavern, a gathering spot for locals, its swinging sign declaring "Sirviéndoles 24 horas cada día." Serving you 24 hours a day.

She pushed through the front doors and walked into a dynamic Saturday afternoon crowd—standing and sitting, heads tilted close in conversation, arms embracing, hands gesticulating, jeers flying, laughter erupting, glasses clinking, bits of flamenco pop percolating through it all from tinny speakers way up on the high ceiling. She loved it and just wished she were here doing anything but buying an alibi sandwich.

She joined the order line behind a young guy with a University of Cádiz logo on his backpack. Just over his shoulder nearer the front, she saw Zapa leaning against the counter talking to a man in a long white apron. She spotted Dani and nodded, making her way over with an extended hand.

"I hear the doctor is in the building." She projected her voice to be heard over the din.

"Yes. Finally," Dani yelled back. "Not that she came to see Jo. She sent Leona with a remote diagnosis."

"A *what?*"

"She sent Leona to deliver her diagnosis which was basically to give Jo more nitro and aspirin."

"The doctor herself never came?" Dani started to respond when someone called out Zapa's name.

She held up one finger and went to the counter to get her plate of food. She lifted it carefully over a couple of heads and returned to Dani in the line.

"I am going to grab a stool over there at the bar. Will you join me?"

"I've got to place a take-out order. And I don't want to leave Jo alone for too long."

"The chicken sandwich?"

Dani nodded and held up two fingers. Zapa called out the order to the man in the white apron, punctuating it with "rápido rápido." He nodded.

They sat next to two older guys working their way through a bottle of sherry.

"This place feels more like a nightclub than a pub at midday."

Zapa smiled. She tapped a passing server on the arm, asked for a glass of water and took a huge bite of the sandwich.

"And that sandwich looks delicious."

Zapa nodded, chewed her food, swallowed and drank some water.

"Lo siento, Dani. I am very hungry and I needed that first bite. And yes, this place is always a bit crazy. But it is Saturday. Everyone is in a party mood. It is contagioso."

"Contagious?"

She smiled. "Exacto. So, tell me again. What did Leona say that la doctora said?" Zapa smirked.

"Yes. Ridiculous, isn't it? More nitro and aspirin plus a procedure Jo refuses to undergo."

"What procedure?"

Dani leaned in so she didn't have to yell the specifics. "An angiogram."

Zapa pulled back with a frown.

"What?" asked Dani. "Why are you frowning?"

"Angiogramas are not performed here."

"Right. They have to bring someone in from another hospital to do it."

"But that is strange. Claro, I have worked here for one month only. But in that short time, patients have needed an angiogram three or four times. And they *never* do them here. Each time, such a patient is sent to Puerta, the public hospital."

"So there actually *are* other patients who come to here?"

"Yes. But not many. So few, in fact, I do not know how they keep the place running."

"That place, Puerta, sure gets mentioned a lot. It's got a good reputation?"

"Absolutamente. And la Clínica has a reputation too but it is a bad one. Ever since Magda started running the place."

"*Who?*"

She held up her hand while she swallowed a bite of her sandwich.

"Perdón. La doctora. Her full name is Magdalena Nieves-Félix. Everyone calls her Magda. It is not with affection, believe me."

"That's odd for a doctor to do, isn't it? To manage a hospital and care for patients?"

"I suppose. She took over when the first manager quit. Magda, well, she is a terror for employees. Her priority is to cut costs. She laid off many people and made all those who remain part-time so she can avoid paying benefits and overtime. No one has a regular shift anymore."

"That sounds familiar. Precarious work is now the norm back home, too."

"Really? In Canada too? I find it so...so...strange, this... uh...desconexión..."

"Disconnect?"

"Sí, sí. I have never understood this disconnect. Do not happy and healthy workers work better? Do not well-paid workers buy more? It seems a perfect match for los capitalistas. And yet..."

"I know what you mean, Zapa. It doesn't make sense."

"Of course, she has done well personally. The doctor has a house in one of the most exclusive neighbourhoods and they tell me she drives around Cádiz in an expensive sports car. And her clothes? Pues, her clothes are always by designers, the best in Spain. Ay dios, that reminds me of the uniform scandal." Zapa shook her head and laughed softly. "It was reported in the media."

"The *what* scandal?"

Zapa covered her lips to suppress some outburst, a laugh perhaps or a curse, and shook her head. "It was increíble. She banned the women from wearing pants. She ordered them to wear dresses with hems shortened above the knee." Zapa gestured to her own hemline. "You see? Too short. And why? Sex appeal. ¡Qué loca! As if sex appeal makes better health care. But she believed it will bring in more patients. Her plan was to only hire women of a certain size. Y los hombres? Ay dios, but the men come in all sizes and walk around in their comfortable pants. The women were very angry. They tried to fight the uniform code. But they had no union. They complained on social media, and finally the national nurses' union took la Clínica to court. The union lost because the dress rule was made by a private institution which was not covered by the law. ¡Qué trola!"

"Trola?"

Zapa laughed. "Bull—shit." Only she pronounced it *bool-sheet*. A strip of fried onion fell out of her sandwich and onto the plate. She picked it up, tossed it into her mouth and turned, using the moment to scan the crowd. She motioned to Dani to come closer.

"Miguel says that even though Magda won the case, the owners were very upset. Her uniform rule got their precious chain taken to court. There were many reporters, much publicity. Everyone was talking about la Clínica Ortega and not in a good way. We all thought this will be the end of Magda. But she is still here. She is una sobreviviente. A survivor."

"How does Miguel know all this stuff?"

"Everybody talks right in front of him while they wait for their coffees. Like he's invisible." She shook her head and smiled. "As if he has no ears. And he is there making coffees for over two years, since it first opened. He knows a lot."

"Tell me, Zapa. Why is the place still under construction?"

"That is a very good question and I do not know the answer."

"You don't like the Clínica much, do you?"

She motioned Dani even closer and whispered in her ear with vehemence, "*No*."

"Why do you stay?"

"Ay dios, it is only temporary. I hope," she said, shaking her head, "I am making some extra money. My dream is to become a lawyer and this job suits my purpose, for now."

"Wow. Good for you." Dani couldn't imagine Zapa's hospital cleaning job making enough money to finance a law education. Still, Dani believed her. Something about Zapa felt good and true. She decided to take her into her confidence.

"I tried to take Jo out of the Clínica and over to Puerta."

"Really? When was this?"

"About a half hour ago. They wouldn't let us leave."

Zapa froze, sandwich halfway to her mouth. She slowly lowered it to her plate before speaking. "What do you mean they wouldn't *let* you leave?"

Dani told her.

"This is against the law."

The pick-up bell rang. Dani went to the counter to pay, took the bag of food and returned to sit with Zapa.

"I can't stay. I'm really nervous about leaving Jo alone for so long. Anyway, they said that it was for her own safety."

"Pardon me, Dani, but that is wrong. You cannot treat a patient by force. And you cannot perform tests against her will. I will suggest something that I normally do not do." She paused.

"What, Zapa? What do you suggest?"

"Call the police."

"Yeah. I was thinking about that actually."

"A complaint would be investigated. You call the police and say someone is being held by force and see what happens. You have a cell, yes?"

"Yes, but it isn't working."

"Have you tried it outside the hospital or only inside?"

"Uh, I guess only inside. I get an error message."

"It will probably work outside the hospital. Try it now."

Dani pulled out her phone and as a test hit the toll-free number for the insurance company. It dialed and started ringing. She hung up. "Wow. That's fantastic. I meant to check it outside. And there ya go. Working. Thank you so much."

"You are welcome."

"So why won't it work inside?"

"I do not know if it is the structure of the building that stops cell phones."

"That's what Jo thought."

"Sí. Or something más insidioso."

"Insidious? You mean like deliberately blocking cell phones?"

"Maybe." She shrugged. "Perhaps I am wrong." Zapa gulped down the last bit of sandwich, wiped her hands on a napkin and downed the rest of her water. "Okay, Dani. You must go back to Jo and I must go back to work. If you decide to call the police, say, 'hay una emergencia en la Clínica de Cádiz y necesitamos ayuda.' Something like that."

"Okay. I got it. And it's 911?"

"No. It is 112 in Spain. I am thinking too that I should talk to Berto."

"Who?"

"He works at Puerta. An intern. A good man. Old family friend. I will check with him if you like. Maybe he can help Jo go there."

"Oh yes, please do that. Thank you so much, Zapa."

"Un placer, Dani. A pleasure. Stay strong. Perhaps you will go to Puerta today. If not, I will see you tomorrow with my old friend the mop." She laughed and waved with the back of her hand as she headed out the door.

Dani immediately picked up her cell phone to call the police. She paused and put it back in her pocket. *I need to run this by Jo.* She grabbed the bag of food and was heading out the door when she stopped and pulled out her cell once more. What the hell, she thought as she called Protection Guy again. This time she left her cell phone number. She continued on through the doors of El Popular, sandwich bag in hand.

She was just passing the blue phone kiosk on her way back to the clinic when she saw them. She quickly moved behind the pay phone.

Thug, a.k.a. Chaco, and Montoya were in front of the hospital entrance. They were beside a police car, talking to the uniformed officer standing next to them. Dani couldn't catch a word, but the handshake between Montoya and the cop, and the cop's pat on the back for Thug, said enough.

She stood frozen, waiting for them to leave the front doors so she could go back into the hospital when her cell phone rang. Dani answered quickly.

"Sí?"

"Dani?"

She didn't recognize the voice and wondered that the sound of her own name could repel her. The male voice continued, "Me llamo Rico, él de la protección." He chuckled. The dirty laugh. It became hoarse and quickly morphed into a cough. *A smoker.* "I am now at a lovely little café a short way down the street from the Clínica. Se llama, it is called La Conchita Rosa. Will you join me for cafecito?"

She wasn't sure she'd heard him correctly. "Perdón?"

He repeated himself and added, "We can talk about how I might be of service to you."

"Uh, okay."

He disconnected. She stared at the phone for a second, turned away from the hospital and headed down the street for La Conchita Rosa. *Angel? This would be a good time for you to keep Jo safe for me. Please? For just a bit longer?*

She found the place in minutes. It was a dingy joint with two men smoking out front. She shook her head. *It's a coffee bar. A public place. It should be okay.* She grabbed the door handle before she could change her mind.

Public was perhaps the wrong word. The small room was filled with tables, chairs and men. Only men. They were older and almost all sported white shirts and black pants. A few sat on the benches lining the walls, but mostly they stood in the center, talking and drinking like an old-time he/him cocktail party. *Maybe they're gay? Dream on, kiddo. It's a flamenco bar.* Una peña. *Machismo plus, guaranteed. Not that gay men can't be—okay, Dan, just stop.*

As if on cue, the room quieted. Two young men dressed in black came through a large, curtained doorway. The one with short hair had a chair. The one with long hair had a chair and a guitar. They sat down, faced the group and then each other. The short-haired man placed his hand on his chest, opened his mouth and sang.

The guitarist watched the singer closely and tailored each stroke and slap of the guitar to the rhythm of the voice. Dani was mesmerized until suddenly, they stopped. Just like that. It was over. She had trouble pulling herself out of the trance, struggled to remember where she was and why she was here. She felt a hand at her elbow and the words, "Señora, con permiso."

He stood out from the rest in white slacks, leather loafers, a silky peach V-neck pullover and thin black leather gloves. A peacock among penguins. His pasty skin and sagging turkey neck made a lie of his jet-black hair.

"You are Dani, the señora from the hospital, correcto?"

"Sí, yes, I am."

"Come this way." He took her elbow and steered her. "I have a table."

It was a relatively quiet corner away from the rest. They no sooner sat down when a waiter appeared and served them cafecitos.

"A little too early for vino, don't you agree?"

Dani nodded.

"Now, una propia introducción. Me llamo Ricardo. Ricardo Montalbán." He looked at her expectantly. When she didn't react, he forced a laugh. "No, no, it is a little joke. But of course, you are too young to know the name of the Mexicano who pretended he was Colombiano, for coffee's sake. Y claro, there is also el Cubano Ricky Ricardo, el alias de Desi Arnaz, y en esta edad, por los jóvenes y los gays, el Puertoriqueño, Ricky Martin. We are an army of Rickys."

He laughed and again coughed. He pulled out a handkerchief from his pocket and spit into it. *No wonder this guy gave Jo the creeps.*

"¿Pero yo? Yo me llamo Monte, Ricardo Monte. But please, call me Rico, agreed?" Dani pressed her lips together and nodded sharply. He looked at her fondly, having declared them first-name-basis friends and brushed a finger across her hand. She pulled her hand away from his.

"What kind of club is this, señor?"

"Rico." An order, not a request.

"Bueno. Rico, I can see this is a flamenco club, but why are there only men here?"

"Ah, sí, sí. This is a traditional club, the way all clubs used to be in my father's father's day. No women are allowed here unless invited by a member." He softened his voice and added, "As you are by me."

Dani managed not to cringe. Just barely. He was the kind of guy who made her skin crawl. He sat a little too close, touched a little too easily, his smile too wide and his voice like velvet on a razor's edge.

"Uh, right. Thank you. So, Rico, please tell me what you do in your business. You used the word *protección* when you visited my friend's room in the hospital. Is that insurance you offer?"

"No. No. I am, how can I say this, un facilitador."

"A facilitator."

"Sí. Eso es. Pues, you tell me. How may I help you?"

"Okay. Well, here it is. My friend in la Clínica Ortega would like to move to another hospital. Specifically, Puerta, the public hospital. Today. Can you do that?"

He didn't pause or even blink. Only quoted his price. 10,000 euros, which roughly translated to $14,000 Canadian dollars, for the immediate transfer of Jo to Puerta. Dani's jaw dropped and her eyes widened. He gave out a low chuckle. She asked him how he would do this. He shook his head and said he could give her no details and, lowering his voice, turned deadly serious and impressed on her the confidential nature of their conversation.

"Be assured. I will do this job for you. I know where your Josefina is. I can go to her at any time. Only to help her, of course," he added.

Ah. There it is. The threat. Why am a not surprised? She thought of the homegrown narco culture Eddie had mentioned. *This guy's a likely candidate.* And then she thought of Eddie mentioning he knew someone he could check with to help her and Jo get out of the hospital. *Could this be Eddie's guy? Nah. Too mafioso for Eddie. I hope.* Before she could stop herself, she asked if he was a member of organized crime.

"No no." He shook his head. "Disorganized crime, perhaps." He laughed again, the laugh deteriorating into a harsh cough and finally, a spit in his empty cup. *So genteel.* "Another bad joke, I am so sorry. There is nothing illegal in my work, la mayor parte del tiempo."

Most of the time? Dani frowned, wondering if she'd understood that right.

"Tell me, Dani, why does your friend not just take herself to Puerta?"

"Uh, well, the hospital, it's also a bit disorganized. They kept her passport and no one knows when we'll get it back. But most concerning is that they don't seem very good at the medical part. The doctor has yet to make an appearance. They've done some tests but still can't tell us just how serious it is. And, most importantly, they won't let her leave."

"Ah. I see. I only ask to make sure I am not stepping into something nasty. If they are preventing her from leaving, it seems that this is perhaps nasty, yes?"

"Hard to say. So, if we do this, how would we pay you? Cash?"

"Si es posible, sería lo mejor. The best. If this is not possible for you, I will take un depósito y un vale. An IOU."

Dani told him she would have to talk to Jo before deciding. He passed her a piece of paper with a number written on it.

"If you decide you want my help, call this number. It is different from the other number you have. Tell the person who answers, 'dígale al señor Rico, sí.' If you decide no, do not call."

They stood and shook hands. Dani walked quickly out of the place white-knuckling the satchel of food, hoping it wouldn't cause salmonella after being dragged around all this time. Once on the street, she ran back to the hospital and room 312.

She found Jo safe and sitting up in bed. She held up the bag. "Sandwiches. If anyone comes through that door, we hide the food."

"Why? I will not have surgery today. Besides, them seeing me eating would be a surefire way of making them stop their angio campaign, right?"

"I guess." Dani looked at Jo more closely. Something had changed. She pulled two sandwiches out of the paper bag, one for Jo and one for herself. "Here. Eat. So. Anything happen while I was gone?"

Jo twisted her mouth to the side. "Later. Tell me what *you* found out." Jo slowly opened the food wrapper and carefully pulled the sandwich apart. Dani smirked. It was Jo's ritual to inspect all food items, double-checking what she was putting in her mouth, just in case something unexpected lurked inside. It drove Dani nuts.

"Nothing in there to hurt you, babe."

"Yeah, okay. I may just remove the green thing."

"It's avocado. Geez, Jo, just eat it."

Jo peeled the slice of avocado away from the bread and held it up for further inspection.

"Tempting. But no." She dropped it in the wastebasket and looked up at Dani. "You look upset. It can't be because of the avocado."

"Eat first and then I'll tell you."

"No, no, no. Tell me. Now."

Dani sighed. She told her almost everything: the message she left for Eddie, the chat with Zapa, the sighting of Montoya and crew with the cop and, lastly, her meeting with Rico.

"You were right, by the way. The guy is very disturbing but he's offering the only fast solution out of here. Don't say it. I know. More against the mortgage. Again. Totally worth it as far as I'm concerned. He says he'll take an IOU in the meantime but damn, he makes me want to run the other way."

To Dani's surprise, Jo laughed.

"I so want to say yes, yes, book him, Danno. And ten thousand? We might be able to cobble that together in cash. But if he upset you, which he clearly did, maybe we should see about Zapa's intern contact first."

"Right. I can't imagine what an intern can do."

"Well, let's find out." Jo was upbeat, almost chipper. "Zapa's guy works at the public hospital? Puerto, right?"

"Puerta."

"Dani. You've got to stop that. I don't care if it's Puert-oh or Puert-uh."

"I'm not being my usual anal self, Jo. There are two hospitals. One is called Puert-UH del Mar—that is a public hospital where you *want* to go. The other one is called el Gran Puert-OH. It's private, part of the same chain as the one you're in. You do *not* want to go there."

"Got it. Puert-UH. And while we're on the topic of Spanish, could you please tell me what you wrote on that card?" She gestured to the business card propped up against the tray. "Leona laughed her way out the door."

Dani picked up the card. "Oops. I wrote 'Ella no habla inglés.' She doesn't speak English. No wonder Leona laughed."

"I don't like being a source of amusement for Leona."

"Sorry." Dani found a pen, scratched out inglés, wrote in español, held it up for Jo to see and propped it against the tray. "Anyway, I will check with Zapa about her contact. She says we can trust him. He's an old family friend."

"Okay. And you still think you can trust Zapa?"

"The more time I spend with that woman, the more I like her. There's something really solid about her. And she's sharp and a bit of a crusader. Says she's going to become a lawyer."

"Really? That's fantastic."

"Yeah. She reminds me a bit of my mum. She says the hospital broke the law by preventing you from leaving, like forced confinement or something. Unfortunately, that cozy little exchange with the cop I witnessed has made me wary of calling them. And that brings me to the last bit of news which I will now tell you, since you've almost finished eating."

Jo dropped the last bit of sandwich. "There's more?"

"Montoya stopped me when I came back into the building and told me you're booked for the angio tonight. They'll be taking you for surgery prep at nine o'clock."

"What the fuck? That's only what—about four hours from now? I can't believe you didn't tell me that first."

"I wanted you to hear everything else first before I dropped the bombshell."

"Fuck. Okay. This means I really, really have to get the fuck out of here. ASAP. Is that why you think we should hire the guy in the bar?"

Dani didn't answer. She stared at Jo.

"I just figured out what's different with you. You're not squinting. Is your headache gone?"

"Almost. It's still there but it's way less."

"Did they change your dosage? Is that it?"

"No idea. She brought me a new patch and"—Jo opened the top drawer of the small dresser by the bed—"a whole box of patches in fact. Told me to change them myself every couple of hours because she had things to do. Self-serve medical care at its finest. But none of that is why the headache has more or less gone away. It's because I took the old nitro patch off and never put on a new one."

"*That's* what you did. You just up and pulled it off yourself?"

"Yes. I decided to go for it. See if it was causing the headache. And I believe it was."

"Aren't you the smart one, not to mention brave, or maybe foolhardy?"

"It's called desperation. I couldn't stand the pain any longer."

"But your heart. That's why it was there. How does your heart feel?"

"I feel better than I have since this whole thing started."

"Really? No chest pains and no headaches?"

"Diminished headache. Absolutely no chest pains. And if anything starts up, I figure I can slap a patch back on. I've got enough here to last a month."

"So it *was* the patch all along. But they're so adamant you keep it on regardless. I wonder why?"

Jo flopped back on her pillow and folded her arms. "You tell me. Maybe it was to incapacitate me. Anyway, let's get a little caffeine in my system. It's time to leave. Somehow."

CHAPTER EIGHT

Zapa was on the main floor, vigorously swabbing down the hallway outside the administration office. She jerked her head up at Dani's approach and nodded in the direction of the women's washroom.

"Come. My office."

She rolled her equipment through the door, held it for Dani, and pushed the heavy bucket back against it after it closed behind them saying it would slow down any interruption.

"Cleaning in progress," she said with a smile.

She went into a stall and sat down with a sigh on a closed toilet seat, holding her mop like a staff, tilted forward to keep the stall door open.

Dani leaned against the sink.

"They're taking Jo for surgery prep at nine tonight."

"Tonight? But that is crazy. Why are they doing it at night when it will require overtime? And where will they perform it? And most important, *who* will perform it. You said they were bringing someone in but that usually takes time. They were talking in the cafeteria about the fourth-floor crew working tonight. Perhaps that is for Jo's procedure. But I do not believe they have the equipment. Maybe they have it upstairs in the private clinic except it is not usually open to regular patients. This is most confusing."

"I still don't get this private clinic thing. Isn't the whole hospital private?"

"Sí, sí. Except the fourth-floor clinic is more private. Like the difference between the regular seats at the movie theatre and the ones you pay extra for and have drinks and larger, more comfortable seats. All in the same building. All require tickets. All private except some sections have more privileges. You understand?"

"So you're saying the fourth floor has the privilege of actual medical care."

"Pues, in essence you are right. The fourth-floor patients receive more attention. At least that is what I understand. I have not been there. It is treated like a separate company. They have a separate staff and I believe they are instructed not to talk to us. I tried talking to them but they walk away, saying they must return to work. And I also tried to go up there to check it out for myself but it is almost impossible without a key card.

"Jo and I saw it from the elevator. The paramedic pressed the wrong floor on the way to the ECG. But when I tried to get back there to find the doctor, I couldn't. All entrances were locked down."

"Yes. That is correct. It is always locked. Tell me what you saw."

"It was like an actual functioning hospital as opposed to the third floor. I saw people, for one thing. Looked like real medical staff. And real medical equipment, like one of those monitoring screens on wheels and also that contraption that rolls around with food trays on it. Like a tall cart. Never seen either down here. There was a nurse standing in the hall with a clipboard, looking rather professional, and I heard a loudspeaker announcement requesting an orderly in room something or other. What do they do there anyway? What kind of medicine?"

"Como dije, like I said, I do not know."

"Whatever they do, it may now include an angio unless I get Jo out of here."

"Did you call the policía?"

Dani told her about the seeing Montoya and Chaco in a very friendly exchange with the policemen.

"¡Qué raro! How strange. Bueno. It is time to call Berto, my intern friend. Here, use my phone. His number is at the top of my call list. While you two talk, I will get some more work done."

"I can use my cell."

"Use mine. He will pick up immediately when he sees my number. He is expecting the call."

Zapa grabbed her mop and bucket and dragged them out to the main hall. Dani followed and continued outside to the phone kiosk. She tapped the first number on Zapa's cell phone.

"Berto?"

"Sí, sí, soy yo. ¿Y usted? ¿La amiga de Zapa?"

Zapa's friend. Dani smiled to herself.

"Sí, sí."

"Pues dígame, ¿qué está pasando allí en la Clínica Ortega?" So tell me…

After she told Jo's story, he said, "Well, Dani, first, I practice oncology not cardiology. Therefore, I have limits in my knowledge regarding your friend's illness. However, I *do* know the angiograma and I agree with Jo. It is not the place to begin, unless of course the reading of the electroencefalograma is extreme."

"Who knows what the ECG reading was. We haven't received the results as yet."

"That is unusual. The readout is immediate. Now, regarding the issue of the medical release, the doctor is correct. Because Jo is a patient of the Clínica, it is best that she leave with its authorization. Without it, she could have muchos problemas. With airplanes, for sure. Also with hotels and car rentals. Comercios, uh, businesses, have much fear of obligaciones, debts, uh…"

"Liability?" asked Dani.

"Correcto, liability, if, god forbid, Jo's illness flares up while on their premises. Regarding the intern going from here to the Clínica, this is very odd. I think this will be a private arrangement between the intern and the Clínica. I am surprised that the paramedics did not bring Jo here to Puerta in the first place."

"They said the Clínica was closer."

"That is true in a geographical sense only. It is not closer if you have a heart attack patient because la Clínica does not have a cardio department. And we do. However, it is too late for this discussion. Tell me, Dani, when is Jo to undergo the angiograma?"

"We just found out that her prep for surgery is at nine tonight."

"Tonight?"

"Yes. I need to move her to Puerta immediately. Can it be done?"

"Admitted here, tonight? I am afraid that is impossible. A fast admission like that will only happen if she arrives as an emergency patient. And with another hospital already involved, it is most unlikely."

"Uh, not to sound...uh...well...dishonest, but we could always lie. Arrive in a cab and say it's all just happening."

"Yes you can try to do this, of course. However, I believe it will become complicated very quickly when they discover what you have done, which they will. Jo will be in the system somewhere and you will not have her passport. I am afraid, Dani, that I do not know what I can do to help you. I know for sure that you will not be able to make this transfer happen tonight."

"So you're saying we're out of luck with Puerta, even with the cardio department there."

"No, not entirely. But on such short notice? Tonight? Yes. You are out of luck with Puerta."

Disappointed, Dani went back inside and rejoined Zapa. Once they had barricaded themselves in the women's washroom again, she told her what Berto had said.

"With Puerta out, I guess we'll have to go for option number two."

"You have piqued my interest," Zapa said, sitting back down on the toilet seat lid. "What is this second option?"

"His name is Rico. He'll charge us 10,000 euros to take Jo out of here and get her admitted to Puerta."

"Ay, dios mío. ¡Qué estafa!" Dani tilted her head. "A robbery," Zapa explained.

"I agree. But he said he'd take an IOU and that he can do it *tonight*."

"I wonder how that is possible when Berto says it is not. What is his name again?"

"First name, Rico. And his surname was…? What was it? He made a joke about it. Oh yeah. He said it was Ricardo Montalbán. And then laughed." Dani closed her eyes trying to remember. "Monte. That's it. Rico Monte."

"You spoke to Rico Monte?"

"Yeah."

"How did you speak to him? By phone, I hope."

"No, no. He called me right after I left El Popular and he… directed…me…to…" Dani's words slowed, seeing the look on Zapa's face. "What? What's wrong?"

"How did he know to call you?" Zapa asked, brows furrowed.

"Uh, well, I called him after he left his card with Jo."

"He was in the hospital?"

"Yeah. I was kind of surprised he was allowed to roam the halls looking for business. But who's around to stop him?"

Zapa pursed her lips and moved her head from side to side, saying nothing. Dani, somewhat concerned by her reaction, rushed on.

"I didn't commit to his plan or anything when he told me about it because I wanted to run it by Jo and quite honestly the guy freaks me out. I'll have to meet up with him again to give him the money and that alone scares me. And I'm not scared of much, well, except maybe empty streets at night and bugs and that fucking stairwell. But you know, now that we're talking about this, and, forgive me, Zapa, but I'm just riffing here, maybe you could come with me, like, you know, for translation purposes? I really don't want to blow it with bad Spanish and also, just to have someone else with me like maybe as a deterrent because he seems like a bit of a loose cannon, and if I'm showing up with a whole bunch of money...?" She paused. "Please? I would pay you for your time too. What d'ya think?"

Zapa sat motionless like a still life. Mop handle held firmly, head tilted slightly, features frozen, confusion flickering about the eyes. American-Gothic-In-The-Can. *No. Española-Gótica-al-Baño. Oh god, that's terrible.* Zapa still hadn't moved or spoken.

"Uh, Zapa? Are you okay?"

"No, I am not okay. First, Dani, I must tell you, that I have never before received an invitation like this. Let me make sure I understand you correctly. You are asking me to be your translator and your muscle?"

Dani guffawed. "Uh, well, yeah. I guess that's about it."

Another long pause.

"The answer is no."

"No?"

Zapa joined Dani at the sink and put her hand on Dani's arm. "It is not because I do not want to help you. Please believe that. It is because no one can help you if you are involved with a man like Rico Monte."

"You know him?"

"Rico Monte? Absolutamente. He is muy peligroso. A very dangerous man."

"But he's our only option to get Jo out of here."

"No, Dani. Rico Monte cannot be any option, first or last or only. With him, you strike a deal with the devil. No matter what you do, no matter what you pay, no matter *how* you pay, he will always be with you. He will own you. Even back in Canada. This man has connections everywhere. And he will not forget you. Guaranteed if there is an IOU. He, or some compinche, uh, some buddy, will appear in your life suddenly and ask for the money. But even after it is paid, he will want something else, probably information but maybe something more. You will not be able to turn him down because he will threaten to hurt you or someone you care about. Or perhaps he will make your life impossible. He will have friends with the police and they will harass you. Or others driving taxis and they will take you to the wrong places. If he has friends at the bank, they will mess up your account. If he has…"

"Okay. Okay. I get it."

Another long moment of silence.

"So I take it that's a firm no?"

"Óigame, Dani. Listen to me. You are about to make a decision that will impact the rest of your life. I suggest Jo might want to brave the procedure she fears rather than invite Rico into your lives."

"It's not a state of mind. The reality is it's a very risky procedure for her, given her family history. And her headaches? She took off the damn nitro patch all by herself and guess what? Her headaches disappeared. Maybe they're giving her the wrong dosage or something. On top of that, she's not being monitored. At all. No heart monitor. No blood pressure readings. If something happened, no one would know. Reminiscent of another patient who just died, isn't it? Everyone says that woman died from neglect. And what if it wasn't negligence? What if it was deliberate? I have no confidence in these people, Zapa. What about the fact that they physically prevented her from leaving? There are too many questions for me to simply go ahead and trust them to perform an extremely invasive and risky procedure on my Jo. So frankly, I'd rather take a chance on Rico."

"I understand what you are saying. I am only telling you what I know. If you must take Jo out now, do it yourselves somehow. I will help you. But not if you involve Rico. I can have nothing to do with that man."

Dani got on the elevator, deep in thought. How would she tell Jo that they were back to charging the front door? The smell of coffee hit her as soon as she stepped onto the third floor.

Right. Coffee. Jo wants coffee. A little caffeine with that bad news?

She rushed along the third-floor hallway to the cafeteria. Through the windows, she saw Thug, a.k.a. Chaco, and a woman she'd not seen before, picking up coffees from the counter. They turned to walk out. They were an odd-looking pair, big burly Chaco in his orange paramedic getup, the rather chic woman in a black suit, silk shirt and black patent pumps. Her getup was topped off by short hair with caramel colours feathered through the black strands. Not a cheap do. *Haute couture paramedic? Nah.*

They walked toward the exit, the woman speaking quietly but intensely. She looked angry. Chaco looked flushed. Dani backed up and cast about for a place to hide. Cursing the lack of corners in the curved hallway, she dove into the stairwell and peered through the slowly closing door. The woman continued to harangue the guy as they headed straight for Dani's hiding spot. She was stuck and could only go up or down the stairwell. She went down and prayed. They pushed through the door and to her intense relief, went up the stairs. They stopped on the next landing. Thug was getting such an earful, Dani almost pitied the brute. Almost. The woman spit out her words and yet still managed to whisper. *Spitting and whispering. Impressive.*

Dani strained to understand the words breezing by her ears. Her Spanish skills were clearly not up to espionage. Dani silenced her mind and focused hard. Thug started whining, grovelling.

"Lo siento, doctora, pero no pude…" Sorry doctor but I couldn't…

Shit. She's the doctor. The great doctora Nieves-Félix. Oh my god.

Dani was about to charge up the stairs and accost the elusive doctor when the tone of the exchange changed.

"Baja la voz, idiota." Keep your voice down, idiot. The doctor's command came low and guttural. She sounded enraged. "Te pago demasiado…I pay you a lot of money…the position you've put me in…they are trouble…" Her delivery sped up until Dani could only grab single words as they whizzed past her ear.

"Improvisar…canadiense…suerte…desastre con Benning… riñón…"

Improvise, Canadian, luck, disaster with Benning, riñón. Riñón? What did that mean? She repeated the words to herself over and over:

Improvise…Canadian…Benning…luck…disaster…riñón.
Improvise…Canadian…Benning…luck…disaster…riñón.

The door from the cafeteria hallway opened inches from where Dani stood. She lurched back and peered cautiously around the banister at the newcomers. From her lower perch, she was eye-level to two pairs of white shoes. Nurses' shoes. Dani jerked back again, far out of sight.

The women seemed stalled there, chattering away. *What is this? A stairwell convention?*

Nieves evidently felt the same way.

"¿Quién es?" she called down.

"Las enfermeras," one nurse called up and they giggled.

The door on the fourth-floor landing opened and thudded closed. The two women exploded in laughter, their boss-nemesis having exited. As they went slowly up the stairs, chatting away, Dani returned to the puzzle.

Riñón. And Benning. That was the woman down the hall. The dead woman.

Dani stilled. Could hardly breathe.

The fourth-floor door banged closed again as the nurses left. Silence crashed down on her, leaving only the ravings of her mind. Why were they talking about Benning, the woman who died, in the same sentence as the Canadian, presumably Jo?

She forced herself to leave the stairwell. She stood in the hall, confused. What was she doing here anyway? She saw the cafeteria. She remembered. It was coffee. That's why she was here. Jo wanted coffee. Such a normal thing, coffee. And yes. That was the best thing to do when the world went sideways. Miguel looked up as she walked into the cafeteria.

"Dos cafecitos por favor," she said. He looked at her and frowned. "Are you all right?"

"Oh yeah. I'm terrific. So, like, is it too late? For the two coffees?"

"No, señora. They've asked me to keep the place open tonight. It seems they're busy upstairs."

"I'll bet they are." She paused. "Uh, Miguel, what does riñón mean?"

"Riñón? Kidney."

Dani stared at him.

"So, señora," he said, watching her while he pulled the espresso, "may I call you Dani?"

"What? Oh, sure."

"Pues, Dani, Zapa said I should tell you what I know about la doctora and the clinic upstairs. It's not a good time right now when she's here in the building. As you say in English, she's got big ears. Orejas grandes. But some time when we can meet away from here, let's chat, okay?"

She didn't respond, only stared at him.

He continued, "I work here most days but I also work many evenings at a restaurant near here, Casa Crema. If you want to drop in there sometime, I'll make a coffee for you, on the house." He put the two glasses on the counter.

She didn't know what he'd just said. She saw steam rising from the coffees in front of her. *Right. I ordered coffees.* She managed a thank you and paid. He gave her a couple of napkins to cut the heat of the glasses. She walked down the hall in a trance, as if someone had pulled back a veil to reveal an alternate reality, something unexpected and ugly. She couldn't imagine how she'd explain it to Jo, what she'd heard. She wasn't even sure what it meant, all those words put together. The doctor had sounded so angry. And why had she talked about improvising? Only one thing was clear. They had to get out of there immediately.

But how will I ever get Jo down to the main floor, let alone out the doors? Jo can hardly walk and Thug is everywhere. Hot coffee splashed on her hand. *Focus, Dani. Focus on not spilling coffee.* It helped, that small task. Calmed her a bit. She and Jo would figure something out, like they always did.

When she reached room 312, she put one of the hot glasses on the floor so she could open the door. She picked it up again and backed into the room, pushing the door closed with her foot. She turned and looked toward the bed.

It was empty.

CHAPTER NINE

Her gut twisted. Barely keeping panic at bay, she put the coffee on the side table and checked the bathroom. No Jo. She started to shake, a cold trembling that gave her goose bumps.

No. No. No.

She opened the drawer in the bedside table. None of Jo's personal effects were there. No nitro stash. She looked under the covers and under the bed. Her paper slippers were gone. On the far side was the leather bag tucked out of sight. She opened it. Everything was there. She'd forgotten that she'd packed Jo's things when they tried the wheelchair escape. Jo must have tucked it out of sight.

Dani moved toward the door, about to run down the hall shouting, "Jo! Jo!" But she stopped herself. *Be still, just for a minute. Breathe. Think.*

She touched the tiny angel in her pocket and looked back at the room. *Wherever she is, when you find her, you must run. You will never come back here.*

She went back, picked up the bag and scanned room 312 one last time to make sure nothing was left behind. She walked out the door and down the empty hall. Her shaking had stopped, but she was still cold. No longer the cold of fear or dread. This was an icy resolve. Dani now had one goal: find Jo and get the fuck out of here.

As she checked all the third-floor rooms, Dani ran through the possibilities. Maybe Jo had tired of waiting and tried to leave on her own? No, between weakness and Thug she would never make it out the front door. Maybe she got tired of waiting for her coffee. Maybe she crawled her way down the hall to the cafeteria and Dani simply missed her. Unlikely but…

She hurried to the cafeteria and asked Miguel if he'd seen her. He said he hadn't seen anyone except fourth-floor staff. She left Jo's bag with him and thought about where else Jo could be. Two guesses: the fourth or the fifth.

They could have taken her for another ECG on the fifth. Or for surgery on the fourth. It was only about six thirty. Way too soon. But what if it was happening earlier than expected? Her stomach turned. She caught the elevator down to the lobby, her heart now matching the manic samba. Once off, she beelined for the emergency room. Montoya was leaning over the desk, reading some papers. She looked up.

"Señora Dani."

"Jefa Montoya, where is Jo?"

"Your friend has been taken to surgery for the angioplastia."

"Where?" Dani asked grabbing the woman by the arm. "Where do they have her?"

"Cálmese, señora, and please remove your hand," Montoya said, her eyes narrowing.

Dani did as asked. "Tell me where Jo is or I will call the police."

"Why would you do that, señora? Why would you call the police? She is in good care and these threats of yours are not acceptable."

For once in your life, rein in the rage.

Dani took a deep breath, forced her muscles to relax and changed her tone.

"But Leona said the surgery wasn't until later tonight. And she ate."

"Sí, sí. The surgeon is coming earlier than expected."

"When?"

"Eight instead of eight thirty? Perhaps earlier. I do not know exactamente. Pero, ¿qué dice Ud., señora? What did you say? She ate food?"

Dani nodded.

"Ay dios. I must tell them. Perhaps they will stop entirely." She paused. "Or perhaps no." She shook her head, rolled her eyes up to the heavens and spoke through gritted teeth. "Ay dios."

"I'm so worried about her. You must tell me where she is, jefa. I wasn't there when they took her. She'll be nervous. She has concerns about the angiogram and she can't understand what's being said. I must go to her."

"She is on the fourth floor, but you cannot go there. She will be fine. You should stay here in emergency or perhaps in Jo's room. They will take her there after the operation, if they continue. Ay dios. She ate. No lo creo. But that is not your concern, señora. You must relax. I believe the cafeteria is open for coffee or you could go to El Popular for something to eat and come back afterwards. The chicken sandwiches are excellent. Y no te preocupes. Do not worry, señora."

With a level of self-discipline Dani didn't know she had, she made herself appear satisfied with Montoya's explanation and nodded.

"You're right. Maybe I will go to El Popular. Something to eat will help."

She walked out the door and stopped. *How the fuck can I get on the fourth?* She could try to steal a pass. That'd be tough. Her sleight of hand wasn't good and her mano a mano skills were nonexistent. Maybe she could convince one of the staffers to take her up there. Montoya? Definite no there. One of the beige nurses when they came down to the cafeteria? That was a real long shot. The surgery could be over by the time one showed up. She looked up and down the street. The ambulance was parked in its usual spot with Scrawny Guy slouched against the side. Chaco was nowhere to be seen. She walked over.

"Hola," she said.

"Hola, señora."

"I have a favour to ask you."

"¿Cómo puedo ayudarle?" How can I help you?

"I would like you to take me to the fourth floor."

His eyes widened. "¿El cuatro?"

"Yes. I am supposed to be with Jo for her surgery. She needs a translator. I was getting a coffee when they took her up there. Now there's no one around to take me. Maybe you could?"

"No, no, señora," he said, waving her off with his hands. "I cannot take you there. She will be back down soon. Surgery will be done."

"But she won't agree to have the surgery at all without knowing what is going on. I must get to her. Do you understand?"

"Yes, yes. I understand. Just wait for her return. Yes, yes. To wait is easier," he said.

Yup. You seem like a "wait-and-see" kind of guy.

"Quizá, señor. Perhaps. But I cannot wait. I have to find her now."

"You cannot go to the fourth floor. You need an access card."

"Yes. I understand. You have one, don't you?"

"Yes, but…"

"Please take me there."

"No, señora. This is not something I do, taking people to the fourth. Chaco decides these things."

"I could pay you, for your time that is." She shoved her hand in her pocket and pulled out a bunch of euros.

His interest rose at the prospect of money and he fingered a pimple on his face while considering the idea.

"No, señora. I do not think so." He shook his head with regret. "I went up there just once, only to see it, and they said next time, I could lose my job."

"You need a better reason, is all."

His eyes returned to the money.

"I will pay you handsomely."

He didn't say anything so she pressed on.

"What's your price?"

He closed his eyes briefly. "A million Euros."

"Come on! I don't have that kind of money. Give me a realistic figure."

He fingered the same pimple. It reddened and grew under his nail.

"Do you have a thousand?"

A million to a thousand. Quite a drop.

"I don't think I have that much" she said. "I have to check the ATM. If I don't have a thousand, will five hundred be okay?"

"Sí, sí, okay."

Dani took off before he could come up with another excuse not to help her. She burst through the doors of El Popular, heading straight for the ATM at the back. She had the one thousand euros easy, but she didn't want him to know that. That was the daily maximum withdrawal allowed by the bank and out it chugged, one thousand euros. She split it into two wads, five hundred for the paramedic and the rest for any other palms she might have to grease. She pushed back through the crowd toward the door and stopped. Zapa was leaning against the counter, sipping from a snifter.

"Zapa," she called out, waving over various heads and pushing her way over. "You're still here."

"Yes. I couldn't finish the cafeteria because it is staying open late. Montoya wants me to wait until it closes. I am not happy about this. I'm having a quick brandy to cheer myself up. The mop won't tell," she said, smiling.

"Oh. Okay." Dani replied automatically without really hearing what she'd said. "Listen, Zapa. They've taken Jo."

"What do you mean, taken Jo? Where?"

"To the fourth floor. They took her when I wasn't there and now Montoya says I can't go up there."

"They're going ahead with the angio?"

"Yes. Well, no. I heard them talking in the stairwell. The Spanish was so fast, I had trouble understanding. But they were talking—"

"What? Who was talking?"

"They kept saying riñón. It means kidney."

"I know what it means."

"Right. Okay, I know this'll sound crazy, but I believe this whole thing is really about Jo's kidney, as in kidney for transplant. That's what I'm thinking, well, because of the stairwell stuff I heard."

Zapa lowered her snifter to the bar top and when she spoke it was with measured words. "Óigame. Listen to me. I do not know what is going on at the hospital. But what you are describing does not make sense, this idea about stealing a kidney. Why would they do this when—"

"For a transplant of course. We don't have time to discuss it. And you know what? I almost don't care what they're up to. I just have to get Jo out of there. Now. Pronto. I will *not* leave her lying on some operating table where they can do whatever they want to her. I've figured out how I'll get onto the fourth floor. I have five hundred euros. See?" She flicked her wad of bills in front of a baffled Zapa. "I just need to know how to get Jo out of the building."

Zapa looked at Dani. It was a detached look, an appraisal. She took a big breath and exhaled slowly.

"Dani, as I have said before, I *will* help you take Jo out of the hospital."

Dani gasped. "You will?" She grabbed Zapa's face, smooshing her cheeks together with her hands.

Zapa gently removed Dani's hands from her face. "Please do not do that. Yes. I will help you. Here is what I can suggest right now: the safest exit is through the basement of the building. You cannot get into the basement without a key card. I will have to accompany you. And pay me? You may have to support me for the rest of my life after I lose my job. But for now, we will not worry about that. If I do this, it is because I believe it is the right thing to do. And I do because I believe *you*." Zapa picked up her snifter and drained it. "Come on. We must get to work."

"Oh my god. Thank you, thank you, thank you."

"Now tell me, why do you need all those euros?"

Dani told her about her deal with the acne-scarred paramedic as they moved through the crowded room. Zapa nodded.

"What a weasel he is. But he can be useful. Stay on your guard. Chaco owns him." She paused again. "Listen, Dani. This is important," she said, practically shouting in Dani's ear. "When you find Jo, take her by the main stairwell to the second floor. It is an open space. Completely empty."

"I know that floor."

"Good. You cannot use the elevator or the cafeteria stairwell. Only the main stairwell will take you to the second floor. Okay? I will wait for you there for one hour. Only one hour, okay, Dani?"

"Got it. One hour to the second floor. Oh and, Zapa? I left Jo's bag with Miguel for safekeeping. If you can get it…"

Zapa nodded. They started pushing their way toward the door. It was slow going. They passed the glassed-in display counters.

"Are those cookies?" Dani asked, pointing to small round brown things on a plate behind the glass.

"Uh, yes. Buñuelos de Viento."

"Wind buns?"

"No. No. Fritters. Lighter-Than-Air."

"Okay. Can you get that waiter's attention and get me a dozen. Fast?"

Zapa's eyebrows shot up.

"You are craving sugar now?"

CHAPTER TEN

A richer but skittish Scrawny Guy walked through the main doors into la Clínica Ortega. Dani followed far enough behind to appear separate from him. Or so she hoped. They headed straight for the elevator. Montoya came out of the emergency room and followed them.

"Buenos noches, jefa," Scrawny Guy said, giving her a mini-salute.

"Pepito, where are you going?"

Shit, the guy has a name.

"Ay, jefa," he whined, launching into the line Dani given him. "Only to the fourth floor to bring un regalito, a little present, to one of the nurses." He held up the bag from El Popular. "Buñuelos de Viento."

"Ay, hijo, ¡qué precioso! You have a sweetheart up there, do you?"

Scrawny Guy a.k.a. Pepito managed a blush. Dani was impressed.

"Bueno. But don't stay long. They're busy up there this evening. And you, señora?"

"I'm going to wait in Jo's room. Did you tell them about the food?"

"Claro que sí. They are proceeding. She did not eat enough to concern them. And they say she will be back in her room in an hour's time. Maybe two. I believe they are almost ready to begin."

Dani almost groaned but she managed a nod and smile for Montoya instead.

Once inside the elevator, she pressed the buttons for both the third and fourth floor, knowing Montoya would be monitoring their stops from her main floor perch. The doors closed. "Blue Moon" kicked in.

"Cómo amo esta canción," he said. How I love this song.

Dani grimaced and nodded. *Don't alienate the guy now.*

The elevator stopped at the third floor. Dani's destination, for Montoya's sake. She also could not be seen getting off the elevator on the fourth floor. She would take the stairs. Pepito held the door-open button, waiting for Dani to get off.

"¿Señora?"

"Right." *Here goes nothing.*

She walked off the elevator and made a sharp right turn into the stairwell, manoeuvred around the ladder and bounded up the stairs two at a time. She was panting when she reached the locked door. She waited. It clicked open. *God bless Pepito.* She went through the door and watched his Scrawny Guy butt as he scuttled off toward the nursing desk. *Now, where is Jo?*

She started down the hall away from the nursing station, checking every doorway and every room. Halfway along there was a stretcher. *Fuck. It can't be the same...* A woman lay there, reading a book. *Thank god. She's alive. And no brown spots on her hands. Hallelujah. No Benning come back to haunt.* She instantly felt badly, remembering the crazy guy weeping behind the nursing post. But this woman was very much alive and absorbed in a book titled *Beautiful and Dark* by Rosa Montero. Dani saw a clipboard at the end of the bed and went closer. It said Robards, Mary Anne, Chicago, in big block letters. The woman looked up.

"Señora, ¿cuándo…voy…surgery?"

"Soon, señora," Dani replied in English.

"You speak English?"

"Yes. But I can't stay to talk."

"Come back? To chat?"

"Okay."

Dani left before the woman could ask something else and continued along the circular hallway. Squeals of delight emanated from the nursing station which was now just ahead. After that was the elevator and next to it, the main stairwell. She'd come full circle. There was nothing in between. No nook or cranny where Jo might be. Footsteps sounded, coming her way. Dani backed herself into a depression in the wall behind a post, noticing for the first time a sign across from her. Sala de Cirugía. An excited beige version of Leona came bounding down the hall and charged into the surgery room.

"Ven. Ven. Un regalito de Pepito. Buñuelos de Viento." A second person let loose a high squeal.

Such excitement over those treats. They must be bored. After they'd hurried off, Dani headed into the room.

It was divided by a curtain that hung from ceiling to floor. Each side had a stretcher but only one held a patient with a white-capped head pointed toward Dani. She crept forward and saw the face of the person lying there.

Jo. Her stretcher held no clipboard name nor paperwork. She was on an intravenous.

"Psst."

Jo opened her eyes and smiled drowsily.

Thank god. Not unconscious.

"You came to get me," she said, slurring her words.

Damn. She's stoned. They've got her on something.

Dani motioned for her to be quiet, unhooked the intravenous as carefully as she could, pressing the bandage against the injection point as she pulled the needle out of Jo's arm, hoping she wouldn't start bleeding. Dani helped her down off the stretcher. Her legs gave way. Dani caught her and barely kept her from collapsing completely.

"I told them I ate. They didn't care." Jo started to laugh. Dani pinched her hard to rouse her out of the drug-induced hilarity. "Ow," Jo yelped.

"Shush. I need your help with this," Dani whispered. "You've got to walk as fast as you can."

Jo smiled and nodded. "Okay, Dani," she whispered, leaning against her, nuzzling her neck affectionately.

They lurched together toward the door when Dani heard footsteps in the hall. The nurse was returning. She pushed Jo behind the door and leaned against her to keep her upright against the wall behind. As the door swung open, Dani grabbed it, held it against them. *If this works, badass angel is truly with us.*

The nurse swore at seeing no one and ran out of the room and down the hall. "Beta, Beta, se fue." She's gone.

Dani pulled Jo out of the surgery room and down the hall away from the nurses' desk. She was losing the fight to keep her upright. They'd never make it this way. She twisted around so Jo fell forward onto her back, Jo's face in her neck, Jo's arms around her shoulders and Jo's feet dragging along the floor. Dani hauled her toward the stairwell door Scrawny Guy had unlocked, pushed through it and started to descend. Her knees threatened to buckle at every step, and she could see them falling headlong to their deaths. But the rough ride had roused Jo.

"Let me down. I think I can do it."

Relieved, Dani helped her stand on her own. Jo kept one hand on Dani's back for balance, the other on the railing for support. Dani led the way, staying close to Jo to block her if she stumbled. They lurched together down the stairs as fast and as quietly as they could, past the third floor and into the minefield of ladders, drywall containers, mud trays, and flying dust. One small trowel clattered to the side. They reached the second-floor door, wedged open as before.

Zapa ran toward them, put her arm around Jo and helped her across the room to a small pile of junk. She directed them to lie down between the wall and a precariously piled stack of old wood flooring about a metre high. Zapa grabbed a broom with a cloth wrapped loosely around it and ran back into the stairwell. Dust billowed through the doorway.

She returned, tucked the broom behind a ladder and squatted down next to them.

"What did you do out there?" Dani asked.

"I patted down the footprints you left in the dust. There is no sense in leaving an obvious trail. Bueno. I have things to do and you must lie low for a while. Now tell me, do you still want your passport?"

"Only if it's an easy grab. Otherwise, forget about it."

"I think it is possible. I will use the time we have now to figure something out. I know where they keep these things in the administrator's office.

"Where do we go from here?"

"To the basement first and then out of the building. But we cannot go now. The search has begun. You will hear them soon. They will race through the building looking for you. They will pound up and down the stairwell too."

"We're trapped here. There's no exit from this room."

"That is why I chose it. I will leave the door open, which is how it always is. To close it will make them suspicious. But open, it is a dead-end route they will not take very seriously. When they search this room, I believe they will only check that spot over there," she said pointing to a dozen pieces of drywall stacked against a pillar.

It looked like the perfect hiding spot to Dani, far preferable to the meagre pile of wood slats. Zapa did not agree.

"They will give only a quick glance to the rest. I realize it is not the best solution. I could have put you in one of the hospital rooms but here we are already halfway to the basement. Our exit. It is the best I could come up with on such short notice."

"Okay."

"Here," she said, giving Dani the bag she'd left with the barista. "Tuck this in next to you. I'm going to cover you with a black cloth. I hope you will look like the shadow of this pile of junk but you must stay very still. And you must remain silent and as low to the floor as possible. Flat, como panqueques. Estoy seguro. I am sure this will work. Casi."

"Almost." The word hung in the air.

"Now, put your heads down and be still, no matter what you hear. Promise?"

"We promise."

A light fabric settled over them, blacking out sight. The soft rustling of her steps along the aged timber faded. And she was gone.

Zapa was right. Minutes after she left, there was much yelling and shouting and cursing. Footsteps pounded up and down the stairs, stopping outside the door to the second floor. In a heart-seizing moment, someone came into the room. They heard a growly male sound. A repulsive *gotcha* sound. As Zapa predicted, he went straight for the drywall pile by the pillar and pulled a number of boards away from the stack. They fell hard on the floor, dust billowing out and rolling along the floor. Dani inhaled it, shoved her fist into her mouth to keep from coughing. He stood there for what felt like an eternity, finally leaving to pound on down to the main floor. Dani coughed out the dust, grateful they were safe, for now.

The two women stayed motionless on the hard floor, bodies blended in their confinement, contours matching, absolutely no room to move. It was uncomfortable yet comforting.

"How do you feel?" Dani whispered.

"Drugged but other than that, okay."

"Chest pains?"

"Nope."

"Headache?"

"Completely gone. Although that intravenous drug they were giving me probably helped. But Dani, it was horrible when they came for me. I tried to fight them off but they gave me an injection."

"I'm so sorry I wasn't there. Please let me know if anything feels off, okay? Don't tough it out. We've got your patch stash in the bag. And we really don't want you to need medical help when we're trying to get the fuck away from these people."

Zapa was gone for over an hour. Despite their fear, they drifted off. When she came back, she spoke softly.

"You can come out now. But we must wait here a little bit longer."

Dani and Jo slowly untangled and moved to a sitting position. Zapa stood before them in her uniform and sturdy shoes as if for work. Over her shoulder was a leather backpack. She placed it on the floor.

"They will soon become tired of all this running around. That will be the best time to leave. For now, you are safe here."

They listened to her talk about the route they would take out of the building. As she spoke, she bent over and took off her shoes and put on a pair of skin-thin leather slippers. She shoved her feet back in her work shoes and began pulling her dress off.

"Uh, Zapa? What are you doing?"

She laughed. "Mira." Look. Underneath her uniform, she wore a black spandex leotard and leggings. "My cat burglar outfit," she said. She grabbed a roll of fabric that lay around her neck and pulled it over her head, covering the thick red braid that she'd wound on top of her head like a snake. Only her dark face and black eyes were exposed. She showed them a thin penlight and her staff keys secured under her sleeve. "I wanted to show you. What do you think?" she asked, smiling.

"*Wow*," Dani mouthed.

"Why are you dressed like a cat burglar?" Jo whispered.

"It is in the story my mama used to read me," Zapa said. "*La Ladrona Muy Felina*. The very catlike thief. I loved that story. I was la Ladrona at a Halloween party last year."

Dani wondered at the woman's state of mind. "Did you just happen to have this outfit on hand?"

"No. I went home for it. And I brought some clothes for you, Jo."

"That was risky. No one noticed you coming and going?"

"No. Well, almost no one. It was just before they sounded the alarm about your escape and so all was calm. I saw Montoya. She waved at me. I told her I would be back after dinner to finish my work. Pepito was by the ambulance. Chaco was there too having a smoke. He ignored me. No soy su tipo. I am not his type, gracias a dios. Y claro que no es el mío." She smiled. And clearly he is not mine.

"But, Zapa, why did you need to go and get a costume?"

"I know it is ridículo, but it is all I could think of to deal with the cameras."

"The cameras?"

"The security cameras."

Dani and Jo gasped in unison. "Security cameras?" Dani blurted out. "Holy shit, Zapa. I've been all over this building and I've never seen any cameras anywhere."

"In the oficina, chica. Where I must go for the passport."

"In that case, you can't go in there."

"Right," added Jo. "Forget about the passport."

"Cálmese, señoras. I am told they are probably not hooked up yet."

"Probably?"

Dani reached out to put her hand on the young woman's arm. "Zapa. This is an unnecessary risk for you. And by extension, us."

"Do not worry. I have learned a lot about this place and its people over the past month. Trust me. This will work. You do trust me, yes?"

They both nodded, clearly unconvinced. "Now please. Josefina? You must change into street clothes and put your hospital gown in your bag."

Jo changed slowly while Zapa put her uniform back on. When they were dressed and seated, Zapa spoke again. "Ahora, silencio." She motioned with her hands, ten fingers three times. "We will wait for thirty minutes."

They sat in silence, tired, each sinking deep into their own thoughts and fears until finally Zapa motioned that it was time to move.

They started down the stairs. Jo almost fell when she swung her foot around an obstructing bucket. She grabbed the railing with one hand and threw the other onto Dani's shoulder. At the main floor, Zapa signalled for them to stand back. She turned the knob slowly, wincing as it squeaked, and pulled the door open far enough to peek into the hall. She nodded at them, brushed the dust off her shoes and walked into the hall in full uniform, pulling the door closed quietly behind her.

"I can't believe she's doing this," Jo whispered.

"I know." Dani spoke close to Jo's ear. "Why is she so determined? She's risking everything. Oh well. Doesn't matter now. It's in play."

They stood quietly, listening.

Dani squeezed Jo's arm. "Are you still okay? Any pains? Headaches?"

"No, nothing. I feel all right. Just weak, a bit woozy. That intravenous was one heavy-duty drug."

They leaned against either side of the stairwell and waited. After about five minutes, a voice startled them.

"Zapatista." A woman's voice. It was Montoya.

Dani grabbed Zapa's bag and their own with one hand and Jo with the other and they crept down the stairs away from the door.

"Zapatista," she called again. "Ven." Come here.

From their perch down two steps, they watched the interaction through the glass labeled primera planta, one-dimensional figures moving like shadow puppets.

"What's wrong, hija. Why didn't you answer me? Gato tiene su lengua?" Cat got your tongue?

Silence.

"Zapa, are you ill?"

"Jefa, forgive me. I was remembering my mama. She used to say that to me. She died a year ago today."

"Ay, hija. ¡Qué lástima! I am so sorry. There is nothing harder than losing one's mamacita. If you can, try not to think about her right now, may she rest in peace. We have an emergency here tonight. You must be alert. A patient is wandering about. She is partially sedated. We are worried about her and must find her."

"Ah, sí. Entiendo," Zapa responded.

So that's how they're spinning it. Someone pounded down the hallway. Dani slunk lower down the step.

"¿Qué pasa?" Montoya called out. What's going on?

"The office was open," came the response. *Shit. Thug.* "And I checked it earlier because of the fourth-floor situation. Were you in there, Zapa?"

"No, Chaco. I was not. No need to clean a room no one's been in since the last cleaning."

"Is it locked now?" asked Montoya.

"Claro, jefa. I locked it up tight."

"Zapa, have you seen anyone near the office this evening?"

"No, jefa Montoya. I didn't see anyone. I was cleaning the bathroom. Perhaps Luci was in and left it that way?"

"Perhaps. Chaco, I suggest you double-check everything once again."

More silence.

"Don't look at me like that. I know you are tired. We are all tired. Carry on."

"A sus órdenes, jefa. I'll check the stairwell first." Dani stiffened.

"I can do that," Zapa said. "I'm right here." The door pushed open. Zapa stood there in her uniform. "There is no one here," she said, motioning to Dani and Jo with a small movement of her hand carefully held out of Chaco's sight. They moved farther down the stairs as quietly as possible.

"That's my job, puta. I'll do it."

"Basta, hombre." Enough. Montoya's reprimand contained a sigh.

"Ay estimada, Zapa. Por favor permíteme hacer un buscado propio." Permit me to do a proper search, esteemed Zapa. His words were laced with sarcasm.

Zapa stepped back and swung her arm out in a wide gesture as if welcoming royalty.

Chaco could not restrain himself. "Puta," he hissed as he passed her.

"Watch yourself, Chaco," warned Montoya.

Dani and Jo had reached the basement door by the time Chaco pushed his way past Zapa and charged up the stairs. A door opened and closed and he was gone. Forever, she hoped. If he came back down and decided to check the lower floor, they were trapped. The door was knobless and locked with a card pass box at the side, as per usual.

The main floor door opened with a soft whoosh and closed with a quiet *thunk*. Someone was coming. They froze. Another door opened farther up the stairwell. At that moment, Zapa raced down the stairs toward them, gesturing toward the basement door, putting her finger to her lips. Heavy feet pounded down the steps from the upper floors. Chaco undoubtedly. *Why can't this guy just fuck right off?*

Zapa slid her pass card through the entry lock. The door clicked open. Dani cringed at the sound but it was lost in Chaco's heavy steps. Zapa motioned them through, pulled the door shut and pushed them to the side behind more stacked drywall. Thank god for renos, was all Dani could think. Chaco stopped at what Dani calculated was the second floor. About a minute later, he started down again, slowing at the main floor door before thudding on down to the basement. Chaco slid his card through the security lock and the door opened. Dani and Jo grasped each other's hand tightly to the point of pain. He did not walk into the basement. Dani pictured him standing silent, watching, listening. Finally, the heavy basement door closed with a thunk and his footsteps retreated up the stairs. They waited, motionless, until they heard the main-floor door shut.

Zapa nodded the all-clear. To the left was the elevator and just beyond it were double doors labelled Laundry. They went to the right, following Zapa into an area with no lights. Zapa flipped the penlight from her sleeve and lit a path through a ghostly thicket of equipment and wood studs coated with drywall dust. They wended their way around jagged edges and looming gray forms, passing an ancient rotund boiler, mummylike in its insulation wrap. They halted in front of a massive steel door with a large sliding bolt. Zapa pulled an aerosol can out of her bag and sprayed the bolt, jiggling it until it loosened enough for her to push it back. She and Dani tugged the door open. Fresh salty air poured in.

"Vámonos. Let's go," said Zapa.

Dani put her arm around Jo's waist and powered her up the steep concrete stairs, the last few steps to freedom. A loud buzz-buzz cut through the air. They froze.

"Shit. Shit. My cell phone."

"Póngalo en silencio, ahora mismo. Right now."

Dani dug it out of the bag and shut it down. Zapa nodded.

They scurried along the lane that ran behind la Clínica Ortega, sticking close to the wall like rats on a night mission. Zapa stopped suddenly behind a bright yellow car.

"Aquí está. Here it is. Miguel's car."

"My god, it's a tad noticeable."

"You want to walk?" Zapa asked, brows crinkling. Jo snickered.

"Sorry," Dani said quickly. "Really. It's fantastic. Love it."

Zapa silently keyed the locks open and tucked their bags behind the driver's seat. She pulled out a couple of bottles of water from a bag lying on the floor and gave them to Dani and Jo, explaining Miguelito always travelled prepared. She started the engine and they slipped away into the sultry Cádiz night.

CHAPTER ELEVEN

Light struck her face. Her stomach jellied. Chaco. She opened her eyes, braced for a fight. A yellow shaft beamed out from the kitchen where Zapa was pulling food out of the fridge: rolls, hard cheese, ham, and fruit. Dani crept off the couch, not wanting to disturb Jo.

"Are you getting ready to go to work?" Dani whispered. Zapa squeezed by her and pushed the kitchen door half shut. Back at the counter, she grabbed an espresso maker and set it and a pot with milk on the stove.

"I returned just now."

"What? What time is it?"

"Nine thirty in the morning."

"I don't believe it."

"Oh yes. You have had a good sleep, I think. Y mira, look at Jo, so peaceful there."

"It's really morning?"

Zapa smiled and shook her head. "I used to say the same thing to my mama. Is it really morning? Son las cortinas. My mother's curtains."

They were a forest green velour, matching the area rug, chair, and pullout couch. They blocked all daylight. Dani looked back at the small room. It was the core of this traditional townhome and charming. It had white plaster walls and low ceilings and shelves laden with books and newspapers yellowing at the edges. Her parents were the readers, Zapa had told them, and she hadn't changed a thing, not one thing since their passings.

Coffee sizzled up inside the brikka pot, hissing steam and threatening to bubble over. Zapa turned off the heat.

"Sit, Dani. Would you like some coffee?"

"I would." Dani sat down on a short bench, the wall-side seating for a compact wood table. "So how did it go at the hospital?"

Zapa poured espresso into two glasses half full of hot milk. She handed one to Dani and joined her at the table.

"Montoya called me last night on my cell phone. Ordered me back immediately."

"Oh my god. What happened?"

"They questioned me about the escape."

"Who questioned you?"

"La doctora and Chaco. What did I see? What did I know? Why was the office door open? Luci, the administrator, told them she'd locked it before she left. Which she did. I was the guilty one. Tal idiota, yo. So stupid. They decided it was me. It was very, uh—"

"Terrifying?"

"Sí. Sí. It went on and on. A couple of times, after Magda got a text, she left me alone with Chaco. He would circle me, cracking his knuckles and saying horrible things. He is a disgusting man. When the doctor came back in, it started again. Finally I pretended to, uh, desmoronarse, uh, to crack. I said Luci was lying and that she often leaves it unlocked and I have mentioned it to her. I told them she says she forgets and made me promise not to tell anyone. And I have not because I did not want to get her in trouble. That's what I told them, god forgive me. All lies. Finally they let me go and I finished my work. And now I am exhausted. I never slept."

"Oh, Zapa, I'm so sorry we dragged you into this. Do you think you should go back there? Ever?"

"I do not want to return, for sure. But I may have to. And please, do not apologize. I am now so angry, I want to bring the whole, perdone, puta clínica down. It has upset me many times since I started working there but this experience is the, uh, la gota que desborda el vaso."

"Something the glass?"

"Overflow. They overflowed the glass."

"Oh. Like the last straw."

"Sí, sí. The way they treated you and Jo. The way they treated me. You did not *drag* me into anything. Believe me. It is time to fight these people. Y claro, it is in my blood to fight injustice."

"Why do you say that, that's it's in your blood?"

"Pues, Dani, when I was twelve, my father was arrested."

Dani looked up, mid-sip. "Why?" she asked, flashing on the possibilities. *Robbery? Fraud? Murder?*

"He was part of the big shipyard strike in the nineties. Today, it is around twenty-five hundred people who build the ships. Back then, it was about fifteen thousand. Can you imagine? So many losing their work. It all began with the closures. The workers said no, it will not happen. They went on strike. It was a bitter battle. The company called in the policía. They went to the strikers' homes, door to door, rounding them up. They came to our house and arrested my father. I was terrified. To this day, I do not call the policía."

They sat quietly for a minute. Zapa's hand lay on the table, one finger rubbing an old scar in the age-worn wood.

"Por otro lado." Her finger tapped out her next words in time. "Era un milagro. A miracle. Here and in other neighbourhoods, people came together. I will never forget it. They set up a small government to make decisions and keep things going. It showed me lo de que es capaz el pueblo. What the people can do. The people took care of each other, protected each other. And the women were fierce. Ay dios. My mother..." Zapa pressed her hands over her mouth like a little girl. "...she was like a lion. I will never forget when they came to arrest Papi and the others. The women tossed pots of soup out the window on the policía." She shook her head as she reminisced.

"Wow. Your parents sound like strong people."

"They were a good pair. She was a student from Cuba, ready for adventure, and he was a shipyards boy. They fell in love. They lived together with big spirits, big passion. They danced and sang. And they fought the fights they believed in, por el pueblo. For the people."

"I'd like to hear more about them."

"I will tell you sometime when we have an entire evening and a good bottle of wine and I am more awake than I am now. I was very proud of them."

"And you know what, Zapa? I'll bet your parents would be very proud of you, too. You saved Jo's life today."

Zapa's eyes widened. She stood up, came around to Dani and took both her hands.

"Gracias, Dani. Por eso, todo lo vale." *That makes it all worthwhile.* She leaned over and hugged her.

Dani was surprised. She admired this strong, outspoken young woman. Up until now, though, Dani had thought her emotionally guarded, not given to hugs and public display and drama. *Although she did wear that cat burglar getup. Yikes!*

Zapa sat back down and picked up her coffee, avoiding eye contact, as if she'd surprised herself too.

"Don't worry. I won't tell anyone you hugged me."

Zapa gasped as if unmasked. They both laughed, politely at first, but becoming louder and louder, raucous even, until finally they stopped, out of breath, wiping tears from their eyes.

"What is going on in here?" Jo spoke as she peered into the kitchen. "What are you two up to?"

"Hi, babe. Great timing."

"Josefina. Sit here." Zapa stood, still chuckling, offering her chair. "Would you like coffee?"

"No to sitting, thank you," she said, leaning against the doorframe. "But a huge yes, please, to coffee."

"Do you think you should?" asked Dani.

"Damn. You're right. I feel pretty good and forgot. Just a tiny bit then and I'll add some extra water to it." Zapa complied. "Yum," Jo said, eyeing the brew skeptically before sipping. "So, what was so funny?"

"Zapa got called back to work and was interrogated by Chaco et al."

"Oh my god. And that's funny?"

"No. No. But her story veered into some family stuff. Had a funny moment. Not important now." Dani turned to Zapa. "Tell her what happened at the Clínica."

Zapa filled Jo in. "I think I satisfied them. I certainly sent them off in the wrong direction. But they will be watching me and definitely looking for you. Everyone is acting crazy. La doctora Nieves stood in the hall with men I have never seen before, whispering to each other. She was angry. And Chaco, well, he was going up and down the halls like a madman, yelling at everyone. Miguel was there too. They called him back in to make coffees all night long. He says everyone is talking about the patient who went missing. But he says the story he is hearing even more is something about a patient being accosted on the fourth floor."

"There was another patient?" asked Jo.

"Accosted?" asked Dani.

"Yes. Miguel and I thought perhaps it is you, Jo, they are talking about. But they are saying there was a second patient on a stretcher in the hall and that she was brutalized by an Anglo woman."

Dani stopped her glass of coffee halfway to her mouth.

"Shit. That could be, uh, that woman I talked to."

"You spoke to someone?"

"Yeah. But brutalized? Hardly. I walked by her when I was looking for Jo and she asked me about her surgery. She thought I was staff. She was obviously Anglo and I said a few words to her. 'It will be soon,' or something. I was only trying to get by her without any fuss. I did *not* accost her."

No one spoke.

"You spoke to her in English. They can accuse *you* because of the English. This will be their cover story for their outrageous acts. It also justifies bringing in the policía."

"You mean they're painting *us* as the criminals?" asked Jo, incredulously.

"Which makes the clinic the victim," added Dani. "Clever."

"Yes. It makes everything more dangerous. There is another, well, development."

Dani slouched, disheartened. "Great."

Zapa reached across to the counter and grabbed a small newspaper. "A reporter for this Anglo publication wrote an article about the woman who died the night you arrived at the hospital."

"The corpse on the stretcher woman," Dani said to Jo.

"Right. Thanks." They leaned their heads together and read.

"An Expat Exclusive" by MAGGIE MILESTONE

MYSTERY surrounds the death of an Irish woman at a hospital in Cádiz.

Calinda Benning of Wicklow, Ireland, was admitted to la Clínica Ortega Hospital Friday evening. The 55-year-old cruise ship passenger was transported by ambulance after she collapsed at a local hotel. According to sources close to the family, she received no treatment and no staff were monitoring her condition.

By midnight, Benning insisted her husband, George, return to the hotel to get some rest. The husband says when he came back to the hospital a few hours later, he was informed that his wife was dead. He also says the doctor told him his wife "might not have died" if he had remained by her side.

"Oh my god. That must have been when I was trapped in the bathroom." Jo grimaced. "Who knew I was the lucky one that night?"

Dani passed the paper back to Zapa. "I can't believe these people are still in business."

"Perhaps they will not be for very much longer with articles like this. It also could explain why they are so desperate to contain the 'Jo' situation."

"I'm a situation?"

"Evidently, babe. And I made it worse by speaking to a woman on a stretcher. But I was frantic to find you after the stairwell thing."

"Okay, hold on here. I'm losing track."

"Me too," added Zapa. "You mentioned this 'stairwell thing' to me before but we did not have time to discuss it. Now, please."

"They were coming straight toward me, so I hid in the stairwell by the cafeteria."

"Who?"

"Nieves and Thug."

Zapa and Jo responded at once:

"Thug? That is Chaco, sí?"

"You saw the doctor?"

"Right. Chaco. The big paramedic," Dani said to Zapa. She turned to Jo. "And yes, I saw the doctor." And back again to Zapa. "She's quite the fashionista, right?"

"Yes. She is."

"Well, they started walking right toward me. I couldn't believe it. They were coming into the stairwell. I moved down the stairs. Gratefully, they went up. They stopped partway up and I listened, well, tried to listen, to what they were saying. I missed a lot. But for sure they were talking about Benning."

"They were talking about Benning? The patient from the cruise ship?" Zapa asked.

"That poor woman came from a cruise ship?" asked Jo.

"Sí, sí. The article said she collapsed at a hotel down the road and was rushed to the Clínica last night. Her ship is still docked."

"Oh my god, I missed that."

"Babe, you're still half asleep. But do you remember at our hotel, how it was all booked up that night? And the guy at reception said it was because of some cruise ship stuck in port?"

"I do. And you pulled me out of the path of the ambulance."

Dani nodded, lips pressed together. "I'll bet that was her ride to the clinic."

"Please continue, Dani. Tell us about the stairwell," Zapa urged.

"Well, what really caught my attention was that they, uh, the doctor and Chaco, talked about both Benning and Jo."

"You mean at the same time?"

"Yes. In the same sentence even. And Nieves was very angry with Chaco."

"Perhaps she was scolding him because of what happened to Benning."

"Yeah. That occurred to me. But why would she be on Chaco's case about it? He's the paramedic, not the nurse. And according to that article, the hospital and the widower said it was lack of monitoring that resulted in her death?"

"Yes, that is correct. Perhaps there was some other issue. An error he made in transporting her?"

"Or maybe the other issue is the riñón thing?"

"What?" Jo tilted her head as she spoke. "What are you saying?"

"Riñón. It means kidney." Dani softened her voice and put her hand on Jo's arm. "I think they were planning to steal your kidney."

"What?" Jo's eyes widened, her voice rising with alarm.

Zapa's eyes narrowed. "You mentioned riñón before. Are you *sure* they said riñón?"

"Absolutely."

"It *is* odd, what you are describing but"—Zapa shook her head and swept the idea away with her hand—"it cannot be that—"

"Why do you keep saying that?" Dani stood up abruptly. "Why? Everything that happened there is so bizarre. Why couldn't it all be about some sort of transplant scheme? Like maybe the fourth floor is actually an illegal transplant clinic?"

"You're really freaking me out with all this," Jo interjected.

"Dani." Zapa placed her hand gently on Dani's arm. "I keep trying to tell you. That is not likely."

Dani continued unabated. "So why did they keep saying"— she stopped and punctuated each word with her fist—"riñón riñón riñón? Maybe you weren't the lucky one that night, babe. Maybe you were part two."

There was silence until Zapa and Jo said simultaneously, "Part two?"

Dani started pacing, which in the tiny kitchen was very close to turning in circles. "Think about it. They were ready to take Benning's kidney for whatever transplant scheme they had going on. And she up and dies. No worries, says Chaco. I'll find you someone else. Or more likely Nieves ordered him to find a replacement. And presto, they have a new donor, that new patient just down the hall."

Jo turned pale. "Okay, stop. I've heard enough," she said dropping her head to the table.

"Yes. Stop, Dani." Zapa grabbed Dani's hand and pulled her down into her chair. "Because you are wrong." She stared hard into Dani's eyes. "¡Escúchame! Listen to me. In Spain, transplants are legal and there is no lack of kidneys or any organ for transplantation. They are automatically taken from people when they die. It is the law. It does not make sense what you are describing."

Dani dropped back onto the bench. She leaned forward and spoke, her voice low and taut. "So what the fuck were they doing?"

They moved into the living room, coffees in hand. Dani and Jo sat on the couch while Zapa took the chair across from them. They agreed to stop talking about what they thought might be going on at the clinic because the topic was making Jo feel ill, Dani angry, and Zapa frustrated. It was time for next steps.

"Yeah," added Dani, "how the hell do we get out of Dodge?"

"¿Qué dices?"

Jo rolled her eyes. "It's a saying from an old western. She means how do we leave Cádiz."

"Ah, bueno. Pues, I have a plan."

"Okay. We're listening," said Dani.

"First I will tell you the why of this plan. I believe you, well *we*, must proceed with the greatest caution and involve as few people as possible." Zapa spoke gravely, her eyes dark and her mouth drawn and serious. "You must stay hidden from them at all costs."

"You make it sound like we really *are* the criminals," said Jo.

Dani nodded. "We are, according to them and maybe even the cops, by now. The crime? My so-called *accosting* of that woman I spoke to on the fourth floor waiting for her surgery."

"And, crime two," Zapa chimed in, "the office theft." She reached into her bag. "Here. I meant to give this to you last night but you both fell asleep."

"Oh my god. My passport. Thank you so much, Zapa. You really believe that by taking this you committed a crime? It *is* mine after all."

"Yes, this is your property that I am returning to you. But this is not your property." She pulled a larger file out of her bag. "This is your medical file. It was risky to take but I thought you will need it. And when you leave Cádiz, which we will now discuss, you will most likely be considered fugitives."

"Fugitives? As in 'fugitives from justice'? All in what, a day and a half?" Jo shook her head. "This is a nightmare."

"And to think, if we'd kept my reservation for Gerardo Núñez, none of this would have happened."

"Oh my god, Dan. I can't believe you're still on about that."

"Ay dios mío. Tenías, uh, you had reservations for Gerardo? Su pulgar es increíble."

"What? Is she talking about that pull thing too?"

"She *is*." Dani laughed. "You know his music, Zapa?"

"Claro, girlfriend. Soy gaditana. ¿Me entiendes?"

"Oh yeah. You're a resident of Cádiz. I understand. See Jo, everybody knows Gerardo." Jo's eyes narrowed. Dani moved on. "Okay, so, Zapa. What's your plan?"

Zapa talked. Jo and Dani listened intently, Jo gradually relaxing, leaning back until she suddenly lurched forward.

"The train? You've got to be kidding."

"No. I am not kidding, Josefina. They will have their people everywhere and you must not give them opportunities to see you and identify you. If you take the bus, the driver checks your ticket and ID before you are allowed to board. And the plane? It is the most difficult. You will face many, many checks of your identification before you are allowed on the plane. Much better is the train to Seville. It is the most, uh, under their radar. We can walk to the station from here. As you board, a train attendant will ask you what car you are assigned to. That is all. They will only check your ticket *after* the train leaves the station. Besides, Chaco and his people will never think you will go by train."

A strangled laugh burst from Jo as she fell back onto the couch. "Ya think?"

"Trust me, Josefina. On the bus or the plane, you are trapped. You cannot walk around and there is only one exit and no place to hide except perhaps the washroom." She twitched and grimaced. "On the train, you can move around and it has many exits."

"She's right," said Dani, turning to Jo. "And we know the train, more or less, from our trip here from Seville."

"Can't we just rent a car?"

"Again, Josefina, too many people will ask for your identification. Your driver licenses, your passports. The train is best. And besides, I have already purchased your train tickets."

Jo leaned toward Zapa. "Maybe we could borrow—"

Dani interrupted. "Wait? You did what?"

"I am sorry but time is a concern and I had the car for just a short time. And we could not borrow it, Jo. Miguel lo necesita." She reached over and grabbed her bag. "Here," she said as she passed them a small folder. "The tickets are inside. The next trains for Seville leave in the early afternoon. One is direct. I did not book that one."

"You didn't?" Jo and Dani asked simultaneously.

"No. And this is why." Zapa explained the rest of her plan, including her belief that they must proceed with extreme subterfuge. The "plan" included two trains, separate seating, and if needed, a refuge that was part of a duchess's palace or something. It left Dani's jaw agape.

"You really think they're *that* desperate to find us?"

"Yes. And to be honest with you, Dani, I don't understand why. Something about this whole thing, the intensity, the anger in their voices last night, the lies, it is making me nervous, for you and for myself too. If they present this as merely a patient refusing their services, it will blow over, I think. But they are making it a very big issue. I thought about calling the policía myself, but we know they are making us the guilty ones. Perhaps they will arrest *us*. And who trusts la policía? Yo no, claro. Some of the men who arrested my father have influence to this day."

Dani stared at Zapa. Jo shook her head.

"But couldn't we just tell the police what happened? I mean, come on. Isn't it more of a crime to drug someone and take her off for an unwanted procedure?"

"The hospital will only deny it, saying it was all part of caring for Jo. And they will succeed in convincing the policía because they are a hospital. Besides, how can you prove what you are saying?"

"Shit."

"This is why I have disguises for you to wear."

"Disguises? Oh my god. Not like cat burglars or anything?"

"No, no." Zapa smiled as she shook her head. "Not really disguises. Some street clothes I believe will fit you. Before you change, pack up your things, including the file. We will leave soon."

"I think we should touch base with Eddie," said Jo.

"Who?" asked Zapa.

"A man I met at the conference. He could be helpful if we get stuck in all this intrigue. I mean I really don't want to involve him in any of this, but it's so crazy now. I might just let him know what's happened and that we're heading for Seville."

"That reminds me." Dani pulled the cell phone out of their bag. She logged on and opened her texts. "Yup. Remember when the cell buzzed, when we were leaving the hospital?"

"How could we forget?" said Jo.

"That was Eddie. I left a message asking him to text me. He did, a couple of times. Said to call him back anytime."

"Please don't. Don't call or text anyone. Not now. They have ways of tracking cell phones. Keep your phone off. And do not tell anyone what you're doing. Even your friend Eddie. Please," Zapa urged, "leave this for later, when it is done and you're safely away. Please."

"Okay. But I'm going to give you Eddie's number, Zapa. Just in case *you* need it. He seems to know a lot of people. Maybe lawyers. You may need one before all this is over."

Jo grabbed the ticket folder, pen in hand. "Yeah, good idea. Read the number out loud, Dan."

"I want to give you some cash too," Dani said, passing the folder to Jo, "but I think we need to hold on to it for now. We promise, Zapa, we'll send you money later for everything you've done. Whatever we can manage. You agree, Jo?"

"Absolutely."

"Ay señoras, gracias, pero no. Do not worry. If you send me money, only for the tickets. Please. And perhaps a reference for a new job." She smirked. "But I will keep the number of your friend. The idea of backup is good. I may need it."

The three women walked separately through Zapa's long-established working-class neighbourhood, Matagorda.

Dani had grimaced at the name. "Oh my god, as in mata la gorda? Kill the Fat One." Zapa couldn't stop laughing.

"Ay dios, Dani, you are funny. It is named after a giant bush that used to grow here."

The exchange lightened their mood before heading out into uncertain danger. Their "disguises" also made them laugh.

Zapa was in the lead, head held high, bright blue baseball cap with bushy red ponytail spurting out the back. Her chiseled arms, burnished by the sun, were guaranteed to make hearts flutter. They were on display thanks to a sleeveless T-shirt with a picture of Regino Pedroso on the front and "¿Por qué y para qué nací?" emblazoned across the back. "Why and for what was I born?" According to legend, Zapa had explained, the renown black Cuban poet uttered those words at his birth when he first opened his eyes on the world.

Jo's gold-toned skin flushed red in the sun, her eyes hidden under oversize sunglasses She moved slowly and with effort, the aftereffect of the drug they'd given her. Or perhaps it was the couple-sizes-too-big high tops and the voluminous blue sweatpants that slowed her down.

Dani, who brought up the rear, carried a small gym bag and sported the most disturbing getup of the lot: white stretch pants straining against her generous thighs and hips, white cotton shirt tied at the waist, a yellow bandana protecting her fairer skin and scalp from the fiery sun while her pale nose and cheeks burned. All together she projected a very dated beach vibe.

As a whole, it was not an attractive group, lead chica notwithstanding, but cute was not the point. Incognito was. They were fugitives, after all. That word, *fugitive*, had lodged in Dani's brain. They'd somehow ended up on the wrong side of everything by running from evil. But they were just trying to survive. She thought of the stories Jo brought home from work, of true refugees: women with children fleeing slavery or sex trafficking, boys eluding conscription as child soldiers, all the rebels, resisters, rights activists, and the truly poor, taking crazy risks like pushing out onto wild seas in overcrowded leaky boats, desperately seeking a way to live better, or simply to live. She and Jo had options. Money for one thing. And contacts. Zapa. Eddie. Carmen, the insurance woman. *Hah! Okay. Zapa and Eddie.* They had shelter. Zapa had told them where she'd hid a spare key. And she'd given them the name of some hotel near Jerez. Just in case.

Dani checked the street and looked at the two women walking ahead of her. *No. We are not real fugitives. But I'm beginning to know what it feels like. Here's hoping Zapa knows what she's doing. That plan. Ay dios. It's confusing.* Dani shook her head and went over it again, dutifully memorizing the details, including the name of the hotel. It was a mouthful. She practiced it now if only to keep her panic at bay, matching the words to her steps, giving them rhythm, turning them into a salsa coro accompanied by imaginary congas: Hospedería Ducal, Sanlúcar de Barrameda—Hospedería Ducal, Sanlúcar de Barrameda— Hospedería Ducal, Sanlúcar de Barrameda. She imagined the music video, the three of them dancing along the street. A conga line perhaps. *Okay. Maybe not.* But the idea amused her enough to get her down to the base of the hill from Matagorda without running for cover.

They came to a roundabout with three roads spinning off: the farthest angled toward the Port of Cádiz where giant cruise ships docked; the second led to the train station; the nearest headed up another hill. As per the plan, Zapa took the road up the hill, no hesitation, no backward glance, no final wave goodbye, her blue baseball hat disappearing suddenly over the crest. Dani and Jo continued on in tandem taking the second road.

As they entered the train station, a cavernous glass building, Dani prayed once again to every spirit-world heavy she could think of along her angels, big and small. *¡Te lo ruego! I beg you.*

They maintained their distance from each other, Jo walking in front. From behind, Dani scanned their surroundings, the cafes and stores and every person standing by Platforms One and Two, where trains bound for Madrid and Barcelona stood waiting. All seemed normal. They continued on to Platform Three where the *Sevillano* stood at the ready. Dani really wanted to board this one, the train that went directly to Seville with no stops, but Zapa had said no. She had insisted on the train now sitting at Platform Four, the one bound for Jerez de la Frontera.

"If they *are* at the train station," Zapa had carefully explained to them, "they will assume you will be on a train that will go directly to Seville, not one that stops in Jerez. Once you are in Jerez, you can decide if it is safe to continue on the same train. If not, get off and board the Seville-bound train originating in Jerez a short time later. And remember, stay separate from each other."

Where the fuck is Jerez de la Frontera anyway? Zapa was either brilliant or a total whack job. The range of possibilities made Dani so conflicted, she found herself coming to a full stop before boarding and praying once again: *Please let Zapa's plan work and don't let the bastards find us.* Then and only then did she board.

Jo sat in Car A, Dani in Car B next to a window. She looked over to the opposite platform and saw two armed security guards boarding the direct train. *Come on. Let's get outta here.*

As if on command, the Jerez train began to roll. She leaned forward like a kid trying to make it go faster. The train dragged itself sluggishly along a bleak railway right-of-way pockmarked by ponds of brackish water and swampy grasses and the occasional sad-sack building. It was the kind of urban setting where movie villains would take their victims for a bit of privacy. Dani shuddered and checked out her fellow passengers instead.

Next to her was an elderly man with an expensive-looking shopping bag at his feet and a copy of the *Diario*, Cádiz' daily newspaper, spread over his knees. In the seat ahead was a deeply tanned woman with an equally tanned little girl. Dani winked at her when the girl took a mischievous look-see over her seatback. Across the aisle from the kid was an older passenger munching daintily on pan dulce, pulling bits of sweet bun from the wrinkled paper bag she held on her lap. Behind that woman and across the aisle next to Dani were young lovers chatting quietly, heads touching in an enviable public display of intimacy.

No one suspicious that she could see.

The train finally picked up speed and moved off the peninsula, every kilometre from Cádiz adding to her relief. She figured it would take about thirty minutes to get to Jerez. Her eyes slid shut mid-hallelujah, but she resisted sleep. She decided to review what lay ahead. Get to Seville and book a hotel for some much-needed peace and privacy and hopefully security. She'd never called Eddie, on Zapa's advice. *We'll call him when we're safely in Seville.* She wished she'd gotten through to the Canadian embassy earlier. *Great emergency number, guys. Thanks. Maybe I should've called one of the Consulates.* There was one in Málaga, the opposite direction from Seville. *Not enough time.*

But I must remember to call insurance. They'll need an update. And Jo has to get to a hospital. She'll need an "okay to fly" from some doctor or other. Today was Sunday. Their flight was Thursday. Ample time, she hoped.

CHAPTER TWELVE

It was a struggle to stay awake. Dani stood up just to get the blood flowing again. She decided to stretch her legs and check on Jo. She went up the aisle and peered through the connecting doors into Car A. She could just make out the top of Jo's head. She was alone in a window seat at the car's midpoint. She seemed okay.

Dani walked back through her car to the washroom at the opposite end. When she came out, she decided to check on the car behind hers. She peered through the door window. More folks passing the time, enjoying the ride. All calm except…

Two men were moving slowly up the aisle in Dani's direction. *Ticket checkers*. One wore a train uniform. Each passenger dutifully passed a ticket and what looked like identification to him. The second man was in plain clothes. He turned in Dani's direction. Her heart stopped.

She walked back to her seat, picked up the gym bag and went into Car A. She motioned to Jo to move onto the window seat and sat down. She spoke softly, without urgency, even managing a pleasant lilt to her delivery, so as not to draw attention.

"Chaco's on the train, two cars back."

The fear in Jo's eyes was instantaneous.

"He's checking tickets with a train conductor," Dani said with a nod and a bright smile.

Jo caught on. She grinned back. "How did he know we'd be on this train?"

"I have no idea. Maybe he's simply covering all the bases." She turned to check that the aisle was still empty. "You know, we're probably going to have to make a fast exit off this train."

"As in jump from a moving...?" She laughed. It was an odd sound that landed somewhere between a mild case of nerves and madness. "You've got to be kidding."

"No, actually, I'm not." Jo's laugh became a groan. Dani continued, "I'm hoping we'll be close enough to the station that the train will have slowed. But if necessary, I'll create some sort of diversion so you can get off first and I'll follow."

"Please don't do something crazy. Don't hurt yourself. We'd be better off just facing the guy with all these people as witnesses."

"They'd only be witnesses for a while."

"Or...or...what about just hiding?"

"I suppose we could hide in the washroom but not for long. The conductor is checking tickets and passengers against his list. If it doesn't match up, Chaco will suspect something. Start searching for us."

"But he won't be sure it's us. Our tickets have assigned seats, but no names. Whereas if we jump off, he'll see us," said Jo.

"I don't know, babe. If we hide in the washroom, there's no way to escape. No back door. If we just get off, well, we'll still have a chance of evading him. I guess I could..."

"What? You could what?"

"Why don't you move closer to the door? I'm going back to see what's happening. If the train stops, jump, hide, whatever seems best and don't look back."

"Oh, Dani, please promise me you'll be careful."

Dani nodded and walked back to the rear door of Jo's car. The train had begun its deceleration into Jerez station. Dani leaned into the corner to take a quick peek back into her own car. The conductor and Chaco were already there, halfway to her seat. She looked back into Car A, where Jo was moving slowly toward the door at the front of the car. She was trying to be inconspicuous, which of course she wasn't. Her fellow passengers turned their heads one by one, out of boredom if nothing else, to watch her progress. Dani grimaced. If Chaco didn't get her, the fashion police just might.

The two men were now only a couple of passengers away from heading into Car A. It was time for a diversion. Dani pulled the emergency cord. Another law broken. The train jerked. Its wheels screamed in protest to the automatic brakes as it skidded along, losing speed. With a long screech and final lurch, the train came to a complete stop. Dani rushed up the aisle to Jo who'd been thrown onto the lap of an attractive older woman seated at the front. She peered over half-lens reading glasses at the person now lying on top of her book and said, "Ay, señora, cuídale, cuídale. Es muy difícil para caminar en el tren." Dani nodded, muttered a perdón and helped Jo stand up. She seemed stunned, smiling obsequiously at the woman. Dani pulled her by the arm while a message played over the loudspeaker: "Por favor, no abandonen sus asientos..." Please do not leave your seats...

"Jo," Dani hissed. "Go hide in the washroom. Get off the train when it's safe and meet me where the taxis are."

Dani waited until Jo was inside the washroom before she hit the emergency "open door" button and jumped off the train. She stumbled slightly as she hit the ground, scrambled to her feet and took off running toward the station a few metres away.

"¡Eh!"

A male voice yelled behind her. She didn't look back but kept her pace, driven on by the heavy feet pounding the gravel behind her. Her gym bag bumped against her back. Her breath came harder. The voice yelled again, "¡Párale! ¡Párale!" Stop, stop.

It was Chaco. She'd recognize that bellow anywhere. It spurred her, running faster than she thought she could, alongside the train tracks, up the metal service steps and into the crowd peering with interest at the train that had screeched to a stop just shy of the station.

She dodged suitcases and people. One woman snatched her small child from Dani's path, an elderly man shuffled to the side. The crowd seemed more irritated than alarmed by the woman rushing along the platform. Dani barged through the doors to the railway building and found herself in a small retail area. She stopped running and tried to match the pace of the shoppers. Just one of many. She considered grabbing a scarf from a display stall to change her appearance, but they were tied to a scarf tree. She could see the whole thing tumbling down if she tried. She kept going, wending her way through the crowd, searching for an escape. She ducked round a corner. Big mistake. It was a dead end. But then she saw it. The sign she'd been looking for. She gasped. Salida. Exit. Relief flooded through her as she started for it, but it was short-lived. A solid body slammed into her, knocking her down sideways. Her cheek smashed into the tile floor and pain cut through her brain and face. Chaco spat out "Qué puta" as he wrenched her hands up and behind her back and hauled her to up on her feet. Her shoulders were about to pop out of their sockets. She cried out in pain. "Cállate," he snarled as he pulled her toward himself, a bull of a man, pressing himself tight against her back, his breath harsh and peppermint-y, as if he'd brushed before ambushing. "I am going to beat you and more, stupid whore, if you don't tell me where the other one is."

Terror flooded through her along with pain and regret and worry about Jo. *I've failed. No, remember? You can't fail.* She was just about to wail like a banshee when another voice pierced her adrenaline haze. A soft and oddly familiar voice.

"Perdón, señor."

She felt the brute jerk and release his hold. She turned, forcing her aching arms up, ready to fight. Her assailant stood, frantically rubbing his eyes, blinded by a brown liquid dripping from his face. She realized it was Jo standing next to him. She held something in her hand. It was a glass. One of those thick heavy coffee glasses designed to withstand heat. Dani watched as Jo raised her arm glass in hand and bring it down hard and fast. She heard the crack as it hit Chaco's skull and the clattering as it dropped to the tile floor in a mess of jagged shards. Chaco staggered from the blow. Jo didn't lose her advantage. She swung her leg back and then forward with wicked force, landing a solid hit to the crotch. Chaco collapsed, howling, cradling his balls. Dani yelped when Jo grabbed her by the arm and pulled her through the exit door. In front of them stood a row of taxis, waiting for their next fares. They tumbled into the closest one.

"Vamos rápidamente…señor, por favor." Dani barely managed to squeeze out the words between breaths. "Hay hombre malo…que está…buscándonos."

The driver twisted around to get a better look at them. "Would you please repeat that, señora?" he asked gently and in perfect English. Dani's jaw slackened as if she didn't understand. She started to shake but said nothing.

"Go, just go," Jo snapped. "Please."

"As you wish."

The two of them fell back against the seat as the cab sped off. Dani was pale, Jo was clutching her chest. Both were panting hard.

The cabbie looked at them in the rearview mirror and said, "Pues, señoras, when you catch your breaths, perhaps you could give me a little more information. I know where we are rushing from. But where are we are rushing to?"

Hearing no answer, he started to slow the car and steer it to the side of the road.

"No, no. Don't stop. Please," Jo said.

"Señoras, surely you understand. I need to know where I'm taking you before I can continue dashing away," he said with an elegant flourish of the hand.

"We're going to…what's the name of that place, Dani?"

Dani remained silent. Her breathing was raspy and her eyes were locked on her trembling hands.

"Are you okay? I really need you right now," Jo said, her own voice strained. "I can't remember the name of that place. Dani?"

Dani stared, still mute. Her mouth slowly opened, but no sound emerged.

"She's in shock."

The cab driver turned for a quick look-see. "Ah, sí. Pues, señora, I can take you to a hospital."

"No, no. No hospitals. The place we're going, it was a hotel or something. Or maybe a refuge. Or both? I don't know exactly. Do you know any place like that around here?"

"There is the women's shelter. Is this what you mean?"

"I don't know. Dammit." She looked back at Dani. "Dani. Snap out of it." She was shouting now and punctuated her words with a well-placed finger flick to Dani's thigh. Seeing her eyes un-glaze briefly, Jo tried again, flicking Dani after every word. "Where…" Snap. "…are…" Snap. "…we…" Snap. "…going?"

"Stop. That hurts."

"Good. Now, tell us the name of that place, the one Zapa told you about. What's it called? The driver needs to know."

"We, uh, want to go to the…" Dani took a big gulp of breath and felt the rhythm of the chant she'd practiced. "Hospedería Ducal, Sanlúcar de Barrameda."

"Ah, the Hospedería. But, señoras, Sanlúcar is about twenty-five kilometers from here. A long drive. It will cost you."

"We have the money—I think."

She looked at Dani who nodded and replied. "Sí, sí, señor. We have it. Please take us there, rápido rápido. It is an emergency."

He reached over to pick up a small mike from the dash console.

"What are you doing?" asked Jo.

"I must call it in."

"No, no, no." Dani was totally alert and horrified, seeing Chaco in her mind's eye. She leaned forward, grabbing the front of the seat. "Don't call it in. Please." She fell back against the seat again. "I feel like I might pass out."

Jo took her hand. "You cannot pass out. I need you."

The cab driver glanced at them in the rearview mirror, brows furrowed.

Dani roused herself. "Sir, we'd rather not have our destination on record anywhere."

"Señoras, why are you running like this? I should be informed."

Dani inhaled deeply and closed her eyes. "It's complicated, señor, and we're frightened."

"In that case, perhaps it is better to go to the police?"

Dani's eyes shot open. "No, no police."

"Oh. Perhaps you are running from the police. Have you done something for which they wish to apprehend you? Señoras, if that is the case, please allow me to drop you off somewhere and I will forget all about you. I won't tell them anything. This I can promise."

"No, señor. No nos dejan—" Dani stopped midsentence. "Sorry. I'm speaking Spanish. You're speaking English. I'm confused." Dani gave her head a shake. "The guy who attacked us knows we got off the train at Jerez station, but he doesn't know where we're going. He will probably check with the cab companies. If you call and put it on the record, he'll find us."

"Ah. Yes. I understand. But forgive me, señoras, I must ask again. Is he la policía?"

"No," they both said in unison.

"But," added Dani, "he might have contacts, bad contacts within the police. We were at the Clínica Ortega in Cádiz and we left without...uh...without permission."

Jo kicked Dani, hissing, "Overshare."

The driver looked in his rearview mirror again, one corner of his mouth curling slightly upward. "He's chasing you because you left the hospital without permission. Perdón, señoras, but even in this crazy world that would be rather extreme, would it not? Even for the Ortega Group." He shook his head, his shoulders moving as he laughed silently.

Dani and Jo looked at one another.

"You know Clínica Ortega?" Jo asked.

"¿La Clínica? Sí, sí, I know that place." He seemed more relaxed now, driving smoothly, snatching looks in the side and rearview mirrors as the city gave way to countryside. "Everyone knows that place. Not the one in Cádiz, however. The one near Jerez. Not the same name, of course. But part of the Ortega chain."

"There's one near here?"

"Sí, señora. El Gran Puerto. My cousin used to work there. She quit. She couldn't stand the people who ran it."

He paused, but only briefly. He pressed a button on the console. Jo gasped and reached for the door handle, as if to leap from the moving vehicle. Dani grabbed her arm and held it, her eyes never leaving the driver's face.

"Hola, Carlito. Sí sí, Malik. Óigame, tío. Tengo un evento familiar en Sanlúcar. Mi hermana. Tengo que llevarla allí." Rapid Spanish from a tinny disembodied voice responded. The cabbie interjected with a lot of "sí-sí's" and a couple of "claro-claros." He ended the exchange with an assurance to the front office, no doubt. "Sí tío, ella va a pagar. Okay. Okay. Nos vemos. Ciao." He looked at them in the rearview mirror, and said, "Okay, señoras, vámonos a Sanlúcar."

Dani squeezed Jo's arm. "He told them he's taking his sister to Sanlúcar."

"Yes. That is what I said. I am keeping your presence secret. Please, señoras, do not make me regret this."

They sat back. Jo thanked the driver for agreeing to the long trip and asked how much it would cost. She pulled out thirty-five euros to show him they had the money.

"Ah, gracias, señora. Pues, it is a lovely day for a drive in the country. And to the Hospedería. It is a place held dearly by all of us here. But you are tourists, no? How did you come to choose the Hospedería?"

"A friend suggested it."

"Do the people there know you are coming?"

"No. Well, perhaps. Our friend said she would try to let them know."

The cabbie nodded and rested his right arm along the top of the front passenger seat, his left hand on the steering wheel, his left elbow resting on the ledge of the open window. Cruising position for a road trip.

Dani turned to Jo. "Are you okay?"

"Yeah. How about you?"

"I'm okay. Shaky. I've never been physically attacked before."

"Well, at least you're not still in shock. You scared me."

"Señoras." Dani and Jo both jumped at the cab driver's voice. "I imagine, given your hasty exit from the train station, you did not have the opportunity to see the architecture of the building."

They stared at him, wordless. He was not deterred.

"It was built en el siglo XV, the 15th century. We have spent considerable amounts of public money restoring it."

Dani loved buildings, especially historic ones. After nailing a prerequisite calculus course in university, she considered studying architecture. At this particular moment, however, she could care less about "Heritage Jerez," aside from the fact that they needed this guy right now. If he wanted to talk about the local architecture…

"The station is beautiful," she said. "But I only got a close-up of the tile floor. It was stunning," she said, gently touching her cheek. Jo poked her leg and rolled her eyes. "My name is Dani, by the way, and this is Jo."

Jo shook her head at giving out more information. Dani shrugged.

"Gracias, señora. My name is Malik."

"Malik," Dani said, "is that a Spanish name?"

"No. Andaluz. My ancestors came here a long time ago. They were the Moors, or Moros, as we say. Andalucía, where we are now, was the heart of the Moros empire. And this," he said with a sweep of his left arm out the open window, "this is the Jerez region. This is where we make sherry thanks to the canals built by my ancestors, the Moors, and before them, the Romans."

Dani leaned forward to hear him better, placing her forehead against the front seat's headrest. She felt calmed by his voice.

"I read the history in a manuscript kept in the archive of the Hospedería. It is a very impressive place. It is the largest private archive in Spain and possibly in Europe containing six million original documents dating back to 1228. Increíble, ¿no?" He continued, not waiting for a response. "It is a passion of mine to find out what I can about our past, uh, my Moro past, ¿me entienden? I was privileged to view an archive document from the thirteenth century. Can you imagine? It told the story of the vines that grow the grapes to make sherry. It is estimated they were brought here by the Phoenecians sometime during the eleventh century B.C. or later by the Greeks. No matter who or even when. Look at them today." He gestured again out the window. "¿Qué belleza, sí?"

Dani and Jo turned and looked out their respective windows.

The land rolled toward the horizon in dusty red waves broken only by swaths of luminescent green. The vines. On the highest hills, towering white windmills flailed a cobalt blue sky. This was fabled southern Spain, of sun and wine and wind power. Dani smiled. *This was our paradise. If only…*

The car motored on along Jerez A-480. Dani lay her hand near Jo's on the hard shiny leather of the back seat, their fingers touching, an unspoken reassurance, each making the other's journey into the unknown bearable. A sign rushed by. Only a few kilometres to Sanlúcar. Dani was almost disappointed. She revelled in the hiss of the tires and the heat of the breeze, the sensation of being on the move, disconnected from the stationary world and all its ordeals. She wanted to keep rolling, simplifying life into the basic needs of food, fuel, and a place to sleep, suspending all problems, mundane and extraordinary, making the mere act of moving superior somehow to standing still, because something better was surely just around the next bend.

When Malik turned off the freeway, he drove into Sanlúcar with confidence, navigating its streets without hesitation. He turned onto a short block and stopped in front of a dignified, three-storey white-stuccoed building with black iron grates at each window.

"Here it is," he said, gesturing with his hand, "the castle of the twenty-first duchess of Medina-Sidonia, the oldest royal title still in existence in Spain, a descendant of the famed Duke of Medina-Sidonia, Guzmán El Bueno who commanded the fabled Spanish Armada." His hand caught the seat back and he swivelled around so he could face them. "Her full name? Duchess Luisa Isabel María del Carmen Cristina Rosalía Joaquina Álvarez de Toledo y Maura. But we have always called her Isabel."

"A duchess? A castle?" Dani's brow crinkled. "An archive? *And* a hotel? Wow. What an unusual mix."

Malik nodded and smiled. "Indeed. Isabel herself was unusual. A strong woman. Who knows what Guzmán would have thought of her?" Malik seemed to find this very amusing, shoulders hunched up and torso shaking in a silent laugh.

Jo looked at him quizzically. Dani merely nodded, not paying too much attention, eyeing instead the place they would stay. They got out of the car. Malik stood with them, still talking, not discouraged in the slightest by travellers too weary to listen, let alone respond.

"All of Andalucía have argued about Isabel and the Fundación. It is like a local sport. Some described her as a brave, forward-thinking woman, others that she betrayed her heritage. And members of the Royal Family, oh my," he said, laughing, and shaking his head. "When she gave away the land and protected the archive, they ranted for oh…well…they are still ranting. Her children took the Fundación to court and last I heard were awarded a large amount of money. But she wouldn't care, I am sure. She was always una populista. For the people, that is. She wanted the land and the archive to stay with the people. That's how she got her nickname, the Red Duchess. But around here, they call her La Duquesita, with affection. The Little Duchess."

"They?" asked Jo.

"The people. El pueblo."

Dani spoke quietly, almost to herself. "I'll call her anything she wants for a safe place to stay."

CHAPTER THIRTEEN

Dani grabbed the heavy door knocker and dropped it three times. Nothing happened. She was about to knock again when the lock turned and the bolt was drawn back. The door opened but just a bit. There was a grunt, accompanied by a word, or rather a partial word.

"Jo," pronounced *ho*.

The door opened another few inches. Now a long groan, and, presumably, the last half of the word.

"—der," pronounced *thair*.

The door lurched open.

Ah. Dani smiled. *Joder. Fuck. One of my favourite words and from such an unlikely source.*

A young woman stood before them, shaking her head laughing, as she leaned her slight frame against the door to push it back and completely open. "Ay dios mío, perdóneme, señoras. ¡Qué esta puerta está tan pesada! Casi rota. Queda atascado frecuentemente." This door is so heavy, almost broken. And it gets stuck all the time.

She was the quintessential Spaniard, or so Dani would have thought, prior to this trip. Pale skin, black eyes and shiny black hair pulled into a tidy knot at the nape of her neck. One could see her raising her arms and snapping her fingers to a flamenco wail, if it weren't for the nose ring, of course.

She straightened up, tucked an errant strand of hair behind her ear, cleared her throat and launched into a more formal greeting: "Bienvenidos a la Hospedería Ducal, Sanlúcar de Barrameda. ¿Cómo podemos ayudarles?"

As Dani introduced herself and Jo, the woman's eyes widened with recognition and she waved them in. "Ay, señoras. Sí, sí. Bienvenidos. Y pasen. Pasen adentro. We received word two Canadienses may arrive but it was not confirmed."

"Yes, well," Dani said, "we had an incident at the train station in Jerez that made the confirmation a last-minute thing. Our apologies."

"We are here to help. My name is María Consuela. Please call me Consuela. I am the front desk clerk, a sus órdenes. And *my* apologies for the front door. It is being fixed later today." She smiled and beckoned them into the foyer, a wide-open space with a vaulted ceiling and blue and cream-coloured floor tiles.

She moved them efficiently through the registration process and led them down the hall to a beautiful vintage elevator. An old-fashioned grate blocked access to its shiny brass door. The young woman pushed the button on the wall and together they stared at the pointer above the door marking the elevator's descent. When it arrived, María Consuela pushed the grate aside and the door opened. It was a tiny passenger box, but recently approved by the local elevator authority, or so the sign on the wall declared. Next to it was another sign with the restriction Carga Maxima 4 Personas. Four very *tiny* people, thought Dani as she squeezed in after the other two. *Look out. I could be two and a half here.* The door closed without setting off any alarm and the elevator started up. *Something's missing.* She smirked at herself. *Ascensión a la samba.*

Once on the top floor, Consuela ushered them into their room, turning down the covers on the bed and pulling back the long velvet curtains from the window. "This is beautiful," said Jo. She tilted her head back to take in the ceiling with its dark brown lattice of wooden beams. Tapestries covered the wall and to one side was a door into a full bathroom outfitted with antique fixtures. Dani walked over to the floor-to-ceiling window and gazed out.

Consuela joined her. "You have one of the best views in the castle. Look. There is the garden and over there? That is the city and the harbour and just beyond is el mar, the sea," she said with a hint of reverence in voice.

Before leaving, she explained the amenities. "There is a washing machine and dry-cleaning service. In good weather, the patio is open to guests. And our cafeteria offers excellent snacks and drinks. Breakfast is complimentary and brought to your room each day. Also, Zapa requested an appointment with the doctor for you, Josefina. It is booked for today just down the street at El Centro de Refugiados, the Refugee Centre."

Because we're now refugees I guess. No wait. We're fugitives.

"You know Zapa?" asked Jo.

"Claro. Es una amiga, she is a friend of the Fundación and el Centro. She knows Viviana as well."

"Who?"

"The director of the centre. Consuela is advising you to rest for a while. It will be a busy afternoon with your appointment, Josefina. And there is a standard intake interview to complete. Viviana will go through that with you. I believe you have at least an hour, maybe two, before then." She pulled the heavy door closed behind her and they were alone. Dani went immediately to the door and checked the lock.

"Are you nervous, Dan?"

"I'm concerned about security here. We thought he wouldn't find us on the train, but he did. I can't imagine this place is any safer."

"It feels safe to me, Dan. I think Chaco really scared you."

"True."

"Maybe if we slept a bit. Do you think you could? Sleep? Because I'm exhausted."

"Okay. I'll try."

They crawled onto the high double bed. The mattress was firm and sheet thread count high. Jo sighed. Dani rolled over so she could see the door.

"They don't seem to have security at all unless you count María Consuela and the cranky front door. No cameras. No actual security people. Of course, good security wouldn't be seen I suppose. And we're on a higher floor."

A soft grunt from Jo. Dani continued, "How did we even get here? Having a nap in a big bed in an actual Spanish castle with not a care in the world except a possible attack-by-asshole. I guess we can consider this an adventure vacation, right, babe?" She looked back over her shoulder at Jo.

She was already asleep, her lips parted slightly. Dani's heart lurched with a sudden rush of love. It was still there, that spark. La chispa. After fifteen years in the relationship trenches, all that emotion still ran hard under skin toughened by daily wear. The realization calmed her. She closed her eyes and let her mind drift toward sleep, sweet thoughts easing her down gently into visions of windmills and wine and Moors riding bareback across red dunes. The desert air was hot. It became too hot all of a sudden. She couldn't breathe. She was starting to panic, desperate to pull oxygen into her lungs, but it was so hard from inside Chaco's beastly arms—

A soft knock pulled her out of her dream/nightmare and back to consciousness. The clock radio showed a couple of hours had passed. She rolled out of bed, stumbled across the room and opened the door.

María Consuela whispered apologetically, "The centre sent a message that the doctor will see Josefina now and Viviana is waiting for you, Dani. It is located down the street. You go to your right out the front door. There is a sign."

"Bienvenidos al Centro de Refugiados de Sanlúcar de Barrameda. Yo me llamo Viviana Rodríguez Sánchez. Please call me Viviana." She walked around her plain metal desk and extended her hand. "Yo soy la directora del Centro, para servirle." I am at your service.

Her grip was firm and her manner no-nonsense. She sat back down behind the desk, moved a few papers to the side, folded her hands and rested them on the desktop.

"Firstly, I must explain the Centro to you, who we are and how we operate."

Dani nodded and settled in, still half asleep. *Please god let this be brief.*

"We are a small group of professionals and volunteers working to serve people who arrive in Spain from other countries, people who seek refuge for one reason or another. We provide basic medical care through a small clinic in this building, legal services also based here, courses to help people navigate the Spanish system of government and education and public health. We also offer newcomers a simple but comfortable room for their use. It is furnished and contains magazines and computers and a small kitchen. It a is safe place to meet others or simply relax on one's own. We do not provide shelter ourselves but we will help you if needed. We are financed through donations. We do not receive any government or corporate money and so we are completely independent. We do not accept as clients anyone who may have been involved in criminal activity, although this is often difficult to determine."

Oh oh. It took all Dani had to keep herself from squirming in her chair.

"You and your partner, Jo, are unusual in that you are essentially tourists. Not refugees. Our help was requested by our friend and supporter, Zapatista Arocena. I believe Jo is taking advantage of our medical services as we speak."

She spoke with ardor, her weathered face moving constantly, her ear-length, gray-blond hair swishing in time like a fan club, applauding her words as she spoke. Two tiny pearl earrings swung delicately from her ears. *Feminine adornment?* Dani looked closer. *I think not.*

Viviana wore a white cotton shirt tucked into tailored slacks with a soft blue blazer and comfortable shoes grounding the whole ensemble. It was a style Dani knew well, one she and a gazillion other lesbians had mastered back in the bad old closet days. She could be mistaken of course. *Nah.* Dani tuned back in just in time for Viviana's wrap up. *Hallelujah. I want to get back to the room. Our private safe zone.*

But the woman continued on—*blah blah blah*—asking how Jo was feeling and if they were enjoying their room at the Hospedería. Dani answered as politely as she could, just barely reining in her impatience. Just when she heard what she thought was the perfect exit point and started to stand up, Viviana's tone changed.

"This is what we call our sesión de ingreso, intake session."

Dani sat back down and nodded again, reluctantly. "Okay," she said, her voice rising at the end.

"Zapa gave us only the barest of details about your situation. If you could tell me, please, how it is you arrived at our door?"

Here we go. Damn. Dani described their experience, avoiding any mention of the times they broke laws and paying special attention to keep Zapa out of it, except in a very general way. She didn't know this woman from Eve and she didn't want to get Zapa in trouble.

She told her about Jo's treatment at the hospital and the dramatic rescue and escape from the fourth floor. She mentioned the kidney-snatching idea briefly, explaining that they dumped that idea because of Spain's default organ harvesting law. "But you know, Viviana, something truly bad is going on there. So they lose one patient? Why would they go to all the trouble of following us to Jerez station? It's bizarre."

"Someone from the hospital followed you to Jerez?" Viviana asked, lowering her pen.

"Yes. And physically attacked me."

Viviana stared at Dani for a few seconds, eyes scrunched in concentration.

"And this attack made you decide to come here?"

"Absolutely. It was terrifying. We were on the train when I saw him looking for us."

"Who?"

"Chaco, the hospital thug. I pulled the cord and stopped the train." *Shit, Dan. Shut up!* She hurried on, hoping Viviana wouldn't catch that broken law. "I took off for the station. I was trying to draw him away from Jo. He caught up to me inside the train station and tackled me to the floor. Jo saved me. After that, we ran. You were Zapa's recommendation if we got into trouble in Jerez. And so here we are."

"You were right to come here. You are describing, however, some rather strange activity on the part of the hospital. Forgive me, Dani, but I must ask, did you leave some large bill outstanding at the hospital or do something that would provoke this extraordinary action?"

"Absolutely not. Jo is insured and everything was covered. Everything but the angio which Jo had refused. It was the doctor who insisted on it. And I quote: No angio? No discharge and no passport."

"Couldn't you have simply walked out and retrieved the passport later?"

"We tried. The same guy who followed us to Jerez physically barred us from leaving the hospital. He was backed up by the head nurse who said Jo wasn't well enough to leave."

"What you describe is concerning. I would like Dr. Pena to hear your story about la Clínica Ortega. He is always complaining about the Ortega facility in Jerez. I would also like to bring in Tomás, our legal counsel. A moment please." She grabbed her cell and texted him. She was just putting it back on her desk when it pinged.

"Ah, it seems Tomás is relaxing in the garden of the Hospedería. I'd rather not make him move. He is just back from a twenty-four-hour legal aid marathon with clients. He's probably exhausted and he feels comfortable there. Is it all right with you that we join him there? At the Hospedería."

"Of course. I'll be going back there anyway. But, uh, I should just let Jo know where I'll be."

"I will let Raúl know."

"Raúl?"

"Perdón. Dr. Pena. He will bring her to join us."

Viviana sent another text and led Dani out of the Centro and back up the street to the Hospedería. They chatted as they went.

"I haven't been in the garden yet. Jo and I got to our room and immediately fell asleep."

"Ah, this will be a treat, then. It is lovely. We all know the place quite well and Tomás stays there when he is working round the clock."

"Does that happen a lot, that people need legal services at all hours?"

"Oh yes. Some refugees are legal, some are not. Sometimes they come over the fence at Melilla. They are on the run, frightened and they can arrive here without warning."

"The fence?"

"In Melilla. It is an independent city on the coast of Morocco that is a protectorate of Spain. Would-be migrants from Africa go there in hopes of crossing into Spain. But they are blocked by a massive fence. It functions like Trump's wall, to our discredit. Some refugees manage to scale it. But once here on the peninsula, more difficulties await them. They cannot get jobs or earn a living legitimately. They face all kinds of challenges and Tomás is dedicated to helping them through it as much as he can."

They arrived at the hotel and Viviana pushed open the massive wood door with ease.

"Wow," said Dani, "they must have repaired it. Consuela could barely open it when we got here earlier."

"This building is very old. Parts are the remnants of the Muslim fortress that was here originally. After the Reconquista by the Spanish kings in 1264, the Guzmanes took possession. Just imagine the vigilance required to maintain a building this old. But isn't it wonderful?"

Dani nodded. It was like she was seeing it for the first time and was left speechless.

They walked through a massive stone archway and along a hall with a rough, whitewashed cobblestone floor. The walls were gleaming white plaster with cutaways exposing original reddish stone and brick work. The walls soared up to a white plaster ceiling supported by massive rough-hewn brown beams, essentially tree trunks. Ahead was a high iron gate spanning the doorway to the outdoors. Viviana opened it and motioned to Dani to go ahead.

Dani was awestruck by yet another glorious scene: the garden.

"It was designed in the sixteenth century for royalty and is open for hotel guests and tourists now. And as you can see," she said, nodding toward a man stretched out on a couch, "Tomás considers it his second home."

The lawyer definitely looked comfortable surrounded by flowers and plants and more cushioned chairs and couches, a bottle of brandy and three glasses on the table beside him. At their approach, he scrambled to his feet, the gold liquid in the snifter he held sloshing over the top.

"Ay, jefa. You came quickly," he said, chuckling and wiping his rust-coloured shirt with a napkin. He was attractive, dark hair and a well-manicured, light stubble beard.

"Claro, hombre. Pues, Dani. This is Tomás Garza de Mondragón, our house counsel. Tomás, this is Dani Papineau. She and her partner arrived a few hours ago in need of a doctor, and as it turns out, a lawyer. Agreed, Dani?"

Dani nodded and shook the hand he offered.

"Mucho gusto, Dani. Estoy aquí para servirle," he said with a warm, generous smile. Viviana and Dani sat down in the armchairs. Tomás topped up his glass from the bottle of Duque de Veragua Solera Gran Reserva. With a hand gesture, he offered the two women brandies but they declined.

"I checked with the staff and there are no other lodgers here right now aside from you and..." He looked questioningly at Dani.

"Jo."

"Jo," he said, nodding. "And the staff are bonded. So your conversations here are safe. ¿De acuerdo, Viviana?"

"Absolutamente. Y gracias, Tomás."

A slight flick of his hand acknowledged her thanks. He pointed to the couch. "¿Con permiso?" May I?

"Claro, hombre."

He sighed as he stretched out on the couch again. "I am so tired, I almost cannot think, let alone speak."

"I understand. I trust your ears are still operating?"

He smiled. "Como siempre, jefa." As always.

"Bueno. The topic of interest is la Clínica Ortega."

"¿De veras?" Tomás's eyes widened. "¿La Clínica? You have my complete attention."

"Relax, hombre. I want Raúl and Jo here for that discussion as well. They should arrive at any moment. In the meantime, Dani, we can talk about your goal. Zapa mentioned Seville?"

"Yes. Our plane leaves on Thursday. Assuming Jo gets the all-clear from the doctor, we need to make that flight."

"We can help you with that."

"I would be so grateful, Viviana. We'll cover any costs, of course."

"Only incidentals. As for doctor and lawyer fees, Raúl and Tomás are both on staff. We do not charge those we help. However, if you can afford a donation at some point…"

"Absolutely. We'll definitely make a donation. When we get back home, if that's all right."

"Perfect. Also, if I may be so bold, before you leave, I suggest that we find some alternate clothing for you."

"It's that bad, eh?"

"Given the attack you described, you may want to be a bit less conspicuous."

"You're very diplomatic, Viviana. We look terrible. I know. We'd love a change of clothes."

"I believe we have some spare gym clothes. I will check with—"

She was cut short by a ruckus at the gate. A man came charging through it with Jo close behind. He was waving a file over his head while shouting, "Jefa. Jefa."

CHAPTER FOURTEEN

Dani and Viviana turned sharply while Tomás lurched up once more, this time holding his glass well away from his body. "Cristo, Raúl. Could you enter like a normal human being?"

Raúl ignored him and slapped the file down on a small table next to Viviana. "Take a look at this," he said with a snort.

"And good afternoon to you, Dr. Pena," said Viviana. "Dani, may I present to you el doctor Raúl Pena. Doctor, Dani Papineau."

The man looked confused, his dramatic entrance diminished by the demands of etiquette. He turned his head to Dani, his little ponytail swinging, and extended his hand. "Encantado, señora," he said, untensing slightly.

"Uh, yes, likewise," said Dani. "And, Viviana, this is Jo." As the two women stretched their hands toward each other, Dani turned to the doctor. "I hope your…uh…excitement…isn't bad news about Jo? Please tell me she's okay."

"Sí, sí. Jo's vitals are quite good. The blood pressure is a bit too high, but we can deal with that. All other markers that I can extrapolate from at this point indicate the condition of her heart is acceptable."

"Oh my god, what a relief. You scared me."

"Ídem," came from the couch. Ditto.

"Perdón, señora. I did not mean to alarm you. *This* is the reason I interrupted you." He frowned and pushed the file closer to Viviana's side of the table.

Viviana motioned to them with her hand. "Please, sit down, Jo. You as well, Raúl."

The doctor seemed reluctant to give up the leverage of standing, but he complied, lowering himself slowly onto the chair, unconsciously tidying himself as he went, smoothing his khakis and straightening his skinny tie.

"Now, Raúl." Viviana turned to the house doctor. "Tell us what has you so concerned."

"The file." He reached over and tapped the papers as forcefully as one could from the sitting position. "Take a look at the file."

Viviana flipped through it and looked up at him. "What am I supposed to see in all this?"

Raúl snorted again.

"Please stop making those sounds," said Viviana. "Just tell us what has you all hot and bothered."

He paused briefly before speaking. "There is so much contradictory information in this pile of paper that it is a wonder anyone knew what condition they were treating. According to the *first* ECG taken by the paramedics at the hotel, Jo did *not* have a heart attack. Neither was there evidence in her blood sample of troponina—perdón, troponin, the post-attack protein released into the blood—which would confirm a heart attack had occurred."

Dani and Jo looked at each other but were silent.

"This is a surprise, yes?" he asked, looking at Jo.

"Yes, although we did think something was off in how they treated me, or I should say, *didn't* treat me. But they kept giving me nitroglycerine? Why would they do that? And it seemed to work because my chest pain lessened. Why would that happen if it wasn't a heart attack? And why did they insist on an angio? And what made me so sick in the first place?"

"Bueno. Muchas preguntas. Many questions, señora. You may have suffered from food poisoning or some kind of food intolerance. An esophageal spasm. Acid reflux, perhaps, which the paramedics' report does reference. It could have been a coincidence that you felt better. Perhaps simply moving around or drinking water helped ease the pain."

He said he couldn't imagine why they continued giving her the nitro, especially given the headaches or why they insisted on an angio. He added that he considered the repeated blood testing and urine sampling unusual because no results from those tests were ever recorded. "Only the results of the hotel test were put on record. Until later on, that is."

"Later on?" asked Dani.

"Sí. I will explain in a moment." He tapped Jo's file vigorously and said, "I just wanted to make clear that this says to me you did *not* have a heart attack and I would suggest that the only explanation for this rather gross misdiagnosis is negligence in reading their own results incorrectly or greed in initiating an unnecessary treatment. Either way, their actions are a betrayal of the Hippocratic oath."

"Ay dios." The lawyer rolled his eyes. Raúl frowned.

"Tomás, welcome to the conversation," said Viviana.

He raised his glass and nodded. Dani smiled to herself. She liked Tomás. His irreverence helped her relax. Raúl had the opposite effect. Riveted as she was by his report, he made her tense.

"That would have been enough but…" Raúl frowned again.

"But what, Raúl?" pressed Viviana.

"Well, this." He flipped through the papers. "This file clipped to the back of Jo's file, which in truth, I scanned rather quickly."

"Qualification noted. Now what did the attached file tell you?"

"That is hard to say, jefa."

"Ay dios, hombre. Qué me hace loca." You make me crazy. "Explain please."

"Bueno." He sat up rod straight and began. "The tests on the attached file appear to refer to different people."

"You mean people other than Jo?"

"Yes. I believe this because the results differ so greatly. Furthermore, the tests are indicative of an entirely different medical issue than a heart condition. And the report itself, how it is set up, the clarity of the results, well, it is simply a far more professional job than the first file, as if it came from an entirely different medical team and—"

"Oh my god," Dani cried. "I wonder if that was done by the fourth-floor team. Zapa said—"

"The fourth-floor team?" asked Viviana.

"That's where the operating room was. Hospital staff told me it was a private clinic with separate staff, only for wealthy people. I mentioned that, right?"

"You did, yes. But every detail is important."

No one spoke. Dani looked at Jo. Viviana broke the silence.

"Are there more details you care to add?"

There was another stretch of silence before Dani finally answered, "Well, actually, there's more I didn't mention."

More silence.

Raúl cleared his throat in little broken hacks. Tomás sat upright on the sofa and poured himself more brandy.

Viviana stared at Dani and Jo with narrowed eyes. And then her look softened. "You didn't know if you could trust us."

"Uh, well, yes. That's it actually. I'm sorry but it's not like we've had many good experiences in the past few days."

Viviana paused, moving from her armchair to a small straight-back one, sitting closer to Dani and Jo now and leaning toward them. "I must explain something to you. Many people come to el Centro during their search for sanctuary. Because of that, we as an institution need to know exactly what we are dealing with from a legal standpoint as well as an ethical one." Dani and Jo both nodded without speaking. "Your experience has, of course, made you cautious."

"Yes."

"I understand. That is wise. However, in this particular case, may I remind you who sent you to us? Zapa. And because Zapa trusts us, perhaps you can as well, yes?"

"Uh, yeah," said Dani slowly. "Good point."

"Excellent. Now, I would like you to retell your story, this time including *all* the details that you may have omitted previously."

"I have a question that I really need answered before we go through the story." All eyes turned to Jo. "I would like to know what you, doctor, meant when you said the tests seemed to be for another medical procedure? What other procedure?"

"Ah, sí, señora. I would conclude from the test results that they were doing preliminary discovery to determine candidacy for organ donation."

"Shit," said Jo.

"I knew it," said Dani.

Viviana grimaced and scrunched her entire face so tightly her eyes disappeared. "Organ donation? Are you certain of this, Raúl?"

"Well…no, I am not *certain*. But what I see here leads me to that conclusion."

No one spoke.

Jo put her hand on Dani's arm. "Didn't Zapa say the transplant idea didn't make sense. Because of Spain's donor law."

Tomás nodded. "Yes, the default dead donor law."

Viviana leaned forward and stared intently into Dani's eyes. "You said earlier you suspected this but dismissed it. Why did the transplant idea come to you in the first place?"

"Because of an argument I overheard between the doctor and one of the paramedics. They kept using the word 'riñón' along with 'Canadiense.' It was all in Spanish of course so I wasn't sure. And there was the other patient."

"The other patient? Bueno. It is clear we must hear the whole story without omissions. ¿De acuerdo?" Agreed?

Before Dani could answer, her cell phone rang. "I'm so sorry, Viviana. I turned it on just before we got here because… and oh my god, it's Eddie."

"Answer it if you must," Viviana said in a weary voice.

Dani walked away from the group and lowered her voice. "Hi. I'm so sorry I never called you back. I'm not sure how to describe what we've been through. And you know what? I can't get into it now because I'm in a meeting. I'll call you later, okay? Yeah yeah. That should be fine. Thanks for checking on us, Eddie." She disconnected and returned to the group. "Okay. Here's the absolutely complete story."

Dani went through it all. When she finished, all three, Viviana, Raúl, and Tomás, fired questions at her:

"You met with Rico Monte?" Viviana asked.

"Two surgical tables side by side?" Raul shook his head in disbelief.

"You know Eddie Muñoz?" Tomas couldn't hide his surprise.

Dani looked at each of them in turn. Her mouth opened and closed as if she couldn't quite decide which question to answer first. Finally she said, "Yes, to all of you."

Viviana sat back down and stared at her hands. Tomás topped up his snifter and flopped back onto the couch. Only Raúl seemed energized by the information. He jumped up with a hearty "Aha," grabbed a snifter and poured himself a shot of brandy. "I knew it. Not the setup for a transplantation at all—"

Jo interjected, "But you said it *was* a transplant—"

"And you said it *wasn't* because of the law," added Dani.

Viviana sighed. "They speak correctly, Raúl. So now, please tell us. Is it a transplant or not a transplant?"

"Mira, jefa, *this* is what I am saying. It is *not* a transplant in the usual sense." He turned to Dani and Jo. "It is *not* the simple harvesting of a kidney from a corpse."

Jo gasped.

"Cristo," Tomás blurted out. "Watch your words, hombre."

"I agree," said Viviana.

"Ay, perdón. I am profoundly sorry. I put that very crudely. What I am trying to say is that I believe this report is…" He flipped quickly through each page of the attached file again and finally set it down. "It is how they have set up this document with letters ascribed to each test result. And each page in the file is headed by another set of letters."

"What are the letters?" asked Dani.

"There are—"

"Who cares about *letters*?" Jo spoke through gritted teeth. "Just tell us what you mean. Is it or is it not about a transplant?"

"A thousand pardons. Again, I have misspoken. It is most definitely about a transplant. It is that these particular tests indicate a certain *kind* of transplant. The extent of the testing on your blood, HIV, Hepatitis B & C, kidney function, liver function, possible virus exposures, test for anemia, all these are quite telling. And look"—he pointed to incomprehensible handwriting on one page—"it shows here a cross-matching test. Your blood was matched against someone else's. A recipient, I presume. Lumping all the tests together and thinking of that operating room with two operating tables, I would say you underwent preliminary testing for *live* organ donation. In other words, the harvesting of an organ from a live human instead of a dead one, in this case you, Jo."

A stillness settled over the room. Dani looked at Jo, who had paled noticeably.

"Live? So they weren't trying to kill me, just steal my kidney? Better than dead, I suppose."

"Geez, Jo."

"What? People do donations, as in the noble deed, from a family member or friend who is a match. Of course, I'm *not* family or friend. They most definitely did *not* give me a choice. And given the quality of care, I probably would have ended up like the Benning woman anyway."

"The Benning woman?" asked Viviana.

"That's the woman, uh, the body on the stretcher down the hall from Jo's room. I mentioned her before." Dani told her more of what they knew about Benning. "So the poor woman died alone. Her husband, who is being blamed by the hospital, is still trying to get her body back. I have a newspaper article about it thanks to Zapa. But I still don't get the *live* donation thing. I mean if you've got all those organs available from dead people…?"

"It is a very desirable choice in many circles," said Raúl, "a way to avoid tainting yourself with someone else's diseases."

"Why?" Jo spoke, her hands clenching and unclenching on her lap.

"It is because people are concerned about corruption, if you will, of an organ taken from a person who has died," said Raúl. "But of course the testing alone would—"

"No, no. I don't give a damn why someone thinks one kidney is better than another. I mean why *me*? Why did they come after me for my kidney?"

"Ah, well, señora. In these circumstances, it is all reduced to opportunity. Quite simply, you were there. You were the *opportunity*."

"So I was right about that stairwell conversation about Benning and the word riñón. Probably not too many people lining up to offer live—" Dani stopped, seeing Jo's face.

Raúl answered the unfinished question. "Absolutely not. Organs for live transplants are very hard to come by, except perhaps, as you mentioned, offered out of love or duty. There is increasing popularity of what's called live-donor cross-over kidney transplants. That is where the family member or spouse is not a viable option for *their own* relative but is perhaps viable for someone else, a complete stranger. The two people register and then the transplant agency searches for a match with another couple looking for a kidney. I believe such a transplant was done at Puerta Del Mar in Cádiz. But they are relatively infrequent and certainly not commonly available to foreigners."

Tomás sat up again and looked at Dani and Jo. "Besides, those arrangements are all legal."

Viviana raised an eyebrow. "Welcome back once again, Tomás. I thought you'd drifted off."

He gave her a lopsided smile. "Claro que no, mi jefa. Bueno, what appears to be going on at la Clínica Ortega is most definitely not legal on a number of fronts. Dáme el dossier por favor, Raúl?" The lawyer took the file and started flipping through it. "Spanish law only allows live donations under very strict protocols regarding disclosure and consent. And there must be absolutely no remuneration. As Raúl said, it's a long process to find the correct matches. The result is a short list of living kidney donors against a long list of recipients."

"So tell me if I've got this," said Jo. "Because they didn't have my consent and are, as you say, breaking other rules, they probably would've had to kill me. I mean I'd be a prime witness, right?"

"Pues, Jo," said Raúl, "I believe there are two possibilities: they take your two kidneys at once and be done with it and you. That is, they allow you to die. Or, they keep you alive as a source donor available on demand, perhaps this way solving future organ requests. The hospital could keep you on some sort of life support and help themselves to your liver, your cornea, any assortment of organs…"

"Stop, stop!" Dani groaned. "Could I have some of that brandy?" Tomás handed the file back to Raúl, picked up one of the empty snifters and poured out a generous portion. He gave the glass to Dani and started to pour some for Jo but stopped when she shook her head, stood up abruptly and started pacing vigorously. Tomás sat back and sighed. "Thank you again, Raúl, for your sensitivity. Now, if you will all permit me, I will try to describe what I believe has happened here somewhat less, uh, graphically. Are you all right with that, Jo?"

Jo nodded as she sat down.

"Bueno. So, the hospital is, it seems, performing illegal live transplants. The donor, most likely some desperately poor person or illegal immigrant with no resources at hand, agrees to sell their kidney. The recipient arrives in town and staff discover the donor has fled, most likely due to fear. The hospital must now replace the missing donor because a wealthy client just arrived and wants his/her kidney. This person is expecting a new lease on life, has purchased it in fact, and is privileged enough *not* to accept 'sorry, we must rebook'. This person will make sure to damage the clinic's reputation for future organ recipients. Since the hospital wants to prevent that at all costs, it pounces on some reasonably healthy person who unwittingly arrives at the hospital for treatment of some unrelated issue. Family or friends are eventually told that the patient has died from some unexpected cause. Something credible. Perhaps a previously undiscovered malignant tumour. They say the body was cremated as per hospital policy or something like that. In reality, the patient is still alive and used as a live donor. The transplants are performed as needed and when he or she is no longer useful, the hospital allows the patient to die and cremates them immediately, leaving the bereaving family and friends none the wiser."

Dani groaned and turned back to Raúl. "That's a fate worse than death. That's a…a…a living death. Is there actually evidence of that in the file?"

"Allow me to describe it this way. I believe they were preparing Jo for a kidney extraction. That is to me a reasonable explanation for what I am seeing in this file."

"Is it possible the Clínica people are after us, not only because they lost their chance to take Jo's kidney, but also because we inadvertently took proof of what they're doing?"

Viviana, Raúl, and Tomás looked at each other. Tomás spoke first. "Absolutely. If they never had any conversation with Jo about a kidney donation, this becomes akin to assault and possibly "—he stretched his legs out in front, leaned back with his hands behind his head and stared at the ceiling— "conspiracy to murder. Not to mention kidnapping and forcible confinement. The list of possible charges is long." Dani noticed the look in his eyes.

"These grisly crimes seem to interest you, Sr. Garza."

"Call me Tomás, please. I am interested in all crimes, but those of the Ortega group are especially interesting for me."

"M-A-R." Raúl announced the letters like a bingo call.

"What are you saying, Raúl?" asked Viviana.

"M-A-R. The letters. Dani asked me what the letters are at the top of every page."

"She did. A delayed response, but thank you nonetheless," said Viviana. "Do those letters mean anything to anyone?"

"*Mar* means sea, right?" asked Dani.

"Yes, but these are initials. There are periods between each letter."

"Can I see, Raúl?"

He handed the page to Dani who stared at it before she spoke. "Mary Anne Robards. The woman I saw on the fourth floor. The one we suspect was waiting for a kidney transplant."

"Dios." Tomás broke in. "Pass me the document again, please." He scanned the pages and started pointing to it. "Look. Down the side are more letters with periods after them. Initials as well? What if they represent individuals being considered as organ donors for the person whose initials are at the top? What was her name again?"

"Mary Anne Robards," said Dani.

"And the fact that I'm part of that list," Jo said tremulously, "was just a wrong place, wrong time?"

"Eso es," said Tomás. "If we are right, their usual donors are desperate people who agree to sell parts of their bodies for cash. This is a lucrative business, certainly not for the donor, but for the broker."

"God, really? Organ brokers?" asked Dani.

"Claro. They exist everywhere. No country has a lock on virtue in these things, including Spain. We have thousands of immigrants and refugees who are easy prey. They will be afraid of going to the authorities if they have entered the country illegally, by sea or over the fence in Melilla."

"Oh right. Viviana was telling me about that. What people go through…"

"Claro. I worked all last night with a young couple in very difficult circumstances."

"They are donors?" asked Jo.

"No. But they are desperate enough that if offered the opportunity, well, in a moment of panic, I can see them accepting. And given time to reflect, they could just as quickly change their minds."

"Not a very reliable source for a serious medical procedure," said Raúl.

"Exactly," said Tomás. "And if the Clínica does not have the donor under lock and key, that person could simply not show up at the appointed time. Or perhaps the donor is rejected for some medical reason. Raúl can speak to that." Raúl opened his mouth to speak. Tomás held up his hand. "But not just yet, Raúl, thank you. So the clinic is forced into emergency mode. Their first target may have been this, uh, this Benning woman you mentioned. What was her full name?"

"I think it was Calinda, Calinda Benning."

Tomás looked at the pages he held and gave them a cocky grin.

Dani leaned over him to see for herself.

"Oh my god. There it is. In black and white. I can't believe it. C.B."

"What do her results say, Raúl?" Tomás passed the file to him.

"It appears she had some sort of pulmonary infection. Imagine their distress to discover la señora Benning was too ill for the transplant. They could not risk using an infected kidney. She died, you said? This Benning woman?"

"Yes. I believe I saw her body on a stretcher covered with a sheet. And later, I saw her husband having a meltdown. That was the same night we arrived at the clinic."

"The death of their donor, their backup donor at that, could spell disaster for their covert business. They must have been frantic. And then you two called for help," Tomás said, turning to Dani and Jo. "Jo's reflux, or whatever it was, would be easily described as a heart condition. From their point of view, it was very much right place, right time. You, Jo, were their salvation."

Jo's eyes darkened. Her cheeks flushed. The muscles of her jaw twitched.

"They are wrong," she said. "I am their downfall."

CHAPTER FIFTEEN

It was late the next morning when María Consuela led Dani and Jo into the garage under the hotel. Tomás was waiting for them, leaning against an old dark-green sedan with colourful blankets tucked over worn seats.

"Connie has agreed to lend us her car."

"Who?"

"That is me," said María Consuela, handing Tomás the key. "I call him Tommie and he calls me Connie."

"Thank you. That's very kind of you."

"I'll do anything for Tommie. Right, compa?"

Tomás laughed. "She lies. She's taken a shine to you two is the real reason. Eh, Con?" She laughed and shrugged. Tomás's tone turned serious. "The reason we need another car is because we believe they could be watching for us. And Connie's car, discúlpame amiga, doesn't look official or noteworthy. It will pass more easily. In addition, we will take a back route to Seville."

"You think they know where we are?"

"Perhaps we're being overly cautious. Let's hope so. But regardless, we're carrying precious cargo," he said, patting the briefcase. "Ortega is a private institution but it receives public money. They are committing crimes with that money and *this* is a solid start to a case against them. I sent these documents to the attorney general's office electronically but they will need the hard copies and your testimony. We should get there by late afternoon."

"That's fan—"

"Dani. Jo." Viviana was waving at them from the other side of the garage.

"Did you get a hold of Eddie?" Dani asked when she reached them.

"No. I called him as you requested. But unfortunately, there was no answer."

"Thanks for trying, Viviana. I really don't want to talk to him. He asks way too many questions."

"How did you meet him?" Viviana asked.

"He's actually Jo's contact."

"Yes. He was at a conference I spoke at in Cádiz. We ended up having a business dinner which is where Dani met him. She called him when we were starting to realize all was not right at the Clínica. I was very surprised you knew him too."

"Oh yes. We *all* know Eddie." She looked at Tomás who shook his head slowly and rolled his eyes. Viviana continued with a small smile, "The non-governmental community dealing with immigrants, and in particular refugees, is not large in Spain and quite interactive. We all know each other, more or less. I made sure he still had Tomás's cell number. That way he will call you and you can be the circumspect one, right, Tomasito?"

"Great," Tomás said sharply.

"Come now, my lawyer friend, you can handle it. Besides, all that is ancient history."

"What's ancient history?" asked Dani.

"Eddie and Tomás used to be, how shall I say it, uh, involved."

"Viviana, mi estimada jefa, deja las detallas privadas por favor." Please, keep the details private.

"Cómo no, estimado amigo." She winked at Dani and pulled two cell phones out of her pocket. "And here, these are for you and Jo. They are new numbers and not traceable to you. You are on speed dial under your first initials, D and J and T for Tomás. Mine is under V. If you have a problem, do not hesitate to use your cells. They are as secure as they can be. You can give them back to Tomás before you board the plane home."

"Viviana, you have been more than kind. We are grateful."

"You are most welcome. I ask for only one thing in return. Well, two, counting the donation you mentioned earlier."

"Don't worry. We won't forget that. As soon as we get home, we'll send it via e-transfer. You've been a lifesaver, literally. So, please, tell us. What else can we do?"

"You mentioned Rico Montes. I ask you to agree to never make contact with him again. He is an extremely dangerous man. To you and to us. ¿De acuerdo?"

Dani and Jo nodded solemnly. "We won't," said Dani. "Zapa had the same reaction."

"Yes. She is a smart woman. Bueno. Be safe, my new friends. À la prochaine, como dicen a Paris." She hugged Dani, walked over to the car, hugged Jo and left arm in arm with María Consuela.

Dani went to stow their gym bag in the trunk, reconsidered, and tucked it under her legs in the back seat. The bag held a backup copy of Jo's medical file, just in case. Jo got in the front passenger seat. Tomás started the engine and they motored raggedly out of the garage, en route to Seville yet again.

Outside the Hospedería walls, their easy talk evaporated. Dani felt apprehensive, exposed, her fear strapped into the seat next to her. Just one more passenger along for the ride.

"Is it usually this quiet on a Monday?" asked Jo, staring at the mostly empty street.

"Hey, we just passed three pedestrians. That's busy for Sanlúcar." He chuckled. "And it's early for the *turistas* to be wandering around. Besides, no one on the road means no one is coming after us."

"Shit," Dani hissed.

Tomás's eyes jerked up to give Dani a quick glance in the rearview mirror.

"Sorry," she said. "I'm just back here quietly freaking out. Empty also means more noticeable."

"No te preocupes, Dani. Don't worry. We'll get there. How about some music to distract ourselves?" He turned on the car stereo. A Spanish version of "I Will Survive," Sobreviviré, blasted out mid-tune. Jo gasped, Tomás shook his head and Dani laughed at first but became serious. "Sobrevivir. To survive. Una sobreviviente. A survivor. That's what Zapa called Nieves. I guess we'll see, eh?"

"We will see. For sure. I can't imagine how she can survive with this clinic. It's jammed with danger. But let's go back to silliness, shall we? Just to relax for a bit. That person singing there? That's Pitingo. Connie is a big fan."

"Who?" asked Jo.

"Pitingo. He's a Spanish performer who sings pop songs al estilo flamenco. Personally I prefer Rosalía."

"Oh I know her," said Dani. "She's recorded with the Weeknd."

"Yes. Yes. She is amazing. But perhaps something more relaxing right now, yes?" He switched the station to one playing a soft jazz vocal. "Ah. Now that's more like it. Carme."

"Carme?"

"Carme Canela. She sings a lot in Spanish but mostly in Portuguese. The guitarist is Jordi Matas. I love this recording."

They headed onto a narrow highway, soothed by the music. Watchful. Silent. Until Dani spoke. "So, Tomás, you and Eddie?"

"Ay dios mío,' he said, turning down the radio. "Viviana does not believe in privacy."

"Me neither, when I'm trying to distract myself."

"Fair enough. What do you want to know?"

"How did you and Eddie meet?"

"We were in a class together at university. He's an amazing guy. Very smart. Talented. But he is driven. He never stops working. There is a name for it. Pathological ambition."

"I've noticed. He took Jo and me for dinner in Cádiz. A very focused and persuasive guy."

"Yes. I always told him he'd be an incredible lawyer. Or politician. He knows how to influence and persuade. Imagine him in front of a jury. But he said no. He said, the way he grew up—single parent mum and poor with childcare workers butting into his life all the time—he figured he knew more about social work than anything else. And the degree was cheaper and faster than law. He's done all right, from what I hear."

"How come you two didn't last?"

"He was too much for me. Too much of everything. Too much wine, too much food, too many clothes, too many parties, too much plotting and planning. I didn't have the energy for it, frankly. And then there were his affairs. It was all drama with Eddie. It was messing up my mind. I had enough trouble dealing with law school. So I left. The relationship, that is."

There was a prolonged silence.

"I don't want to cross a line here but is Viviana gay?" Dani asked with a raised eyebrow.

Tomás looked at Dani and laughed. "You're serious. I thought you were joking. Yes, absolutely. There must be something in the water, right?" They looked at him blankly. "You know what I mean, don't you?"

"No. We don't," Jo said. Dani leaned toward the front seat.

"Isabela. La Duquesa. I must tell you about her. La Duquesa was the most amazing woman. She acted on her beliefs and got into trouble as a result. While the dictator Franco was alive, Isabela stood against him and was exiled to France. She defended the archive, refusing to hand over control to any other royals because she didn't trust them with it. She believed they would destroy archival records that prove Spanish royal lines are mixed with Moorish blood."

"Why does that matter?" asked Jo.

"Who knows. Something about being able to claim they are 'puro español' perhaps? Isabela also believed there are documents in the archives that show the Moors ventured to the Americas long before Columbus. She wrote a book about it. *It*

Wasn't Us is the title. She wrote other books too. She was jailed for protesting the destruction caused by the accidental drop of an American hydrogen bomb. It spilled radiation near a Spanish town and impacted farmland. I loved that woman. She grew up as a royal but she was never one of them. And she knew just how to press their buttons. There are so many great stories about Isabela. Here's one of my favourites. Now remember. She was a royal. A lesbian. A feminist. A republican. A socialist. And what a sense of humour. And irony. She went to a fancy dress party and took her female partner of the time as her date. They both dressed as medieval lepers, complete with bells to warn other guests of the danger of contamination from their company. ¿Increíble, no? La Duquesa, may she rest in peace. Always a rebel to her class and a hero to her gender. It is a pity you never met her."

"When did she die?"

"2008. It was very sad. She married her secretary of twenty some years on her deathbed. Some say she only did that to keep the archives from falling into *royal* hands. But there are others, like myself, who believe it was love first, and only later, practicality."

"Wow. I guess that's what Malik was—"

They all jumped at the ring of Tomás's cell phone. He grabbed it. It was Eddie. There was a terse exchange.

"Sí. Las dos se alojan en la Hospedería. El doctor nos dijo que Josefina tiene buena salud. Solo está exhausta. ¿Qué dices? Ah sí, sí. Todavía Raúl, claro. Bueno, mira, hombre, es que estoy conduciendo ahora. ¿Podemos hacerlo breve?"

He went silent, listening to Eddie.

"Sí. Entiendo." His tone had changed. "Bueno. Claro que voy a decirles. Gracias, Eddie." He hung up.

"What did he say? That sounded serious at the end there."

"Pues, ah, he was glad you were safe and in good health, Jo. I told him you were still at the Hospedería. He offered you both a place to stay in Seville if you need it. But he said that Zapa had left a message that she needed to talk to him."

"We gave her his number in case of emergency. I hope she's not in trouble."

"The message said she thought security from the Clínica was following her. That was early Sunday evening. He called her shortly after she left the message and couldn't get hold of her. He figured she was at work. But he said he tried again later in the evening and at regular intervals since then, including this morning. She has not answered. He wanted to know if Zapa has contacted you or if you know where she is?"

A chill gripped Dani. "No. Tell me again, when did she leave her message?"

"About seven yesterday evening."

She closed her eyes and thought.

"Could she have had an unusually long shift at the hospital?" Tomás asked. "Or got drunk and gone off with some guy?"

"Look, Zapa's shifts are unpredictable but *she* most definitely is not. She's rock solid. Although she *was* afraid of how they were going to react at the hospital when she went back to work. What do you think, Jo?"

"Agreed. I think she was concerned about their reaction."

"He said he was going to make a few more calls to see if he could find her. And he asked you to text him your number, although Viviana suggested keeping that number private. It's up to you of course."

No one said anything, each deep in their own thoughts. Dani began to hope Zapa *was* having some wild fling. She couldn't imagine her going AWOL, though. "Not bloody likely," she said out loud.

"What did you say?" asked Jo.

"I can't believe Zapa would, what, just take off with all this going on? But the idea of her being in trouble, and because of us…If that bastard…If Chaco…It makes me sick to even think about it."

Jo turned and reached behind her seat to touch Dani's knee. "She's okay. We have to believe that until we hear otherwise, especially since we can't do anything about it right now."

Dani groaned through clenched teeth. "Why is this psycho on the loose, anyway, running around attacking people?"

"Who knows?" Jo said with exasperation. "And we aren't sure if it's actually Chaco involved in this thing with Zapa," Jo said.

"Come on, Jo. We know they're capable of anything. And he's their enforcer—" As she spoke, an image flashed through Dani's mind: Chaco dragging Zapa off. *Fuck, fuck.*

"Yeah," said Jo. "That hospital seems to have its reach everywhere, even in Jerez."

"Ah sí, Our delightful regional hospital." Tomas's voice was laden with sarcasm. "Private yet receiving tax dollars on top of their own investments. And still they manage to offer substandard service."

"You said something last night, uh, something about how you were especially interested in the Ortega chain. Why is that, Tomás?" Jo asked.

"My aunt died there and they cremated her without the family's permission. That's my personal experience. I am still angry about it. And Raúl has so many stories. Negligent care, extraordinary wait times…"

Dani tuned them out. She couldn't compartmentalize like that. Zapa was her only concern. *Where is she? She never mentioned family beyond her parents. As for friends, only Miguel. Damn. Eddie. You've got to find her.*

"…It's so bad we now joke about it. We call it 'El Morgue Ortega.' People drive over an hour to the public hospital in Arcos de la Frontera just to avoid going there."

They slowed to a crawl behind a tractor turning onto the narrow road ahead of them. They all watched silently as Tomás manoeuvred around it and picked up his train of thought as well as their speed, once past it.

"I've wanted to get a class-action suit organized, especially since they get public money. I'd do it pro bono. But I've never been able to get anyone to sign on. People are too afraid. I tried to get my uncle to do something when my aunt died, but he said no. He was heartbroken and just wanted to move on."

"Maybe he'd consider joining a lawsuit now that some time has passed," said Jo.

"I'll bet that guy Benning would sign on," said Dani.

"Do you know how to contact him?"

"No. But he talked to a reporter, the one with a local expat newspaper. Her name is Maggie...hold on a second." She rummaged around in the bag under her legs and found the article. "Maggie Milestone."

"I'll contact her. If we can put personal experiences like those of Benning and my uncle and Jo's together with the documentation you have, perhaps we would further strengthen the case. Finalmente."

Dani and Jo exchanged looks.

"Is that why Viviana is helping us?" said Dani. "Because we've got ammunition and could help?"

"Our mandate is to help all who come to our door in need, as long as they are not engaged in any crime, etcetera. You came to us first in need, but second with proof of illegal activity on the part of an institution. That takes our engagement to another level. We are obliged to offer you legal advice about you own situation but also to follow up on what you have described."

"We'd both be happy, uh no, happy isn't strong enough, ecstatic is more like it, at the prospect of bringing those bastards down."

"I agree absolutely. The idea of working with—" Jo stopped short when Tomás's cell phone blared.

"I must change that ring," he said. He pulled to the side of the road and grabbed his cell. "Diga. Ah sí, Eddie. ¿Qué has oído?" He listened intently, nodding sometimes and occasionally groaning. "¿Por qué a ti?" Another long silence. "No sé, mano. Okay. Bueno."

As he hung up, Dani leaned forward to see him better. He shook his head.

"What? What happened?"

The decision was unanimous. They were going back to Cádiz.

The message had been short and clear: give us the files and we will give you Zapa. Eddie said the speaker hadn't identified himself and had hung up immediately after adding instructions.

"The bar is on Plaza San Antonio? Isn't that...?" asked Jo.

"Yup. That's the square where your conference was held. And where Gerardo was playing. Different bar, though."

"Gerardo?" Tomás shot Dani a quizzical look in the rearview mirror. "Nuñez?"

Jo turned to Tomás, aghast. "Seriously? You too?"

"Uh, maybe later for that," Dani said. "Eddie said we were to meet an intern? Did he give you a name?"

"No. Just said you were to meet *the intern* at nine tonight at Bar El Andaluz."

"I wonder if it's Berto, Zapa's friend. Probably not. He sounded like a decent sort. And from the way he talked, there was no love lost between him and the Clínica. Unless he's being coerced somehow. I think it's more likely the intern who was going to do the angio."

"So like what, now he's ransom guy?" Jo shook her head. "And why did they call Eddie?"

"I asked him and he said all he could think of was that he was trying to reach Zapa and he left messages including your names and his phone number. If they have her, they have her phone. And with the phone, they probably figure Eddie's a path to you since they couldn't find you themselves."

"Maybe they only have her *phone* and not *her* and figured out their play from that," said Jo.

"That would be a best-case scenario if she's safe." Dani's voice cracked. "But if they have her phone, they know what we have. Proof of the goings on at the clinic. Zapa took pics, remember, Jo? That was before she gave us the file, so there'd be another copy."

"Yeah, she did. So they're trying to get all the copies back, including the hard copy we have. Tying up loose ends, I imagine."

"Sí. And like the attorney general, everyone values the original documents," said Tomás.

"You know, I don't care about the file or prosecuting them anymore. The only thing that matters is Zapa's safety." Dani rested her forehead on the back of Jo's seat.

"We should bring in the police. We need expert help," said Jo.

"They told Eddie, no police."

"And remember what I saw, the police cozying up to Chaco and Montoya."

"One corrupt policeman, maybe more. But Cádiz is not any more corrupt than any other police force," said Tomás. "They all have manzanas podridas."

"Bad apples. Maybe," said Dani. "But I agree with Zapa, that it's more than that. It's systemic. A lot of cops see themselves as the thin blue line, protecting the existing order, which is usually wealthy, white, and male. In this case, the existing order is the Clínica, wealthy, Spanish, and female."

"Individual or systemic, it doesn't matter now. Eddie said that they were very clear we should not involve the police or it will not go well for Zapa."

"They actually said it like that, threatening her?"

Tomás nodded. "That's what he said, and I know what Eddie sounds like when he's exaggerating. He was not."

"Oh my god," said Jo, turning from the window to look at Dani. "So we're completely on our own with this."

"Well, okay then," Dani said, touching Jo's shoulder. "Let's figure out it out."

"C'mon, Dan. You think we should meet with these guys without any professional help or backup?"

"What I'm suggesting is that we do some investigating. See if we can find out where she might be, or at least where she was last. We've got to think like detectives."

"But we aren't detectives. We're tourists."

"I'm painfully aware of that, Jo. But since we got Zapa into this, let's just try to find her. If we fail, we still have the meeting in the square. We'll give them the damn file it if comes to that and hope they keep their end of the bargain. What do you think, Tomás?"

"We should not give them the file, but I agree, we should try to track her. Where was she before she disappeared? No one's really looked for her. No one in Cádiz, that is. Eddie made all his calls from Seville."

"That's right," said Dani. "Okay. We know she went back to her house after leading us to the train station. Let's head there first. Check around the neighbourhood. And of course, there's Miguel. She's pretty tight with him. If I could get online, I could find the restaurant he works at when he's not at the hospital. It's in Old Town. Crema something." Dani pulled out her cell phone.

"I think your cell is only talk and text. Here," Tomás said. He handed his to Dani. "The search engine icon is bottom right."

The car moved steadily along the old highway back toward Sanlúcar. Jo looked out the window. The sun was higher now and heat rose in waves from the desert sand. She looked at Tomás.

"Tell us again exactly what Eddie said."

He repeated it all, adding new details. "He said no police. He did ask me about the file. He wanted to know what was in it to make these people so angry. I told him I didn't know. Maybe I should have been honest with him but I think the fewer people who know the details the better."

"I agree," said Jo.

"He did *not* sound like himself, though. I mean we have our differences, but they're personal. We have always been respectful professionally. Sometimes even friendly. He was cold as ice, this time."

"I wonder if they're threatening him."

"Shit," said Dani. "He wanted me to text my number. I totally forgot. But now I'm glad I didn't."

"Look." Jo pointed to a highway sign coming toward them, reflectors gleaming: Sanlúcar De Barrameda 4 km, Jerez De La Frontera 27 km, Cádiz 52 km. "We're almost back where we started."

Dani glanced at the speedometer. "How much time till we get to Cádiz, Tomás?"

"About forty-five minutes."

"Okay, let's talk about this meeting. In a bar of all places. So, not really in full view. Probably dark, offering some cover for the intern and maybe backup of some sort tucked out of sight."

"Do you suppose he'll bring Zapa to the bar?" asked Jo.

"I can't imagine they'd risk having a person held captive in a public place."

"Exactly," said Tomás. "The message was, 'You will give the file to the intern and the intern will tell you Zapa's whereabouts.'"

"Her whereabouts?" Outrage infused Jo's words. "So we're supposed to, what? Race across town to some location and hope to god she's there and okay? That's not very reassuring."

"Right now, they're dictating the terms," said Dani. "We should take control. They want those papers? They don't get them until we *see* Zapa and know she's safe. So we should stash the papers somewhere and tell them where once we know Zapa's okay."

"We have to assume the intern's just a go-between," said Jo.

"But someone who makes decisions," Tomás interjected, "will be accessible, like a phone call away. He won't be acting on his own."

"This bar meet-up is disturbing."

"I agree, Jo," said Tomás. "In fact, it makes me think that you should not be there."

"He's right. You're the riñón." Jo grimaced. "It's too risky for you. We could take you back to the Hospedería. We're just coming up to the turn off."

"Now wait a minute, you two. There's no way we're splitting up. I'm going where you're going."

"Consider this, Jo," said Tomás. "We know they are willing to kidnap people. What would prevent them from grabbing you along with the file, just to have all their worries dealt with. File and prime witness in one operation. And don't forget. They still need that kidney."

"Face it, Jo. You don't need to be there."

"Dani and I will give them the file, Jo, and we will keep you out of it."

"Okay, just stop. We are not splitting up. I won't do it. I will *not* go back to the Hosp...Hosp—"

"Hospedería."

"Yeah. That place. Besides, what they really want is the file. That's the real danger for them. So just forget about leaving me behind."

Dani leaned forward and talked softly into Jo's ear. "Babe. You gotta understand. When I walked into that hospital room and you were gone, well, I broke. My heart broke. My knees gave way. It took everything I had to start figuring out how the fuck I was going to get you back. And then by some miracle, I got my sorry ass onto the fourth floor. I was so fucking scared walking along that hall. I didn't know what state I'd find you in: unconscious, cut open, some angio catheter already plodding along some artery? I didn't have a clue what I was going to do then. We were so damn lucky you were still conscious, sort of, and not under the knife and that there was still time to *get* you out of there. We might not be so lucky next time. *I* might not survive that, let alone you. So please, I'm begging you here. Don't ask me to go through that again. You've got to stay somewhere—"

"Oh just stop."

Dani shook her head. "I see I've really moved you."

Jo paused and changed gears. "Look. I get it, Dan. But how can I stay safe and cozy in Sanlúcar while you two do battle in Cádiz? I mean, come on."

"One less horror to worry about, I'd say."

"Only for you. For me, the flip side: I'll be worrying about you two. So how about a compromise? I won't go *into* any of the places we check out. But I *will* stay *with* you, just in the car."

"Frankly, I'm nervous about that too, that you're sitting in the car where anyone can see you."

"Suck it up. I will stay in the car but I will not, repeat, *not* wait in Sanlúcar."

"Uh, señoras? You can stop debating this," said Tomás. "We have passed the last turn off to Sanlúcar. Next stop? Cádiz."

CHAPTER SIXTEEN

The green sedan cruised over Cádiz Bay by way of the Bridge of the Constitution of 1812.

"It's nicknamed La Pepa, also like the constitution." Tomás spoke, eyes glued to the road as the car crested the bridge's high point. "That document was considered one of the most liberal and inclusive constitutions of its time. A group called the Cortes of Cádiz came together in defiance of Napoleon and his armies who were occupying Spain. Those brave souls wrote it all out here."

Dani stared down at the city before them. She wondered if that courage was still there, lodged somewhere between stone and time. *We're going to need it if we're going to find Zapa and get home safely.*

The midday sun heated the buildings. The sky, clear and deep blue, offered no relief.

Far below, the Atlantic churned, whipped up by the same winds buffeting Consuela's little car as it came down off the bridge. At its base, Tomás took the second road off a traffic circle and their search for Zapa began.

They'd decided on four places worth investigation: Zapa's home, Dr. Nieves's office near the dock, Miguel's after-hours restaurant, Casa Crema, and la Conchita Rosa, Rico's lair. Jo reminded them of their promise to Viviana to stay away from Rico Monte. Dani argued they'd made the promise before knowing Zapa had been abducted and as one of the worst guys around town, he most likely knew or was their prime suspect. They had to go to there.

Zapa's place required no such discussion.

Tomás parked the car around the corner from the townhouse. His task was to ask neighbours and store owners when they'd last seen Zapa. Dani's was to check out the townhouse itself. Jo's was to stay safe and out of sight in the car.

"I don't think you should go in alone," she said, not for the first time.

"We've been over this and we're doing what we agreed was best under the circumstances."

"But not at the cost of you, Dani. Please remember that."

"Got it."

Dani left the car, shaking off Jo's fear because she had enough of her own. She walked up to the small building, found the key under the planter, unlocked the door and ran up the stairs, hoping she would find her new friend at the kitchen table, waving her in for coffee. How they would laugh at the idea of…

She stopped short at the living room door and slumped against its frame. The room had been torn apart, books dumped from the shelves, the green velour curtains shredded as if by giant raptor claws.

She made herself go into the kitchen. It was worse. Broken dishes, food and garbage strewn everywhere. The little espresso maker that Zapa had used to make their cafecitos was bent beyond repair. Zapa's bedroom was similarly trashed but with uglier focus. Her clothes had been ripped to pieces with her undergarments placed on top of the pile in a sinister aside. Dani groaned. It went beyond looking for a file. It was a "fuck-you" from a very disturbed individual. *Chaco. Has to be.*

She headed back downstairs but paused to check the street before opening the door. From the window, all seemed calm. A woman was walking a dog. Dani watched her. The pooch sniffed and peed on a pole and looked up at its mistress as if to say, "Okay, I'm ready to go now." The woman did not move. She turned her attention from the dog to stare directly at Zapa's house.

Dani ran to the front door, locked it quietly and took the back exit into a common courtyard shared by other ancient townhouses. From there she took a passage to another street, stopping only to text Jo about the dog walker.

The mood in the car was grim.

"What's wrong?" asked Tomás, looking at their faces after he'd closed the driver side door. "What's happened?"

"Dani thinks there was a watcher. I saw her too walking a dog, but she didn't seem off to me."

"It's much worse than that woman. Zapa's house was viciously ransacked."

"Viciously?" asked Jo.

"Yes. It was more than a search. It was a really ugly message."

Tomás turned in the driver's seat and made eye contact with Dani and Jo in turn. "I believe at least one of these folks after you is crazy."

"Thug," Dani and Jo said at once.

"A.k.a. Chaco," Dani tagged.

"The paramedic?"

They nodded.

Tomás shook his head and gave them his report. Everyone he spoke to knew Zapa but said she hadn't been around for a couple of days. "Except for the woman at the bakery. She saw her on Saturday. But that was before you left the hospital, right? I didn't knock on any doors. I didn't think we had time for that."

"No, we don't," said Dani. "Are you okay?" she asked Jo.

"Me? I'm fine. But I didn't leave the car. Are *you* all right?"

"Yeah. But that was pretty horrible. I'm sure it was Chaco. That level of hatred just oozed out of him at Jerez station. If he's got her—"

"Don't go there, Dan. We'll get her. Time for target number two."

The Santa María district in the north end of Cádiz's Old Town was just a short drive from Zapa's place. It was an historic area with small businesses and restaurants and flamenco houses and museums. The only available parking spot was in front of 23 Avenida del Puerto, a modern structure housing a bank. After Tomás cut the engine, all three of them twisted their heads like robo-spies to look back at their actual target, número 21. It was a lovely eight-story, art deco-style building, its entrance flanked by a café and a bookstore. The retail outlets didn't interest them of course, only the office inside that housed the medical practice of la doctora Nieves.

"I can't believe it," said Tomás. "I know that building. It was included in a course I took on Cádiz architecture."

"You took architecture?"

"Briefly. But I changed my mind and went for law. No math to worry about. So. This building. The architect is renowned. He's a local man. Esteve. It was built in the late forties, early fifties. And here I thought that course was a waste of time."

"Any good place for hiding a kidnap victim?" asked Jo.

"Yes, lots of places." He paused and threw his head back. "Si recuerdo, uh, if I remember correctly, it has an underground tunnel that goes to the port."

"Really?"

"It was designed to protect wealthy merchants and their goods from bad weather."

"In the forties?"

"No, no. The building was built on the foundation of an older structure."

"I'm going to check it out. Anyone want a coffee?" Dani asked.

She got out of the car without waiting for an answer. She walked past the café and went through the main entrance. Two etched bronze elevator doors dominated the foyer; to the left were a couple of chairs and a small coffee table. On the wall above one of the chairs was the building directory. Dr. Magdalena Nieves's office was on the fifth floor. Dani went back outside and into the café, ordering three cortados, one decaffeinated.

Back in the car, she passed the decaffeinated one to Jo and then remembered.

"Sorry, babe. I keep forgetting you didn't really have a heart attack. Next time, solid espresso."

"Not a problem, Dan. Anger is my new caffeine."

Dani jumped when her cell buzzed. "Miguel. ¡Qué bueno!" *You got my text*, she wrote. *We've got to talk.*

He replied immediately. *I agree. ¿Puedes después de las seis? ¿En Casa Crema? Tengo algo para darte.*

Okay.

"Who was that?"

"Miguel. We're meeting at Casa Crema after six. That's when his shift starts. Now, Tomás." Dani touched his arm. "Nieves's office is number 507. Are you *sure* you want to do this?"

Tomás nodded. "Absolutely. Tell me what I should be looking for, aside from a woman held against her will."

"We need to find any sign that Zapa might be in there, or anywhere nearby for that matter," said Jo. "Given we have nothing at this point, any bit of information or insight will help."

"You know, it's ridiculous for Tomás to be going in there," Dani said.

Jo shook her head. "Absolutely not. Nieves might have seen you at the hospital."

"Really?" countered Dani. "That's a long shot. And Tomás doesn't have a clue what Nieves looks like. Or Chaco for that matter. That puts him more at risk. Actually, do you even know what *Zapa* looks like." She reached across the seat and touched his shoulder. "I mean she could be sitting right there and you wouldn't recognize her, would you, Tomás? Aside from her being a gorgeous black woman with brilliant red hair, of course. But her hair could be under a cap or something."

"I did meet her once, but that was a long time ago. She was nine. I'm *sure* she's changed."

"Geez, what were you? Ten?"

"I was twelve. But you're right. I might not recognize her today."

Jo reluctantly agreed Dani should go in. "But please be careful. If you see Nieves, turn around and walk out." She passed Dani a pair of sunglasses and a scarf. "I found them in the glove compartment." Dani donned the glasses and tied the scarf around her head, bandana-style.

Twenty minutes later, she returned.

"That was a lot of walking for nothing. No sign of Zapa. But I did learn a few things. I checked out the basement first. The elevator doesn't go there so I took the stairs down and ended up at a solid brick wall. I went back up and talked to the guy in the bookstore. He said they filled in the tunnel and sealed the wall about ten years ago because the tunnel was leaking ocean water during big storms. I went up to the top floor and walked along every hall except the fifth. There are four offices per floor and I checked every one of them. Lots of vacancies. One guy was hard at it in an accounting business on the eighth. There was some sort of web server company on the seventh. Most were dark. I asked everyone I saw about other occupants. And I listened at every closed door for activity. All negative."

Tomás shook his head. "If Zapa is being held in an empty office, she could be drugged or gagged, unable to make a sound."

Dani nodded.

"What about the fifth floor and Nieves's office?" asked Jo.

"I saved that for last. Nothing happening that I could tell so I went inside her office."

"You're crazy," Jo said.

"It's pretty much your standard office setup. A few people sitting, waiting. The receptionist asked if she could help me. I told her I was checking out which doctors in the area were taking new patients. She said Dr. Nieves was closing her office at the end of the month, but she wouldn't say why. Told me I could ask the doctor directly, but I said I didn't have time to wait. I left immediately. An elderly woman left at the same time. She was walking with a cane. You may have seen her come out of the building ahead of me."

They shook their heads.

"Anyway, we were on the elevator together. I asked her about Dr. Nieves. She said it was a pity she was leaving. There weren't many doctors in the area to choose from. I asked her if she knew where Nieves was going. She said some island somewhere for her health, but she said she didn't know what was wrong with her. It was all rather sudden, she said. She's probably headed to someplace like the Cayman Islands, where she's got her money stashed."

They sipped their coffees and returned to the topic of Zapa's house.

"Why would they think we'd leave the file at Zapa's?" asked Jo.

"Who knows. Worried about taking it with us? Or maybe they thought Zapa had plans for it?" said Dani. "Which of course would be right."

"Well, there's not much more we can do here" Tomás inserted the key into the ignition and paused. "Shall we keep going?"

"The sign said Nieves's office closed at five. We could wait for her to leave," Dani said, pulling off the scarf, "and follow her."

"She wouldn't necessarily go to where Zapa is," said Tomás. "And we don't know for sure that she's involved."

"Oh, she's involved. I guarantee it," said Dani sharply. "One of us could stay here."

"No. No splitting up," countered Jo. "I think we should stick with the plan and come back later. There's still enough time before five. Right?"

Dani and Tomás both nodded.

He manoeuvred the car along Old Town's narrow streets and parked within spitting distance of Clínica Ortega.

Target number three: La Conchita Rosa.

"I guess it's finally my turn, yes?"

"You got it, hombre. I'd prefer to avoid Rico at all costs. I suggest you avoid him too if he's in there. He's got a table at the back, his regular spot I think. And he looks like the sleazoid he is. Older with jet black hair."

"I don't think the black hair part is a particularly defining feature here in Spain," said Jo with a wry smile.

"Right. But it's an obvious dye job. And the guy acts like he owns the place, which of course he may. Zapa considers him evil incarnate. As does Viviana. I think he's only of interest here because he's knee-deep in nasty goings on in Cádiz. And if anybody has an idea of where Zapa is, he will. That said, I'm feeling kind of guilty letting you go in."

"Don't. I have my own stakes in this. Zapa *and* el Grupo Ortega. Besides, as we say in Spain, gato con guantes no caza ratones. A cat with gloves cannot catch mice."

"Meaning?"

"Don't overaccessorize." Tomás got out of the car and then leaned back through the open window. "It may limit your options. Or…if you're going to do something right, you may have to get your hands dirty."

Dani leaned toward him and whispered, "Seriously, Tomás, you maybe don't want to test that with this guy."

He raised an eyebrow. "Just don't tell Viviana. More scared of her." He winked. "Ciao."

The two women sat in silence, waiting for his return from the demon's den. It was taking too long. It seemed like an hour. No. Longer. Like an eternity. Until suddenly, he emerged, walking quickly to the car. He got in, closed the door, started the engine and pulled into the street, all in one fluid motion.

"What happened?"

"¿De veras? Not much."

"Oh come on, Tomás. You were in there for"—Dani checked her phone—"fifteen minutes. Seemed a hell of a lot longer. But okay. Tell us. What happened?"

He turned a corner just down the street from the La Conchita Rosa, pulled over to the curb and stopped the car. "Bueno. This is what I found out," he said, turning sideways with one arm over the back seat. "No one knows anything about Zapa and her whereabouts. But when I asked about Rico—"

"You *asked* about him? Shit."

"Well, I decided to see what happens."

"And?"

"He isn't there. The bartender said Rico took off without notice. Closed down his backroom table operation yesterday leaving a huge unpaid tab. The bartender was very angry. He asked me if I was one of his henchman and if I knew where he was." Tomás was clearly shaken by the experience, growing paler with the telling. "Other patrons in the bar gathered around me. I thought they were going to try to beat it out of me. Of course, I have no idea where he is. It was nonetheless quite unnerving." He sat back around, put his hands on the steering wheel as if to brace himself and took a deep breath. "You were absolutamente correcto, Dani. It is advisable to stay as far from these people as possible. But like I said, I have no new information."

Jo leaned forward. "Oh but you do. The bartender said that Rico closed down his operations. Remind you of anyone else we checked out today?"

Tomás's eyes met Jo's in the rearview mirror. He smiled. "Nieves."

"Yes. We now know that two of our chosen targets are on the move, Nieves and Rico. A coincidence? I think not."

"Maybe Nieves is not going to her island to be with her money. Maybe she's feeling vulnerable because the incriminating file is now out of her hands," said Tomás.

"Possibly. But Rico? Why would he run off?" Dani shook her head. "No. The way he talked, he wasn't connected to the hospital. He seemed like an independent operator to me."

"Whatever he is, I would prefer we not wait around to find out," he said.

"We're too early for Miguel," said Jo.

"We could take a break. La Duquesa has a safe house not far from here. Or we could go back to Nieves's office?"

Dani looked at Jo who nodded. "Let's go back."

Tomás had found them a good spot behind a couple of other cars with a clear view of Nieves's building. They'd arrived just before five and it was now five thirty. After thirty minutes watching the front door of Nieves's building, they were getting restless.

"Are you sure the sign said five, Dan?" Jo asked.

"I am. Maybe she has things to do before she leaves. I'll go in and check."

Dani was back after a couple of minutes.

"Her office lights are still on. I heard someone moving around. We still have some time to spare. I say we wait."

After another thirty minutes, Tomás jerked his chin toward the building entrance. "Mira."

Nieves pushed her way through the front door with a large rolling suitcase in tow and an oversize bag over her shoulder.

"Wow. Looks like she's all packed up."

They watched her get into a cab and followed it down Avenida Puerto into the newer part of town, a section Dani and Jo had not seen before. The cab stopped on Calle Tolosa Latour. Nieves got out and headed into number 17, bags in tow.

"This section is known as lawyer's row. Lots of law offices along here. And she just headed into a bar that's very popular with the Cádiz legal crowd." Tomás parked the car a half block from the bar and opened the door. "I'm going in."

Five minutes later he returned.

"She wasn't there but a guy at the bar had the shoulder bag sitting in front of him. I knew his face but can't remember his name. Definitely a lawyer. Did you see her come out?"

"No. No one came out," said Jo.

"She must have gone out a back exit because she wasn't inside. I even checked the women's washroom."

"She couldn't have gone far with that big suitcase."

Jo nodded. "That's right, Tomás."

"I'll bet she had a vehicle ready out back," he continued. "Did you see any cars come out of the lane?"

"Actually, yeah. A big black SUV."

Tomás slammed the steering wheel. "I'll bet that was her."

"Do you think she knew we were following her? I was really careful inside her office building," said Dani.

Tomás shrugged. "I don't think so. But she was clearly taking precautions."

"What do you think she's doing, Tomás? Any ideas?" Jo asked.

"That big shoulder bag could carry files. Or money," said Tomás. "She is perhaps tying up loose ends?"

"Don't like the sounds of that," said Dani.

Dani stood just inside the door of Casa Crema, an Old Town dining spot. She spotted Miguel at the espresso machine with his back to the room. She took a stool at the bar as quietly as she could and was mesmerized watching performance art à la Miguel: the espresso and milk were his mediums, the glass his canvas, the steaming black and white artfully poured into the tall glass. Et voilà! His creation.

"Miguel," Dani said softly when he was finished. He turned and looked at her. She lifted her sunglasses and pushed them up onto her bandana. His face lit up.

"Ay, Dani. I am glad you are here. Please sit over there." He nodded to a table in the corner. "Vengo ahora mismo." I'll be right there.

He finished his task and joined her with a warm smile that quickly turned serious. "I am so worried about Zapa," he said. Dani believed him and was relieved. She'd been nervous about seeing anyone from the hospital, but Zapa had sworn by this guy.

"She simply disappeared." He spoke in Spanish, voice soft, words fast. "She came into the cafeteria late yesterday afternoon. Twice actually. The first time she bought a bunch of little cakes and cookies for the women in the laundry, she said. But she came back later too. She wanted a cafecito to take for herself."

"Miguel, más despacio por favor."

"Slower? Yes, of course. It must have been around six because the cafeteria was empty by that time."

"I can't believe she went back to the hospital." Dani scrunched her face in disbelief. "Chaco gave her a really hard time about the administration office not being locked."

Miguel's eyes widened. "¿De veras? No lo sabía. I didn't know that. That explains why she looked…well…almost scared. I asked her about it but she wouldn't tell me what was going on. I called her later last night and again today to check on her but there was no answer. I left messages. I even called others at the hospital to ask if they had seen her but everyone said no. I called the police this morning. They insist on twenty-four hours before they will act. They think, 'oh a young single woman, she is off having some fun.' But Zapa is not like that."

Dani nodded. "Miguel, I have some news about Zapa and it's not good."

Miguel's face darkened. "¿Qué, qué? Dime."

"A friend of ours got a call with a message for us. The caller said Zapa was taken as a hostage in exchange for a file she took from the administration."

"Ay dios, no no no. Mi amiga."

"We were warned not to involve the police. But honestly, the way things are going, we may not have a choice. Has anyone called you asking questions about Jo or me or Zapa or some medical files?"

"No. I have received no calls about you or any files. But the reason I wanted to talk to you is this." He held up a folded paper. "It is from Zapa. When she came into the cafeteria the last time she said if I see you, to give you this."

"Zapa left this for me?"

"Sí, sí. She told me it was the address for her gym."

"Her gym?"

"Sí. Mira." He opened the note. "Gimnasio Greco. Calle Cristo de la Misericordia 10 Bajo. And she added this." He pointed to some words and numbers: Número 224. L1 R4 L25. "Quizá es la combinación de su taquilla, uh, a locker." Miguel glanced back at the bar. "Ay, Dani. The manager is starting to pace. We have some big reservations coming in soon. I do not know how I will be able to work knowing this. I am heartbroken. But thank you for telling me. What can I do?"

"Honestly, I don't know. But if we think of something, we'll call. Right now time is running out and we have to meet some guy at a bar later tonight."

"Be careful and remember, I am here all evening. If I can do anything, anything at all, call me. I will simply walk out and go wherever you want." He stood up and started to walk away but turned back. "She said you would not forget about her."

"Really? She said that?"

"Yes. No offence, Dani, but I said to her, *ellas son turistas solamente*. They are only tourists. I told her to be careful putting herself at risk for you. But she said, 'I believe in them. They need help. They would help me if I needed it. I know it.' Those were her words. Exacto."

Back in the car, Dani relayed the conversation.

"That was a leap of faith for her," said Jo.

"I just hope we don't let her down."

"De acuerdo," said Tomás. "I agree. And since our investigating time is quickly diminishing, perhaps we should split up. One of us will check out the gym while the other two go to the meeting?"

"No, no," Jo said vehemently. "We stay together. Besides, it's now just after seven. If we get to the bar around eight, that's early enough to get in position. So we've got at least an hour."

"Good, because we *have* to check out why Zapa is directing us to her gym," said Dani. "It could affect how we handle this exchange at the bar."

"The gym is close by," said Tomás, starting the car. "We should be able to manage it."

The night manager of Greco Gym escorted Dani and Tomás to Zapa's locker.

"When did Zapa usually work out here?" Dani asked.

"Because we're open twenty-four hours, she worked out around her shifts," he said. "But most often she came on Saturday and Sunday plus a couple of evenings during the week. She was here yesterday."

"Really?"

"Yes. In the evening. Around nine. I haven't seen her today, though."

"She left a phone message that sounded urgent but we haven't been able to get hold of her," said Tomás. "And she left us this note with another friend around six yesterday evening. We came to check it out. We are very concerned because her phone message was, well, worrying."

"I understand. I don't normally allow anyone to open someone else's locker. Thank you"—he nodded at Tomás—"for allowing me to check your reference with Viviana and with the Hospedería. Both confirmed that you are who you say you are. I don't know Viviana personally, but I certainly know the people of the Hospedería. My family is from Palomares and my father met the Duquesa. She was a good friend of Palomares."

While Tomás and the manager chatted about what Isabela had done for his hometown, Dani opened the locker. A blue satchel was inside. She took it and closed up the locker. Tomás was now completely engrossed in a trip down memory lane with señor Gimnasio. Dani put her hand on his elbow and squeezed a wordless "let's get out of here." He understood.

"Ah, sí. Pues, Sr. Calixmo, we thank you for your help. Muchísimas gracias," he said as Dani steered him back to the main door and out of the building.

"Geez, Tomás, you two definitely got into it."

"Yes. He used to live near the village where that hydrogen bomb was accidently dropped from an American military plane. I was telling you about that. What the duchess did? Remember?"

"I do." They left the gym building and walked over to the car. "When was that, Tomás?"

"It was in the mid-sixties."

"I read somewhere that there was an accident like that back home. Some bomb fell off a US plane over a small town in Quebec. But that was in the fifties."

"¿De veras? Really?" They continued unabated as they got in the car, Tomás turning to include Jo. "Well, the damn bomb is still in the ground in Palomares leaking radiation it's said. It's still a big issue diplomatically between the U.S. and Spain and—"

"Uh, excuse me. Sorry to interrupt, Tomás," Jo said, staring at the blue bag, "but is this about the bag?"

"No, Jo, no."

"But it *is* information that will help us find Zapa?" Tomás shook his head slowly. "No?" Jo said, confirming his response. "Okay then, it can wait. Let's go."

He squinted at her, his mouth opening and closing as if his brain had short-circuited.

Dani cocked an eyebrow at Jo and turned to Tomás "Jo is very smart and *very* focused. Some call it rude."

He looked back and forth at the two of them.

"Drive," Jo ordered.

Dani cracked a very small smile.

CHAPTER SEVENTEEN

Plaza San Antonio was filled with people, mostly locals, reveling in spring, Andalusian style. They were crammed around outdoor tables topped with tipsy umbrellas, colour-coded for the various cafés and bars on the square. Orange for Mama Pronto. Red for Bar Casino. Blue for El Serranito. Green for La Prensa. Dani pointed to the black awning on the other side of the square: El Gato: Vino Jazz Tapas it declared in big white letters.

This was the Spain of Dani's dream vacation, hanging out on a plaza like this, a convivial place surrounded by gaditanos, where they could kick back after a long hot day at the beach, drink and eat, catch the amazing Gerardo Nuñez performing at that little jazz joint right over there, the place she'd booked before the working dinner detour with Eddie.

She smiled to herself, imagining Zapa and Tomás there too, how they would all sit down together and how Dani would jump up at some intoxicated moment and declare in her biggest on-stage voice: "Te saludo, Cádiz. ¡Qué bellísima!" Jo would of course be appalled at such public antics and pull her back down into her seat. Tomás would roll his eyes. Zapa would cover her mouth and rock with laughter.

But no, this was no vacation in paradise. This was a vacation in hell. There was no boisterous laughter, no washing away the fear with too much tinto. Zapa was out there in the hands of... someone.

They'd taken a quick look inside her gym bag. All in all, disappointing. Just a bunch of clothes and on top, a note that didn't reveal much in a quick read. They'd have to give it a better look later because now, their deadline loomed. The meeting with the intern. Dani realized she was walking into it with no more information on Zapa's whereabouts than they'd had back on the Sanlúcar highway. With a cold knot lodged in her chest, Dani headed inside Café Bar El Andaluz. The meeting place.

The room was dark as if all joy and light were squeezed out of it. *Damn. The kidnappers picked a good spot.*

She had about twenty minutes to spare, time enough to suss out the place. Dani picked a table in a corner, her back against the wall, a small bag on the floor secured between her feet. Her heart was racing. Her mouth was dry. She studied the room, wondering if the intern was there already, wondering who else might be about, wondering how she could ever gain control of this meeting.

An unexpected trumpet riff cut the air. Dani jerked at the sound and then relaxed. Just the bartender trying to liven up the joint by upping the volume. She saw Tomás come in. He headed to the bar, leaned against it and ordered. She was comforted by his presence and the fact that another small part of the plan had fallen into place.

She went back to surveilling the crowd from her dark corner like some night creature, eyes glittering from its hidey hole. No one seemed curious about her. She thought about the intern. He would take delicate handling. She had to strike the right tone, sound conciliatory but not weak. She must show strength. She hoped Zapa was close by so they could get to her quickly once the deal was done. Where could they have stashed her?

She saw a young man in a wrinkled white shirt and red tie come in. He headed for an empty table near the bar. She glanced at her cell. It was exactly nine. He was short and chunky and looked exhausted. He dropped heavily into the seat while calling out to the bartender for una botella. He pulled out his phone and punched in a number. Dani looked around to see if anyone answered the call, but he'd already snapped the flip cover shut, the conversation over before it began. He chatted up the waiter who was uncorking the wine. A call came in on his cell. He answered and got into a heated exchange, gesticulating with his free hand while pulling at his tie to loosen it. She decided to get closer to him so she could hear what he was saying. She put on her sunglasses, tucked the bag under her arm and started walking across the room.

First problem. She couldn't see. She wanted to stay more or less incognito if only to confirm he was the intern. The glasses however might be her undoing. She moved slowly around tables and chairs, trying not to fall over something or someone. She managed an acceptably nonchalant walk-by of the man. He looked up and away, ignoring her. When she reached the bar, Dani grabbed it, grateful for the mooring, ordered a tempranillo to make sense of her trek across the room and tuned her ear to the cell phone conversation now going on at the table next to her.

Second problem. She could only understand the useless bits, exclamations and various conversational connectives. But the rest of it, the meat of it, was all a blur of rapid-fire Spanish. *Idiota. When will you remember you're trying to eavesdrop on Spanish.*

Her self-harangue was cut short by two words. "Clínica Ortega." So, he *was* their guy after all.

She glanced down the length of the bar to catch Tomás's eye. She gave him a subtle nod, took a couple of sips of wine and shuffled back across the room and into the washroom. She doffed the bandana and sunglasses and stuffed them in the bag. She pulled off her T-shirt, put on the blouse Zapa had given her so long ago and looked at herself in the mirror.

"Okay. This one's for you, Zapatista."

She strode back across the room all brassy and bold in tight gym pants and blouse, extended her hand and gave him her best "hi there" smile. "Bueno, señor. Me llamo Dani. Y usted?"

He snapped the phone shut, jumped up awkwardly, knocking over his chair, and took her hand. Clearly, he was not expecting such an aggressive approach.

"Bueno. Dani. Me llamo Luis."

"The intern, I presume?"

"Sí, sí, señora." He gave her a quick nod, leaned over to right his chair.

"I hope you speak English," she said with a strident tone. She wanted to have the upper hand.

"Sí, sí, yes. I speak English, well enough, I hope. I have been required to meet with you and collect the files. I am an intern, not a spy. But la doctora asked, well, insisted I do this. So I am here."

"Come on, Luis. You're up to your eyeballs in this. I'm not an idiot."

"Pues, claro, señora, of course you are not an idiot. But I do not know what you believe I am up to my eyeballs in. You are making me very nervous."

"Fine. You're nervous. So let's get on with it, shall we? Tell me where Zapa is."

Luis looked everywhere but at her. "Zapa? Who is Zapa?"

"Come on, Luis, she works at Clínica Ortega and she's been missing for over twenty-four hours. You know all about her. She's why we're here. So don't give me that shit."

"No, no, señora. I assure you I do not know her. I am only here to receive the files you stole."

Dani squinted at him as she tried to figure whether he was really this ignorant about what was going on or lying to protect himself. "Look," she said, making herself chill and give him the benefit of the doubt temporarily, "it's a debatable point if taking one's own medical records is stealing, but I won't get into that." She softened her voice and leaned into him. "I came here to make a trade: the file for Zapa, who we were told, is being held by your people. That's the deal."

"But, señora, truly, I do not know about any missing woman. I am sure I would remember this name Zapa. It is unusual, yes? However, I do not have any idea who she is or where she is, I assure you. As for the files, many were taken from their rightful owner, el Grupo Ortega, and I was told you would give them all back."

"You're full of shit, Luis." The intern startled at her changed tone and leaned away. "There is only one file and you know exactly who Zapa is. And if you want the file, we need to know where Zapa is. It's that simple."

"I do not know what is going on, if you are saying this Zapa is missing. I work at Puerta del Mar and I only help la doctora Nieves from time to time. It is usually help of the medical kind, but this morning I received a message from her asking me to pick up files here at El Andaluz. I was told to meet you here at this time and that you would give me the files. I was told not to ask questions. That is all I know. Truly. I do not know anyone named Zapa and I have no idea where she is."

Dani tried another tack. She put her hand on his arm.

"Look, Luis. I'm not here to get you into trouble. You take the Hippocratic oath here in Spain, don't you? That you have to swear to as a doctor? Isn't that right?"

He nodded slowly, watching her closely, like one watches a prankster, expecting a trap.

"What is that oath, Luis?"

"Do no harm."

"Well, Luis, there *is* harm happening to some people and *you're* part of it. A couple of former patients of Clínica Ortega, in fact. One is out of there now and safe. But the other one is dead. And of course there's Zapa. So, Luis, if you honour your oath, you will tell us what you know about where Zapa is."

"Señora, I say to you again that I was told to get the files from you. Six files to be exact. No one gave me any information about this Zapa person to pass on to you. I realize they are somewhat, uh, taciturnos…"

"Taciturn?"

"¡Sí, sí!" He managed a strangled laugh at the similarity in words, but clearly did not feel the humour. "They are indeed taciturn at the Clínica. Mucho más, uh, much more than at Puerta del Mar. Information is hard to come by. I count on other staff to tell me what's going on. The best place to find things out is in the cafeteria. And of course, the laundry. Cierto. They know everything down there. Isn't that strange?" He expected an answer.

"Excuse me?"

"Ay, lo siento. I'm sorry. It is only that I find the Clínica a difficult place to work compared to Puerta. They joke about it, the staff, that those women in the basement laundry have more information than bedclothes."

Dani frowned. "What are you talking about, Luis? Don't play me."

"Señora, it is the truth. I know nothing about any Zapa. I am only trying to help."

He stared at her bag, which she held securely at her side.

"Please, just give me the files you have and I'll leave now. I am too tired to continue." He pulled out his cell phone. "Otherwise I must do as instructed and let my contact know this meeting has failed."

This was the moment. If she didn't give him the file, he'd make that call to god knows whom. And who knows what would happen to Zapa. Dani couldn't decide what to do. She stood up.

"Look, Luis, let me check with my friends before you make that call. I'll be fast, I promise."

He stood up too. He didn't say anything, but he looked at her, his eyes narrowed. Dani wondered whether he'd understood what she'd said. Maybe he was going to try to grab the bag.

"Please, Luis, just a few more minutes?"

He came out of whatever daze he was in.

"Friends?" He looked around, concerned. "I didn't know anyone else was here with you. But okay. Please don't take long."

Dani picked up the bag and headed toward the exit at the back, moving into the shadows as soon as she could. She looked back at Luis. He sat down, took a sip of wine and tapped the screen on his cell phone. She swore quietly and headed for the door as quickly as she could. One more glance back added to her panic. Two men had walked up to Luis's table. She exited and walked briskly along the side street. It was dark and silent. *Get to the car. It's just around the next corner.* A quarter of the way down the block, footsteps sounded behind her. She picked up her pace. *Stay calm. Don't panic. Just a passerby. They couldn't have caught up to you that fast.* The footfalls sped up and her brain finally screamed.

Run.

And she did, as fast as she could, but her pursuer gained on her. Now he was close behind her, a faceless entity breathing hard. She was terrified but couldn't make her feet move faster. A hand struck her back and she was shoved into a store doorway.

"Dani, it's me. Tomás," he hissed through clenched teeth.

"What?" she said, trying to turn her head. "Tomás?" He pushed her hard into the wall. She could scarcely breathe.

"Shhh. Be quiet," he whispered.

Seconds after they'd ducked out of sight, she heard running and shouting, getting closer and closer. Tomás eased his hold on her and she looked over his shoulder. Two men ran by so close she could hear their clothes rustle. They were the same two who'd entered the bar to talk to Luis.

"Jo. If they see her…" Dani whispered.

They kept still until the footsteps were gone, then hurried toward the car, staying tight against the walls of the buildings. The car was dark. It looked empty. She tried the door. Locked. She knocked on the window, calling softly to Jo. Her stomach turned. She wasn't there. And all of a sudden, she was, popping up from the car floor like a jack in the box. She opened the doors for them and they jumped in. Tomás started the car while Dani and Jo ducked down out of sight.

"Good idea," he said. "Stay down, both of you. If they see only me, we should be all right."

"I heard people running. Who was it?" she asked.

"Part of Nieves's gang, I'd say." Dani's words were muffled by her facedown position on the floor. "Goddammit I'm tired of being chased. And, Tomás, thank you for pushing me into that doorway. But I gotta say, you scared me to death."

"I am very sorry, Dani," he said, slowing to take a tight corner. "I couldn't risk calling out."

"Fill me in, you two. What happened in there?"

Dani rolled onto her side. "Luis is either a liar, a complete idiot or a pawn who knows nothing," she said. "Or maybe he's part of some bizarre double cross. He kept talking about files, plural. Said we were supposed to have six files to hand over. And he claimed he didn't know who Zapa was. He had no info to give us, other than telling me about his arrangement with Nieves."

"Did you give him my file?"

"No," said Dani, voice rising, annoyed. "I wasn't giving it up for nothing."

"Sorry. It would be understandable. It wasn't a criticism." Jo reached for her hand, awkwardly, across the drive shaft hump in the floor.

"I know. I'm a bit stressed."

"We are left with the file and still we know nothing about where Zapa is," said Tomás.

"And I would say the fact that those guys came after us means there is never going to be a trade, the file for Zapa."

"Yes, Dani. I also believe we must not meet with anyone connected to the Clínica again," said Tomás. "They are too much for us. We must regroup."

Tomás drove south for a few minutes and pulled into a parking spot just before their road teed into Avenida Campo Del Sur that ran along the coast. Dani and Jo groaned as they emerged from their hiding spots on the floor. They grabbed Zapa's bag and scrambled after Tomás who waited for them at a gate in a wall surrounding a house. He swiped a fob over a pad and the gate clicked open. He led them through the garden to a side door where he punched numbers into a keypad. They walked into a bachelor apartment with a living/bedroom and a galley kitchen.

"This is owned by a supporter of el Centro and available for our use. We can rest safely here for a while."

"Oh yeah. Grateful," said Dani, flopping down on the couch. "Now, let's get a better look at that bag."

Jo sat next to her. "Start with the note, Dan. We need to figure out what Zapa was trying to tell us."

Dani pulled it out and began reading it loud. "'Queridas. Si están leyendo...'" She paused and started over, translating as she went. "'My dear friends. If you are reading this note, I must be gone. Hopefully I am only missing and not dead.' Smiley face. I can't believe she put a smiley face in a note about her possible demise. Tomás, here." She passed the paper to him. "I think you should read it. You might notice something in the Spanish..."

"Yes," said Jo, "and we should break it down, word by word this time."

He took the note. "Bueno, but it's all very vague, as you know." He stared at it briefly and began. "After the 'not dead' part, she says, 'I say this because I now realize that these people are capable of anything. I believe they have followed me since you left town this morning. I am afraid to go home. If you go back to the hospital, my ID and keys and some other things are here to help you. Please say hi to the women in the laundry. They work in the basement where the lockers are.'"

"What is it with those women in the laundry?" Dani asked. "That's the third time I've heard about them today, from Miguel, who said Zapa took cookies to them and from that fucking intern Luis who went on and on about how poor communication is at the Clínica, and now Zapa."

"She continues, 'And there is also Descubrimiento Tres for a view of the port area.' She added her signature too. And that's it." Tomás handed the note back to Dani. "I don't see anything unusual in the language itself. But it's clearly some sort of message."

"Okay then. Let's break it down. This laundry in the basement. Have you ever seen it, Dan?" asked Jo.

"Nope. But we walked right by the entrance to it when we left the hospital."

"This is a rather common thing, is it not?" asked Tomás. "In a large institution where official information is scarce, gossip abounds. Everyone ends up talking on their breaks, speculating about what's going on."

"Right. Zapa told me that's why Miguel knows so much. People chatter away right in front of him like he's not there. But the laundry? I mean who hangs around the laundry, aside from the actual workers?"

"True. But everyone uses the lockers. See?" said Tomás, leaning over her to point to a line on the note. "She said, 'where the lockers are.' I'll bet that's a clue. Another part of the puzzle."

"Good catch. She already used one locker to leave us stuff. Maybe she's got a locker in the basement with another message? That means, of course, we have to go into the hospital to find out."

"I strongly suggest we put that bad idea on the back burner. Go back to that big word, des…des-cub…?"

"¿Descubrimiento tres?"

"Yes. What does that mean?"

"It means discovery." Dani turned to Tomás. "Discovery three, right?"

"Yes. It could be an address too. She says, 'for a view of the port.' There is an Avenida de Descubrimiento near the port. It is an odd area." He took out his phone and pulled up a map. "Aha. Descubrimiento Tres is a Cádiz address and it appears to be very close to the office of la doctora."

"You're kidding. Any idea what it is?"

"By the look of it on street view, it's an old warehouse. That could be out of date, of course, but there are a lot of those types of buildings around here."

"It's still worth checking out. Okay, let's leave the note for now. What else is in the bag?" Jo reached in and pulled out a gym suit. "Not surprising. Oh, but look. It's her blue hospital uniform. Now why would she leave that in here?"

"We've got to speed this up." Dani said, taking the bag. She tipped it over and dumped its entire contents on the couch. Out fell a can.

"Pepper spray," said Tomás.

Followed by a set of keys, a sturdy canvas pouch about the size of a toiletry bag and a hard plastic strip that held six bullets standing upright. Dani held it up. "Shit!"

"One guess what's in that small bag," said Tomás.

Dani picked it up, surprised at its heft. She opened the zipper. "Fuck!" Dani pulled the gun out slowly, two fingers around the metal grip. "Do you know guns?" she asked him.

"Barely."

She held it out to him.

"That actually meant I know nothing," he said, taking it gingerly from her hand.

"Is it loaded?"

He pointed it away from himself and the others, pulled the top of the shaft back and looked into the small opening on the top of the chamber. "No. No bullets inside. She must have felt very unsafe to have all this," said Tomás. "You don't obtain a gun last minute, at least not legally."

"She never let on that she was in so much in danger that she'd carry a gun. Well, not before all this."

"Until we came along, that is, and put her in even more danger," said Jo. "If she was being followed or something, how did she manage to stash the bag?"

"The gym was her regular workout spot," said Dani. "Anyone following her wouldn't think anything of it. But she left her credentials and uniform here too. That's gotta mean that she left the bag after her last shift at the hospital."

"That was yesterday morning, right?"

"Right. Miguel told me he saw her later, around six that evening, remember? Although she didn't really need her ID to go to the cafeteria."

"She would if she went to the laundry, wouldn't she?"

"That's right. Miguel told me she bought some pastries or something to take down to the laundry."

Tomás shook his head. "We know she called Eddie around seven saying she was worried. That was after she went to the hospital."

"So, something happened at the hospital to put her in emergency mode, calling Eddie, stashing this stuff at the gym. Maybe she even thought she'd get back for the bag if everything was okay," said Jo, "but she never made it."

"They grabbed her," said Dani. "That must have been after nine because she showed up at the gym around nine. It means Mr. Gym Guy…"

"Señor Calixmo."

"Yes. It means he was probably the last one to see her."

No one spoke. Tomás started tapping his phone.

Jo reached over and picked up the gun. "If we assume she added the gun to the bag for us to find, she must have figured we needed it more than she did."

"And it leaves us with a decision," said Dani. "Are we ready to carry a gun? Or rather, are we ready to use one?"

"I am," said Jo without hesitation.

"Well, I'm not."

"Come on, Dan. I'll bet you wish you'd had one in Jerez Station."

"I had a gun once. A rifle."

"You never told me that."

"Yeah, well, it wasn't a good experience. I totally freaked myself out. I thought someone broke into my house and I was too afraid to go downstairs and check. I sat upstairs all night with the fucking rifle loaded, ready to blow someone's head off. I discovered the next morning that some books had fallen and knocked a glass off a shelf. The shattering glass made the one sound I'd figured someone would have to make to break into the house. Just having that rifle in my possession took me to a 'stand-off' mentality. I decided two things after that: I'd always check things out before hitting the alarm and I did not want a gun."

"Okay I get it, Dani. But this is a bit of a different situation. This is not some hypothetical risk. We *know* Zapa's in big trouble and she clearly thought we needed a gun. Which leads me to think that we should, pardon the expression, bite the fucking bullet and carry the damn thing."

"There is another problem here, if I may interject," said Tomás. "I am not certain of this, but I imagine as foreigners you are not allowed to carry a weapon. However, even if you are, you will, without a doubt, be required to follow the same rules as Spaniards, which is primarily that you must be licensed, which you are not. So, if you continue to hold on to the gun, you are probably committing a crime, which incidentally, makes me an accessory to a crime. I can be disbarred for much less. Also, I have just texted Viviana, updating her on what has happened. She has indicated before this that she is uneasy about the direction we are going, meaning this kind of thing, active engagement, is not our role at el Centro. I can almost guarantee when she hears about the gun, she will say that it is all too much for me to be involved. She will want us to turn the whole case over to the authorities."

"What are you saying?"

"Pues, mis queridas amigas, it means that, if you keep the gun, I will not be able to help you find Zapa."

"You're saying we have to choose: the gun or you?" asked Jo.

"Oh my god, Tomás. You can't leave us."

His cell phone buzzed. He checked it and looked up. "Bueno. It is now official. Viviana is saying she cannot risk my reputation and the reputation of el Centro. She is quite emphatic about it, with regrets to you both."

"We can't give up the gun," said Jo.

"Jo, really?" said Dani, looking at her with astonishment. "If we had a little time, maybe we could get a license."

"No," said Tomás, "there is not enough time to deal with bureaucracy. It would most likely take a few weeks for anyone applying for a gun license, even me, a Spaniard. Background checks and so on."

"What if we put it in the trunk, not on our persons?"

"That is just as much against the law. One, it's Consuela's car which would involve her. Two, as a lawyer it would be an issue for me. I *know* there is an unregistered gun in the vehicle. And three, perhaps lo más importante, Viviana said no. Besides it is not just the gun. As I said, it is the investigating as well. And I know you aren't ready to give that up."

"I don't know if we can do this without you, Tomás."

"Yes, Dani. You can. And I am proposing to Viviana that I stay in Cádiz and monitor but from a distance."

"Damn."

CHAPTER EIGHTEEN

"I can't believe Tomás is gone. I got used to him being our…our insider legal guy." Jo sighed.

"Not to mention our ride," Dani interjected.

It was early Tuesday morning, still dark by the ocean and quiet but for the screeching of hungry seagulls and the soft-hard cadence of joggers' shoes hitting the sidewalk. Few cars were on the road and not a cab in sight. They'd eaten and caught a few hours of restless sleep before they'd parted company, Tomás retreating to his car and Dani and Jo heading off on foot.

Dani touched Jo's arm. "But he's not really gone, you know. Just keeping his distance."

Jo turned and placed her hands on Dani's shoulders. "So it's up to us. *We* just have to find her ourselves."

Dani stared into Jo's eyes and finally, nodded. "You do realize what the next step is?"

"Yes. The hospital. The very idea makes me shake."

"Which is why you aren't going. Just me." Jo's mouth opened to speak but Dani held her hand up in front of her. "No. There is no debating it. Let's use our energy to find a ride instead."

"Look," Jo said, pointing to the corner. A white vehicle was moving slowly in their direction. "It's a taxi." They started to wave at it but stopped when they noticed the roof top sign declared the car "ocupado." It kept moving forward until it pulled alongside them and stopped, its driver unseen behind windows awash in sunrise gold. Slowly, the glass lowered.

"Buenos días, señoras."

The driver's green eyes gleamed from his dark brown face, his chin glistened with silver bristles.

"You are Dani and Josefina?"

"Yes?" Dani answered, voice trailing up, laden with suspicion.

"I am here at your disposal. Where would you like to go?"

"But your sign says 'ocupado.'"

"Yes. Ocupado, a sus órdenes. Occupied by you. My cab is at your service for the day. Gracias al señor Tomás."

Dani looked up and down the street. *So you're still with us.* She smiled and got in the back seat.

When they reached El Popular, they left the cab waiting and hurried inside. The place was starting to feel like home to Dani, the faces of workers and students almost familiar. She led Jo to a table near the back. Jo placed the gym bag beside her on the bench, keeping her arm through its straps. It was invaluable. It contained the original file plus a few clothes and the can of pepper spray. Tomás had taken the copy of the file, just in case. And the gun wasn't there. They'd agreed to leave it, for the time being, at the safe house in a locked storage room until it could be returned to Zapa or if necessary, the police.

Dani went to the washroom, carrying the other bag, Zapa's blue bag, and hauled out her uniform. When she got back to the table, Jo looked her up and down.

"You look sadly authentic," Jo said with a smile.

The Zapa-size outfit proved a bit snug on Dani, the regulation above-the-knee-length skirt just skimming her butt, the short sleeves pinching her arm flesh and the cap slightly askew.

"I'll take that as a vote of confidence."

"Now it's my turn," said Jo, getting off her chair.

"What are you doing?" asked Dani.

"I'm going to change up my clothes. I figure I can make myself look different enough to get in unrecognized, like a visitor or something."

"No, no, no. You can't go back to the hospital. Come on, Jo. We already agreed on this. It's too dangerous for you. Besides, if we both go in, we'll stand out. And if they grab us both, no one would be left to find Zapa."

"Dani. If you go missing, there would still be no one left to find Zapa. To put that another way, if I have to choose between finding you or Zapa, I'm afraid Zapa's on her own. You are and always will be my priority."

"Okay. That makes it even more critical that you stay here so you *can* save me if it comes to that. Remember. To them, you're just the *kidney*."

"I really wish you would not say that."

"Pass me that can of pepper spray? It could come in handy."

Jo pulled out the can and gave it to Dani. She tried various spots on her body but the uniform was too tight. Finally, sighing and bending down below the table and out of sight, Dani slipped the little can under her breast.

"Thank god Zapa has a larger cup size than me. Room at the inn, as it were." She looked down, wondering if anyone would notice the deformed boob.

"I am not happy about staying here," said Jo.

"So who's happy? Our vacation is a fucking nightmare." Dani started to walk away but came back. She leaned over close to Jo. "I love you," she said, voice husky. She leaned in close and gave Jo a long slow kiss and a smile. "Hasta luego."

Dani walked out of the bar and past their cab driver, who didn't recognize her. At the main entrance to Clínica Ortega, she fell into step behind a couple of uniformed nurses heading inside. *Must be an early shift for the fourth floor.* She turned her head away from Pepito, a.k.a. Scrawny Guy, in his usual spot slouched against the ambulance. Next to him was a different partner, a stranger to her. *Chaco must be on special assignment, hunting us.* She shuddered and focused on the two in front, trying to appear "with" them. Together, they walked through the main doors and over to the elevator. She went past them and into the washroom. Once she heard the elevator door slide shut, she headed straight for the stairwell. Her forehead was covered in a sheen of sweat and her chest was tight making breathing difficult. She was afraid she might pass out. *Hang in there, kiddo.*

Once at the basement door, she slid Zapa's access card through the slot and the door popped open. She looked around for any new securities but saw none. She walked by a row of lockers and stopped in front of a door with a big sign—La Lavandería. The Laundry. After a brief hesitation, she used Zapa's card again. It was possible each swipe left an electronic fingerprint but it couldn't be helped. She pushed the door open.

It was a humid and noisy industrial world of high-gloss green walls, polished concrete floors, exposed pipes and ductwork, hissing valves and shouting workers. Dani steeled herself and approached the women standing amid giant roaring machines.

Two of them were feeding washers with armloads of dirty laundry and a couple of others heaved lumps of wet clothes into the gaping mouths of empty dryers. This was more staff than Dani had ever seen in the place. Their uniforms were different too, more standard issue than sexy getups. Some even wore pants. She smiled as they began to notice her, nodding and smiling back, accepting her as one of their own thanks to Zapa's staff blues. Dani approached the closest worker and yelled over the din, saying she was looking for Zapa. The woman beckoned Dani to follow her behind a large glass door, which when closed, dampened the noise.

"This is a busy place."

"Sí, sí," she said wiping her hands on her apron. "Estamos muy ocupadas ahora…" Yes, we are very busy right now.

"I didn't think the Clínica had enough patients to produce all this laundry."

"Oh, but we are not part of la Clínica Ortega. We are separate and belong to the public system. We are a centralized service, you see, to reduce costs. The laundry comes from the other facilities like Puerta del Mar. Also from some of the smaller care facilities in the city. Pues, you are asking about Zapa?"

"Sí, señora, por favor, I'm wondering if you've seen her lately."

"Claro. The last time I saw her was on Sunday afternoon. Late. Around five o'clock. Just before our shift ended."

"The laundry works all weekend?"

"Sí, sí."

"And Zapa was here, in the laundry?"

"Disculpe, señora. Who are you exactly?" She looked Dani up and down with skepticism. "Not a regular, by the look of the fit."

"I'm a friend."

"And what is your name?"

"Dani."

"Ay dios, Zapa mentioned you to me."

"She did?"

"Sí, sí. She said that Dani will come to collect the things in her locker. But I thought this was only if she took a trip or something. Dani, is everything all right?"

"Uh, Zapa may be in trouble. We don't know where she is and I'm trying to find her."

"She is missing?"

"Yes. We are very concerned for her safety."

"Ay dios mío. Bueno. Entiendo. Pues, como dije, like I said, she was here on Sunday and she was fine then."

"Señora, why was Zapa down here on Sunday? I didn't think she was working that day."

"She wasn't. She wanted to put some things in a locker."

"Right. One of the staff lockers out in the hall?"

"Yes. Most of them are outside the laundry room itself but there are a few here for our use only. Zapa said she wanted one of ours because they are more private here than in the main hall. We like Zapa and we gave her one."

"That was kind of you. And she used her locker every day?"

"You misunderstand, señora. She has a locker outside the laundry for her daily needs, just like the rest of the hospital workers. But this one, inside the laundry, she only took on Sunday. She made two trips down here that day. I remember because we were all very tired, only wanting to go home. But when she came down with the little chocolate-covered cakes and sweet tortas and pan de Cádiz from the cafeteria, we were charmed. It was fun. Like a party. But she came down a second time with a bunch of papers for the locker. She has not been down here since."

"She did all this on Sunday? Brought down treats *and* papers?"

"Yes. Exacto."

"I don't suppose you could show me inside her locker?"

"Lo siento, señora, but you need the key to open it and Zapa has it. Perhaps, for emergencies, someone in the building has a master key."

"Do you see it on here?" Dani asked, pulling Zapa's key ring out of her pocket.

"Yes, here it is. Ay, señora, qué suerte. How lucky. Zapa gave you these?"

"She left them for me and I'm trying to figure out why. Perhaps something inside the locker will help me understand."

The woman hesitated briefly, then nodded, taking the key to open the locker. On the door was a picture of Zapa's parents, whom Dani recognized from a photo at the townhouse. Below it was a small poster.

"Ismael Serrano," said the laundry worker, "a famous Spanish singer." And she began singing, gaining volume as she warmed to her performance:

Rebelión en Hamelin…No me seas conformista…
Acuérdate de vivir…Que no te engañe el flautista.

Dani's jaw dropped. The woman burst into laughter.

"Señora, perdón. I couldn't help myself. Ismael is very famous and much loved."

"Wow. Great performance, señora."

"Gracias."

"I'm surprised Zapa did all this on Sunday, got the locker and decorated it and all."

"Sí, sí. She came prepared. She had these things in her bag. She said it made it look more personal, less institutional. She is such a romantic."

Dani nodded. She looked down and noticed a pile of papers on the floor of the locker.

"May I?"

"Pues, if Zapa gave you her key, I guess she gave you permission to look at the contents."

The pages were stapled into sections. There were six of them each labelled "Técnicas de Limpieza." Cleaning Techniques.

"Have you ever seen these kinds of files before?"

"No."

"Could I take them? Would you have a problem with that?"

"Me? No. And since you're Zapa's friend, I'll even get you something to put them in. How about a laundry bag? We Marías have lots of those." She walked back to the main room, laughing softly and shaking her head at her own joke.

She came back and put the files into a worn canvas sack.

"If you don't mind my asking, what do you mean by *we Marías?*"

"That's something the management here calls us, the laundry staff that is."

"But I thought you said you didn't work for Clínica Ortega."

"We are employees of the public system and members of the union. But because we are in this building, we come under the company's immediate management around security and the use of the equipment. The Clínica is happy to have the basement space rented but they don't like us being here much. Maybe because we tried to unionize them upstairs." She smiled. "Ay dios mío, the owners were mad at us. Now, as a little token of respect I am sure, they refer to us as Marías. No names."

"Wow," Dani said, shaking her head.

"Ah sí, señora. We are María One, María Two, María Three and so on. I myself am María Five," she said. "But I don't care what they call me. I am just grateful I do not work upstairs. They are bad bosses."

"Yes, I've heard that."

"Oh yes. They are all casual workers. No regular jobs. And they can't wear pants, only dresses like yours. Speaking of which, yours is a bit off. Too small I think."

"Yeah, someone else said that too."

"You need a work bib. I have an extra one here."

She pulled one out of a drawer and helped Dani into it, pinning the front in place. "There, that's better. Covers the too-tight parts."

"Of which there are many," said Dani. She hoisted the sack on her back. Nurse Santa.

"Thank you, María Cinco," she said, squeezing the woman's arm lightly to emphasize the joke. "And if you hear from Zapa, could you tell her…." There was pounding on the glass. One of the other women stood there, jerking her thumb over her shoulder toward the metal door.

"Mierda. Someone is here."

A male voice boomed from the entrance to the laundry. Dani couldn't make out the words but she knew who the speaker was immediately.

"I'd like to get out of here without being seen. Is that possible?"

"Dios mío. Are you doing something illegal?"

Dani put her hand on the woman's arm and looked directly into her eyes. "I swear to you on the soul of Zapa's mother, whom she loved dearly, I am trying to help her." María Cinco hesitated before pointing to a door on the other side of the lockers. "Go through there and follow the hallway to your right. You'll have to wait somewhere until they leave. Maybe in the closet."

Dani nodded. "When it's safe for you, could you take this bag across the street to my friend?" She rolled the bag off her shoulder and held it. "Her name is Jo, and she's in El Popular waiting for me."

The man's voice was louder now, sounding as if he was in the main laundry room. Dani thrust the bag into María Cinco's hand. The woman shook her head and muttered something. Dani rushed out the door wondering if she'd ever see that bag again.

She sped down the hall to its end and found the closet, a hiding place for now. She squeezed in between mops, buckets and brooms, Zapa's stash no doubt, and closed the door just as heavy steps sounded along the concrete floor. There was a button lock on the doorknob, which someone had installed backwards. Dani pressed it.

The male voice was now yelling, "Catch that bitch. I want her. You hear me?"

Charming Chaco. Dani started to shake so hard her arm jerked, hitting something with a long handle in the closet. She cursed herself silently. The footsteps paused outside her door. The doorknob rattled. Chaco yelled again from farther down the hall.

"No, you idiot. Go to the rear exit. That's where she'll head." The footsteps pounded off, one set up the hall, the other down. The heavy exit door creaked open and closed with a thud.

She waited motionless, her heart pounding, scarcely able to breathe. After about ten minutes, she unlocked the closet door and pushed it open a crack, and then a bit wider so she could look in both directions. She eased her way out of the closet as quietly as possible, and hurried toward the exit door. She opened it and looked up. Someone's shadow fell across the concrete steps beyond the door. The "idiot" was guarding the back door.

She pulled back inside and took the stairwell up to the main floor. Leona was standing there, glued to her cell phone. Dani walked by her quickly, face averted. She made it out the front door and immediately headed for El Popular, hugely relieved to be outside.

"Buenos días, señora."

Chaco and Pepito stepped out of nowhere, grabbed her one at each elbow. She struggled to get free, but they just tightened their grips. She called out to a passerby, "Help me, please." But Chaco countered her words.

"Ignórela, señora. Ella está loca." He twirled his finger next to his head and spoke to Dani in his best caregiver voice. "Señora, cálmese. Todo está bien. Venga con nosotros, por favor." They hauled her to the ambulance, practically lifting her off the ground. Pepito opened the back door. Chaco pushed her inside, jumped in next to her, and speed-dialed someone on his cell.

"La tengo." I have her.

CHAPTER NINETEEN

They marched her from the vehicle without blindfold or restraint but held hard on both sides. She twisted under their bruising grips, struggling to be free. *But where will I run?* Derelict warehouses surrounded them and across the street, an empty parking lot. Further on, she caught a glimpse of waves smashing high over concrete sea walls. A river cruise ship was pushing its way into port, its merry whistle a harsh contrast to her terror. The damp, salty air anointed her face. Last rites.

They propelled her toward a building behind a building. Tres, said the sign. *Tres. Descubrimiento Tres. Discovery Three. Tomás was right.* Her eyes darted around, like an animal's mute plea before slaughter: *please—stop this—save me.*

Once inside the main door, they pulled her to the elevator. Pepito walked away when the door slid open. Chaco yanked her into the small box. The door closed and the elevator rose. There was no floor indicator to watch so she counted the pings on their way up. Five.

Okay great, Dani. Good intel. You know what floor you're going to die on.

He pushed her down a hall past solid-steel doors. He stopped at one, unlocked it and forced her inside. It was a sad little room dimly lit by sunshine leaking through a shuttered window, furnished with a small Formica table, a straight-back chair and a bare mattress on the floor. On one wall was a small fridge and a sink. The air was stale and hot.

"I'll be back, puta." *That word.* Whore. He slammed the door, his key turned the lock. She sank to the floor, her breathing hard and uneven. Something jabbed under her breast. The pepper spray. She shoved it under the mattress. Just in time. The lock turned again and the door swung open.

Not Chaco. A smaller person stood there, backlit from the hall. They approached, and smelled of lavender.

La doctora Nieves-Félix.

From her prone position, Dani reviewed the woman from the bottom up: comfy flats and form-fitting black jeans, a long white shirt open over a tight red camisole, black hair pulled back, exposing long gold-chain earrings that played nicely off her tawny, sun-kissed skin. Dani had never seen her close up. *She's quite attractive. Even in her warehouse warden get up.* They stared at each other, each assessing the other. *This would be a great time for a badass warrior angel appearance.* But Dani knew that might be a bit of a stretch in her current condition. Hair askew, blue uniform wrenched off-kilter, bib torqued high against her neck, legs splayed. More ragdoll than anything. *Damn. Not a good look for defiance.* She sighed. *Oh, what the fuck.*

"Finally. I get to meet the almighty doctora Nieves-Félix. Tell me, doctora, what do you want from me? Why have you kidnapped me?"

"Dani, Dani. Kidnapped. Such a strong word. You are not kidnapped. I only want to talk to you. I need you to tell me where my files are."

"File-zzz? As in plural, more than one? We only took one and that was Jo's medical file. She has a right to that one."

"You're lying. Six files were stolen from the administrator's office. Six and that does not include Jo's."

Damn. Six. The intern said six. Zapa stashed six in the locker. I sent those six to Jo. Six fucking files called "Cleaning Techniques" and they're going to get us killed.

"I don't have them. Ask Chaco. I was empty-handed when he grabbed me. Where is Zapa?"

"You should be more concerned for yourself. I am warning you, if you do not give me my files, it will not go well for you."

"Really? It's gone so well already. I was just mentioning what an amazing vacation it's been."

"It will be worse. Believe me."

"What the hell is in those files? Details of some nasty activities? And now that it's come up, why does a woman like you, who seems to have everything, looks, smarts, a medical degree no less and a busy little practice, great hospital, well potentially great—it's got some issues—why does a woman with everything hire a creep like Thug and run a place with essentially no staff, like it's a secret undercover operation or something. Is it? Illegal? Are you really that desperate for extra euros?"

Nieves walked to the other side of the room, leaned against the wall and folded her arms. She stared at Dani silently for about a minute.

"I do not explain myself to you, you pathetic *tortillera.*"

"A tortilla maker?" Dani remembered the pejorative. "Oh, I get it. You're saying we're not worthy of your concern because we're lesbians? Really?" She paused. *Must push harder.* "What about Benning? Nice het woman. What quality did she have that made her expendable? And what about Mary Anne? She can't be happy about the endless delays in her surgery. How's she doing, by the way?"

The smugness left Nieves's face.

Finally. A strike. Dangerous but oh, it feels good. Come on, Dan. Do it again.

"Oh yes. I know all about Mary Anne. Robards, isn't it? She's in from Chicago, right? Had a little chat with her in the hallway there when I was searching for Jo who you fucking kidnapped! You've got quite the sordid little racket going on there. You proud of your business model?"

"I am a healer."

Dani groaned. "A healer? You're delusional. You're a power-hungry, money-obsessed killer I'd say."

Nieves made a low sound in her throat, like a growl. Her fists clenched and unclenched. Dani was surprised.

She seems to care what I think? Why? Perhaps someone else called her a killer? A nurse? The widower Benning? Her kindergarten teacher?

"Why are you smiling?" Her mouth twitched. "Something amuses you?"

"You amuse me."

"Not for long, Dani, because you see, I am not delusional."

It's the word delusional that upsets her?

"I am a realist. I make the decisions that must be made to achieve success. It is rarely the easy path and this situation we find ourselves in is a case in point. Let me be very clear, Dani. If you do not give me my files, I will hand you over to some medical friends. They are not interested in talking or playing games. When they have finished with you, I will give you to Chaco who seems to be quite taken with you. After that, I will find Jo. Not a pleasant future for either of you, I assure you. So, I will ask you only one more time. Where are my files?"

Dani's bravado was seeping away. She had to switch it up fast before the dread nipping at her soul took over. Nieves had left the door open to the hall. Maybe she could make a run for it. But first there was the issue of getting on her feet without raising alarm. She leaned back against the wall and began slowly leveraging herself into a standing position, talking as she went.

"Honestly," she grunted, only partially for effect, "I don't know where those files are. And we only have Jo's and it's…" She groaned, further playing up her weak state. "Well, honestly? I don't have a clue where *it* is, either."

She was finally upright, pretending exhaustion at the effort while readying herself to head-ram the doctor—but Nieves moved first, calmly delivering a two-fisted punch to Dani's chest, knocking her to her knees.

Her windpipe closed. She couldn't inhale. She started to panic and tried rolling on her side to give her lungs room. All the while, she screamed silently at herself. *No. No. You can't stay down. Get up. Get up. Get up to breathe if nothing else.* She managed to push herself up again and suck in some air, all the while bracing for the next push down. It never came. By the time Dani was completely upright, Nieves had retreated to the other side of the room. Dani moved slowly over to the chair and sat down. While her breathing returned to normal, her mind scrambled for a next move. She looked over at her opponent. *Keep her talking.*

"Fuck"—Dani's voice was raspy—"you must have some powerful secrets in those files." She took a breath. "'Cause they sure have all you folks going crazy! I mean, worse-case scenario, the whole story gets out. Hey, did you hear? La doctora Nieves is running some kind of crazy clinic for the rich, kidnapping people and maybe killing a few through neglect at the very least. Who cares? They're only a bunch of ne'er-do-wells by your account, right?" Dani paused and took a few more breaths. Her thoughts began to clear. "But maybe it's not about *who* you mess with. Maybe it's about who you serve. Got some pretty high-up folks on your client list, do you? I mean a woman like you, you've gotta have great connections. So is that what the panic's about? Surely they'd help you if you got in trouble, like that lawyer guy in the bar? The one you gave the big bag of...what was it...more files? Or maybe money so you can make a run for it, or stash it away so you don't have to give up that cushy lifestyle you got goin' on."

Nieves strode across the room and Dani ducked. No punch this time. The doctor shoved her face up close.

"Óigame"—she spit out the word—"listen to me. There is nothing 'cushy' about my life. I built it all through sheer force of will with no help from anyone. I earned every single euro to put myself through school. I studied and worked two jobs while the rest of them went off drinking and dancing and fucking, knowing *daddy* would always take care of them. I endured endless sleepless shifts as an intern grunt. I did it all by myself and I earned my *lifestyle*. I deserve my house in Sotogrande. No one will take it away from me. Not you. Not them. Because I. Am. La jefa."

She inhaled deeply and exhaled, her eyes widening, as if suddenly aware of some inner bulwark breached. She backed away.

So this is the face of evil. Gorgeous, well-educated, clever and greedy.

"Well, *jefa*"—Dani's lip curled at the word—"your *reign* is about to end. Enjoy it while it lasts. Meantime, consider this. I don't *have* the files. I don't *know* where they are. And guess what, I'm your *only* chance at finding them. You need me *alive*. Capisce?"

Capisce? She'd never said the word before. Not once in her entire life. The fact that it flew out of her mouth now, when her very existence was at stake, almost made her laugh. But nothing was funny here and that ill-timed chuckle curled up in a corner of her brain to await a cheerier moment, after she was rescued perhaps, or, given the way things were going, in her next lifetime.

Nieves's face reddened. Her fists clenched and unclenched and when she moved this time, it was so fast Dani didn't have time to duck. Nieves smashed her knuckles into Dani's cheek. Pain burned through her skull as she dropped back to the floor. She stayed still this time, too afraid to move. Nieves walked out of the room, massaging a sore hand, and slammed the door hard behind her. The lock clicked.

Dani forced herself to crawl over to the corner. She propped herself against the wall. She needed that wall behind her. She needed to face out. Needed to see the door.

It crashed open. Chaco grabbed her with both hands and dragged her off the floor and onto the chair. His face zoomed in like a viper, first on one side, then the other, mouth open, wet tongue moving inside red cavity, breath sour. Recollections of Jerez Station. *But no peppermint.*

"You forgot to brush."

"¿Qué? ¿Qué dices? Óigame, cabrona. You think you are funny? They will sell you piece by piece to the highest bidder. ¡Ja Ja! And then, when it is done, if you are still alive," he said, trailing his finger lazily down her arm, "you'll be a little stump of a woman. Useful for some things still, perhaps." He let out a strangled sound, a snigger. That was the only word for it. A low, repulsive sound that made her stomach turn. She wanted to push back against his threats, show bravery and strength, but her resistance dissolved before his brutality.

They'd made him look a fool, he said. A couple of cunts. They'd made him look bad to la jefa. But she would pay. He bent close and spoke softly, a soothing tone that turned her bowels to liquid.

"Do you know how it feels when the knife enters the body? How the mind stops? How the heart squeezes and the lungs close down? You will, soon enough, puta. You will." He went on enthusiastically detailing her torture. He trailed his finger along her cheek. "If you do not please la jefa, she will let me take you on this painful journey." He let out a strangled sound, a laugh turned snarl that became a whisper. "I hope you never give them back, los archivos."

The files. The fucking files. Her thoughts came slow, mucked up. She couldn't quite remember why they were important. Maybe she never knew. *That's it. That's true. I don't know what's in those files. I don't even know where they are. I only know I don't have them. Jo does. And I don't know where she is.*

The realization that she *couldn't* give them what they wanted brought some relief. At least she wouldn't betray Jo and Zapa, because she couldn't. She dodged the thought that she would give them all up to save herself, if she could. Why torment *herself* when Chaco had that well in hand? Her fate was sealed. He would wield the knife. And she believed him, that he'd done it all before and was good at it.

He yelled more, kicked her chair, coming at her from every side. She put her head down on her arms but he didn't miss a beat, slamming his hands down on the table on either side of her head. She flinched at each strike, expecting the next one to make contact, waiting for that ham fist to hit. *Ham ibérico o serrano?* She was losing it until a thought pierced the chaos in her mind. She realized that, despite his bluster, he hadn't actually hit her yet. Not once. She dragged this idea from the muck, mulling it over until finally, she understood. *He's not allowed to hit me. Nieves will not appreciate a bruised and bloodied donor.* Her spirit wrapped itself around that tiny seed of hope.

A knock on the door gave him pause.

"Ay, hombre. Tranquilo. You're upsetting the others," someone yelled.

The others? There are others?

He leaned in close, his lips brushing her ear, hot moist puffs hitting her tiny aural hairs. "Hasta el próximo, puta." Until next time.

He left.

She stayed in place, paralyzed. Her ears still burned but kept working, tracking his steps down the hall, away from her door, away from her. She heard the elevator door slide open and closed. He was gone. Release.

She tried to stand but couldn't. She lowered herself off the chair to the floor and crawled back to her corner. She sat facing the door again and her thoughts drifted into a dark daze filled with images of Chaco pounding her, Nieves cutting her open and probing with tiny surgeon hands. She heard voices arguing in a language she didn't recognize. A woman cried out. *A dream. A nightmare.*

CHAPTER TWENTY

Dani lurched awake. *Where am I?* She felt pain, touched her cheek and winced. Nieves's punch. The room was suffocatingly hot. How long had she slept? Was it daytime still? Light leaked in along the edge of the closed shutter. Was it even the *same* day? She had no way of knowing. She looked around the room. She focused on the table and chair. She remembered Chaco's threats.

No. No. No. No. Only courage. You're only allowed courage right now. No dying in terror. So here's a thought. How about getting the fuck out of here?

She started deep breathing, focusing her mind on anything but her fear. If she was going to fight back, she had figure out how. And with what? And then she remembered it. She felt around under the corner of the mattress.

Hello, weapon.

She tucked the can of pepper spray under the waistband of her bib, and braced herself, armed and ready for her next ordeal. She prayed it wouldn't be Chaco. Her ears remembered his voice, the feel of his lips brushing her skin. But there was something else. Something good. Wasn't there? Something she heard? What was it? She remembered, the voice in the hall. "Shut up, Chaco. You're upsetting the others."

There are others. I am not alone.

For a chilling moment, she wondered if Jo was among the others. But she rejected the idea as too much to bear. It would bring her to her knees. Better to focus on Zapa and a group of nameless "others" all trapped in the same hellish warehouse. This gave her hope, somehow, that she wasn't the only one fighting for freedom. From this she could draw the strength to act and somehow get herself out of here. She stretched and massaged her cramped and sore limbs, and, for the first time, walked around her cell. She had to find a way out. *There has to be a way out.*

It was a depressing little room, about ninety square metres with a bathroom off to one side. The slatted metal hurricane shutter was locked down so opening the window was impossible. She squinted through the slats but could see only the brilliant blue Andalusian sky. Five floors up, she remembered. The idea of falling that far in order to escape overwhelmed her. She returned to her corner, dropped down on the mattress and studied the place from there.

The walls were painted yellow. It might have been cheery once but was now dirty and faded. It was even darker behind the mattress, where the heads and torsos of other prisoners had pressed back, staining the paint over time with sweat and anxiety.

She saw no vents for heat or air-conditioning or cooking. Apparently no actual living went on here. It was a blank room, save for the mattress, table, and chair. What looked like an old-fashioned milk delivery box was built into the wall next to the door but there was no handle. The main door was of steel. It too had no handle. There was no escape.

Stop thinking that way. You can not give up.

Dani got on her hands and knees and crawled around the perimeter of the room, checking every joint, seam, electrical outlet, anything that might be worked into an opening. To where? she asked herself. *It doesn't matter where as long as it's out of here. Just keep looking. There must be something.* She thought of the *others* and the voices she'd heard. Was Zapa here too? Maybe she could find her? She pushed herself harder. There had to be some way out of the room.

High up on the wall was a large tin plate embedded in the plaster. She pulled the chair over, reached up and tapped the tin circle. It sounded hollow. An opening for a stove pipe when the room was heated by coal or gas? *No, not gas, not this high up in such an old building. Coal. Had to be coal.* The opening most likely led to the roof or the side of the building. She had no tools to pry the plate off the wall. And even if she could, she herself would have to be smoke to waft her way to freedom through that small opening.

She checked the two drawers in the cupboard under the fridge and found them empty. She opened the fridge. There was a bottle of water. She grabbed it and drank with abandon, water spilling over onto her chest. She was surprised at her thirst. When she was sated, she continued her search.

She went into the bathroom. The mirror had been removed from a small medicine cabinet. *Not much need for primping?* Or perhaps to keep the occasional poor wretch from breaking the glass and ending it all. *Stop it, Dani.*

The handle to the medicine cabinet was also missing. She pried the door open. Empty. The tub and shower were old and rarely used, given the black mould munching its way along the grout. Plastic hooks hung empty from the curtain rod. She tried to take the rod down. It was fixed in place. Dani sighed. The place was escape-proof.

She looked back at the medicine cabinet. It was old-fashioned, made of flimsy tin with tiny pink flower decals climbing up the sides. Someone *had* lived here once and taken a small stab at pretty.

Screws held it to the wall. She grabbed it on either side and yanked. Nothing. She tried to wiggle it sideways. Was it wishful thinking or did it move? She repeated the motion and was sure that the fixture gave way ever so slightly. She started pushing and pulling the cabinet back and forth, back and forth, over and over, ignoring the tin edge cutting into her fingers and the fine dust drifting onto her hands, blood and sweat and plaster dropping in pink globs onto the sink. She stopped briefly to wipe off sweat and tears with the back of her hand and got back at it. One corner of the cabinet pulled completely away from the wall. She was exhilarated. That changed abruptly to fear. She'd made noise. *There are people around. And who knows what's on the other side of this wall. Another locked room? Or maybe freedom?* At that thought, she decided noise be dammed. She took an aggressive stance and imagined herself the strongest fucking woman in the world and began pushing and pulling the remaining corner still fixed to the wall. And then she froze. There was a noise at her door. A key was being turned in the lock.

"Señora," came a female voice. *Not Chaco.* "Tengo comida para ti." I have food for you. The voice seemed muffled, at a distance. "Venga," she continued. "You must eat and keep yourself healthy for the surgery."

Dani cleaned herself up as best she could, dust flying everywhere. She started choking and ran for the bottle of water in the fridge. The main room was empty and the door remained closed. The little milk box hatch was open, however, and a hand pushed through a carton of juice with a straw. "Toma, señora." Dani grabbed it, hoping she wasn't about to be drugged.

"Gracias," she whispered after her coughing jag subsided. "No estoy aquí voluntariamente, señora. Ayúdeme, por favor. *Help me, please.*" She was pleading to a hand, the hand in the milk box. The woman's face was still unseen on the hall side of the wall.

"Sí sí, señora, es lo que dicen todos aquí. That's what everyone here says when they realize it's time to give up their kidney. But they all get their money. I see them get it. I know they are okay. It's not so bad. You'll be sore but just for a while. And you will have your many euros. Don't worry. But you've got to stay healthy to get your money. So here. Eat, hija. Eat."

The hand passed through a small plate with cheese and bread and an orange. Dani took it.

"Señora, is there someone here named Zapa?"

"Pues, no sé cómo se llaman. Everyone here is new. Just arrived."

"She's a tall black woman, red hair, about thirty-five years old. Maybe you've seen her?"

"There are only two women here. A Sudanese woman and a Spanish woman."

"¡Qué bueno! Quizá sea la española. Please, if you wouldn't mind, could you ask her if she knows Dani? Tell her Dani is here too? What room is she in?"

"She is on the seventh floor. I don't know the room number and I am not supposed to deliver messages."

"Señora, we shouldn't be here. We never offered to sell our kidneys. They threatened us. They said they'd kill us. Please, help us."

The woman was silent and when she spoke, her voice had changed.

"Señora, I don't know what you're talking about. This is a residence for people who sell kidneys to rich people. It's a business deal. No killing. Really, señora, you've just had a bad dream. Eat your food and you'll be okay."

The hand pulled the little rope on the hall side of the box. The tiny door began to close.

Grab it. She moved, arm outstretched, fingers reaching forward. Too slow. It slammed shut and its lock clicked.

"Don't go, señora," Dani shouted. "Por favor, no me dejas. I'm frightened."

"Cálmese, hija," came the voice, muffled by the door. "All is good."

"What time is it? Can you just tell me what time it is? Please, please."

"It is about nine thirty in the morning."

"Is this your job?" Dani asked, pressing her cheek to the door of the box, desperate to hear and be heard by this unthreatening human contact a little while longer.

"No, señora, es un favor por mi hermano." I do this as a favor for my brother.

"Who's your brother? And maybe do you know when will my surgery be?"

"Ay, señora, I'm not supposed to say his name ever, so I can't answer that question. But I can tell you that surgery is usually a day or two after people come here. It depends on when the person needing the kidney arrives. They often come from far away, from another country. I have to go now. Buen provecho, good eating, señora."

The wheels of her cart rattled as she pushed it down the hall. Dani listened as she stopped and unlocked another milk box, spoke a few words and left. She heard the elevator door open and close. *That means the room with the other person in it is closest to the elevator. The room beyond the little medicine cabinet must be closer to the outside. Hopefully harder to hear any noise because I will get out of there.* She figured there were only two of them on the fifth. And Zapa was on the seventh. She would go to Zapa first, when she'd broken out and was free. The very word charged her. *Free.* She rushed back to the bathroom and attacked the medicine cabinet with renewed vigour. She tugged it back and forth, exhilarated by every micro-loosening from its moorings. Chunks of plaster fell into the sink and flew across the floor. After about twenty minutes, her arms ached so much she could hardly move them. She rested for a moment but then she lost it. She had no more patience. And where the patience had been, anger and fear welled up like lava from a volcano. She took hold of the cabinet once more and yanked the damn thing with all her strength, whisper-yelling, "fucking give" at the stubborn little fixture. It responded and came out in one piece so suddenly she practically fell backwards into the tub. Stifling another coughing jag from the dust, she put the cabinet down and ran to the kitchen for a drink of water, hurrying back to the bathroom to see what she'd accomplished.

A large piece of plaster had come off with the cabinet. Underneath was the wall's rigid frame: narrow wood strips running horizontally with hard white plaster bulging between the slats like icing on a layer cake. Old-style lath and plaster. Dani stood stunned. She needed a tool. She wound a screw out of the cabinet and started pecking at it.

This will take a lifetime.

But the more she scraped with her little screw, the more fell away from the wood frame. She started clawing at the small gaps she'd made, breaking off chalky chunks. She found a crack in one of the slats and widened it, prying it loose. She used the broken lath as a tool. Eventually, she reached the other room's wall and the backside of its layer of plaster hardened by age. She grabbed the screw again. She pecked away to make a hole. She saw light. It really was there. Another room. Since no one had sounded the alarm yet, she decided it was unoccupied. She began pounding the small hole with the lath stick. It broke. She switched to her running shoe. It was useless thanks to soft soles. She used her fists, flailing at it until she bled. Finally the plaster gave way. Peering through the hole she'd made, the size of her head, she saw a room like hers but with bright sun pouring through unshuttered windows.

She went back to pounding, grabbing and pulling off bigger chunks of plaster and longer strips of wood. It was hard to gain purchase because the hole was over the sink forcing her to lean over it. But she didn't stop, hell-bent as she was to get out of prison. When she'd cleared away enough of the wall's frame, she got the chair. She raised it behind her and swung as hard as she could into the remaining plaster and prayed no one heard nor cared. She climbed onto the sink and pulled herself through the opening. Its rough edges grabbed her bib and scraped her arms and legs. She didn't care. She allowed herself to fall into the other room with nothing to break her landing. She stifled a cry of pain, too giddy to care.

She lay there for a few moments to catch her breath, pulled herself up and went to the window. Below was nothing but a concrete pad, five stories down. There were no intervening roofs or fire escapes or balconies. She thought she could probably get the window open but that five-floor drop horrified her. And then there was the concrete waiting at the bottom. She went over to the door. She pressed her ear against it. Silence. She looked down. It had a knob. *Locked, no doubt.* She placed her hand around the hard metal and was shocked when it turned. She held her breath and pulled. It didn't move. She pulled harder. The door lurched open.

The hallway was empty. No sign of cameras. She closed the door behind her, ran to the stairwell at the end of the hall and dashed up two flights of stairs to the seventh floor. She started knocking softly on every door, whispering as loudly as she dared, "Zapa?"

At the third door, a male voice answered, "No, no está aquí. El próximo cuarto, quizá." The next room, perhaps.

Holding her breath, Dani knocked on the next door, calling again a little louder this time, "Zapa."

"Quien es?"

Dani's spirit soared at the sound of her friend's voice. "Zapa, it's me, Dani."

"Dani. Gracias a dios. Can you get me out of here?"

"Yes. Don't know how yet. But hang on. I'll find something."

"Please hurry," Zapa said, sounding uncharacteristically plaintive.

Dani took stock of the door. Like her own, it was steel with deadbolt and handle. No visible hinges or anything to pry open. She went down the hall, found a door next to the elevator. She tried the doorknob. Locked? No. Stuck. She grabbed it again and pulled hard. It gave way suddenly, throwing her against the opposite wall. Inside it was a classic utility closet offering her an old mop, a bucket crusted white from dried cleaning liquid, and a couple of nasty looking rags. Nothing of use. She turned from the door breathless with frustration and excitement and fear. She'd need either a blow torch or a key to open that door. She smiled.

"Hola, señora."

She found the woman bringing food on the third. At Dani's voice, the woman turned and blanched, face-to-face with a rogue donor.

"¿Cómo es que estás fuera de tu habitación?" How are you outside your room?

Dani pulled the pepper spray from her waistband and pointed it at the woman like a gun.

"Open that door," Dani demanded, jerking her head toward the closest door, room 303.

The terrified woman complied.

"Do you have a cell phone?"

She nodded.

"Give me your phone and your keys."

The woman held out her hand. Dani snatched phone and key ring and motioned her inside. A young man stood freeze-frame, staring at them holding a piece of bread loaded with cheese midway to his mouth. Dani pushed the woman further into the room and closed the door, locked it and ran back upstairs to the seventh.

Praying this was a universal key, she inserted it into Zapa's doorknob. *Yes!* The key worked. She pushed the door open and the two women embraced like long-lost sisters.

"Thank you for not forgetting me," whispered Zapa in her ear. Dani pulled her toward the door, but Zapa broke away to grab a pen from the table.

"What's that?"

"A pen. For the handwritten confession that I'd stolen the files."

"And you need the pen now?"

"Yes. To write a phone number. We must free the others."

Dani hesitated but one look at Zapa's face and she knew her friend was right. "Okay. Let's go."

They went for the man in the room next door first. Dani kept nervous watch.

"Cómo se llama, señor?" Zapa asked, as she hustled him into the hall.

"Hayyan."

"Bueno, Hayyan, me llamo Zapa. Dime por favor. Are you here to sell an organ?"

He looked at her with suspicion.

"I am not police or immigration or any kind of security. If you want to find out your options, here," Zapa said as she wrote a number on his hand, "call this place. They will help you without wanting anything from you. Pues, ándale, Hayyan, si quieres." Go, if you want to, she said to the bewildered-looking man.

They left him standing there deciding and ran up to the top floor, the eighth. They went door to door, checking each room. All were empty. They checked the remaining rooms on the seventh and the sixth floors. All empty. There was a woman on the fifth floor. Dani had heard her crying. Zapa repeated her message but it was unclear if the woman could understand. Zapa wrote the same number on her hand and said that was all they could do. They continued down to the fourth and finally the third floor.

They opened the door to the room Dani had forced the food server into, ready for anything. They found two people standing on opposite sides facing each other. They looked at Dani and Zapa with alarm and disbelief. Dani pointed the pepper spray at the woman while Zapa waved the man over.

"Come out. If you want to. We have a phone number for you to call for help." She kept talking until finally he moved toward them. She showed him the pen, grabbed his wrist and wrote down the number. He fled. They locked the woman back in and headed down to the second floor. All the rooms were empty.

"All right, Zapa, we have to get the hell out of here. Now."

Zapa nodded and they rushed down to the main floor. Dani placed the food server's phone on the floor in plain sight and they headed outside. They charged down the walkway toward the street when Dani stopped cold. About two hundred metres away, at the curb, stood Jo with Pepito and Chaco next to their ambulance. Dani couldn't quite figure out why Jo was there with the two men until she saw the gun in her hand. *What the fuck? Where did she get…Oh no.*

Dani watched horrified as Jo raised the gun and pointed it at the two men, holding them at bay. She leaned into the driver's side of the ambulance and grabbed the vehicle's hand-held mic and yanked, tearing it from the dashboard and throwing it on the ground. She barked something at them, and oddly, given her lack of Spanish, they both complied, even the dreaded Thug, dropping their cell phones on the ground next to two bags at Jo's feet, a gym bag and a gray laundry bag. Dani watched, mouth agape, as Jo directed Pepito into the driver's seat and Chaco into the back with a flick of the gun barrel. She aimed the gun through the back window and fired. By the screams, she'd figured Jo just shot Chaco. Jo seemed oblivious to her own action, yelling something at the two men and waving her gun around. The ambulance took off, siren blaring. Jo turned back toward the warehouse with such a ferocious look on her face that Dani stepped back involuntarily, bumping into Zapa.

Jo saw her, shoved the gun under her waistband at the back and ran up, pulling a shocked Dani into a tight embrace.

"Oh my god. Who are you?" asked Dani.

Jo was breathless. Was it from exertion or excitement at the act of shooting? Dani wasn't sure.

"You shot him. I can't believe you did that," Dani said, breathlessly.

"No choice. I needed them to go away. It motivated the little guy to get Chaco to the hospital. He's too dangerous to try to hold at bay for ever."

Dani crooked her head. "Uh, okay. Didn't know you had it in you. Anyway, later for that. Look over there. Look who I found," she said waving at Zapa to come closer.

"Zapa! Thank god. And take a look over there."

Jo pointed to the parking lot across the street. Dani saw a man standing there.

"Holy shit. It's Tomás."

Zapa started to wave, but Jo grabbed her hand. "Sorry, Zapa. He's here. He helped me. Found this place in fact. But he's in deep cover, you know what I mean?" Zapa's eyes narrowed. She looked confused. Dani nodded slowly, frowning slightly at this new covert Jo. "Hey, Dan," she said snapping her fingers. "You listening?"

"Uh, yeah. Yeah. Okay. We need to figure out next steps," said Dani, "definitely away from here."

"Over there," said Zapa, pointing to the port parking lot. Dani was about to object but Tomás had already disappeared. Zapa continued, unaware, "Do you have any money?"

Jo nodded. "A bit. There's some leftover—"

"Okay. Let's go," Zapa ordered, pointing to the port entrance.

"Could one of you take that?" Jo pointed to the laundry bag. "I've been lugging it around since that lovely woman brought it to me at El Popular."

"María Cinco," said Dani.

Zapa grabbed it. "Andamos."

They formed a line reminiscent of a forced march at double time like the French Foreign Legion—Zapa bounding along in front, the gray bag over her shoulder, Jo next with the gym bag, Dani in the rear. They jogged across the street, through a construction zone and into the parking lot.

"María who?" Jo asked over her shoulder, panting.

"The woman in the laundry," yelled Dani.

"Y qué bueno, that you found them," Zapa said without breaking the pace. "The files."

"The what?" yelled Jo. Zapa didn't slow down to answer until they'd run up the steps of the Port of Cádiz Maritime Building and charged through the main doors. She slammed on the brakes just shy of the ticket booth and took a moment to catch her breath.

"The files I took from the administrator's office."

"Oh my god, did they get me in a heap of trouble. I almost didn't survive."

"I am not surprised. They appear to be some sort of financial reports but they are labelled *Cleaning Techniques*. We do not have 'cleaning techniques' at Clínica Ortega." She made a snorting sound. "Why would the administradora have so many files on a topic that does not exist? They were in a pile under your file, Jo. They called to me, 'take us with you,' and so I did. Perhaps that was a mistake."

Dani snorted. "I don't know about a mistake but Nieves and crew kidnapped you and were about to kill me...for those files."

"Hopefully these files will help us end the horror at the Clínica. Now, please, give me the money and your passports."

Jo picked up the gym bag, rifled through it and pulled out the envelope and passports, which she handed to Zapa.

"What are you going to do?"

"Did you stay at the Hospedería?"

"Yes."

"Okay. I assume something happened that made you come back to Cádiz."

"You happened. We were on our way to Seville with Tomás who you seem to know. We were supposed to meet with the attorney general. When we found out you'd been kidnapped, we turned around and came here. We couldn't just leave you."

"Ay queridas, mil gracias por haber vuelto." Dear ones. A thousand thanks for returning.

"Zapa. After what you did for us, we would never leave you."

"Gracias. Gracias. And it appears that Viviana and el Centro understand how serious this crime is. It involves their clients as well I believe. Los refugiados."

"Absolutely. It was with them and Raúl that we figured out what was going on. It *is* illegal organ transplants, just not the way we were thinking before."

"Okay you two. We don't have time for this," said Jo. "What's next?"

"Bueno. This is how you must proceed. You are going to take that cruise ship over there," she said, pointing to a mini-ocean liner rocking in the water dockside. "It goes up the Guadalquivir River to Seville."

"The boat?" gasped Jo.

"Yes. It is an instant exit from Cádiz. They will not know. And they will follow me if they see me. When you arrive in Seville, you can go to the hospital or wherever you want to go. You must take the files with you. I'm afraid to take them. If they do find me again—"

"Understood," Dani said quickly and took the bag from Zapa. "But where are *you* going to go now?"

"I am going to find Miguel. He is in danger because they have my cell and I called him so many times. And I saw Tomás earlier, right? Or did I imagine him?"

Dani and Jo shook their heads. "He was in the parking lot watching the whole show," said Jo.

"Bueno. Tengo que encontrarlo. I must find him."

"We can text him to meet you somewhere," Dani said, opening her cell phone.

"Oh no, no. Do not use your cell phone. They can track us."

"No worries there, Zapa. Viviana gave us new ones. So they're safe to use."

"Okay. Tell him I will meet him at Café Crema. Then Tomás, Miguel, and I can go to Sanlúcar together."

"When you get a new phone"—Jo pointed to the pen in Zapa's hand—"text us your number."

Zapa nodded and wrote their numbers on her wrist as Jo recited them. "And you have the gun, right?" she asked.

"Yes." Dani cocked an eyebrow, disapprovingly. "It seems Jo does have the gun."

Zapa continued unaware of the contentious nature of the gun. "I do not believe there are metal detectors on the cruise ship but there may be one you must go through before you board. Be ready to get rid of the gun somehow."

"I don't know how we can just dump it, like last minute. Why don't you take it?" asked Dani. "You may need it more than we do."

"I would love to take it, but I will feel better if you two have it," said Zapa. "You are in danger because you have those files in your possession."

"Look. We know having the files is dangerous. But we have the pepper spray. Having the gun may cause us more problems down the line. Just be sure you tell Tomás you now have it. He probably won't be happy. But you are the registered owner, right? So just tell him and he can decide what he needs to do for himself."

Zapa pursed her lips. "Bueno," she said, taking the gun. "Estoy un poco confundida. Confused. Pero no importa. It is not important. We are all free. Not out of danger just yet but so much closer than before." She paused and turned to Dani. "Now, amiga, I think you must change out of that uniform. You are too visible. There is a washroom over there."

"You're pretty visible too, Zapa," said Jo, pointing at her wild red hair. She grabbed the gym bag and pulled out the scarf. "Use this. It's yours."

Zapa laughed. "Fantástico. Gracias." She twirled her hair into a knot and tucked it under the scarf. "Okay, now I will buy your tickets."

A few minutes later, they walked out the back of the building toward the dock. Shouts echoed in the distance. Dani looked around and was relieved to see that they were well hidden from the street behind the port building. Ahead was the ramp onto the ship with a large banner draped above it. Bienvenido a *La Belle de Cadix*. Welcome On Board *The Beauty of Cádiz*. Their escape vessel gleamed in brilliant sunshine. *Perfect. She's beautiful!*

"This is insane, Zapa," said Jo. "How long will it take to get to Seville by boat?"

"Eight or nine hours. It is one o'clock now. You'll be in Seville by evening. They will never imagine you will take this route."

"Uh, ya think? Because maybe it's impractical?"

"Please, Jo. Like you did with the train, you must trust me with this. They will not find you on the ship."

"But they did find us on the train."

"They did? Ay dios. We have much to talk about. But that cannot be helped for now. I have no other idea how you can leave here and stay safe. They will be searching the area for you."

"How will *you* hide from them?"

"With great difficulty. But easier one than three. I will not be caught off-guard by these people again. And you two, please, when you go on board, stay out of sight. What is happening at the hospital is big but I don't believe we understand it all yet.

You must proceed with caution. Do not talk to people on this route along the river. It looks idyllic but most of the hachís, uh, hashish for Europe comes from Morocco and is taken up the Guadalquivir. Probably not on your cruise ship. They use dinghies and shrimp boats. You will see them, abandoned and burned boats, along the river. It is very disturbing. Please be careful at every step."

"Okay. And thanks for the tips," said Jo. "And you too, Zapa. Please be careful."

"Yes. I will, Jo. And thank you both. You saved my life and your own life, Dani, and perhaps the lives of those others held in that building. We did good work today."

"I really wish you were coming with us."

They hugged and parted, Zapa slipping into the shadows, Dani and Jo walking down the gangplank. *Ramp, Dani. Ramp.*

CHAPTER TWENTY-ONE

"I'm so tired I can't speak."

"Amazing how a little gun action will take the good right out of you, eh, Jo? I can't believe you lied about stashing that gun at the safe house."

Jo looked over at Dani. They lay on either side of the queen bed in the deluxe cabin Zapa had purchased for them, the only one available. It was beautiful but in their post-adrenaline state, they didn't really care. Jo pursed her lips.

"I did *not* lie. I *did* stash it at the house. I went back and got it after you disappeared. Tomás helped me. It was clear we needed something, at least temporarily. Damn glad I had it too. But having it wasn't enough. I decided to pretend I was Jessica Jones and convince Chaco I was deadly serious about him leaving and never coming back."

Dani's eyes widened. "It was a *cautionary* shot?"

Jo nodded. "My aim was a bit off. Didn't really mean to hit him...much."

Dani was silent for about a minute. She rolled on her side to face Jo and said, "I gotta admit. You were pretty impressive with that gun, even if having it was potentially criminal and using it? Well—"

"Okay, okay. I'm more shocked than you that I actually shot the guy. It was wrong, even by mistake. But frankly, Dan? I have had enough. In the world of fight or flight, I choose fight. Of course, right now it's time for the flight part. But I'd do it again. I'd shoot Chaco without hesitation."

"Very Jessica Jones-ish, my love. Not the gun. She didn't need a gun."

"Okay, throw that in my face."

"My big battle with Nieves was pretty intense. She punched me. I hurled insults at her. No gun, but I assure you, I used a very nasty tone."

They chuckled softly together. The whistle blew and they felt the boat move away from shore.

"Thank god," said Dani. "Outta here."

"I guess the upside of this slow boat to Seville is that we can sleep for an hour or so. But after that, we have to tackle those files." Jo leaned over her side of the bed and pulled her cell phone out of the gym bag on the floor next to her. She gave it to Dani. "Could you text Viviana so she knows where we are? And maybe Eddie too? I'd do it but everything's in Spanish on the phone. And I'm going to nap now."

Dani watched Jo. Her eyelids slowly shut. She looked peaceful in sleep. Dani was envious. She was afraid to close her eyes, afraid of what she'd see. She looked at the phone in her hands. Jo asked her to text something to someone. *What was it, exactly? Oh yeah. The ship. We are on a ship. Yes.* She could feel the ship rocking gently beneath her, lulling her like a baby in a cradle. Her eyelids closed and she too succumbed as *The Belle de Cadix* motored out of port and onto the open sea.

She couldn't breathe. She couldn't see. Her heart was pounding. Her first thought. Where was he? Where was Chaco? She bolted upright and looked around. She could just make out the form on the other side of the bed. Jo. Sleeping. The room rolled. The ship. They were on the ship. Bound for Seville.

She got up. Something fell to the floor. Later. She'd find it later. She had to get to the bathroom. She was nauseous.

She returned to find Jo sitting upright in bed with the bedside light on.

"Here's the cell. You dropped it when you got up."

"Thanks. Did you give it to me? I can't remember."

"Yeah, Dan, I did," she said, looking at her curiously, "so you could text Viviana and Tomás that we're okay? And maybe Eddie too?"

Dani opened the cell and checked the text box. No messages out and none in.

"Shit." She looked at Jo with dull eyes.

"Are you all right?" Jo asked.

"I must've fallen asleep."

"You mean you never texted Viviana or Eddie?"

"No. I was so tired, Jo. Sorry."

"Okay. Just do it now."

"I'll call them. That'll be faster."

"Texting would be better, in case they can't talk."

"Right. I'm not thinking clearly."

"If you haven't texted them, they don't know we're on the boat," Jo muttered while Dani tapped away on the cell phone. "They won't even know you were kidnapped or that you found Zapa and she's okay. Unless Tomás got the word out, they probably think we're still in Cádiz, looking for Zapa. I hope she found Miguel. I hope they're all okay."

Dani put up her hand. "Jo, stop talking please. I can't think."

When she finished, she read the message out loud. "Hi Eddie. Jo and I are on our way to Seville. We're coming in on the river cruise ship today. Just so you know we're okay. And maybe, if you'd like to meet us? Text me back when you get this."

"Now the folks in Sanlúcar," she said, composing a similar message for Viviana.

She closed the cell and started to lean back when it pinged.

"Wow, that was fast. It's Viviana."

"Read it out loud, Dan."

"I am so glad you are both safe. Tomás called to say he was with Zapa and a colleague of hers and they were about to leave for Sanlúcar. We will wait to hear from you after you arrive in Seville and can confirm that you will make your meeting with the attorney general. Otherwise, Tomás and I will go to him ourselves."

Another ping and part two of Viviana's text came in. *Eddie called and left a message asking where you were. Tomás told me Eddie's phone was not secure and I did not call back.*

"Shit. I wrote Eddie. Maybe that wasn't a good idea. But if Zapa's safe it should be…"

Another ping sounded. There was more from Viviana.

Tomás told me about the files. And about your dramatic exit from the warehouse. I advise you not go to the police. Go directly to the attorney general's office in Seville. I have alerted his assistant and they are awaiting your arrival. We will talk later. Be safe my friends.

"Geez, Jo, she's making me really nervous."

"Are you *sure* you're all right?"

"No. I don't feel right. Do you think they could have drugged me?"

"Oh god, Dani, there hasn't been time to ask you. What happened in there, in the warehouse, when they had you?"

"I was more frightened than I have ever been."

She told her about Chaco. Her terror. His leering and violent words. How he threatened her with torture and death but left her untouched. She told her how emotional Nieves became and how she'd pummeled Dani's chest with her fists and later punched her in the face. And finally, she described how she finally clawed her way to freedom.

"That's amazing, what you did. And terrifying. My god, Dani. No wonder you feel tired and drugged. I've been pushing ahead with stuff but maybe you just need to rest."

"No. We've got to look at the files. We have to figure this thing out before we get to Seville, if we can."

"Okay. But is there anything I can do for you right now?"

"Is there any drinking water? I'm so thirsty."

"Yeah, there in that little fridge. I'll get it. You stay here."

Dani took the bottle Jo brought to her and downed it on the spot. Jo sat next to her and raised her arm to put it around Dani.

"No. No. Don't. Sorry. I'm feeling a bit claustrophobic."

Jo pulled her arm back. "Really? So, Dan, you've thrown up. You look white as a sheet. You don't want me to touch you. Maybe you're suffering from some form of PTSD. Maybe there's a ship's doctor who could give you something?"

Dani turned her head slowly and squinted at Jo, as if puzzled. She started laughing, falling backwards on the bed. "Call...a... doctor?" she blurted out the words mid-laughs. "A doctor? Seriously? Have we learned nothing?"

Jo started laughing too. And then they couldn't stop, their faces reddening and tears coursing down their cheeks. "Oh my god, stop. I've got to stop. My sides are killing me."

The hilarity had just started to die down when Dani started laughing again and shaking her head.

"What? What are you thinking?"

"I just remembered seeing you standing at the ambulance with those two guys and waving the gun around. I couldn't fucking believe it. Where exactly did you end up shooting the guy?"

"In the knee."

"Oh my god. You may have crippled him for life. That is *not* funny."

"I'm handling it. I only wish I'd aimed a bit higher than the knee."

"Yikes." Dani grimaced. "Maybe you should change professions."

"And be what? A security guard? A cop? A PI? I couldn't handle it. These scenarios were blind luck combined with an overwhelming desire to protect the woman I love. I seem to lose all fear when someone is hurting you. And you know, you're the same way. You carried me on your back out of that fourth-floor clinic, and this morning you went back inside that den of horrors and to the basement no less. I know I said I wanted to go with you, but I don't think I could've gone back inside that hospital."

"You would have if you had to." Dani smiled, feeling more relaxed now. She moved from the couch to the window and pulled the curtains back for a full view.

"Oh my god, this is beautiful." She swept open the Juliette balcony doors. Warm, humid air rushed in.

Jo joined her and they stood hand in hand as the ship turned toward land. For a tense moment Dani thought it was making some unscheduled stop until she realized it was heading exactly where it should: up the Guadalquivir River.

"We must have just passed Sanlúcar. It's right at the mouth of the river. Weird, eh? We have friends there now."

They stayed at the window watching the ship's wake roll onto the shores of the hot, arid plain of Andalucía. Everything shimmered in the midday sun, a golden panorama dotted by village casitas of white walls and red clay roofs.

"I love you," said Jo, not looking at Dani.

"I love you more," Dani responded, pressing Jo's fingers, a cue to the next line in their well-worn exchange.

"I love you most."

"I love you more than that."

"That's impossible. There is no more than most."

Dani took Jo's hand and pressed it to her lips, and pulled her close.

"Oh yes there is."

They pulled away from each other reluctantly, neither of them wanting to break the warmth and safety of their embrace. Too many unknowns pressed in around them, beyond this moment, beyond the door to their cabin. They didn't want to talk or even think about what lay ahead. Dani's stomach had finally settled down and she discovered she was ravenous. They called room service. Once they'd finished their meal, they sat contentedly side by side on the couch, pinioned by their bellies.

"So, whaddya say," Jo began, eyeing the laundry bag across the room, "would you like to check out those files?"

"That would involve getting up, wouldn't it? Not to mention discovering some new horror in all that paper."

Jo laughed as Dani pushed herself off the couch like a pregnant woman. She brought the bag over to the coffee table and flopped back down. "Not sure what sense these'll make without Zapa or Tomás here to translate."

Dani refilled their glasses with water, pulled out all the files and spread them across the table.

"The intern had the number of files right. There are six."

Jo picked one up and scanned its pages. "I don't know why *I'm* looking at this. I can read the numbers, and there are lots of them, but the names of the sections are in Spanish. So over to you, babe," she said, tossing it to Dani.

"Okay," said Dani. "The label on all the covers says *Cleaning Techniques*, like Zapa said. But, up in the corner is a different name. Look. Cádiz on this one. Here's el Gran Puerto, the hospital near Jerez. And the rest of these, well, I've never heard of them. They're probably the ones in eastern Andalucía or somewhere. Leona was going on about them. Six files, six different names, six different hospitals in the Clínica Ortega chain, just like she said. What do you think?"

Jo flipped through a couple of files. "They're definitely some sort of accounting record, year-end financial reports by the look of them. Nothing extraordinary, except for the labelling. *Cleaning Techniques*. That's pretty weird."

"So there's something in here they're hiding?" said Dani, turning the pages. "It's got to be pretty damning, whatever it is."

"Something worth kidnapping for."

"Yeah. And killing for. Nieves made that very clear."

Jo took Dani's hand and squeezed it.

They went through the reports again, this time laying them out in a row so they could compare the pages side by side. They appeared to follow a template with only the amounts varying from hospital to hospital. All the reports looked more or less the same, except the Cádiz clinic report.

"Why would there be more pages for Cádiz?" Jo asked, flipping through the extra pages at the back of the report.

"Maybe that location is bigger than the other places. Or they include more detail since these reports were located in the Clínica."

Jo ran her finger down the items listed on one of the pages. "These figures look like they're for something separate. But they do say income and expenses, or I think they do."

Dani looked and pointed. "Gastos is expenses. Ingresos is income." Her cell phone buzzed.

"There's a column labelled pacientes," Jo continued. "Is that patients?" Dani nodded. "And what's that word mean?" Jo asked pointing to it on the page.

"Just a minute," Dani said, opening the cell. "It's a text from Viviana. Zapa said we must be very careful. Miguel told her more about the anger over the missing reports but I think we're pretty up to date on that part."

"No kidding. I wish Zapa would call us directly. I'd like her to explain what it is about these documents that has everyone in a frenzy. It looks like regular business accounting to me."

"She has to get a new phone before that's going to happen. But if she's with Tomás—"

"Dan? Look at this word. Or-gah-nos?"

"Shit. Really? The word órganos is there? Show me."

"Here," Jo said, pointing to the page.

"Órganos. Yes. And you say it like I just did. Emphasis on the first syllable."

"Yes, dear." Jo spoke through gritted teeth.

"Anyway, it definitely means organs. And look. It's in the gastos column. Expenses. That means that these pages are specifically about the transplant clinic."

"Maybe the transplant clinic is a separate legal entity and its financial reports have to be separate. What's that entry?"

"Renovation costs. Wow. That's pricey. It must mean the fourth floor because we know nothing was done on the third. Looks like Nieves spared no expense. Where did she get that kind of money? And these two pages here are both annual reports, I think, covering the transplant clinic's costs and expenses. But it's kind of weird because they're for the same year. Actually, they look like duplicates except for the fact that the amounts are hugely different. Like, here, look. On this page it says there were eight transplants all of last year but on the second sheet it says there were twenty-five."

"Are they different kinds of transplants?"

"You mean like heart instead of kidney? Yeah, that would explain the money differences. But I'm sure I heard someone say that they only did kidneys."

"All right," said Jo. "So look. The first report says that last year they spent 65,000 euros and took in 65,000 euros. Broke even. But the second report, also for last year, tells a totally different story. It says the total gross income from twenty-five procedures is over 2.5 million euros. But the expenses remain the same as on the first report. The difference?" Jo tapped the page. "Here. Look. In income, it shows the amount charged the patients for the organs. It's more than ten times the cost, which is shown here, in expenses." Jo grabbed the cell phone and tapped numbers into the calculator app. "So compare: in this report, let's call it report A, the transplants cost each patient 8,000 euros. And here, in the second report, or report B, they paid 100,000 euros. How can that be? How can the charges for the same procedure involving the same organ be so wildly different?"

There was silence between them, both women staring at the pages, pondering the possibilities of the different numbers. Jo started drumming her fingers on the table and stopped abruptly.

"What?" asked Dani.

"The only reason to put together different financial reports like these is to hide money, uh, more specifically, to hide income. Maybe they're trying to avoid paying taxes."

"So," Dani said, picking up one of the pages, "in reality they make way bigger bucks but only declare the lower amount? That's a lot of earnings to hide plus a lot of extra activity."

"That explains their reaction. They didn't want to be exposed."

They sat in silence for a while, pondering the reports, until they both spoke at once.

"Or how about—"

"I know why—" Dani gestured to Jo to go first.

"Let's say the first report lists less expensive legal transplants while the second report lists the expensive and illegal live transplants. Remember Tomás said some wealthy clients would pay a handsome sum for a live and healthy donor's organ? The purity of it and all?"

"Yeah, I do. That makes sense. And it would explain why they want these reports back so badly. It documents their illegal activity in black and white. It seems crazy they have these reports all nicely printed. They've basically recorded their own crimes on paper. Or maybe the printouts are for Nieves. Maybe she's old school. Wants some kind of record and prefers paper."

"Could be," said Jo. "Some people believe hard copies are more secure than computer records. Paper you can shred, but god help you if people are looking into your computer trail. Maybe they keep track of their real business, the illegal business, only on paper. They create a document to track the illegal transplants, print it off, and only enter the lower figures, which may be fabricated. Like, do they even *do* legal transplants there?"

"I'll bet they cover their asses by doing legal ones now and again."

"Anyway," Jo continued, "when they're done and they save the document, there would be no record of the illegal numbers in the system to be found by some forensic auditor."

"Listen to you. *Forensic auditor.* Aren't you the one."

"It was in a workshop I took on how to maintain client confidentiality for refugees. Aside from anything that might indicate criminal activity or terrorism or fraud or whatever, there's all kinds of stuff that the authorities really don't need to know."

"Like what? Gender issues?"

"Exactly. Responsible agencies collecting data on people like that often attempt to protect a claimant's privacy one way or another."

"Of course. Less recording is better in some situations. Another possibility is that maybe these hard copies are for Nieves to feed her huge ego."

"Vanity accounting."

"Yeah. I wouldn't be surprised. She's quite a piece of work I discovered."

"So report A, the one the government requires every year, is incomplete and report B, the illegal and complete one, is for Nieves's private file. It's still odd."

"Why, Jo?"

"If their big challenge is keeping the government from finding out how much money they're actually earning, why did they spend all that money on the renos? I mean, the government surely wouldn't spend that kind of money on an elite private clinic when the main hospital is such a mess. Maybe it was Nieves's own money?"

"Possible I guess. She did say she'd done everything herself. But there's no way we can extrapolate that from these records. Besides, Nieves seemed way more interested in her own buying power than tarting up the hospital. What blows my mind is that this second report basically lays out the monetary value of their crimes.

"In other words, it spells out their motivation. That's one more piece for the AG."

"She's one gutsy doctora: running an illegal transplant clinic inside a legal one."

"And we have the written report to prove it. I can't believe the administrator left the reports lying around. That's something else that doesn't make sense, Dani."

"That woman is related to Nieves, so she was a family hire. Maybe nepotism won over office smarts."

"When did Zapa take these?"

"Late Sunday afternoon, after we left town. Remember, when we were walking to the dock, she said something about having grabbed them off the desk?" Dani flopped over on the couch. "That was quite a risk, but it looks like it was worth it."

"It also explains why they want to kill us."

"Yeah. And why Chaco's so invested. They probably told him to get these no matter what. Shit. I wonder if they'll send him to Seville. They've got to know we're heading there."

"They might, but he'll be walking with a limp."

They smiled at each other and jumped in unison when the cell phone buzzed.

"Eddie texted," Dani said, opening the cell. "He's going to meet us at the port."

"Good. I'm glad someone we know will be there."

They stood in the middle of the crowd, waiting for the gangway to be lowered. Dani glanced up at the flat-screen monitors positioned around the ship's exit gate offering muted information for tourists. One featured the final events for cruise passengers: registering at their hotel and a farewell party at "Seville's renown flamenco club La Carbonería." Another had the national and local weather, reporting a pleasant twenty-two degrees. On the third monitor, news headlines scrolled beneath large on-screen images. One story caught Dani's attention.

"Uh, Jo. You seeing that, on the TV there?"

Jo's eyes turned to the screen.

"Boletín: Médico de la Clínica Ortega encontrado muerto en la playa de Cádiz. Circunstancias sospechosas, según la Policía. El pueblo de Cádiz está sacudido por el asesinato. Un médico asesinado y un residente desaparecido en Cádiz."

"Translation please."

"Doctor from Ortega Clinic was found dead on the beach in Cádiz. And the whole town is 'sacudido'...whatever that means...by the killing. Police say it's a suspicious death and an is intern missing."

"That can't be connected to—"

"Yes, it can," said Dani as the image of Dr. Nieves flashed on the screen. It was a professional-looking photo. *She looks attractive and her eyes are almost kind. Ha! And now she's dead?* "There's karma for you."

"Oh my god. But who...?"

"Exactly. She was the one in charge. La jefa, as she liked to remind everyone."

They were momentarily silenced.

"Maybe somebody she owed?" Jo suggested.

"Or maybe Chaco got fed up with being treated like shit. Given the game she was playing, the possibilities are endless."

"Maybe it was the widower."

Dani's eyes widened. "Actually, I can see that. He was crazy with anger and grief. I could've gotten to that point if I'd lost you."

Jo quietly took her hand. "But you didn't lose me. Thanks to you. And Zapa."

"I hope she's not mixed up in this."

Jo turned to Dani, eyes narrowed. "Zapa wouldn't kill anyone, would she?"

"No no. Not what I meant and you're absolutely correct. She wouldn't. I just meant that with all this stuff going down, I hope she's got herself to Sanlúcar. And I really wish *we* were going directly to the airport. The doctor's murder—presumably, because she sure didn't seem like the suicidal type—is weird, don't you think? That means there's another killer out there because the woman who was going to kill *you* is now dead."

Jo shrugged. "She really had it coming. What goes around…"

"I wouldn't be so cavalier, my love. I mean they could even suspect us given the…" Dani dropped her voice to a whisper. "*G-u-n.*" Jo looked at her, aghast.

The ship's crew was gathering now, talking to people, laughing, explaining how deboarding would take place. Dani saw their cabin steward. "I'll be right back."

She returned just as the gangway rumbled into position and the doors slowly rolled back. It was, as the weather monitor stated, a beautiful evening in Seville. Sun just beginning to set. Air balmy with a hint of cool. And mayhem. On one side of the dock, a flamenco guitarist was performing a rousing rasgueado, while a cruise staffer used a mini-megaphone, directing the eighty or so passengers to small vans that would take them to their various accommodations. On the other side was a boisterous and happy group waiting to greet debarking passengers. As they were herded down the plank, Dani and Jo looked around, searching for Eddie…or for trouble.

"I see him," said Jo. Dani followed her gaze. They slowly worked their way over. He was meticulously dressed: snug fitting jeans, a light cotton sports jacket and a black T-shirt. Dani was amazed by how much Eddie now seemed a valued old friend.

He gave them hugs and air kisses on both cheeks, managing both warmth and respect. He pointed to their laundry bag and gym bag and laughed.

"Cape Breton luggage," Jo countered with good humour, raising her voice above the din of the crowd.

He tilted his head, not understanding, and picked up the bags.

"Eddie, it's so good to see you," she shouted.

"I'm very happy to welcome you to Seville, Jo, and to know you're out of that hospital," he yelled in return. "But let's get going."

"Eddie, hold on a sec. I have to…"

There were yells and whistles as a flamenco dancer joined the guitarist and started stamping out a rhythm.

"No delays, my friends. This noise is unbearable."

"But, Eddie…?"

He seemed oblivious to irritation coming through in Dani's voice.

"No buts. Come on."

Before she could say more, he pushed forward through the crowd and led them to his car: a long sleek silver Porsche Panamera 4 eHybrid with a licence plate that read "El-Ed." He stowed their bags in the trunk and opened the rear door for them to get in.

Dani shook her head and tried once more. "Eddie, I have to…"

Eddie pointed to his ears and the car. "In, in, Dani. Too hard…"

She conceded. They closed their doors. The hubbub was instantly muted.

"That's better," he said, starting the engine. "I will be your chauffeur. The front seat is taken as you can see." He nodded at a couple of bags of groceries in the front passenger side. "I went shopping just in case I could persuade you to dine at my home. But first we must go to meet the attorney general."

"No, Eddie. Stop, please. Like I said, we can't leave until I go back and—"

"There's no time, Dani. I have to get you to the attorney general. That is the priority. After that, we will go to my place. You can shower. Call Zapa. She's very anxious to talk to you. You have her number, right? Anyway, I have it if you don't. It will be wonderful to enjoy a glass of wine together while I make us something for dinner."

"You have her number? That's great. Did you speak to her? Is she okay? Where is she?" asked Dani.

"She said she was at her townhouse and that she's fine. And she congratulated you both on taking those reports from the office." He started the car and drove slowly along the dock, turning his head toward them briefly as he spoke. He smiled and nodded. "Very smart, she said."

Dani looked at him sharply. "When did you speak with her?"

"This afternoon, when you were on the cruise ship. She said you now have good evidence to give to the authorities."

Jo leaned forward. "Ed—"

Dani squeezed Jo's hand, and, out of Eddie's line of sight, touched her finger to her mouth.

"Ah yes, my darlings. I am happy you are going to finally have some peace after this long ordeal. We will go to the AG's home as he is already there after a long day at his office. Which bag are the papers in? The gym bag or the laundry bag?" he said.

"Eddie, we can't leave yet," Dani said. "I need to find a washroom. I haven't felt well since I left Cádiz. Could we stop, please? There's got to be a washroom around here somewhere."

"We cannot stop now, Dani. That will make us late for our meeting. He will allow you to use his facilities or we can find a nice place to stop after we leave him. So please, señoras, sit back. We must be on our way."

"Eddie, please, I can't wait that long," said Dani as she reached for the door handle.

At that moment, he reached down between the seats to a small control panel and hit a switch.

Click. The sound was small but soul-shattering.

CHAPTER TWENTY-TWO

"Eddie, what are you doing?" Dani said, trying to open her door. "Did you just lock us in?"

"I am so sorry, señoras, but I have promised to deliver those reports immediately."

The two women looked at each other, horrified, as the implications of his act sunk in.

"Eddie. Open the doors," Jo ordered in her rarely heard comandante voice.

"Please, sit back and there will be no trouble."

They screamed at him to stop the car. They pounded on their windows to people standing on the crowded sidewalk, but no one took any notice.

"Please. You must be calm." Eddie manoeuvred the car off the pier road and onto a bigger street. He sped up.

"You aren't going to the attorney general's house, are you?"

"All will be fine, Dani. I will simply give them the files and you will promise not to say anything to anyone and you will be on your way. And in case you have any foolish notions of overpowering me, please notice what is in my hand."

They looked down. He was holding a semiautomatic pistol, small, black, and gleaming.

"Oh, Eddie. You'd shoot us?" asked Jo.

"Yes, my dear Jo, I would. This is life and death to me."

"What are you talking about?"

He was silent while he manoeuvred the car around a slow-moving truck. "It is enough to say that the reports are extremely important."

"We know they are, Eddie. But why do you care? You don't work for Nieves? Or do you?" asked Dani.

"No. No. I could never work for that...that...puta."

"Really? Wow. Okay. I mean I agree actually. But language, Eddie, language. Don't you have another word for a conniving, murderous megalomaniac?"

"Who cares what he calls her." Jo leaned forward. "Eddie, please tell us, what's the life or death thing to you? Surely this has nothing to do with your Caballero group?"

"Please, sit back. I am so sorry, Josefina, I cannot discuss this further. I do their bidding. And right now it is to return the reports."

"Who? Whose bidding do you do?" asked Jo.

"Caballero Andante." Eddie stepped on the gas. The vehicle sped along a road next to the canal, its water heading the other way, back to the river, Sanlúcar, the sea and the setting sun.

"What are you going to do, Eddie?" Dani was sitting behind Eddie and leaned toward his ear. "What? Hand us over to them?"

"Don't worry, they won't hurt you. They promised me."

"Fuck that," countered Dani. "You are a fool. They won't just let us walk away. Look what they did to Nieves."

"What do you mean? What have they done?"

"She's dead."

He said nothing, but his jaw clenched and he tightened his grip on the steering wheel. "That cannot be true."

"It is true. I saw it on the TV screen on board the ship. It said her body was found. The intern's too. Suspicious deaths."

Eddie paled and swore to himself. "You realize that this is all your fault. You threatened everything when you stole those reports. And now it is even more critical that you give them back. It is the only way to keep everyone safe, including me. The only way."

"Why did your guys kill her? It was your guys, right?"

"Oh please, Josefina. This is much bigger, much more important than Nieves and her little clinic."

"What are you talking about?"

He drove aggressively, weaving his way through the traffic. "My darlings, I think I might love you both but it doesn't matter. I cannot allow you to destroy what I have spent so long building. You don't think I could afford this car or my wonderful dinners on a social worker's salary, do you? I perform little jobs for powerful people who pay me handsomely. What you carry in those files will destroy everything I've worked for."

"What kind of *little* jobs?" asked Jo.

"Pues, nothing important. Only information, to let them know what things will be done when and where and by whom."

"I still don't understand," said Dani. "What's in those files that's more damaging than Nieves's kidney stealing and accounting fraud. And how does any of it impact you?"

He blew a puff of air and curled his lips. "Her crimes are not important. It is that they may lead to investigations which will bring everything tumbling down. This silly attempt of hers to make a few extra euros is absurd."

"That's exactly what I said to her."

Eddie shot a confused glance at Dani.

"Well, actually, it's in the millions," said Jo.

"Ah. So you have read the reports. Please do not refer to that with my friends. That will not ensure your safety."

"Okay fine," snapped Jo. "But what does your group have to do with Nieves?"

"Any scrutiny of her financial statements will cause great inconvenience for my company."

"Come on, Eddie." Dani grabbed the back of his seat. "Get specific. What's going on?"

He slowed slightly as he steered off the highway and onto a busy roadway called Paseo de las Delicias just as the streetlights were flickering on. "Dios, the traffic. Yes. All right. Why not tell you? But do not forget, I have my weapon here and I will use it. So please. Sit back. Agreed?"

"Yes, yes. Agreed."

"Bueno." He sighed. "So, my friends, this is what it is: Caballero Andante is an umbrella corporation for many companies, Caballero Ético, el Grupo Ortega—"

"Your company owns the Clínica?" Jo asked.

"Please do not interrupt." He manoeuvred around a traffic circle and headed in a different direction through a large park area. "Caballero owns the Clínica, yes, but indirectly. The companies Caballero owns are el Grupo Ortega which includes the six hospitals, of which the Clínica is one. El Grupo builds and renovates hospitals, just like Caballero Ético builds and renovates housing for immigrants. CA owns the buildings and the infrastructure. Each of the six manages its own staff and doctors, equipment, all the general operations. In the case of la Clínica, la doctora Nieves was in charge. Each one of these operations is costly to operate and above board. They do not make much profit, but that is how Caballero Andante prefers it. Profit is not the purpose. Because these facilities operate in the public interest and relieve the burden on the public health system, the government reimburses CA for a large percentage of its original investment and operating costs. And so, the money that was originally invested becomes clean. But enough. I have said enough." He slowed.

"Money laundering," said Dani.

"I don't like that term, money laundering. Consider it more like a fair exchange. Our friends give us money that we use to provide facilities of various kinds for people in need. And in return, they are repaid from money the government gives us."

"And the original money is drug money, isn't it, Eddie?"

He shook his head.

"Oh my god. Drug money is paying for the immigrant residences?" asked Jo.

"Some newcomer housing. Some hospitals. All good work, don't you agree? And in return we are paid a modest fee. Why is this so bad?"

"Because, by extension, you actually work for the drug cartels. Remember that night we first met you? You were bemoaning the growth of a local narco culture in Cádiz? How it was 'scandalously exploiting the desperate'? Yeah, those are the exact words you used. I was impressed. So was that all just a performance to impress us? Or do you not like the Cádiz crew 'cause they're competition for your precious Caballero Andante? Eddie, the cartels destroy lives. Think of the murders and tortures, the addictions, the communities given over to crime, the corrupt politicians and police, the thousands of people who just go missing. You're *cleaning* money that can never be cleaned because it was printed in hell and inked in blood."

Eddie said nothing. He drove around yet another traffic circle. Cars were turning on their lights now in the evening dusk. Dani saw a University of Seville sign. Where was he taking them? She looked back at him. His eyes were locked on the road. His face was frozen, completely devoid of emotion.

"What cartels are you connected to?" Dani asked. "The ones in Mexico? Columbia? I know a bit about this stuff, Eddie. My brother-in-law is a criminologist and cartels are his specialty. Is it the Sinaloa cartel? Los Zetas? Or maybe they aren't Spanish-speaking. Money is the universal language. So it could be the Russian mob is here on the continent. Or maybe some gangster types in Morocco, just across the water. How does the money get into the country? I mean, there've been huge issues with banks around the world improperly tracking drug-related money. HSBC, Deutsche Bank. And don't forget there's Wachovia. That's one for the history books. And let's not forget the Canadian banks. They were found negligent in monitoring some of their depositors. That's according to a secret government report uncovered by the CBC a few years back. I mean this is all old news about the banks. So how's it happening here, Eddie. How are your *friends* as you so endearingly call them getting their money into Spain?"

"Stop asking questions. You will get us killed."

"Killed, like Nieves?" Dani asked. She reached over and grabbed Jo's hands, her eyes directing Jo's attention to Eddie's gun. "Maybe you weren't really surprised to hear she was dead.

Maybe you were the one who killed her with that nice little gun you have there."

"Absolutely not. I did not know she was dead. Besides, I am a humanitarian working for the poor immigrants."

"Wow. You're really screwed up if you believe working with drug cartels is a humanitarian act. And if you're in this business at all, you did kill Nieves, even if you didn't actually pull the trigger," said Jo.

"You're wrong. I do not kill people. It was probably Rico." Dani's jaw dropped. "Besides, Nieves deserved to die. She double-crossed them with her little scheme."

"You *know* Rico?"

"Of course. My company hires Rico from time to time. He is very useful in many scenarios. How do *you* know Rico?"

"He came to Jo's room in the hospital and offered protection."

"Ah, I understand now. My company is very sensitive to any, uh, unusual activity at the Clínica. The uniform fiasco taught them what can happen if problems go unattended. The good doctor has a way of drawing attention to herself *and* the business. There must be talk." He sighed. "And so when I talked to Rico about your situation, Josefina, he decided to check it out for himself. I told him not to approach you directly. To call me back for a confirmation. But I see he ignored me. It's possible that is when he learned the details of the Benning woman's death along with this craziness involving you and the transplant operation. He must have alerted Caballero. And so, my company decided it must step in. I tried to warn you it had moved out of my hands. Why didn't you answer my calls? I could have protected you. And now, because of you two, everything is ruined. In fact, *you* are the reason for the death of la doctora."

"How do you figure that?"

He slowed and turned along a much smaller road with businesses and parked cars and homes. "It is because of the files you took that this became something much more urgent and, uh, dangerous. The details my bosses gradually learned about this *illegal clinic* that they never knew existed must have sent them into a panic. And the proof of its existence was out there, available to whomever gets possession of the files. Competitors, media, the attorney general. Ay dios…it is increíble. Unbelievable. Caballero Andante will surely be exposed. And so I am sure CA called upon Rico to deal with the situation. He is most reliable in circumstances like these." He shook his head. "Why didn't you just call me? I informed you of the cleaning woman's fate when they took her. I assumed you would stay in touch with me. I could have managed this situation. Why didn't you trust me?"

"Fuck, Eddie. I did call you. You weren't there. I left a message. You never called back. And then it was too late. We were hiding and when we figured your phone was compromised, there was no way we would've called you. Of course, now that we know who and what you really are…" Jo shook her head.

"Pues, you have dragged me into it. The only hope now is to give them the files. That will make it right. I assured them I would bring the files. They were very happy with this and in return, they promised not to hurt you."

"And you believe them?" Jo snorted. "They're going to kill us."

"No, no, they promised they wouldn't."

"You know they'll kill us, Eddie. Let us go. Keep the files. All you have to do is stop the car. Please."

"Ay, señoras, no puedo." He scrunched up his face like he was fighting back tears.

"Párate, Eddie," Dani pleaded. "Stop. Let's talk this through. There must be other options. You could come with us to the AG's office. Be a witness against them. You'll go into a protection program or something. You can stop this insanity now. Don't let them kill us."

Tears rolled down his face. He shook head slowly and whispered, "No. No va a pasar. Me prometieron." It won't happen. They promised me.

He turned onto a side street and they came to a crawl. It was getting dark. Streetlamps were few. Pedestrians were everywhere walking without regard for vehicles. Eddie struggled to avoid them. They drove past brightly painted walls rising high on either side with ornate tile signs labelling streets and plazas.

Seville's Old Town. Dani wondered where he was taking them. On one wall of weathered orange was the word "Judería." *The Jewish Quarter. We're in Santa Cruz.*

"Lo siento amigas. Siento siento siento."

Dani and Jo looked at each other.

Now. The word screamed through Dani's mind. Without stopping to think, she grabbed Eddie around the neck. He cried out. The car lurched but he held control with one hand while he twisted around and aimed the gun into the back seat with the other. She let him go and both women ducked down.

He swore, panting. He kept the gun aimed toward the back seat, his eyes switching back and forth between the road and the rearview mirror, while they drove further into the district.

"Stay back or I will shoot you," he said when Dani straightened up.

Dani kept on. "Eddie. This is madness. How did you ever get involved with these people? You aren't like them. You're a decent man."

He didn't speak but his face softened yet again.

"Ay, queridas, my dear ones, it was so easy," he said. "They helped me out a few years ago with some money I owed. And, as is proper, I helped them in return. It became a beautiful relationship."

"With the devil."

He turned a corner and drove along a narrow, darkened lane. It ended at a large cobblestone yard in front of a grand white house. A lantern lit up a black door surrounded by ironwork. Eddie stopped the car and kept the gun pointed at them.

"I will not let you destroy everything." He tapped the horn.

A man stepped out from the shadows next to the building.

Rico.

The car doors clicked open.

"Eddie. What are you doing?" Jo said, her voice rising with panic. Dani reached over and laid a hand on Jo's arm. When Dani spoke, her voice was hard.

"Eddie. We don't have the reports. They aren't in the bags."

He turned to stare at her. "¿Qué dices? What are you saying?"

"I was nervous after I saw that news about Nieves. I asked a steward on the ship to hold them for us until we came back for them, once we knew we were safe. I was trying to tell you that when you locked us in the car and drove away."

"You stupid bitches. You've killed yourselves."

"No, Eddie. We were already dead," said Jo as she watched Rico approach the car. "I think we just killed you."

Eddie glanced at Rico, who walked closer, fists clenching and unclenching. Eddie clicked the doors locked, started the car and reversed it, frantically backing into a car parked in the lane behind them. Rico raced toward them, pulling a gun from his belt. Eddie accelerated into a squealing turn. Bullets slammed into the trunk. He gave it more gas and they fishtailed down the lane.

Once out of the lane, speed was impossible. They were forced to a crawl by pedestrians, mopeds and other cars crowding the roadway around Plaza de Santa Cruz. Dani looked back.

"He's still coming, Eddie. He's running after us."

Eddie tried to turn onto Calle Santa Teresa to get out of the plaza jam but traffic was at a standstill. They were stuck. He honked the horn as if that would force someone ahead to move. He was ignored.

"Where are you trying to go?" Jo asked.

"Back to the port to find the steward. We must get the files."

"Come on, Eddie. Let's just get to the AG's office. Give yourself up."

He was silent, trying to move the car forward. A bunch of motorbikes were in front of the car. He touched the closest one with the bumper, trying to nudge the driver to get out of the way. The driver gave him the finger. Eddie inched the car forward, leaning on the horn. A couple of bikers moved out of the way. The others soon did the same. There was a short space open ahead but he still couldn't manage a turn off the plaza road. He looked at the pedestrian walkway that headed into the centre of the square. Pretty lanterns on black cast iron poles lit the way. He turned the car onto it, forcing his way along. Sharp branches on bushes scraped the side of the vehicle. Pedestrians screamed and fell out the way. Ahead was a massive tree.

Eddie slammed his hands onto the steering wheel and screamed, "You've destroyed my life." He sped up and aimed for the tree. Dani and Jo both yelled at him to stop. At the last minute, he slammed on the brakes, throwing them both hard against the front seats. He clicked the door locks open, got out and took off running.

"Shit. Come on." Dani grabbed Jo's hand and pulled her out of the car. They started to run but spotted Rico coming into the square. They swerved and fled, heading away from both of them.

They dodged people and scooters and signs and made a hard turn out of the plaza. The streets began to narrow and twist and turn until they found themselves deep inside a medieval maze. Dani knew exactly where they were, the irony of its history stoking her dread. She heard footsteps thudding behind them. Rico. She grabbed Jo's hand and propelled them both forward along the cobblestones, past buildings so close together the sky almost disappeared. This was the Jewish Quarter. There were times of peace. But there were also times of running, and everyone had their turn. The Christians from the Moors, the Moors from the Christians, but most often and most recently, it was the Jews fleeing slaughter by the soldiers of the Catholic royals. She felt the panic, heard the screams and the relentless pounding of horses' hooves in her head. She wondered if she was going crazy or was it her own blood pounding through her veins? The two women were slowing down, losing steam. Dani spotted a darkened place in a recessed doorway. She remembered how she and Tomás had hidden from the men chasing them that night in Cádiz.

She pulled Jo into the dark space, pushed her against the wall and pressed herself into Jo, trying to make them both invisible.

She felt Jo's chest expand, her breath coming as hard as Dani's. She placed her lips against Jo's neck, moist with sweat, and took in the smell of her. They had to live. They had to have more time together.

"Please. All you who ran for your lives. Help us now," Dani chanted softly.

Shouts and sirens and sounds of a chase drifted into their lane. They heard the pop-pop of gunfire in the distance, followed by the oddly normal sound of a car lock beeping nearby. The screams and pounding hooves were gone from Dani's ears. Nothing was happening on their lane. It seemed surreal, almost peaceful. Were they safe or still in danger? Dani couldn't tell.

When she finally spoke, her voice was raspy. "We've got to get out of here, if for no other reason than my knees are killing me."

They walked together holding hands, relieved when they found their way safely out of the maze. The plaza was a hive of police activity, lights flashing and sirens blaring all around them. A police motorcycle was stationed by Eddie's abandoned car. An ambulance was parked on the other side of the square. The pedestrians had fled. The joyful atmosphere had long evaporated.

Dani and Jo stayed in the darkness, expecting Rico to pounce at any moment. They ducked inside a crowded restaurant. Talk of a crazy driver and guns being fired filled the place. Dani grabbed a waiter's arm and asked for a telephone book.

"We do not have a book, señora, but I will check the Internet for you. What number do you need."

"The office of the attorney general. Please. It is urgent."

The woman's eyebrows rose. "The attorney general? Urgent? Will anyone be there at this hour?"

"Yes. They are expecting our call."

"Bueno. Lo tengo pronto." *Soon, my friends.*

When they finally got through, the agent on duty told them to stay where they were, out of sight. They sat together at a table in the corner where they could watch the door. They finally ordered coffees and buns to pay for dallying so long.

Eventually, a little yellow car with a badly dented passenger door pulled up directly in front of the restaurant.

"Zapa," they both said at once and rushed to meet her.

"How did you know where we were?" Jo asked.

She smiled. "That is for later, señoras."

CHAPTER TWENTY-THREE

They sat together in the restaurant on the airport's departure level. Dani, Jo, and Zapa.

They had been kept apart for an entire week while they were separately and repeatedly interviewed by investigators from the attorney general's office. Once done, Dani and Jo were told they could go home on the condition they would give testimony either in person in Seville or by Skype or Zoom if schedules didn't permit.

Zapa touched Dani's and Jo's arms. "Tomás sends his regrets. He had to work. But he asked me to tell you that he will perhaps be in Canada for a visit soon."

"Really? That's great news. Any particular reason?"

"He has a new friend. A special friend. Someone he met thanks to you and me, Dani."

"Who?"

"Do you remember Hayyan, the guy we freed from the room in the warehouse?"

"Of course."

"He came to the Centro. He is asking for refugee status because he will be killed if he returns home. He is gay, you see."

"No. You're kidding. And so he and Tomás?"

"Yes. ¿Increíble, no? His original plan was to go to Canada but Tomás is trying to change his mind." They laughed. "Now, I must ask you both this. Are you angry that I put you on the cruise ship?"

"No, no," said Jo. "It was the only option at the time. You acted fast and saved us."

"I was so worried, seeing you sail off with those reports. You did not really know how dangerous they were to have in your possession. But I—"

"Zapa. It's okay," said Dani. "Besides, it gave me time to start breathing again after the captivity thing, and Jo and I time to analyse those documents. Of course, it was Eddie who finally explained most of it. We *never* suspected he was involved."

"I wondered about him when you told me he got the call about the kidnapping. That struck me as odd. I did not know you would contact him once you were on board the ship. I thought he was out of the picture until I saw him portside."

"You were there?"

"Yes. I decided to try and meet your ship when it docked in Seville. But I got there just as Eddie was driving off with you two waving and pounding on the windows. I was afraid to intervene, afraid Eddie might do something crazy and hurt you. I alerted the AG's office that I thought you were in danger and I followed you. It all happened so fast. When I saw Rico—"

"You *saw* Rico come after us? You were there too?"

"Absolutamente. I saw his gun. I was going to ram him with Miguel's car but Eddie threw his into reverse. He crashed right into me."

"*That* was you?"

"Sí, sí. The hit almost knocked me out. I ducked when Rico rushed by. But I followed him in the car. I was grateful it still moved. I saw Eddie's car stop fast before hitting the tree in the square. Ay dios, I thought that was the end for you both. And then Eddie ran off in one direction and you two went the other way. Rico saw it all too. He stopped and called someone on his cell. When he disconnected, he turned and started after you. That's when I doored him."

Dani and Jo both gasped. "You doored *Rico?*" asked Dani.

"It was a pretty hard hit, that broke his leg or a rib or something. He was writhing on the ground in much pain and very distracted. I removed his gun and I called the police. I told them Rico had tried to snatch a child. I waited a minute or two until I could hear sirens getting closer before I left because I didn't want to be there when the police arrived."

"Why not?"

"Everyone there saw I had hit him. It would have meant endless explaining and there wasn't time. I wanted to get your bags from the car, which I did, yours and the laundry bag with magazines in it. Very clever, Dani. That's when I went looking for you. I was very afraid Rico had called an accomplice, perhaps another killer to join him in the hunt for you. I called Tomás at el Centro and he said they had not heard from you. I was very worried. Finally I called the AG's office and that is when they told me you were in a restaurant called El Trompo."

"What a story, Zapa," said Dani. "I love that you brought Rico down."

"But I'm surprised the AG's people told you where we were," said Jo. "You could have been a threat too."

"No. They would not think that. You see, I have not been entirely honest with you. De verdad, uh, actually, I was investigating the Clínica, only informally you understand."

"Holy shit. You're an undercover agent?"

"No. Not exactly. It happened by accident. You see, I *am* starting school in the fall. It is not to study law exactly. I got this scholarship from my father's union that made it possible for me to go to school and I chose criminal investigation. I wanted to specialize in fraud by corporations. Now I think I will narrow that down to health care fraud." She laughed softly. Dani and Jo stared at her quizzically. "Bueno," she continued. "It is not the time for a joke. So, to continue, I got the job at the Clínica to make extra money for day-to-day costs when I was at school.

I worked there only for a couple of days and I could see that something was very wrong. I went to my advisor at the union and she talked to people she knew in the attorney general's office. She told me that yes, there was concern about the owners of this hospital, el Grupo Ortega. I decided to do a little investigating of my own, listening, catching glimpses of papers in the administrator's office, only very passive activities you see, and only about the money the clinic made, you understand. What do I know about medical care? I was not discovering much until you two, well, happened. When I saw you both that first morning, I thought, perhaps I can learn more from the individual patient's experience. ¡Y cómo! And how! I hope you are not upset by this."

"Are you kidding? We have everything to thank you for, Zapa."

"¡Y cómo!" said Jo.

Zapa looked at her and shook her head. "Óigala. Jo está hablando español."

Dani nodded. "Yup. She's speaking the lingo. Doesn't that just make it all worthwhile?" She squeezed Jo's hand. "We took down an illegal operation *and* Jo learned Spanish. Sort of."

Jo rolled her eyes. "Yes, well, frankly, I'd rather learn in a classroom, thank you very much."

"De acuerdo, Jo. Me too. I will take the classroom. At least for now." Zapa giggled. It was an incongruous sound from this powerful woman. It made Dani start to laugh first. Then Jo. Soon all three of them were laughing hard, drawing wary looks from other people in the small airport resto. But they didn't care. When they calmed down a bit, Zapa reached out and took Jo's hand and Dani's hand.

"Y también, amigas, I must tell you what is going on with this case. Eduardo, Eddie, is now a witness for the prosecution. He will go into witness protection I believe as a result. Chaco has not been found."

"Isn't he crippled?" asked Jo. "I shot him in the knee."

"Ah no, not crippled. Walking in pain evidently, but mobile, according to Pepito who *is* in custody by the way. I have worse news, however. Rico has been released."

"What? Rico? Free? How can that be?"

"In a way, it is my fault. He was walking when I hit him. I removed the gun and put it in my vehicle. There were no fingerprints on it because he wore gloves."

"Oh god, those fucking gloves."

"Yes, well, they saved him from facing justice. They did not have enough evidence to charge him. He is free but I am told he is on their watch list, whatever that is worth."

"Wow. Okay, that's worrisome. But you probably saved our lives by dooring him, Zapa. I mean he would be in prison if he'd managed to find us and—"

"No, no. No lo diga. Do not say it. He will face justice some day."

They stayed a while longer, reluctant to say goodbye to each other. Zapa bought another round of coffee and they hashed through more details about their nightmare experience. At one point, Dani excused herself to go to the washroom. Outside the nearest one, a member of the ground staff was placing an out of order sign in front of the door.

"Where's the closest one?" Dani asked him.

He smiled at her. "Allá." He pointed to a washroom sign farther down. When she got to that sign, she found more signs placed at regular distances apart, that took her farther from the main passenger area and its kiosks and snack bars. She turned a corner and looked down a long empty hallway. A now familiar finger of fear traced its way up her spine. She mocked herself. *Chill, Dani. It's over.* She took a deep breath and hurried into the washroom at the end of the hall. By this time, she really had to go. She went straight into a vacant stall, dropped her pants and sat down. Instantly, the lights went out. She was in total darkness.

"Hello-ooo. There's someone in here," she called. Once the echo of her own voice faded, it was utter silence. "Hello-ooo," she called again, loudly, thinking that it was some stupid janitorial misstep. She finished as fast as she could and tentatively opened the stall door. She could barely see in the darkness but gradually her eyes adjusted.

Something moved near the sinks. It groaned, low, not from pain. And then, a voice.

"Puta puta puta."

Dani froze.

Chaco. Fucking Chaco. Fucking Thug. When will this end?

"Puta mía. I have waited for this moment, you and I alone together at last. And here you are leaving without saying goodbye. ¡Qué vergüenza! Shame on you. I must give you what I promised." He waved something. She heard a click and his cell phone flashlight beamed brightly. He pointed it at the item in his hand: a long, silver, serrated-blade knife. He shone the light directly in her eyes, blinding her once again. "And I need to pay you and the other one back for the pain I now suffer."

Rage flooded Dani's being. She was furious. Furious with him but even more furious with herself. She had allowed herself to be caught in his trap. *For god sake, Dani. You're smarter than him. Surely. So prove it. Stand up straight. Square your shoulders. Brace those muscles you know you have. Play the goddam game. Play it smart. Do not hesitate and do not back down. You're tougher than you have ever been in your life. So fucking prove it. Now.*

Dani screamed and, despite still being blinded, drove her foot forward toward what she hoped and prayed was the location of his knee. Chaco cried out. She was emboldened by the pain in his voice and followed the kick by throwing herself at him with every bit of strength she could muster.

In retrospect, it was an incredibly stupid thing to do, some might argue suicidal, because of his size, his strength and most importantly, the nasty weapon in his hand. But in that moment, Dani didn't care. She'd heard one too many "putas," one too many disgusting taunts involving knives, and the pleasure he got from using them. In fact, his brutal recital had unwittingly released a rage she'd accumulated over a lifetime: rage over the fear of walking alone at night or down an empty hall or into an underground parking lot or along a street past a bunch of whistlers and jeerers or in a crowd beside some guy copping a feel; rage at the almost daily news of women being assaulted or raped or abducted and murdered. Threaded through it all, was the white-hot rage that burned in her soul after her mother's death. Bottled up for too long, it now exploded out of her and landed squarely on Chaco. She had merged with her badass angel and was going to tear the man to shreds.

Her offensive had stunned Chaco. He clearly underestimated the thrust of those Celtic thighs, but at the last second he managed to dodge her attack. That resulted in Dani hitting the sink flat on. Pain tore through her chest. She struggled to breathe. But Chaco hadn't fared so well either. While a strong man, he was not an agile one, especially now with a bum knee. He lurched sideways to avoid her attack and threw himself off-balance, landing hard against the next sink, its edge jamming into his kidney and rib, his knee twisting beneath his weight. He let out a deep male bellow of shock and pain. For a brief moment, the sound filled Dani with joy.

But Chaco rallied before she could, pushing himself up and off the sink. He raised his right arm over his head, the oversize serrated blade in hand, and drove it down to where Dani lay. She rolled away, leaving the knife to slam into the enamel countertop. He cried out again and dropped the knife on the floor. Dani grabbed it and rolled farther away from him. A jab in her side reminded her of the pepper spray still tucked in her pocket. She'd kept it because it comforted her, even though she knew she'd have to dump it before going through airport security. When she was close enough, she aimed it at his anguished face and pressed the nozzle. The spray hit him full force. He fell, fists to his eyes and howling in pain. She ran out and called for security. Her last view of Chaco was the police hauling him and a man in an airport staff vest off to a waiting van.

Two days later, they were finally given permission to leave the country. The three women returned to the airport and said their goodbyes, bittersweet but joyous at surviving yet another assault.

Dani and Jo settled into their seats. They had two flights, the first one to Frankfurt and the last stint over the ocean on an Air Canada plane home. They were flying first class all the way thanks to someone in the attorney general's office. At the moment, the flight attendant was coming around with freshly baked cookies.

"I don't think I'll ever recover from sitting in first class. Who knew they had it this good?" Dani thanked the attendant and asked her if there were any Toronto papers available. She brought copies for both of them and they sat happily reading the news from home, including the story of the money-laundering gang in Spain taken down by two Canadians. They shook their heads and muttered expletives at the size of the organization they had faced. They finally put the newspapers down and waited for takeoff. Dani smiled. *Okay. It's time. Bring on the wine. And food. And more cookies, please. And the stupid movies.* She turned to Jo. "Babe. We may be strapped into chairs, but they're big chairs, and these kind folks seem willing to bring us treats on request. So this is it. No more waiting for fun. We are going to party. We are going to make this flight our vacation paradise." She took Jo's hand. "So? What do you think?"

Jo seemed distracted, staring out the window when Dani spoke. "Uh, yeah, sure, babe. Whatever." The plane started to roll along the tarmac when she squeezed Dani's hand. Hard. Dani jumped.

"Ow. What are you doing?"

"Look," she hissed.

Dani leaned over and peered out as directed by Jo. "What? What am I supposed to be seeing here?"

"Look. Look at the waiting lounge window."

Dani squinted to see better. There was a person, more form than face, staring through the glass at their plane. Pale complexion, black hair, a closed-mouth smile distorting his old man face. He raised a gloved hand, waved and was gone.

Dani gasped. "Rico."

Disclaimer

Paradise Pending is a work of fiction inspired by a real event. However, names, characters, businesses, events, locales and incidents are either the products of the author's imagination or used in a fictitious manner. Certain long-standing institutions, agencies, and public offices are mentioned, but the characters involved and their actions are wholly imaginary. Reference is made to historical events and figures in Spain and these are very real.

Bella Books, Inc.
Women. Books. Even Better Together.
P.O. Box 10543
Tallahassee, FL 32302
Phone: (800) 729-4992
www.BellaBooks.com

More Titles from Bella Books

Mabel and Everything After – Hannah Safren
978-1-64247-390-2 | 274 pgs | paperback: $17.95 | eBook: $9.99
A law student and a wannabe brewery owner find that the path to a fairy tale happily-ever-after is often the long and scenic route.

To Be With You – TJ O'Shea
978-1-64247-419-0 | 348 pgs | paperback: $19.95 | eBook: $9.99
Sometimes the choice is between loving safely or loving bravely.

I Dare You to Love Me – Lori G. Matthews
978-1-64247-389-6 | 292 pgs | paperback: $18.95 | eBook: $9.99
An enemy-to-lovers romance about daring to follow your heart, even when it's the hardest thing to do.

The Lady Adventurers Club - Karen Frost
978-1-64247-414-5 | 300 pgs | paperback: $18.95 | eBook: $9.99
Four women. One undiscovered Egyptian tomb. One (maybe) angry Egyptian goddess. What could possibly go wrong?

Golden Hour - Kat Jackson
978-1-64247-397-1 | 250 pgs | paperback: $17.95 | eBook: $9.99
Life would be so much easier if Lina were afraid of something basic—like spiders—instead of something significant. Something like real, true, healthy love.

Schuss – E. J. Noyes
978-1-64247-430-5 | 276 pgs | paperback: $17.95 | eBook: $9.99
They're best friends who both want something more, but what if admitting it ruins the best friendship either of them have had?

CPSIA information can be obtained
at www.ICGtesting.com
Printed in the USA
JSHW022217110423
40225JS00001B/1

9 781642 474381